Noontime
in Yenişehir

Sevgi Soysal

Translated by Amy Spangler

Milet Publishing
Smallfields Cottage, Cox Green
Rudgwick, Horsham, West Sussex
RH12 3DE England
info@milet.com
www.milet.com
www.milet.co.uk

First English edition published by Milet Publishing in 2016

Copyright © Milet Publishing, 2016

ISBN 978 1 84059 770 7

First published in Turkish as *Yenişehir'de Bir Öğle Vakti* in 1974

Funded by the Turkish Ministry of Culture and Tourism TEDA Project

Sevgi Soysal was born in Istanbul in 1936. She grew up in Ankara with her father, an architect-bureaucrat originally from Salonica, and her German mother. She studied archaeology in Ankara. Soysal's first volume of short stories was published in 1962. She went on to write *Tante Rosa*, a novel of interconnected stories based on her colorful aunt Rosel. *Yürümek* (*Walk*), her 1970 novel addressing male-female relationships and marriage, was banned on charges of obscenity. Soysal won Turkey's prestigious Orhan Kemal Award in 1974 for *Yenişehir'de Bir Öğle Vakti* (*Noontime in Yenişehir*), translated into English for the first time here. In 1975, she followed with another novel, *Şafak* (*Dawn*), in which she criticized the 1971 military coup in Turkey—a time during which she was imprisoned for her opposition. Her memoirs of prison life, which originally appeared in the newspaper *Politika*, were published in a single volume as *Yıldırım Bölge Kadınlar Koğuşu* (*Yıldırım District Women's Ward*) in 1976. Soysal died of cancer that year, leaving behind an incomplete novel, *Hoşgeldin Ölüm* (*Welcome, Death!*).

Amy Spangler was born in Ohio in 1978. She graduated from Bryn Mawr College with degrees in Near Eastern and classical archeology and German language and literature. Spangler is the cofounder and director of literary agency AnatoliaLit. She is translator of the novel *The City in Crimson Cloak* (2007) by Aslı Erdoğan, and co-translator and editor of the collection *Istanbul Noir* (2008). Spangler's English translations of Turkish short stories and novel excerpts have been published in numerous books and magazines, including the Milet collections *Istanbul in Women's Short Stories* (2012), *Europe in Women's Short Stories from Turkey* (2012) and *Aeolian Visions/Versions: Modern Classics and New Writing from Turkey* (2013).

Editorial Notes

Throughout this novel, we have retained the Turkish for several types of terms, including personal names, honorifics, place names and foods. For these terms, we have used italics in their first instance and then normal text for subsequent instances. We have not italicized the Turkish honorifics that form part of a name, such as Bey and Hanım, to avoid splitting the name visually with a style change. We have included a glossary of the Turkish terms that appear in this book.

Guide to Turkish Pronunciation

Turkish letters that appear in the book and which may be unfamiliar are shown below, with a guide to their pronunciation.

c   as *j* in *just*

ç   as *ch* in *child*

ğ   silent letter that lengthens the preceding vowel

ı   as *a* in *along*

ö   as German *ö* in *Köln*, or French *œ* in *œuf*

ş   as *sh* in *ship*

ü   as German *ü* in *fünf*, or French *u* in *tu*

^   accent over vowel that lengthens the vowel

Glossary of Turkish Terms

Abla: Older sister; also used as an honorific for women.

Ağbi: Older brother; also used as an honorific for men.

Ayran: A lightly-salted beverage made from plain yogurt mixed with cold water.

Bacı: Sister; often used by leftists as a way of addressing women in the sense of "female comrade."

Bakkal: A person who runs a small shop selling sundry foodstuffs; also, the shop itself.

Bey: A respectful term of address used after a man's first name.

Beybaba: A respectful term used by children to address their fathers; also, a respectful way of addressing older men.

Darbuka: A single-head drum played with two hands.

Dolmuş: A shared taxi or minibus that travels a fixed route.

Dönme: A community of Jews in the Ottoman Empire who publically converted to Islam but privately held onto their original religious beliefs; this movement was centered in Salonica.

Efendi: A title of courtesy, equivalent to the English "sir."

Gazino: A restaurant that serves alcoholic drinks and hosts musical performances.

Gecekondu: Literally, "set up overnight"; a dwelling built illegally on public land.

Goralı: Traditionally, a sandwich containing grilled meatballs, pickles and potato puree with butter and carrots; a goralı can also be made with salami or sausage.

Hanım: A respectful term of address used after a woman's first name.

İnşallah: God willing.

Kanun: A type of large zither with a trapezoidal soundboard; in Turkey, kanun usually have 26 courses of strings with three strings per course.

Kaymakam: Title for the governor of a provincial district in Turkey.

Kıraathane: A tea- and coffeehouse where patrons often play backgammon, rummy tiles or other games.

Kolcu: A watchman or overseer of an office, such as a customs office.

Kolej: A type of private school in Turkey commonly focused on foreign-language education or occupational training, ranging from primary to secondary level.

Kolonya: Scented water sprinkled on the hands or daubed on the face for refreshment, or used as a medicinal tincture of sorts.

Maşallah: An expression used to indicate appreciation, joy, praise or thankfulness.

Menemen: A breakfast dish made with eggs, onions, tomatoes, peppers and spices.

Muhtar: An elected head of a village, urban district or neighborhood.

Namaz: The Muslim prayer which is performed five times a day.

Palikarya: A person of Greek descent; usually used derogatorily to mean a ruffian.

Pavyon: A type of nightclub where there is generally a woman singer and "hostesses" who accompany male clients at their tables.

Puf böreği: A pastry that puffs up when fried, usually filled with cheese or meat and finely-chopped vegetables.

Rakı: An anise-flavored alcoholic drink.

Saatli Maarif: A calendar with tear-off pages for each day; each page includes the Gregorian and Islamic Hijri calendar dates, the times for namaz (prayers), and often religious or famous author quotes.

Simit: A bread ring covered in sesame seeds.

Sucuk: Spiced, fermented sausage usually eaten cooked.

Takke: A white skullcap worn by devout Muslims.

Tarhana: A dried food based on fermented yogurt, grains and vegetables, often reconstituted into soup.

Tespih: Muslim prayer beads.

Yarabbi şükür: Thanks be to God.

Ahmet the clerk meets with defeat in the department store basement

The poplar swayed as if about to collapse with a thunderous crash. Those who failed to see those things that happened, that changed with each passing moment, failed to sense this. It was noontime. The crowd coursed towards Piknik, the liveliest, noisiest, most frequented haunt in the neighborhood of Kızılay, with the fastest service too. The sales manager of the department store Tezkan, located on the opposite side of the boulevard, was still at his desk on the ground floor. He had just closed the installment sales ledger. The fastidious customers wading through the ironing boards, blankets, and clothes hangers in this particular department had not yet tired of touching the same items over and over, of testing the woolen texture of the blankets, expecting their fingers to display extraordinary talents, or of opening and closing the doors of medicine cabinets they contemplated hanging in their bathrooms, or of scolding their snotty-nosed children who knocked over ironing boards as they sprinted from one end of the store to the next, or of trying to wrest their future curtains or divan covers out of wrinkled paper wrappings. Husbands sick of scowling at their wives when confronted with "necessary" items that absolutely had to be bought for the home, narrow-minded housewives who mistook household amenities for the center of the universe, families who never tired of change and innovation when it came to appliances, certain that each would spice up their bland lives (and indeed, it was perhaps in this regard alone that they made any so-called progress in their lives), fiancees who derived incomprehensible pleasure from decorating the nests they were about to build, imprisoned birds who spent endless amounts of money and labor on their cages, and those who bemoaned the act of shopping all the while they were engaged in the very act . . . But amongst these types, the store manager could not distinguish one from the other. For it wasn't his job to do so. Distinguishing different types of customers was the clerk's job. In short, the clerk should know how to distinguish newlyweds from oldyweds, and fiancees from both; that is, he should be able to distinguish those likely to lay out a small fortune from those liable to pull tightly at the purse strings.

The sales manager was responsible for installment payments; he was responsible for making sure that payments were made to the right places at the right times, for the traffic of money coming in and out, and for making sure that there were no disruptions in the flow of that traffic. He had spent all morning identifying those customers who had not made their payments on time and then undertaking the necessary procedure. Meanwhile, he had also registered new install-ment plans, and made sure the business was, on the whole, securely anchored. That is, as securely anchored as financial figures can possibly be. For example, though for many one or two hundred was nothing to sweat over, like anyone who deals in numbers the sales manager knew the tempests that a figure of one or two hundred was capable of whipping up. Or at least, how misleading the apparent stability of a hundred lira could be, and the villainous hoaxes one might encounter when trying to deal in hundred lira bills. One hundred liras might be good for a blanket one day, and just two clothes hangers the next, to give the simplest of examples. That much the sales manager knew. Therefore, he was responsible not only for making sure there were no disruptions in the incoming and outgoing traffic of figures, but also for being vigilant so as to ensure that, when it came to the insidious volatility of numbers, it was the customers and not the store that got screwed in the end. Looking at it this way, his job was equivalent to the jealous sailor who attempts to sequester the regiment's whore yet himself spends months at sea. It was a tough, calculating task, trying not to get cuckolded by money. Customers turned the goods over in their hands with the incomprehensible idiocy of husbands doomed to be cuckolded, with the logic of husbands who assume that they can protect their honor by objecting to the revealing nature of their wives' attire, no matter how slight it might be. They wearied themselves, as if squeezing the wood of the clothes hanger twice and inquiring after the price thrice would somehow subvert the preassigned roles in this game of shopping with its rules that never changed and never would. The salesmen would take part in the same wearisome game, running themselves ragged and running their mouths nonstop. The purchasers were the righteous who must never know that their rights were being violated. The clerks dashed about, wet with perspiration, repeating the same words over and over, lighting up with smiles for snot-nosed children, submitting to the insane demands of crotchety housewives, convincing husbands that their precious money was not being wasted and thereby striving to cover up the crime that no one would admit to. There were spoilsports out there trying to ruin the game of shopping, but who were they? According to the sales manager, it was the clerks' job to make sure that none of the customers became a spoilsport and to endure all manner of suffering in the process. Suffering was part of their job. And for them to think it was they themselves who cheated the customers, that was part of the game too. Their own salaries a constant from one month to the next, like bewildered eunuchs they kept a meaningless watch over the natural friskiness of numbers. In truth, such thoughts never occurred to them or the sales manager. This was not a place for thinking. And it was not a place for watching and observing either. They were all slaves under the whip of an unjust division of labor, obliged to bear for months and years on end a weight which they did not ponder.

On this day too the sales manager was tired. He picked up the ledger and locked it in the safe. He placed the calculator in front of him. He began crunching the numbers, punching them into the machine and then pulling down on the handle again and again. There weren't many customers left in the shop. Now the salesmen were busy trying to return the goods which had been strewn all over the counters to their rightful places. Customers who plunged into the store in a sweaty rush, filled with the sense of panic that strikes once the closing time announcement is made, attacked the salesmen, as if the store were closing for good, never to open again. The clerks, weary from having exhibited good intentions all day long, were trying to palm off to the customers whatever goods happened to be in front of them.

A couple intending to purchase a trash can and wallpaper for a newly furnished home grew angry at the clerks' hastiness:

"Look, darling, that wallpaper with the violets is by far the prettiest!"

The woman really loved violets. And to have her nails done too. When they first started dating, Hayati had always brought her violets.

"That way you won't forget to bring me violets every now and then . . ."

The exasperated salesmen reached for the scissors.

"How much do you want?"

"Wait, no need to rush, dear. Look, that there with the birds is awfully pretty. Take that one down too, would you?"

The salesman was just about to hang the violets back up and take down the birds when he was interrupted:

"Wait, don't hang it back up. Take down the birds too. Not that one, that one. Do you have it in pink? Not in the storeroom either? Okay, so do you have the bird wallpaper with violets?"

The salesman put down the scissors. Even the most infatuated of men would lose patience pandering to such whims.

In a dimly lit corner of the store, an old woman was analyzing a suitcase.

"How much can this hold?"

"It can hold all kindsa things."

"Give me a proper answer son, will you? What do you mean exactly, 'all kindsa things'?"

"It'll hold all of your stuff, ma'am."

"I'm not buying it for myself, I'm buying it for my son. He's going to America. How much of his stuff can it hold?"

"It can hold a lot of stuff, ma'am. Look, you can put yer dress shirts here."

"Who puts dress shirts in a suitcase, son? They'd get all wrinkled. I'm going to put those in his hand luggage."

"Look at how soft the leather is, ma'am. Luggage with soft leather like this can hold all sortsa stuff."

"But then the clothes will all get wrinkled. How many suits and how much underwear will this hold?"

"It holds a lot, ma'am. Enough that you can go anywhere with just one suitcase."

"Who goes all the way to America with just one suitcase, son?"

The salesman leaned against the suitcase for a moment. He stared at the old woman with vacant eyes. With full eyes the old woman was calculating how many suits her little boy could fit into the suitcase.

In front of a counter where the latest patterned bed sheets were displayed, a middle-aged woman with hair dyed golden blonde and wound in a neat bun, wearing plain but clearly expensive clothes, ran into a heavy-set young woman with glasses who, as was apparent from her attire, had spent a long time in America, and who, as she would soon make apparent, had studied at a fancy private high school.

"Ohhh, Mine, my dear, how are you?"

"*Just fan-tas-tic!*⃰ I'm about to lose my wits."

"Well, I'm in a wretched mood myself. What's up with you? I swear, if you ask me, you're just fine. You're always just like this, *always* so active."

"Don't say that. *It's enough* already."

"*Don't be cross.* Tell me what's wrong."

"Well, you see, I've been without help for months, my dear. Cooking, cleaning, getting two kids to do their lessons, the whole burden is on me. And just when the ladies' auxiliary is starting to have their teas."

"Do you know who's going to be the next *Madame President?*"

"Not yet. We're going to hold the next tea at the Ankara Hotel again. The entrance fee is a hundred liras."

"Oh, how wonderful!"

⃰ In this dialogue, the words and phrases in italics appear in English in the original Turkish text.

"There are cheaper *solutions* but then the next thing you know it'll be a disaster and *at the end everyone will be talking* behind our backs. Last year was better, I tell you. I mean, *nothing's new*, you know, haha!"

"Oh, I almost forgot. A woman called yesterday. She wants to join."

"Who?"

"I'm not sure, actually. Her husband works for the air force, I think."

"Does she know English?"

"*If you want my opinion*, I don't think we should dwell on that anymore. I'm sick of people just showing up and giving *speeches* left and right. We need some members who are actually useful. Look, last year we got everything we needed for the dinner for cheap from the Army Solidarity Cooperative thanks to Muazzez Hanım's husband. *By the way*, she'll improve her English as she comes and goes."

"True. You've put on a little weight, dear."

"All because of those *anti-baby* pills. They said it wouldn't do me the least bit of harm, but then I started bleeding. We tried all kinds of doctors. Hüseyin Bey told me to lie still in bed. Faruk Bey tried to give me an abortion. Meanwhile of course it was just sleep and eat, sleep and eat. Anyway, I'm better now. With a little help from the sauna and regular massages, hopefully I'll be able to shed the pounds."

The sign on the door had already read "closed" for some time. Customers, bearing their packages, left the store reluctantly. Under his breath, the clerk Ahmet, who had plans to meet his girlfriend in front of the record store at exactly half past noon, cursed the customers before him who never tired of choosing cloth. Finally the door to the store was locked from the inside so that no one else could get in. Ahmet rolled up the bolts of cloth that had been strewn across the counter and returned each ream to its rightful place, with a swiftness and dexterity calculated to please the ever watchful storeowner who was sitting at the cash register. He took his comb out of his back pocket and carefully ran it through his hair, which had grown curly at his neck. He patted the cuffs of his bellbottoms, ridding them of dust. After tightening his belt one more hole, he made a swift exit out of the store and onto the boulevard. A young mustached man, his unbuttoned shirt revealing a hairy chest, stood next to an open suitcase containing a pile of Orlon sweaters, yelling:

"Wrap 'em up 'n' take 'em home! They're fifty liras in the Kızılay shops, but we got 'em for thirty! On the cheap from a merchant that went bottom up! There's no obligation to buy. But I'm talkin' genuine Orlon brother, genuine American Orlon! Buy it! Wear it! Wash it! If it shrinks, bring it back! May we be cursed with cockroaches if we don't take it back, brother!"

A crowd of people eager to get something on the cheap, cheaper than everyone else, for the cheapest price before anyone else, had amassed around the suitcase. At that moment, a "shill" who practiced the art of facilitating sales by taking advantage of customers' idiocy and greed, was busy doing his job. He pushed aside those gathered around the suitcase and started grabbing the sweaters out of the hands of everyone left and right, as if he'd struck gold. He paid immediately. And then a few seconds later of course he furtively returned the goods, getting his money, and then some, returned in the process. It was a highly effective tactic. Just as it was in the stores. Of course, in the stores there wasn't any professional involved, just a slew of greedy, aggressive customers who never failed to sway the undecided, leading to the outbreak of a property struggle over goods not yet purchased. Ahmet couldn't count the number of customers who'd fought over the last bit of a certain ream of cloth, even while there were reams and reams of better quality cloth. Just as he was thinking this, one of the birds perched on a tree crapped on him. His new shirt was ruined. For a moment, he just stood there, stunned. Then he grabbed his shirt and shook it, a meaningless motion, as if that would make it clean again. He glanced around. He felt as if all the pedestrians on the boulevard were gawking at the bird crap on his shirt. His right shoulder began to twitch, like it always did when he was upset. If he'd had a gun he would've shot all the birds he could, that's just how particular he was about his appearance. "Damn birds! If I could get my hands on you . . . Ah!" Grumbling, hopeless, he started walking. But who wouldn't be angry, downright furious in the same situation? It wasn't for nothing that he spent the better part of his salary from Tezkan on clothes from Amado. Of course it wasn't. You had to invest if you wanted to be at the height of spiffy all the time. Were the shop windows of Amado not designed for the sole purpose of realizing Ahmet's dreams of being the handsomest of the handsome? They sold stylish, unique, original things there. The clothes they sold were the same ones worn by the young people Ahmet strove to emulate. Patterned shirts, pants with thick belts. But these weren't enough to make Ahmet stand out to the degree that he desired. Even in Samanpazarı there had sprouted up young men with a predilection for such novel attire, even if it wasn't of the best quality. But their garb was hardly on par with Ahmet's, of course. As soon as Ahmet walked out onto the street, young men went green with envy, neighboring housewives shook their heads in disapproval, and blood went rushing to the heads of old geezers. And that's what mattered. Anyone who was a real man stood out in Samanpazarı. Anyone who didn't stand out was a slovenly, ragtag twit, a member of that inconspicuous hoard known as "the people"—the people! If you asked Ahmet, any self-respecting man should be dressed so as to turn at least half a dozen heads as soon as he walked out onto the street. He stopped in front of the record store. Şükran hadn't arrived yet. While studying the cover of a "Love Story" record displayed in the window, he was startled by the sound of a shrill voice:

"Brothers and sisters and fellow citizens . . . Come closer, closer still . . . Look! I've been to sixty-six counties, three hundred and ninety townships and one thousand five hundred villages in Turkey, but a crown befitting my head have I yet to find. May Allah deliver us from destitution of every kind. My Muslim brothers, we just performed our Friday prayers together at that mosque right over there. So do not, I bid thee, seek to detect in my words falsehoods, hypocrisy, or untruths. Now you wake up in the morning and you feel an ache in your head, a pain in your back, but try as you may, you can find no antidote. Well, our factory, esteemed customers, will supply the cure that you have sought in vain in stores and apothecaries, and for the mere recompense of one hundred and fifty lira. Now dear respectable brothers and sisters, when I shake this jar I am holding right now, not once, not twice, but three times, this snake, beknownst to you as an asp, which thirty-six hunters chased for fourteen days in the African jungle, will poke its head out to greet my dear respected brothers and sisters . . . But first, I beg you to turn your attention this way and I shall take these boxes you see me holding in my hand . . ."

Ahmet was surprised. Such hucksters usually set up shop in Ulus, but now it seemed they too had made their way down to Kızılay. The Tezkan store used to be in Ulus too. Over by the hill. But now all self-respecting residents of Ankara did their shopping in Kızılay. Even civil servants looking to get their vittles on the cheap went to Gima, not to the old open-air marketplace. For Ahmet, goods purchased in Ulus were worthless. Even as a child, when speaking about something he'd bought, he wanted to tack on the sentence, "I got it in Kızılay." Perhaps

this was due to the indoctrination he had been subjected to throughout his childhood, that incessant refrain of his mother warning him
that shopping in Kızılay inevitably meant getting cheated. Whereas
for Ahmet, this indoctrination translated into the idea that anything
bought in Kızılay was a sign of privilege and superiority, and so as
soon as he began earning his own money, he made sure to do all of his
shopping there, and at the most expensive stores to boot. Whenever he
thought of Ulus or the open-air marketplace, it was the boring sacks
of potatoes and onions and the grimy tins of cheese and olive oil that
his father used to bring home en masse at the onset of each winter
that came to his mind. How could such thoughts possibly mesh with
a stylish wardrobe? But what did they mesh with? With miserliness,
with poverty, with the idiotic naivety that one might conquer poverty
by means of miserliness. He read the words on the record displayed in
the shop window: Love Story. A beautiful, delectable girl and a puny
boy wrapped in each other's embrace. Was the girl a virgin? *C'mon now,
even if she was getting it on with that puny guy, she wouldn't really qualify
as a non-virgin . . . The girl possessed both beauty and an innocent-looking
face, a rare find*, thought Ahmet . . . He thought of Şükran's chubby
face, of the crude, wide nose that protruded from beneath eyebrows
thinned out from too much plucking, and her knobby knees. But still,
she was of course a thousand times better than the girlfriends of his
buddies (his mother absolutely insisted that they call her "auntie"),
those awful girls whose faces were always red, as if they got their peri-
ods every day, whose eyes were always downcast, who didn't know
how to walk or talk properly. For one, Şükran knew how to dance.
She committed the names of singers and new songs to memory, just
like that. She stood up to Ahmet when she had to. She let him touch
her, and she could burst into laughter at any moment. She talked. She
instantly recognized celebrities walking down the street. She could tell

you Fikret Hakan's street address and the name of Salih Güney's ex-wife in a snap. She never flagged when it came to fashion. As soon as small talk became fashionable, she mastered the art of blah-blah before anyone else. In this regard, she completely outdid Ahmet. That was Şükran for you, every bit the girl; he looked at the girl on the record sleeve again. *That girl wouldn't let the likes of us near her, son. As for the boy embracing her, who knew whose son he was? In the movie they're always ice skating, or playing ice hockey, or something like that, and the girl just adores it. Ice hockey, way out of your league, son.* He looked at his reflection in the window. *How about I get me some of those striped pants next month! I'd do well to wrestle some money from my mom; a little conniption fit should do the trick. Being a fastidious dresser isn't a bunch of silly nonsense like my father thinks. His father spent his life dressed like a janitor, and where did that get him?* Alain Delon used to be a waiter. Şükran had told him about how Alain had caught the eye of a film producer thanks to his good looks, fashionable clothes, and of course his cunning. *Good looks could make you rich, like winning the lottery, or if not that, it at least got you the girl, kept her happy. But what did walking around all sheepishly, dressed like a janitor, filling the house with sack after sack of potatoes and onions get you but a depressing, wearisome life?*

Every week, when he played the lottery, Ahmet liked to think about the clothes he'd buy if he won. He'd tour shop window after shop window, imagining buying himself countless shoes, pants, shirts, sweaters and jackets. As he looked at more and more shop windows, he'd would begin to dislike the items he had originally liked, start eliminating them from his initial list, and then add on the newer, the more recent, the very latest items that struck his fancy instead. Shopping, compiling a wardrobe was nothing less than a science. Not the kind of thing you could learn by buying secondhand pants in the used clothing stores in Samanpazarı. Who knew what his father would do if he were to enter ABC? Imagining the pathetic scenarios his father would live through if he were to set foot in the store, Ahmet laughed to himself, but then he felt ashamed. *And he thinks he's smarter than me, when he doesn't know the first thing. Once you've gotten yourself some sharp clothes, then you get yourself a car. Once you've got a car, there isn't a door you can't open; it's a thousand times better than money in the bank. Who's going to know about the money you've got sitting growing moldy in the bank and respect you for it? Besides, it's hardly like money has any real value anymore these days. But a car? A car is something completely different. It's a must, no matter what. I'm perfectly happy to go hungry, to go without house and home, anything for a car! "The way you think, you never fail to shock me."* Ahmet frequently engaged in such spontaneous imaginary discussions with his father. It was as if his father were responsible for all of the obstructions he encountered in life; he stunted Ahmet's growth, and deserved to be squelched. *If only I had a dad like theirs.* He turned his eyes away from the reflection in the show window and galloped down the record store's stairs. On the doors of two record stores facing one another hung the same sign: "Selda's albums available at this store only." *Are customers really so gullible?* Ahmet thought. *You walk into the store whose sign you see first; that's what they're counting on. The people of this country are lazy, that's what they think, that once they've read the first sign, they won't even question it when they see the second one.* But Ahmet knew well and good that customers were anything but lazy when it came to shopping. Forget about the huge letters on such signs, they'd sniff out even the tiniest print on the most obscure part of an item and shove it under your nose. Both of the record stores were closed. He walked back up the stairs and resumed waiting. What did she have to give him that gave her the right to keep him waiting like this? He saw Şükran approaching from the opposite side of the street.

"Where've you been, girl?"

"Why? It's not like you kept a taxi waiting for me, now is it?"

"Cut it out. Look, if you keep me waiting like that again . . ."

"I'll keep you waiting just as long as I want. Now what do you say to that?"

Ahmet didn't respond. It was no use arguing with Şükran. Like all streetwise girls, Şükran could hold her own and then some in any quarrel. If he were to drag this one out, soon she'd be harping on about this and that, stomping heavily on every word: "Now. You. Look. Here." They heard a whistle. A civil servant was dragging away the hawker who'd just been screaming bloody murder in his efforts to attract customers. The hawker, his goods strewn all over the ground, was crying: "Brother, please, I'm begging you, I'll kiss your feet . . ." They paused at the sight. Şükran shrugged. *Long live the snake that doesn't bite me.* Ahmet threw his arm around Şükran's neck. They began walking uphill.

The sandwich place was packed. Grilled cheese with sausage, with mustard, with ketchup, and *ayran* to drink; no one ever tired of eating these same old foods, which were served at each and every sandwich shop, and to which no one ever thought of making any changes, of introducing a few innovations. For most, eating a *sandviç* was enough of a change as it was. Although the claim that it was a cheap meal was hardly believable to those used to cooking a very cheap meal on the stove, it was something new, something different for those sick and tired of dishes comprised primarily of potatoes with a wee bit of ground beef and a heavy dose of onion thrown in, dishes that boiled on the stove for hours and hours. How many years ago did sandwiches first become available? The first sandwich shop had opened in the arcade next to The Big Movie Theater. The owner had hung up a sign above the boulevard sidewalk that read, "Hot Dog." As soon as it opened, it was chock-full of boys and girls from the private high school, the Yenişehir *kolej*. At first the sandwich shop was a place that the majority viewed with suspicion, the latest hangout of the *kolej* kids who were more open to innovation than anyone else. It was a nuisance to parents who got angry at their children for spoiling their appetites with a sandwich when there was a delicious meal waiting for them at home. And then, suddenly, sandwich shops popped up throughout the city. All over Kızılay and Yenişehir, all of the unoccupied corners in all of the stores which would have been good for nothing else, the vestibules of apartment buildings, any space that could be squeezed out of coal bunkers, all of them became sandwich shops. The sandwich shops spread near and far, all the way to Ulus, Cebeci, Maltepe, everywhere, to Yeni Mahalle, and even to Altındağ and Telsizler. Now anyone able to equip some corner of his fly-ridden, dusty old shop with a rusty, cruddy toast machine began to sell toasted sandwiches which they made by putting a membrane of cheese in between two stale slices of bread and slathering some margarine on the outside. These sandwiches and grilled toast, no matter how disgusting, always found a buyer. Perhaps it was an insurrection against the onion-reeking hands of mothers, against the meals that always tasted the same regardless of the season, always made of the cheapest ingredients, meals that had become tasteless as a result of housewives skimming off a portion of the money allocated for foodstuffs in order to go sneak off to the cinema or secretly buy a pair of nylon stockings. They were capable of overthrowing the system (and this system only) in homes, a system grounded upon sacks of flour, potatoes, and onions lugged into the home with the onset of each new season.

Ahmet and Şükran each ordered a *gorah*. This particular sandwich was designed for those who like to walk into the sandwich shop thinking they're in for a feast; a sandwich into which all of the ingredients put into other sandwiches individually are lopped en masse; in other words, a sandwich that doesn't have a particular taste, and gives you the impression you're eating everything at once. As she ate her sandwich, Şükran studied her reflection in the mirror across from her, focusing on her brows that had recently been plucked. It was horrible the way thin brows had come into fashion. Şükran actually had thick, dark eyebrows. She'd shed sweat, blood, and tears to get them thinned out, that's how determined she was. And now her skin revealed where the brows had once been thanks to its surprising paleness, and a day would not go by before the bases of the recently plucked brows made themselves visible once again as individual dots. Şükran worked at Spor Toto, the government-run football pool. On certain days of the week, that is. "Tomorrow's Wednesday; I'm off." Tomorrow she was going to get a wax at Günseli's. This time she would try using wax to remove her brows. Günseli was a pro when it came to waxing. But then, Günseli was incredibly skilled in every way. Maybe it was because she'd gone to boarding school? Günseli had spent years on a full scholarship at a boarding school for students studying to become teachers. Her memories of those days knew no end. Still, school did get you ready for the world. Şükran had dropped out the first year of middle school. *So Günseli completed her studies, so what? She works at Spor Toto, and so do I. But no, I have to give it to her, she is one brazen gal. I guess that's what a proper taste of school and a little living does to you. Nothing stops Günseli. There's nothing reserved about her. She does whatever comes to mind, her heart's desire. "If I get desperate, I'll just do some tailoring, or knit some baby's clothes, or do some manicuring at the hairdresser. What's there to worry about?" That girl really could do anything. Well, sure, but after all that time studying to be a teacher, she barely made it through two years of teaching in a village, and put up with a hell of a lot until she finally found her place at Spor Toto.* Şükran whined a lot about her troubled childhood in Hamamönü, but that childhood, spent begging her mother for this and that in vain, and shedding tears when her wishes were not fulfilled, was seventh heaven compared to Günseli's years as a teacher. As kids, our heads were in the clouds, our hearts set on the boy next door, and our purses never empty, at least. The village where Günseli taught was a nightmare. She very well could have had the unfortunate fate of being born there. Still, she should be grateful. The more she heard Günseli's stories, the more Şükran thanked God for her good luck—after all, she could have been born a villager.

Günseli could not shake off her memories of Şahinler, the village where she had taught. It had a wooden schoolhouse which consisted of two parts. One side was a stable, and the other the school. The villagers had prepared a room for the teacher above the stable. "I didn't get lonely much during the summer nights; they tied their horses up in the stable. But during the winter I'd cry as I listened to the sound of wolves' howling." Günseli's room would fill up with the winter cold that seeped in through the gaps between the wooden boards. She still shivered when telling about those cold, frightening winter nights she spent all alone. "Şahinler was a tiny mountain village. Nobody ever passed through there during the winter. They got their winter supplies from town in the summer. A villager would bring me wood every morning. They even lit my stove until I finally learned how to do it myself."

"Weren't you scared of those villagers, girl? That they'd come in in the middle of the night and rape you?" Şükran would ask. "No, they wouldn't do that, they were good people. They were good people, but still, I was afraid. They always had respect for city dwellers, but they always considered me a stranger. They always kept me at a distance. I was a stranger, but at the same time something they wanted to emulate; it was weird like that. My room never seemed to heat up in the winter. The first winter it got really cold and so I stayed in the *muhtar's* house. Even the gas in the lamp in my room froze. And so while I was staying at the muhtar's, I woke up one morning and what should I see: all of the village women were gathered around my bed studying my hands and my fingers and this and that. You can't possibly imagine how shocked and frightened I was. People rarely moved from the village to the city, so it's a pretty insular place. But sometimes guys who'd gone to the city to work and ended up settling there would take a girl from the village in marriage. She'd be considered the luckiest girl in the world. The same as high society here. You know those slum houses we call *gecekondu* that we find so distasteful, well, a bride from Şahinler who moved to a house like that would be mighty impressed. Compared to my village, a gecekondu is paradise, paradise I tell you. As soon as anyone lands a place in Ankara, from that moment on the entire village would start using all sorts of excuses to go and stay with him. They'd pretend they had some disease that could only be treated in the city, or start looking for a job. And so then after a while, the guy who'd moved to the city would start getting peevish and looking for a way to cut his ties with the village."

"You know what a *kolcu* is? The kolcu's the highest ranking man there." "Were there a lot of trees there?" "It was a mountain village, smack in the middle of the forest—it was heaven."

One day, and this would only happen once in a blue moon, mind you, a *kaymakam* came to the village and talked and talked, and the villagers listened and listened. And then finally one of the villagers said, "Oh, Mister Kaymagam, if ya'd only studied a wee bit more, ya coulda been a kolcu!"

Günseli had countless more stories like that. These are some of the more boring ones actually. But she had some racy ones too. She'd have Şükran and the other girls rolling on the floor with laughter. "I'm telling you girl, there wasn't any sneaking around; you'd be shocked by the stories the village women told me." So she could leave the village and come to Ankara, Günseli got engaged to a third lieutenant. The guy had a relative who worked at the Head Office of Spor Loto. He got her a job there. She even got the guy to pay off her compulsory teaching service. But at what cost? Later on they broke off the engagement. If you asked the girls, the third lieutenant had been scratching his itch with Günseli. And so, both giver and taker came away from the deal satisfied.

In their waxing session the previous month, the wax had got stuck on Meral's leg like glue. They nearly skinned the girl alive trying to get it off. As Meral screamed in pain, Günseli once again recalled the villagers. "Girl, I hear a scream and the first thing that comes to my mind is the village. One day I was playing ball with the kids in the playground when a gunshot rang out. And just what should I see? The kids are all lying on the ground. And there I am, screaming my lungs out, just like Meral. They told me later I yelled out that there was a bandit. I walked all the way around the school building three times. I ran out to the field. That's where the gunfire was coming from. And then I saw her, this old woman holding a big gun. I lashed out, telling the old woman she'd shot the kids, goddamn her, and she immediately started crying. 'Oh, my sweet girl, please don't turn me in to the gendarme.' I grabbed that old woman and took her straight to the gendarme station. I had the gendarme lock her up. They took the children to the city. All of them were fine. The buckshot barely grazed them. It turned out the old woman was known for taking shots at chickens who wandered into the fields. She shot any chicken that entered any field, regardless of who the chicken or the field belonged to. I'm telling you, even old hags abide by their own laws out there.

And that's just the beginning. The things I could tell you . . . There was a girl named Döndü. She was as beautiful as the actress Türkan Şoray. Her older brother caught her in the hay shed with her brother-in-law no less. He dragged the girl by her hair and threw her in the barn, locking her up next to the cattle. One night, there was a loud banging at my door. It was the muhtar and a few villagers. They were holding a lantern. "Miss Teacher, we've come to take you with us." "Why?" "You're going to act as a witness. Döndü's family's going to sentence her." We went to the barn, with me still uncertain about what exactly was going on. Döndü lay on the ground, nearly passed out, her hair all a mess, with this sad look in her eyes. They'd beat the brother-in-law up real bad too, he was standing up though, his face covered in blood. Before I even had a chance to ask what was going on, the muhtar explained everything. The girl's family was saying she was no longer pure, that she had to be sentenced, that they should set up a court and throw the hussy off a cliff. The muhtar heard about the sentencing bit and called on me to come and talk to the girl's father and older brother, thinking I might be able to change their minds. I pleaded with them for an hour. But the father and son wouldn't give an inch. And the village's muhtar, and the elders, they all just waited to hear whatever verdict came out of the father's and son's mouths, as if there was no such thing as actual laws in this country. If I'd let 'em have their way, they would've tossed her off a cliff, just like that. The gendarme would've arrived in the morning to work things out, but by then the girl would've been long dead. Finally I put the fear of God in the muhtar, telling him they'll do this to you and that to you, and that I'd have him put on trial for being an accomplice to the crime. That lit a fire under him, and so he pleaded with the family all the more passionately. Everyone else was still backing the father and son. Anyway, the decision was left to the village tribunal. Finally, the entire village stoned the girl in the middle of the village square—based on the tribunal's verdict. The girl ended up almost worse off than she would've been if they'd pushed her off a cliff. The gendarme got wind of it and intervened in time, otherwise she would've died for sure. The whole village just went mad, rabid. Especially the old hags, they didn't show an ounce of pity, didn't once say anything about her also being one of God's creatures . . . I'll never forget that girl's dark eyes."

"Why are you looking at yourself in the mirror like that, all forlorn?"

Şükran was startled by the sound of Ahmet's voice.

"No reason. I just felt bad for Döndü."

"Which Döndü?"

"You know Günseli, sweetheart, well, the Döndü in the village where she taught . . . She was caught fooling around in the barn you see and . . ."

"What's it to you?"

"You men are all like that, you don't think of anything but your own pleasure."

"Now where did that come from, girl? This Döndü, now she . . . I'm going to start swearing because of you, God help me. I don't know who the hell the girl is. So what if she got caught, what's it to me? What do I have to do with any of it?"

"But of course you would say that! You men are only concerned with getting your nasty desires out of your system. Her father and brother wanted to throw her off a cliff, 'cause she's damaged goods . . ."

"It's a matter of honor, it's nobody's business."

"But of course, and so why don't they throw the bloke off the cliff, huh?"

"He's a man . . . If the girl doesn't bother to protect her honor, why should he?"

"Oh, right, I get it, I get it. Of course that's your reaction, it would be a mistake to expect anything less!"

Ahmet didn't like what was happening. Oh no, he didn't like it at all. This unsavory little tiff—out of nowhere!—was not working to his advantage. He tried to smooth things over.

"Şükran!"

Şükran frowned.

"What is it?"

"Şükran, girl, red really suits you, you know."

"Really?"

Şükran softened up. How could she not? She was crazy about Ahmet. Ahmet was a good-looking guy. Other girls were mad with jealousy, she was sure. *But the blockhead, the only thing he thinks about is . . . But then he wouldn't marry me, never in a million years.* Şükran was confused.

"Ahmet?"

"Yes?"

"Do you think Günseli's still a virgin?"

"What's it to you?"

"I just wondered!"

"Better you start thinking about me than wondering about her. We've been hanging out for how many months now, but not once have you—"

"Enough . . . Watch your mouth!"

"Is Günseli stupid like you? No way, she doesn't play around. Goodness knows how many times she's done it already."

"How do you know?"

"Girl, we can tell whether or not a girl is a virgin from ten meters away."

"So you mean she's not a virgin?"

"Her maidenhead's been through some serious devaluation."

"What's that supposed to mean?"

"Guy talk. You know how money's devalued when you exchange it, well, that's what it means, she's been exchanged a few times too many."

"If you only heard the stories Günseli tells . . . Look, one day a boy went out into the forest to gather kindling. These two young men from the village followed him and then they, you know, and so then the villagers went after the young men, beat the crap out of them, and then tied them onto the back of a donkey. They completely humiliated those guys there in the village square."

"I really got to meet this Günseli, up close and personal!"

"Why?"

"From the stories she tells, I bet she's loose."

"There's no talking to you."

"I was just kidding, girl."

"Alright, alright. In one of the villages neighboring Günseli's village they have this pit called God's Command. The villagers themselves try anyone who commits a crime and then throw them in the pit if they're guilty."

"Would you like another sandwich?"

"No. I'm trying to tell you something. But you never listen. Besides, you just want to—"

"I asked because I don't want you going hungry. Is there anything wrong with that?"

"I don't want one. I'm getting fat. Just look at me."

"Şükran?"

"What?"

"What's up with you today? You're awfully hot under the collar. What's on your mind?"

They would have these weddings, Günseli had said, that were like funerals. Nobody spoke a word. They transported the bride to the groom's house as if carrying a corpse—no instruments, no songs. In one of the villages, they would immediately punish anyone who got a little boisterous or even cracked a smile. "After a wedding like that," she had explained, "I aged a thousand years, it was as if I'd been buried alive six feet below the ground. I couldn't stay there a minute longer, I had to get to Ankara; at that point, if they'd told me I'd had to register as a whore at one of the brothels in Bentderesi to do so, I would have been more than willing . . ."

Ahmet elbowed Şükran.

"Hey, I'm asking you a question."

"What? Oh, right. I'm upset. Of course I'm upset. Am I wrong to be upset? What's going to happen to me? My auntie's boy saw us together. My dad's wearing a long face all the time. And my mom yammers on and on about how rather than contributing to the household, I spend all my money on clothes and makeup so that I can look pretty for some punk bastard . . ."

"What business is it of theirs what you do with your money?"

"Riiight, what business is it of theirs? And I suppose it's also none of their business that I'm hanging out with you, right?"

"So don't!"

Şükran looked at Ahmet sidelong, hurt and resentful. *The prick, he knows I won't leave him* . . .

"The devil tells me I oughta just agree to marry one of the guys who's already asked for my hand and get it over with."

"So do it!"

Şükran glared at Ahmet. She would have given him a good flogging with her eyes just then, if only that were possible. *The swine! You're gonna run around with me, have a good time, feel me up, and if it were up to you, do everything under then sun, and then some random guy's gonna strut over like a pasha and take my hand. 'Cause we're all just a pack of idiots. You wanna dirty the laundry and let someone else wash it.* Şükran's rage was swelling by the second . . . *I should just abandon this asshole in the middle of the street . . .*

Ahmet was by now aware of the fact that he had upset the apple cart. Why go getting on her nerves when he could wrap her around his finger? Was that any way to win over a girl?

"Şükran?"

"Yes?"

"Girl, look, I mean, if I were in the position to marry, I mean, I wouldn't think twice, you know that, but what with military service and this and that . . ."

"What's 'this and that'?"

"Oh, c'mon, don't go ruining my day already by making me talk about these things."

Suddenly he paused. He grabbed Şükran's hand and squeezed it. Şükran quivered ever so slightly. Ahmet was certain that he had won Şükran over again.

"Şükran, girl, I'm crazy about you."

. . . .

Again, he paused. This time he put his arm around Şükran's shoulders and gave her another gentle squeeze. Again she quivered.

"Şükran?"

. . . .

"Shall we go to the basement again?"

Şükran didn't respond. They crossed the street at Kızılay and arrived at The Big Store over by the square. After walking past the *dolmuş* stop and down the road built for the vehicles transporting merchandise, they came to the basement of The Big Store.

Çetin, a friend of Ahmet's from the neighborhood, was the watchman at The Big Store's warehouse during the day. He was a student at the Academy of Economics and Commercial Sciences. Whenever Ahmet was in a pinch, such as now, he let Ahmet in. Ahmet banged his keychain against the iron rails of the warehouse. A few moments later, Çetin opened the door. He talked with Ahmet without even looking at Şükran, ignoring her very existence. Male friends do not look at the women their buddies seduce.

"What's up? Did you manage to take care of that cloth business at Sümerbank?"

"Sure did. You'll get your hundred lira cut."

"Let me see the cloth first."

They didn't talk for long. Çetin sat down at the desk located in the center of the warehouse. Ahmet and Şükran walked to the back of the warehouse, their steps revealing a familiarity with the locale. After shoving aside some boxes of Piyale macaroni, Fay dishwashing soap and Omo detergent to make room, they sat down on the floor. Ahmet immediately leaned over and squeezed Şükran's breast.

"Hey, watch it, you're hurting me, ouch!"

"Are ya givin' it up or not? You are, right? I swear I'm about to explode, c'mon!"

"Why should I give myself to you? Let your sister do it."

Ahmet shoved Şükran. She fell backwards. Boxes of Piyale, Omo, and Fay came tumbling down on top of her.

"You beast! I shouldn't be surprised. Why are you shoving me?"

"Don't mention my sister again."

"And why not? As if I don't have a big brother too. Since you're so good at keeping a watch over your sister's honor, well you should know that I have two big buff brothers myself!"

"I know that."

"Well then? Your sister's an innocent little lamb and I'm a whore then, right? What if you saw your sister here, like this?"

"Look here, girl, you're trying my patience. I told you not to mention my sister."

"Well, you can't stop me. I'll mention her all I like. As if I don't know the shit she's up to . . ."

Ahmet slapped Şükran. She began to cry. Ahmet suddenly realized that he'd gone too far. He cupped his face in his hands. He was upset. He'd ruined everything again. *And my pants are all dirty now from this floor. Dumbass, you dumbass, what did you expect? I spent a fortune trying to hoodwink the hussy. Now show me the empty pockets you've got to show for it. I could've bought that purple sweater I saw in the shop window for that much money. And now the little trollop's playing the honor card. The girl's been turning tricks all over the neighborhood since she was just a kid. Murat told me all about it, in mouthwatering detail. The cow. She thinks I'm going to ask for her hand? Are you the type of gal a man marries, for God's sake? Do I look like the kind of dimwit who would marry a girl willing to come down to the basement of The Big Store with a boyfriend she barely knows?*

Şükran, now standing, brushed the dirt off her skirt. She'd broken one of her nails. *The pig, but then what did I expect. Just 'cause you took me to the cinema three times, bought me a few sandwiches and some cake, and took me to Gençlik Park, now you're going to make me pay for the service, right here, right now? He'll sleep with me, and then go marry one of his sister's snotty-nosed girlfriends. Well, I won't do it. He can sleep with them. And even if I were to sleep with him, it wouldn't be in a place like this, the dark, damp, cold basement of The Big Store. Who does he think he is? I haven't fallen that far. If I were going to be a whore, I'd do it right. In the movies, even the most villainous men take the girl to a motel at least, or a luxury hotel or something, and they dance, and drink, and*

even, sometimes they eat expensive meals, get furs and jewelry, or what-
ever . . . It'd end up costing him more if he went to a brothel. The shameless
brute. No good will ever come of this guy. Günseli told me so, many times.
That girl knows what she's talking about. Even she made sure her fiance
brought her to Ankara before she took the bait. Of course, that girl's lived,
it's not for naught that she tells me any man who's constantly looking at
his reflection in shop windows isn't husband material. If you lose your
heart to somebody, fine, have a good time, but whatever you do, don't take
it seriously, whatever a guy like that wants to do to you, you do the same
to him, have fun with him, seduce him, and then walk right past him
without so much as a hello, do that and see how he goes raving mad, his
masculinity going straight to his head, and he might even try to shoot you
out of jealousy. That Günseli, she's a smart one, knows what she's talking
about. Şükran looked at Ahmet again. *But I love him, I love him, what*
can I do? I know damn well that no good will ever come of this scoun-
drel, why would I follow him down here otherwise? Ahmet enters her
dreams, her crazy, crazy dreams. But ah . . . a mad, gushing heat ran
through her body. She took another look at Ahmet out of the corner
of her eye, sizing him up once again. *The spitting image of Alain Delon,*
God so help me. An exact copy. She wiped away her tears. Her eyes had
softened—now the look in them was one of having been offended.
If the boy had any luck, he'd be famous all over Europe, and then of course
he wouldn't give me the time of day. So why was she rebuffing him?
Hadn't she come down here of her own accord, on her own two feet?
If he didn't make me feel all tingly inside all the time, then of course I'd
be able to flirt properly and take things slowly, just like the next girl! Her
brother had always told her that the heavier the gold, the greater its
worth, the coyer the girl, the better husband material she'd catch.
But now tell that to my heart! I'm scared to death that Ahmet won't call
me. If I knew that he'd never call me again unless . . . Then I would . . .

right now . . . Goddamn honor, it's a curse, one that girls like me have to worry about. Look at Elizabeth Taylor. I bet she didn't snag five husbands by being coy. If I had furs, diamonds, cars, worldwide fame like that, he'd be dying to have just two words with me, let alone my hand in marriage. The dirty bastard, he'd go so far as to pimp me out, just so he could take the credit for my worth.

Şükran's face had grown red from the chain of swiftly changing thoughts running through her mind. She wasn't that used to thinking, actually. Seeing her crimson cheeks, Ahmet got excited. *Truth is, Şükran's not such a bad catch. Those nice firm tits. I ruined it with all that stuff about my sister.*

"Şükran?"

"Yes?"

"Do you want to go to a movie tonight?"

"I don't know."

"We could see *Love Story*. Tickets are hard to come by, but as you know, I've got a friend who works at the ticket booth."

Şükran looked at Ahmet again, and again she melted. If he asked her now, she wouldn't be able to say no. She went limp. A warmth spread down to her stomach, and then all through her body. *My legs. I let the hair grow out on them because I was going to get a wax. My leg hair is so long. It's disgusting. If Ahmet sees them, he'll never look at me again. Günseli joked that we'd have to tie a bow on them before long.* She'd been wearing pants so that no one could see her legs in that state. Her first time, with those legs . . . Never in a thousand years. She paused for a moment, pretending to study the cardboard boxes.

"I don't know, maybe. Actually, I was going to visit Meral but . . . Give me a call, just ring me at work, okay?"

Ahmet brushed the dirt off of Şükran. The touch of his hands made Şükran quiver once again. Ahmet stopped. *Now?* He paused.

Seeing the toppled boxes, he recalled what had happened just a little while ago. Şükran looked at the boxes too. She recalled Ahmet's slap. She was overcome with rage. "You'll see. I'm not giving it up to you. I'll make you beg and plead, get down on your knees, kiss my hand. And still I won't give it up. You'll have to walk over coals to get me." Tossing her hair back, she marched off. She was glad now that she hadn't slept with him.

They walked past Çetin without a word. Afraid that Çetin would understand what a failure he was, Ahmet put on a confident air and grabbed Şükran's hand as they walked past him. Çetin didn't pay any attention to Ahmet. He could already tell from the look on Şükran's face what had happened, or rather, what hadn't happened.

They walked out onto the boulevard, wading through the crowd that was waiting for The Big Store to open for the afternoon hours. Ahmet bumped into a middle-aged woman determined to be the first to scramble her way in as soon as the store opened. Thinking only of the warmth of Şükran's hand, Ahmet walked.

Hatice Hanım defends her rights

Hatice Uzgören, who became furious after Ahmet bumped into her just as she was preparing to barge her way through the crowd gathered in front of the Big Store, hissed between tightly stretched, nearly invisible lips: "Goddamn you, ya twerp." Ahmet marched right past Hatice Hanım, thinking only of Şükran's tits.

The truth is, Hatice Hanım wasn't swearing only at Ahmet. For her, Ahmet was just one of a mass of young people who were nothing more than walking specimens of boorishness, mischief-making, impertinence and ineptitude, transcending comprehension or definition. It was always these guys, the beginning and end of all things troublesome, these so-called youth who, being rotten to the core themselves, sought to spoil everything, who bumped into people on the street and marched right by without even so much as an apology, who smoked on the dolmuş, who crossed one leg over the other before the very eyes of their elders, who prostituted themselves, unabashedly holding hands in public, who let their hair grow long like the sons of infidels and grew moustaches like measly porters, who laughed raucously, who wore tight pants that revealed their every attribute, and who then with the veins in their necks swelling disparaged everything right and good and manly. These were the so-called youth of today. It wasn't as if this was the first time Hatice Hanım had ever encountered a member of the youth, of course! She had seen her fair share of real, genuine youth: Good through and through they were, quiet and reserved, never venturing to touch even the hand of their fiancee in front of their mothers or cross their legs in front of their elders.

But those youth didn't exist anymore. Instead, these rascals had sprouted up in their place. It was impossible to find decent white cheese at The Big Store anymore. And the taxi drivers too had grown rude, just like the youth. And day-wage cleaning women had upped their daily wages. The doormen no longer wore themselves ragged to take care of your every need; they stopped by once in the morning and once in the evening, and that with barely feigned reluctance. Taxes were constantly on the rise. Being a property owner increasingly became a burden. Because of whom? Soot rained down on the balconies, housework was never-ending, and these guys incessantly bumped into people without so much as an apology, as if their other crimes weren't enough as it was. There was no such thing as a decent neighbor anymore—all of the local businessmen had turned into crooks, and you couldn't find any meat at the butcher's. They were all incorrigible culprits of the same crime, claiming to go to university while they constantly yelled out slogans in the city squares, constantly engaged in shameless dancing at disco-theques, constantly flooring the gas pedals of their fathers' cars in front of patisseries, constantly trying to teach their elders a lesson, their voices brazen, their arms in motion. And so making do with an exclamation of "Goddamn you!" directed toward all of these criminals deserving of punishment, she began to storm her way through the crowd. Confident in her right to be at the very front, she shoved all others aside. Hatice Hanım was always in a hurry because she always had an important job to do, like washing the dishes and getting them put away as soon as possible. That's why she never let anyone at the breakfast table swallow a single bite in peace, and why she always whisked away the glasses before anyone was actually done drinking their tea. The house had to be cleaned as soon as possible, for she had to leave and go to the open-air market and get the best oranges for the best price before anyone else. Many a moon ago she had been a teacher at one of Yenişehir's elementary schools. Now she was retired. Back then too she was always in a hurry. During breaks between lessons she'd go grab Gülsüm or Fatma from their homes in the gecekondu neighborhood of Deliller Hill, drag them to her house located right next to the school, and have them wipe down the stone pavement at the entrance. Later, she kept one of them, Fikriye, bound to her for years. In the mornings, she'd shake Fikriye to wake her up and oversee her to make sure that the house was cleaned as quickly as possible before anyone woke up.

The household would wake up to a salvo of commands:

"Fill the bucket!"

"That's enough!"

"Don't let it overflow!"

"Turn off the faucet!"

"Turn it off good I said!"

"Wring the towel!"

"Wring it good! Now mop over there too! But don't get the carpet fringe soggy!"

Most mornings Hatice Hanım's husband, who had always worked in the same division of the Finance Ministry, would leap in fright from the bed which quaked as Fikriye mopped beneath it. If you were in a hurry, it meant you were on to something, and knowing what was being sold when at Sümerbank was a natural outcome of this state of vigilance, this hurriedness. Yes, she was fast on her feet. She despised hesitation. She herself searched store after store in Ulus trying to find a faucet to match the one that had broken at home so as not to get cheated by any of the faucet dealers. She cashed in the savings bonds of everyone in the family on the very day they matured.

And now, like always, she was hasty and determined to have her own way. She had to reach the lower floor immediately. If it had arrived, she just had to reach that cheap, delicious, usually-out-of-stock white cheese before others got to it first and snatched it all up. Hatice Hanım had to marry her daughter off before everyone else to the son of a good family who had received a better education than everyone else, who had done his military service and was more than capable of putting bread on the table and then some; for her son, she had to secure the most ladylike, the most virginal of the candidates who showed up when it was her turn for the regular get-togethers of the neighbor women. Because she deserved it, and that was that, she deserved it.

Determined not to let someone else seize the rights she had gone to such lengths to earn, she dashed into the store before anyone else. The escalator glided downwards at its normal pace. The same faces rushing to get the same Vita butter, the same Lüx biscuits at the same price, glided down according to a meaningless arithmetic like oranges, apples, and bananas sliced for the purpose of becoming bar snacks. Hatice Hanım looked at the meat in the window display.

"Don't you have any ground meat, son?"

"We do."

"I said ground veal."

"No, we don't."

"Why not?"

"We're out."

"The store just opened, son, how can you be out?"

"We didn't get any today."

"Is that so? And why not?"

Her voice grew louder and louder. She became increasingly stern, and a terrifying shade of red spread from her lips to her neck, and then up to her ears. The salesman was not afraid. Yet Hatice Hanım was accustomed to scaring people. Even on the bus, a simple glare from her was enough to frighten the other passengers into surrendering their seats. Her voice rang out in the school hallways, echoing as it crashed against the windows and the walls; the echoing spread fear, piercing the not-yet encrusted hearts of young babes and intruding upon the indolent slumber of the janitors. The number of those who were frightened gradually decreased. And it was always because of those who were not frightened, always because of them, that there was no ground veal.

"Now you look here, who's your manager? You need to give your customers proper answers! I asked you why there wasn't any ground veal! When will you have it?"

It was imperative that he cower. It was every bit as important as the ground veal that he cower. It was imperative that he abandon all the other customers and cower before Hatice Hanım, hanging his head, which was incapable of finding ground veal, in shame like a slave aware of his crime. Yet the salesman had turned his back to Hatice Hanım and was weighing chicken for a customer who had come along after she did. Hatice Hanım looked around, left and right, searching for whistles, police whistles, police chiefs, fists, nightsticks and even prison sentences; he wasn't afraid, the salesman; the heart of the salesman did not explode like popcorn, like the hearts of elementary school students who, half out of fear and half out of not having done their homework, were incapable of providing the right answers.

She filled her lungs with air, she wanted to break out in one of the most terrifying screams she could recall, one similar to the scream she let out the day Fikriye ran away. Fikriye, who, while about to put some tea on to brew, let the top half of the teapot fall from her grasp, breaking it, and who then, before she was able to grow accustomed to the terrifying change created by the broken teapot, finding herself face to face with Hatice Hanım, threw the bottom half of the teapot aside and ran straight out of the house. With her screams Hatice Hanım first caused the household, and then the apartment building residents, and then the street, and then the stores at the corner to rise to the rescue, and it soon became clear that Fikriye had run off to a house in the neighborhood downhill with some help from the local *bakkal*. Thanks to the incessant screams that she never wearied of emitting, Hatice Hanım succeeded in taking the bakkal who had led Fikriye astray, the neighbor lady who had put the idea into the bakkal's head and Fikriye, who had the nerve to try and abandon her post before she was fired, to the police station. Although Fikriye kissed her hand a dozen times and the chief pleaded with her, for some time she refused to take Fikriye back; finally, at least partially convinced that everyone was sufficiently frightened and terrified, that the bakkal would no longer try to sell her expired milk, that the neighbor lady had completely abandoned the idea of leading the Fikriye's of the world astray, and that even if every bone in Fikriye's body were to be broken she would not leave, she returned home, her head held high, a snotty nosed and red-eyed Fikriye trailing half a dozen yards behind her. Hatice Hanım always held her head high, always. Thank God! She always caught the criminals and always terrified them; she frightened the criminals, put them back on the right path, made decent human beings of them, showed them what was what. And now this impudent salesman was blatantly committing a crime right here, right now, against a customer who was always right and who, by right of turn and right of money, demanded only what was, indeed, her right, that is, against Hatice Hanım, and yet his crime was going unpunished. In her eyes, there was nothing more unbearable than this: to witness and suffer the fact that an offender engaged in constant misconduct should go unpunished. No one should hold back when it comes to such violations. Every citizen should do her part to ensure that these criminals be punished, that they never again be allowed to freely saunter about like this. They should not be permitted to jauntily stand in the way of the sour meatballs that she had decided to cook for dinner that evening, that is, the sour meatballs that absolutely had to be cooked. And she wasn't going to make only sour meatballs from the ground veal. She was going to brown half of the ground veal and put it in the refrigerator and then make spinach with ground veal the following day. And she was going to separate the spinach leaves from the stalks and use the stalks to make spinach salad. Now how dare some insolent salesman indifferently turn his back upon all of these certainties?

She took a breath, she was going to scream; her breath would be enough to buoy her scream to the police, the chiefs, the courts. It was at that precise moment that she was startled by the voice of Colonel Zeki Bey's wife.

"How are you, Hatice Hanım?"

"Praise be to God, we're doing very well. We all kiss your hands. And how is the colonel, is he well?"

"Well, thank goodness he's finally back on his feet. May God protect us from any worse catastrophe. It's been just awful, just horrendous, my dear Hatice Hanım. God as my witness, this is the first time I've left the house."

"Oh my, well, I'm happy to hear the worst is behind you. I was just thinking of you."

"Is that so? Well, I know you're more than a fair weather friend. I'll be expecting you at our get-together tomorrow, Hatice Hanım dear."

"But of course I'll be there . . . What were you going to buy?"

"I thought I'd get some roast beef, the man of the house is on a special diet of course . . ."

"Well, let me tell you, they don't know how to treat their customers here, not at all. Et-Balık is still your best bet. With this service, they make you sorry you ever shopped here, I tell you."

She spoke these words loudly, peering at the salesman out of the corner of her eye, yet the salesman couldn't care less. But of course this wasn't the end of it, no siree, not for Hatice Hanım, and so she continued to stand there as Colonel Zeki Bey's wife began telling the story of her husband's illness from the very beginning for the umpteenth time. Hatice Hanım had no choice but to listen to her with a sympathetic expression on her face. A sympathetic face was never a good beginning for punishing criminals. She finally parted ways with Colonel Zeki Bey's wife and began filling her metal shopping cart with the other items she had come for. However much laundry detergent was needed for a month's worth of laundry, however much salt, sugar and soap would be consumed, however much Hatice Hanım would allow to be consumed, however much olive oil and flour would be used, is exactly how much she bought of each. Never overdoing it, never veering from the precise amount, knowing very well and never disobeying the laws she herself had made. Disobeying the law was the greatest of crimes in the eyes of Hatice Hanım, yet nevertheless, laws were disobeyed; the amount of money she paid for a month's worth of soap powder increased each month; seeing as Hatice Hanım always used the same amount of soap powder and abided by this law with unwavering precision and great earnestness, there must have been others responsible for transgressing the law. Every time she walked out onto the street Hatice Hanım identified the transgressors and punished them in her own way, and she knew now that this salesman was one of those responsible for raising the price of soap powder; however, she reserved his punishment for later. Hatice Hanım never ever forgot; criminals were not forgotten, punishments were never forgotten, and forgetfulness was not reparative, it was not constructive. Forgiveness was unhealthy. Forgiving was like not using medicine to fight germs, like not applying tincture of iodine to a wound. According to Hatice Hanım, a civilized person neither forgave nor forgot; forgiving and forgetting were barbarian, primitive, it was due to the softness of hearts that this country failed to make any progress.

She thinks about the get-together that is to take place the following day. Nezihe Hanım would undoubtedly be in attendance. Tomorrow Hatice Hanım will rub Nezihe Hanım's nose in the fact that she has not kept her word regarding the doctor's report her husband asked for so that he could take early retirement, that is, regarding the fact that her doctor husband acted duplicitously. She continues walking. There is a new kind of biscuit available. Newly available goods are of great interest to her. She wants to know in which stores which companies put new goods on the market and at what price. With great generosity she shares this newly acquired knowledge with friends and neighbors, and she desires for her personal judgments regarding the newly released goods to be heard out. She likewise expects others to inform her of newly released goods. And then later she says things like:

"That plastic tablecloth Ayşe mentioned isn't worth a cent."

"Our neighbor Zehra Hanım ran and bought the glasses that just arrived at The Big Store as soon as they came out. The woman has absolutely no taste, really."

"I listened to your father and bought this pan. It turns meat into a sponge . . ."

She looked at the tea biscuits which had just been put on the market. She was an attentive listener of advertising programs on the radio. She had never heard of this brand. Should she try it? Not out of nowhere she shouldn't. If it were anything worth its salt they would have broadcast some ads. But then the packaging wasn't bad, not at all. She looked at the price. It wasn't any more expensive than the biscuits she usually bought. Her suspicions soared. If only the colonel's wife would see them and buy a tin. She would offer them at the get-together tomorrow, and that way she'd get to try them. She could hardly reign in her curiosity; if she were certain no one would see her, she'd open it up and take a bite. But, buying biscuits was not on her list today. Otherwise, she definitely would have bought them. But it wasn't right to just buy something out of the blue; she looked around, searching for Colonel Zeki's wife—if she could only spot her she would call her over, and together with a litany of other comments, she would recommend the biscuits. And maybe the little woman would buy them, with the following day's get-together in mind. But she couldn't spot her, and so she walked away from the biscuits in a huff and approached the tableware section. *I should buy some tea-spoons*, she thought. *Actually, I need saucers even more.* She patiently and unflaggingly inspected each and every one of the saucers lined up in a row. She desperately desired for the ones that she bought to be without a doubt much better and much stronger than the others that she didn't buy. Yet all of the saucers looked alike and this created an extremely frustrating and exhausting situation for Hatice Hanım. It was extremely difficult to separate amongst so many similar saucers those worth buying from those not worth buying and thus acquire the feeling that she had bought the best and had not been cheated. Finally, she separated out the ones that had accumulated the least amount of dust.

The teaspoons were displayed right next to the saucers. All of them were the same length and very shiny. Hatice Hanım looked at the teaspoons. How on earth they ever disappeared was beyond her. Once again, there were none left at the house. All because of that cleaning woman. The addlebrained peasant kept tossing them in the trash. She did more damage than good, that woman. Rage welled up inside of her, because she wasn't able to punish the cleaning woman at that very moment; actually because she wasn't able to punish her because she needed her. The feeling of desperation that she felt only served to stoke the fires of her anger. She spotted the meat salesman from a distance. He was oh so casually, oh so carelessly weighing meat. All of a sudden, she reached out her hand. She grabbed a handful of teaspoons, the exact number of which she was uncertain, but which she guessed to be around a dozen, and put them in her coat pocket. With swift steps she walked away.

She got in line at the cash register to pay for the goods she had filled her metal shopping cart with. While waiting she complained loudly.

"This place has gone completely to pot. It's bloody chaos in here, I tell you, bloody chaos."

As she was paying she asked the cashier:

"Isn't there an office or something here where one can report an impertinent salesman, young lady?"

The harried cashier looked at her, boredom written all over her face, and did not respond. She shrugged her shoulders in the face of Hatice Hanım's anger.

Hatice Hanım walked up the stairs towards the exit. She was going to go home. She was of the belief that of everyone at home, her presence was most essential of all. The house belonged to whomever spent the most time in it. The chateau belongs to whoever surrounds it with armed men, to whoever raises its bridge at night. She began to wait by the traffic light. It was red. She grumbled after a young man who dashed ahead without waiting for it to turn green, and to the policeman who saw the young man yet failed to react:

"Look here, son! Everyone and his uncle is sprinting to the other side while we stand here waiting!"

The traffic cop continued to blow his whistle. While Hatice Hanım proceeded to explain to him the situation, starting from the very beginning in a louder voice, the light for pedestrians turned red again. The traffic cop left Hatice Hanım standing there across from the red light and began blowing his whistle after a car.

That so very familiar redness once again spread over Hatice Hanım's face. It was impossible to go out at all anymore. There was injustice everywhere. There was rudeness everywhere. When the light turned green, she marched forward in a huff. On the other side of the street, right in the heart of Kızılay next to that lovely building, right next to that so carefully decorated shop window, a crouching Gypsy woman was begging, in her lap a child that appeared to have gone blind from nitric acid. The beggar woman rocked the baby, those cliches of "ma'am," "fer God's sake," "fer the fergiveness of your sins" falling from her lips.

Hatice Hanım gave the beggar a piercing glance. These scoundrels had infiltrated the very heart of Kızılay. This city was absolutely out of control. *It used to be you never saw any of these ragtag types on the avenues of Ankara*, she said to herself; there used to be order, there used to be an authority, there used to be a system; servants used to seek the favor of this person and that person in the hopes of getting a position for their peasant relatives amongst the household help; the local bakkal didn't know how he could possibly thank Hatice Hanım enough when she paid her monthly bill. All it took was a phone call and the butcher would have his apprentice running right over to deliver the finest meat. The apprentice wouldn't accept any tips, he would just leave the meat and return with dignity to his post. But now? The thought of how things were now sent the blood rushing to her head. She looked at the Gypsy's hair, with its filthy, sticky strands clumped together. *Fine, so* we *might be used to it by now, but what a shameful sight for the foreigners.* Her husband had gone to Germany when he was young. He used to talk about those spic and span avenues that had not one piece of trash or a single beggar. You could lick the avenues and not be disgusted at all, it was that clean. A land of working, discipline, and order. One day he was walking down the street, behind a mother and child. The child tossed a banana peel onto the ground. The mother noticed a short while later. She immediately sent the child back to pick up the banana peel. And she gave the child an earful too. How many times Hatice Hanım had told that story to the children at elementary school, after picking the lice out of the hair of the children from the gecekondu neighborhood on Deliller Hill. *If we want to be proper people, we have to be more like the Germans, who don't toss banana peels onto the ground. But that would be a long time coming! We will never become proper people.* She looked at the beggar with an expression of rage, as if the beggar alone were to blame for the utter failure of this population to become proper people. She wished for the harshness of her gaze to pick the woman up and send her on her way to wherever it was she belonged. But the beggar woman persisted in her begging, as self-assured as ever. Hatice Hanım had given up all hope for her country's recovery. She walked; she didn't notice the greeting of a man in golf pants as he walked past her; she didn't see any faces, she was careful to walk on the right side of the pavement, she held on tightly to the teaspoons in her pocket; she was freezing, her body was ice cold, as if it were freezing outside; despite all of the blood that had shot to her head, her cheeks were like ice; it was as if her face were an apple forgotten in the refrigerator, as if only the palm of her hand, the hand wrapped around the teaspoons she had snatched from The Big Store, were warm, as if her heart were beating at that very spot, as if all the blood in her body flowed from that very spot; the heat spreading from that spot rescued her from the deadly cold; it gave her the strength to continue walking, to make it home and put away all the things she had bought, to cook them in the way they must be cooked, to begin and continue her life from that infallible point known to be necessary.

The hem of Necip Bey's pants comes undone

Necip Bey was upset that the greeting he had bestowed upon Hatice Hanım with informed courteousness was not returned. *They're boors, the whole lot of them, complete and utter boors, male and female alike.* He wasn't someone easily overlooked, with his plaid golf pants, bowtie, and long-handled umbrella. *That uncouth lowlife, and to think she was a teacher! So long as "éducation" remained in the hands of people like her, well . . .* He recalled the French *frères* at the parish school where he had studied, refined men who could recognize a fine wine, who knew which fish to eat in which season, who had no tolerance for those incapable of maintaining a rare center when cooking beefsteak, and he did so with gratitude. And how could he not? The education he received later during his university years in Lausanne, his refined nature, his ability to make a strong impression despite his dwindling inheritance, all of that he owed to what he had learned from them. That's the way it was. That's the way it was, even if uncouth, rude people like Hatice Hanım did fill up all the apartment buildings, even if they did constantly yell at the apartment building attendants, even if they did find a way to have the attendants at their beck and call, that's just the way it was. And to think that he had tipped the hat he bought in Paris ten years ago to greet that uncouth woman. He was very proud of the hat. He had seen a similar one in the Atatürk Museum located adjacent to Atatürk's mausoleum. "Atatürk's traveling clothes!" At the museum there were dozens more pieces of fashionable attire. Atatürk was a refined man with impeccable taste. Perhaps it was because he was from Salonica. After all, Salonica qualified as Europe. But it shouldn't be said that he was from Salonica. Necip Bey's mother got very upset at the mention that they were from Salonica. What was that supposed to mean, "from Salonica"? Of course there were *dönme*s, *palikarya*s, Bulgarians, and other immigrants who were from Salonica. But we, *we hail from the gentry* of Salonica. There was a seemingly infinite number of Greek and Bulgarian sharecroppers at the farm where Necip's father worked in Pişona. Whenever a member of the family died, the death notice would begin with the phrase, "A member of the gentry of Salonica," and all members of the family, even the most distant of cousins, would be mentioned one by one. Whenever Necip Bey's mother didn't take a liking to someone, she would say, "What do you expect, he's Anatolian, those people have no sense of courtesy, they're a bunch of boors, you cannot blame them for their faults . . ." That's the case with Hatice Hanım as well. Every time he turns around she's coming over to Necip Bey's to use the phone. As if the phone belongs to her own daddy! She gives all of her acquaintances, close and otherwise, Necip Bey's number. Necip Bey can't count the number of times he's had to interrupt his bath to go and give word to Hatice Hanım that she was wanted on the phone, or the number of times he's had had to get up in the middle of a meal, all because of Hatice Hanım's phone calls. But Hatice Hanım, well, she sees nothing out of the ordinary about this state of affairs, nothing at all. What's more, she makes him listen to her own litany of complaints about her husband's ineptitude and faint-heartedness, which always begin with, "I listened to the man of the house and cancelled our number when we moved, and we just haven't been able to get a new number since." She has a right to everything, including Necip Bey's telephone, and she will thank him for it, or not, as she darn well pleases. It's the gratitude issue that gets on Necip Bey's nerves more than anything else. The differences between them should be obvious. It should be obvious who gave and who took. It should be obvious who is bestowing a favor upon whom. Necip Bey considers himself to be a man of good manners. He is, he believes, the kind of man who willingly helps a neighbor who lacks a phone. Ever since he was little, he listened to so many stories about how his father helped numerous people in one way or another. And he too loves to help in any way he can, as long as it does not involve money . . .

He's philanthropic like his father, but he doesn't actually remember much about his father. In his mother's words, his father died of "the Aleppo boil," just like Sultan Selim. Right after the Greek-Bulgarian war. The Greeks had imprisoned all of the gentry of Salonica for some time, including his father. His mother had filled the house with hodjas and a bunch of old hags who used combinations of haricot beans for some curious manner of fortunetelling. Then there was a huge fire, and his father either died, or he did not; it was the homes of Jews or merchant dönmes that burned down in the fire. Nothing happened to the Turkish neighborhood because it was at the top of the hill. No, his father did not die just then; in fact, he had rented out a few of the empty rooms upstairs to some Jewish merchant acquaintances. As a gesture of good will.

After all, those Jews were multilingual people who had been

through a lot. They had great respect for İzzeddin Efendi. On every holiday they would come bearing presents to ask for his blessing.

Hatice Hanım, on the other hand, was living in Necip Bey's apartment as if *she* were the one doing *him* a favor. Each month when she handed the rent over to the building attendant, she'd complain of this or that problem with the apartment building. As soon as the central heating flagged even the slightest bit, she complained; she never missed a beat. She was utterly devoid of any manners, how else to possibly describe her?

Yunus Bey, one of his father's dönme renters in Salonica, now *he* was one polite gentleman; on the evenings when he came to chat with Necip Bey's father, Necip Bey would listen, mesmerized, his mouth agape, until he fell asleep on the divan. Yunus Bey knew everything. He talked about Europe, Paris, operas, the churches in Rome, the paintings in the churches. He was particularly interested in painting. One day when they had removed the upholstery from the divans for cleaning, he found Necip Bey hidden behind the divans drawing; seeing a Muslim child take such an interest in drawing brought tears to his eyes. He convinced İzzeddin Efendi that he should foster the development of the child's special talent, and finally, İzzeddin Efendi allowed Necip Bey to take lessons from Yani Usta, a professional painter who lived in the neighborhood. Necip Bey did not come to master the art of painting while working alongside Yani Usta, but he did paint in various shades of blue the skies of the paintings of angels and saints that Yani Usta produced on order for three different neighborhoods. The Ottoman gold pieces İzzeddin Efendi paid for those lessons! Still, may Yani Usta's soul rest in peace. Necip Bey always says that it was he who first instilled in him a sense of European culture.

That thick-legged daughter of Hatice Hanım is taking lessons at a ballet studio, he'd heard. Already an insolent hussy, that one. When

Necip Bey gets into his car on Saturday afternoons, wearing his white shorts, white rubber shoes, white sweater and cap, to go play tennis, she and her friends make fun of him; he hasn't said anything, but he knows, he can tell from their laughter. At one point they had gotten Necip Bey's daughter mixed up in their business and convinced her to let them make all sorts of calls from Necip Bey's phone. Every single day they called the flower-seller located at the intersection, Mehmet Horoz, whose last name means "rooster," to ask, "Hey Mr. Rooster, how's Mrs. Chicken?" The man filed a petition to track the calls. Next thing you know, Necip Bey is served with a court warrant. Necip Bey would never in a million years be caught dead in a courthouse; courthouses are for peasants. As far as he was concerned, the judge should have understood immediately, as soon as he saw Necip Bey's name, that a man such as himself could not possibly be capable of a trick like that, and he then should have convinced the flower-seller to that effect. But that's not what happened. Necip Bey was sentenced in abstentia to pay 50 liras. The very thought of it drove him mad. He refused to speak with his daughter for weeks because of this incident. He forbade his daughter from fraternizing with Hatice Hanım's daughter. His daughter didn't listen.

Compare those girls to the daughter of the owner of the pension where he stayed while studying in Lausanne—apples and oranges! Every time they ran into one other, she would bow and curtsy, never failing to bid him a good morning or a good evening, which she conveyed with smiling lips. She played the piano, went to concerts, played sports. Even though she was the daughter of a pension-owner, she was a very respectable, very ladylike, very well-mannered girl. Sometimes, when he got upset at something or other, Necip Bey would think, "If only I had married *her* . . ."

And now, he and his wife were going to court. His wife didn't want to get a divorce. Not because she loved Necip Bey, of course, but because she intended to get her hands on the apartment building, because she didn't want to be denied the alimony she'd been granted by the court. Otherwise, if only he could be certain that he wouldn't be put to shame in the eyes of his friends, Necip Bey would get her good . . . The divorce case spiraled out of control. His wife went around shamelessly sharing this and that detail about Necip Bey with their friends, gathering witnesses to back up her case. And all of those so-called friends, rather than talking some sense into her, only riled her up that much more. But then, of course, his wife *had* bestowed upon them a topic which would serve as a source for endless gossip during their card games at the club. And now all of them were prepared to perjure themselves. The judge meanwhile just sat back and enjoyed the show. He made sure the trial dragged on and on. If it were up to him, he would have had every socialite in the city take the witness stand, and he nearly did. The peasant ass. Necip Bey's wife maintained that she put up with all kinds of bullshit from Necip Bey, but hadn't divorced him for the sake of the children. She didn't even have the decency to refrain from telling stories of Necip Bey's perversions, right there in court. The judge meanwhile drew out the questioning, relishing every moment. "And just what else would he do, ma'am?"

"Your honor, honorable sir, I'm too embarrassed to say. He had very odd desires, sir."

"Like what?"

"It's an improper thing to say, but I will say it here sir, so that the truth can be known. I apologize in advance, but, you see, he used to take chocolate and spread it on my sexual organ . . ."

Just like that, shameless as could be. Yet all the while daring to act the lady . . .

Now Carla, she was different. One night, when he caught her on the stairs and kissed her, she simply sighed shyly. And then, one day, when it happened just like that, she calmly and silently put her clothes back on, and she didn't say a word about it to anyone, nor did she have any expectations of Necip Bey. And she continued to conduct herself with utmost respect towards the renters. When he was in Lausanne, every morning Necip Bey would leave the rooming house and go to one of the cafes looking out onto the lake. Those who were studying at the same university during that time say that in all the four years Necip Bey was in Lausanne, he never even set foot on campus, but instead spent all of his days sitting at the cafe. Necip Bey is greatly angered by such claims, because his French is excellent.

As for Hatice Hanım's daughter, she would neither become a degenerate in the full sense of the word like Necip Bey's wife, nor was she capable of becoming a full-fledged homemaker like Carla. Later Carla married; she kept a spotless house, and children whom she brought up impeccably. That daughter of Hatice Hanım, even if she did get an education, should she actually manage to land a job, she would be nothing but the embodiment of tactlessness, harping about this and that, talking her superiors' heads off: "It's time I got promoted," or "I still haven't used up all my vacation time." Not only would she always be late for work, but there would never be anything for her to do at work anyway and so she would spend her days knitting or gabbing, and never tire of either. *Why am I so obsessed with Hatice Hanım today? The whole lot of them can just stew in their own juices. It's not like I don't have enough concerns of my own.*

Necip Bey's rather upset today. The money he got from the parcel of land he sold in Istanbul has run out now too. And business isn't good either at the store on Sakarya Avenue, where Singer sewing machines are sold, for which Necip Bey put up the capital, and his friend from the French school, Hüseyin, puts up the labor. Hüseyin told him that he needed to find more money. It's always money, money, money. *What, am I a money factory or something? I was wrong to trust him, just like all the others.* But Hüseyin's persistent. "C'mon, I know you've got something stashed away somewhere. You say you don't but then the next thing you know, another apartment building or shop of yours magically turns up." And it was true that the property İzzeddin Bey had left back in Salonica had, during the population exchange, thanks to his sister's husband, a talented lawyer whose close acquaintances included some highly useful high-ranking statesmen, proven so bountiful, so fertile, that no matter how much property they sold, there was always more to sell. While his father was still alive, Necip Bey's older brother had secretly taken the Reşat gold coins from his mother's chest and gone off to Vienna. When Necip Bey's brother left, their mother locked herself up in a room, wrapped her head in a mourning scarf, and didn't talk to her husband for four days. Her son's departure had devastated the poor woman. Besides, the fact that the Reşat gold coins had left, the act of leaving itself was a bad thing. Equivalent to dying. Staying was good, especially staying at home. If you asked Habibe Hanım, if only her husband İzzeddin Bey had granted his oldest son the capital he had asked for and allowed him to start a business, then neither the gold coins in the chest nor his son would have left home. After his son left for Vienna, the enraged father told everyone that he had renounced his good-for-nothing son. But for the mother, her poor son was in some strange foreign land. Whether he went off to Vienna or off to fight in Yemen, it was all the same to her, so long as he wasn't at home by her side. Bad things happened everywhere; in Yemen he might be stabbed in the back by a treacherous Arab, in Vienna he could be robbed by bargirls. Woe was she, no longer would she be able to boil mint and lemon when her little boy's stomach ached—and her little boy's stomach often did ache, especially on the mornings after he'd spent the night slumming around the taverns of Salonica. She would no longer be able to surreptitiously feed her little boy the best piece of baklava on the tray, stored in the coolest corner of the refrigerator, when he got up from his midday nap. She didn't leave her bed, she spent all her time worrying about her son, and in her heart the hatred she felt for her husband planted firm roots. Some time later, Necip Bey's big brother wrote a letter from Vienna, where he had arrived after stirring up such tempests in the family. He was engaged in the commerce of snails. And he would grow filthy rich doing so. Vienna was incredibly beautiful, it was a full-fledged city, and compared to it, Salonica was but a village. He would buy a villa there, once he'd gotten rich. He was going to bring his mommy dearest over and give her the best days of her life, ah, it was these words that really made Habibe Hanım shed a flood of tears. And, ultimately, her son wanted capital for the big business venture he was about to embark upon. After the letter arrived, Habibe Hanım didn't speak to anyone, no one at all, for several days. She had a son who would talk to her, a big son brave as a lion, in the grand city of Vienna. Her husband could rail on about him as he pleased, but just what, she begged, had *he* ever done for her, his wife? Where had he ever taken her? How many months had he spent in Athens, and in Istanbul, without ever once taking his wife along? Was it not he who, according to what she had heard from a variety of sources, may God forgive them for their lies, took his Greek mistress along on one of his trips? What's more, he hadn't even tried to win his wife over on his returns, hadn't even brought her a single gift. Sure, he had looked after his children and his home, but then it's not like he could neglect these most basic of duties, right? Habibe Hanım inherited a farm from her father. That was another reason why she held her head high and stood her own ground against her husband. Ah, her son, her little boy, he often asked his mother for money, but many, many times he had bought her gifts of embroidered lace handkerchiefs. Stubbornly dwelling upon such thoughts, and stubbornly believing in the righteousness of her ways, she refused to back down. Finally, her husband, unable to stand the look on his wife's face or her incessant nagging any longer, sent to his son in Vienna the capital he had asked for, swearing it would be the last time.

Necip Bey let out a sigh. If only that had been the end of it. But had his brother not taken all of his mother's jewelry and sold it, piece by piece, as well? His mother preferred to remain blind to this fact; she was always in awe of her biggest boy. The more Necip Bey thinks about it, the greater the wave of discontent within him billows, urging him to insurrection. For if his brother hadn't sold that jewelry for peanuts, or blown that first or that last bit of capital in Vienna, Necip Bey would be much better off now. Necip Bey always measured his current situation in terms of his brother's mistakes and misguided passions and that was an appropriate measure. According to him, what he possessed or did not possess today was a result of his older brother's successful and unsuccessful endeavors. Had the inheritance from his father not dwindled away because of his big brother's profligate commerce, or rather, the masking of his debauchery under the guise of commerce? Necip Bey didn't know the details of the snail trade in Vienna. What he did know was that much later, on another of his journeys, his big brother had told one of his nephews that he stayed in the royal suite of one of the most luxurious hotels in Vienna, and then proceeded to show the suite to said awestruck nephew.

This is how the snail trade panned out: İzzeddin Efendi learned from a Jewish friend of his who had gone to Austria on business that the capital he had sent his son had been spent in a mad spree with a Viennese woman, and so this time, he disinherited his eldest son for good. Necip Bey was fixated on this whole disinheritance issue. And how could he not be? Because when his father died a short time after this incident, his mother appeared to have forgotten all about the disinheritance, and so continued selling this and that for the sake of her eldest son, finding him capital again and again.

Before the population exchange, Necip Bey had come to Istanbul, dressed as a shepherd, to study. His big brother had moved to Istanbul much earlier and started an import company together with several easternized Europeans. Before Necip Bey left for Salonica, his mother had taken him down to the basement and showed him the gold hidden there inside a huge earthenware jar. "Look, son," she said, "this is the last of the gold. If your big brother tries to take it from me, stop him!" Necip Bey left for Istanbul, shocked at his mother's expression of distrust towards his big brother, and with the jingle of a jar full of gold in his ears. And his departure, well, that was a whole other story now, wasn't it! Necip Bey's life essentially consisted of stories of his better, brighter past. While wandering the streets of Salonica, he encountered a group of Albanians gathered around a mosque, and when he heard they were going to Istanbul—*and think about it, I was just eleven at the time*—he ran home and dressed up as a shepherd before returning to join their ranks. The issue of how much gold the Albanians demanded to transport him, and consequently of how much of his mommy dearest's gold he parted with, is always left out of the story. Necip Bey tells this story to his children as an example of what a person can achieve when he really puts his mind to it. As soon as he and the Albanians arrived in Istanbul, he went and found his big brother.

His big brother lived in an apartment he rented in Teşvikiye Palas in Nişantaşı. He had the apartment decorated by one of Istanbul's famous Italian decorators. The place was like an antique shop. The walls were covered in luxurious wallpaper. It was an odd bachelor's pad with stylish furnishings that besieged one like a hostile force. But then, it would be wrong to call it a bachelor's pad, for it also boasted the constant fixture of his big brother's big-breasted Greek mistress who, ignoring the surrounding luxury, spent all day in the kitchen frying mezes and dousing them in olive oil. She was a joyous, spirited woman; Necip Bey liked her. It was around this time that his big brother took a fancy to the shipping business. Later, he sent his Greek mistress packing, in order to appear sympathetic to his Armenian shipping partner who had a spinster sister living at home. The Greek mistress left one day, crying a river and planting wet kiss after wet kiss on Necip Bey's cheeks. Necip Bey felt sad after she left, for just as her departure marked the end of decent meals, soon the possessions in the apartment, which grew increasingly unkempt, began to be confiscated. And thus did the shipping business come to an end.

Necip Bey strolled along, these thoughts running through his head for the umpteenth time, until he found himself in front of Piknik. Whipping himself into a state of consternation over the thought of all the money his big brother had squandered was a daily task of his. He definitely needed to withdraw some money from the bank today. His business partner had spelled things out pretty clearly. If he didn't put up more money, the store would go under. But after he withdrew the money, his account would be empty. And for Necip Bey, that was something akin to death. He viewed the future with suspicion. He watched the faces of passersby with an expression of anger, as if they were the ones depleting all the money at the bank with their unnecessary expenses. God only knew how many chocolate bars and ice cream cones their snotty-nosed kids were wolfing down each day, or the amount of money their ostentatious wives were throwing around in an attempt to show off to all and sundry. Together they conspired to consume Necip Bey's inheritance, paving his future with dark dangers by frittering away all the money at the bank. It was just as these thoughts were passing through his mind that the button on the hem of the left leg of his stylish trousers came off, allowing the hem to unravel until it hung down over his Swiss wool athletic socks.

Necip Bey stopped. He was very upset. He leaned over and searched for the button. It would be impossible to find an identical one. They were original Scottish buttons made of yellow metal and decorated with a coat of arms. He had gotten the pants themselves in Scotland too. Growing more and more aggravated by the moment, he looked around trying to find the button. At just that moment, someone walking down the boulevard stepped on the button, crushing it. Sweat poured out of Necip Bey's forehead. Never again would he be able to go to Scotland, never again would he be able to sit in the cafes of Paris, never again would a new death bring to him new inheritances.

Once he withdrew the money from the bank, he wouldn't have any money left, just one single apartment building, that was it. And the revenue from the store wouldn't be enough for him. That spring he had renewed his membership at the tennis club. But that place always cost him a fortune. One had to have some money in his pockets for bridge following the tennis match. A little whiskey in the evening, quality brand filter cigarettes, those were necessities. If he didn't have those, then the unfathomable fee he paid to gain entrance alone would be wasted. Plus he ate his lunch there on Sundays. If he could not do that, if he could no longer do even that much, then he might as well just die. For one, Necip Bey rightly deserved all of this, and, in fact, even more. He remembered the jar full of gold that his mother had shown him in the basement of their home in Salonica. The things one could do with that much gold. Necmi, a friend of his from the French high school—who, according to Necmi's standards, was a poor child—was hardworking and ambitious. After he graduated from high school, he went on to study engineering at the Technical University, from which he later graduated. His father, who owned a wee bit of land in Anatolia and had settled in Üsküdar, had given him very little spending money. Necmi never took a bus or a taxi, never even drank a single cup of coffee at the coffeehouse, sold his books at the end of each school year, and always walked around in the same old clothes. It was this very same Necmi that Necip Bey had encountered the other day at the club. He'd gotten fat, grown a spare tire. He was so relaxed, so confident. That uneasy, sunken-cheeked, complex-ridden boy of yesteryear had been replaced by someone who laughed boisterously as he played chess, treated those at the table to round after round of whiskey, and tipped the waiters heavily without even bothering to check the bill. It was as if all those coffees left undrunk, all that junk food left uneaten, all those trams left unboarded, all those cinemas left unvisited had just accumulated and accumulated until they became a rainbow under which Necmi passed to emerge a completely transformed guy. He greeted Necip Bey warmly, though it must be said, a bit dismissively. God only knows how he must have envied Necip Bey when they were in school. But then Necip Bey was certainly worthy of envy. His big brother, truth be told, used to give him a large allowance. And his clothing was tailored just for him by the fanciest, priciest tailor in Beyoğlu. Necmi Bey's industriousness back then may have been due in part to his envy of Necip Bey. After the Greek mistress left, the home in Teşvikiye in a way became Necip Bey's bachelor pad. To have a bachelor pad in Teşvikiye Palas at that age! On the weekends, when Necip Bey's big brother was out of town on business, Necip Bey and his friends would amass at the place and make a point of drinking, and drinking lots. Necip Bey would use his pocket money to buy the most expensive mezes. Once, on a dare, he phoned Park Hotel and ordered a bottle of champagne to be delivered by a waiter. His friends still talk about it. But now, Necip Bey has become very stingy. Actually, that's one reason why his wife turned her back on him—the way that he constantly insisted she account for this and that, his unbelievable miserliness, which was fostered by an overwhelming feeling of insecurity at the thought of the future, and which depressed him a little bit more with each passing day. He would have the maid dry out the grounds of a cup of Turkish coffee she'd prepared for one guest and boil it again, and he paid all of the expenses that needed to be paid at the last possible moment, including his children's tuition. It was that French bread factory his big brother, the good-for-nothing piece of rubbish, established later that sent Necip Bey to his ruin. Once the apartment building was sold, that was it, there was nothing else, no more hope, certainly no hope of a new inheritance, the end.

His son and daughter were going to study at university. But they gave no sign of hope for the future either. They didn't show Necip Bey a modicum of respect, let alone instill in him any confidence for the future. His daughter answered none of his questions, and his son let his hair grow out, grew odd mustaches, and had a poster of Fidel Castro in his room. He did it all to spite Necip Bey, purely out of spite. Yet Necip Bey was a liberal man, that's how he thought of himself; he never neglected to read the Swiss newspaper in the mornings. He insisted that he knew what communism was, and who communists were. It was an old-fashioned worker's religion; at one point it raised a ruckus in Europe, but the Europeans took the necessary precautions, and by keeping those greedy laborers sated, they rescued their jaundiced minds from the darkness of that dogmatism. And now some particularly spoiled youths had rediscovered this fashion, but it didn't matter, because once they inherited their fathers' money, or began working, they would certainly forget all about that youthful craze. But then what was going on with his son? In Turkey, his son said, the state of the laborer was different . . .

What was it to him? Was he not the grandson of İzzeddin Efendi, a member of the gentry of Salonica? So let the laborers worry about their cause themselves. *None of that stuff would work in this country anyway. The people are ignorant. At this rate, with his mind, he'll never make anything of himself. In the end, he'll be worse off than a mere laborer. So be it . . .* Necip Bey grew furious. *All of them, all of them stole my property, they made me sell it all.* An insurrection had long ago been carried out against Necip Bey, its perpetrators unknown. *Of course, my big brother and those other bloodsuckers have left me with nothing. If I still had that old inheritance, I bet you our little lord wouldn't be neglecting his lessons because of a bunch of nonsensical ideas and growing a mustache that made him look like one of those Bulgarian sharecroppers on the family farm back in Pişona.* Recalling what had happened the other evening when he walked into his son's room sent a shiver down his spine.

Seeing, upon rising in the middle of the night to get a drink of water, that the light in his son's room was still on, Necip Bey grew angry. The electric bills were astronomical enough as it were. He marched into his son's room. Actually, he was not in the habit of entering his son's room because he was not fond of being the recipient of rude rebukes. Right, oh yes, and so when he entered the room, he found his son playing with a gun.

Necip Bey's face went sallow. All his life he had been terrified of guns. Fearing that his son would sense the fear in his voice, he decided not to get on his case about the lights.

"Where did you find that?"

"What's it to you? I didn't use your money to buy it."

"What do you mean, 'what's it to me?' Am I not your father?"

"Is someone denying that? But that's between you and me, the gun has nothing to do with it."

"Where do you get the money to buy these things? First finish your studies and start earning money, and then you can do whatever you damn well please. To think of all the expense I've gone to for the sake of putting you through—"

"So don't. Who told you to put me through school?"

"I'm not like you, I have a conscience. I know that if you don't finish school, you'll go hungry."

"Oh yeah, right, we're not getting an inheritance like you did."

"Have you no shame? Why, when I was just eleven years old—"

"You came to Istanbul dressed up as a shepherd so you could study. Then you moved into Teşvikiye Palas with your big brother. Then, with a suitcase full of clothes made of English fabric, you took the luxury coach of the Orient Express to Switzerland to study. And you didn't study."

This was just too much. The blood rushed straight to Necip Bey's head.

"Get out, get out I tell you."

"Right now?"

"Right now."

His son got up ever so slowly. And as he did so, the barrel of the gun turned to point straight at his father. Seeing Necip Bey turn white as a sheet, the boy laughed.

"You cowardly Jew you!"

It was that word, the word "Jew" that reverberated in his head like a bolt of lightning. Had he searched far and wide, never would he have been able to find a word capable of angering him more. His son had used the word only in jest, had not chosen it especially but only randomly, to make fun of his father's cowardice, but for a moment Necip Bey was devastated. Once he had come to Istanbul dressed as a shepherd and started studying, after learning that he was from Salonica, all of his friends had asked him at least once, with more than a hint of insult, "Are you a dönme?" And so to prove that he wasn't, and indeed he really wasn't, Necip Bey went to such great lengths that he always got the feeling that the other person never believed him, and that all of his efforts only served to reinforce the other person's belief that he was Jewish. And he was never able to shake off that feeling. When he was studying in Lausanne, the Nazis were having their golden age in Germany, anti-Semitism was popular in Switzerland, and all manner of people frequently began to assume that Necip Bey, with his dark skin and rather Roman nose, was Jewish. Even Carla told him about how one day her friends had asked her, "Why are you running around with that Jew?" With time, this feeling had assumed the form of a downright complex. He hated Jews.

But one day, his wife said to him, "It's obvious that you're not a dönme because you're lazy as a sloth and you fail at everything you do . . ."

When his son attacked him with that epithet, the blood suddenly rushed to his head. He marched straight over to his son and slapped him twice, hard. His son, shaken by the unexpected slaps, fell backward, bashing his head against the corner of the chair. As Necip Bey watched the blood flow from the gash on his son's head, his son looked at him with perfectly round eyes that grew deeper and deeper, resembling a well, a well that wanted to pull his father in and drown him. And that look drove Necip Bey even madder.

"You swine!"

"That's right, with a snob like you for a father, what else could I possibly be!"

"Shut up or I'll hit you again."

"Do it, go for it. It'll be the only action you've ever taken in your life. But don't make do with just hitting me, take that gun and shoot me, if you've got what it takes. But you can't. You'd shit yourself. Look, I'm telling this to your face. Do you know what I think about when I play with that gun? I think about ridding the earth of parasites like you!"

Necip Bey's face had gone from yellow to red . . .

"Get out . . . Get out, you ungrateful wretch!"

"I'm not leaving. C'mon, kick me out if you can. Hit me, if you can. But no, you can't, because you're scared shitless. If someone held a gun like this at you, you'd shit right in your golf pants."

Necip Bey didn't listen to the last of his son's words. He saw himself punching his son and pulling his hair. His son didn't fight back, but he yelled. The echo of his son's voice grew louder and louder in his ears: "That's right, you're a shit-filled pair of golf pants!" He turned out the lights and left his son's room. Despite all that had happened, he was still thinking of the electricity bill. As for kicking his son out, he didn't dwell on it. Because if his son left, he would go to his mother's, in which case the court would find his mother even more justified in her demand for alimony.

When the button on his golf pants came off and the hem unraveled and fell over his sock, he got the feeling that there was something in his golf pants, something that was going to fall out. His son had gotten to be too much. Everyone had gotten to be too much since his inheritance started running out. Everyone had joined forces to destroy him, to devastate him in his weakest moment, to spend all of his money down to the very last dime. The gold that his big brother had spent on only God knows what appeared before his eyes. Forgetting that he and his sister had always gotten by on what remained of the inheritance, he believed that all of his woes were due to the fact that his big brother had gotten away with that gold. Whose fault was it then, if not his brother's? He walked into the bank, angrier than ever at his brother.

Mehtap's nightmare

Mehtap wore her long, light brown hair in a single braid that ran down the back of her neck. She saw Necip Bey as he was coming into the bank. She knew him well. He was a frequent customer. Yet he had rarely been seen depositing money. Necip Bey always withdrew money. Mehtap was very surprised by this. For her, a bank was a place to deposit money, accumulate money, invest for a better future. How was it that Necip Bey, rather than multiplying his money at the bank, constantly withdrew it, making it dwindle further and further? Ponder it as she may, the matter remained cloaked in mystery in Mehtap's mind.

Mehtap was from an immigrant family hailing from Caucasia. She was a reserved, hardworking, tall, blue-eyed girl. The bank's management was satisfied with her performance, and the customers even more so. She grew up in Konya. Her father was a master welder who had worked for years as a public servant on the railway.

He had worked on the railway for thirty years, during which time he would leave for a welding job on the construction of a bridge in some far-off mountainous region to return home only weeks later. He spoke of endless toiling in snowy, isolated places inhabited by roaming wolves, and returned with arms burnt from welding and a body depleted of strength. Mehtap and her mother and older brother would spend days, sometimes weeks, waiting for him, usually half-starved to death. Mehtap's mother was enlightened enough to busy her children, who had not yet started school, by teaching them the alphabet. She would try to make up for their feelings of destitution by telling them stories. She had raised her children to be content. When, every once in a blue moon, she fried slices of stale bread dipped in egg, the kids would celebrate: "Mom's making bread fish!" When still just a small child, after she began to understand the meanings of words, Mehtap made up her mind to do something for her parents who, though good people, never seemed to have experienced a truly good day in their lives. She became hard working so that she could put a smile on the faces of these two good people and hoped that by working, by working hard, at school and then later on too, she would be able to change their doomed fate. Her family didn't have the means to put her through school. But Mehtap had to study; if she didn't, the dreadful nightmare she'd had as child would come true. The nightmare went like this: while welding in the snow on the shore of a frozen river, her father is attacked by a pack of wolves whose eyes are shinier than the sparks of the welding machine. Her father uses the welding machine to try and stave off the wolves. But one of the wolves, clearly the alpha, whose head is much bigger than those of the others but whose body is the size of a normal wolf's and who has flames coming out of his mouth, swallows up her father together with the welding machine. And then, from between his pointy teeth he spits out her father's skinny bones, which still have bloody pieces of flesh on them. Then, the other wolves pounce on the remains still clinging to the bones. Finally, the alpha of the pack spits out the welding machine. The sparks of the welding machine, which continues running next to the stripped-bare bones of her father, melts the ice of the river, and the overflowing waters of the river turn into a sea. And in that sea, her father's bones, together with watermelon rinds and pieces of straw, gradually drift away. It was this part of the dream that hit Mehtap hardest of all. Her throat knotted up when her father was being ripped to pieces, of course, but when her father's bones drifted away, as if never to return, that's when she was overcome by an incurable feeling of melancholy and she would wake up crying. The tears wouldn't stop flowing for hours. That day, she swore to herself that one day she would rescue her father from that job. In middle school, she studied at a vocational school of commerce; she had heard that those who graduated from this school found work more easily, and it wasn't long before she had already begun making money whenever she had time left over from her studies. She and her older brother had struck up a deal with one of the shops across from the Mevlana Museum. At night they reproduced portraits of Mevlana on the bottoms of copper bowls. They got fifty kurush for each one. As soon as she had saved up enough money, she bought her father a first-rate Bursa knife. Perhaps so that he could protect himself against the wolves. After graduating from vocational school, she had gone to Ankara to pursue more academic studies. Meanwhile, her older brother had gotten married and started a family and ultimately, in a way, had broken the pact that the two siblings had made to change the fates of their parents. Now, he had to worry about putting bread on the table for his own family. There were others he had to make happy now. If he were going to change anything, he should change it for his own wife and kids. That's why Mehtap was so upset with her brother. For the longest time she could barely bring herself to look him in the face. Once she had finished vocational school, Mehtap found a job at a bank in Ankara. One of the teachers at her school, observing her industrious manner and seeing the predicament she was in, had asked a friend to give her a job. Now, she had a day job. She had brought her parents over to live with her. Her father was retired. Yet even with his pension and Mehtap's salary combined, they barely got by. The landlord was going to increase the rent once again. They lived in Yenimahalle in a cheaply built apartment, where the faucets and everything else were in a constant state of disrepair, where water leaked through the walls of the kitchen, an apartment which didn't have a radiator and also didn't qualify for coal from the government. Even their home back in Konya had been better than this, almost. At least it had a backyard with two apricot, one mulberry, and three cherry trees.

Whenever her father returned from one of his exhausting trips, her mother would set a table out in the yard, dish out the money for a bottle of Yeni Rakı, and fry some liver and peel some cucumbers, which she would serve along with white cheese and melon. If it were winter, she would celebrate by smoking pastrami on the heater. The heater kept the old, thick-walled house plenty warm, and her father, once sufficiently pie-eyed, would fantasize about his retirement, telling his loved ones about the days to come when they would all be able to relax and enjoy themselves. The fairytale her father told during the summer, in the faux fairytale atmosphere created by a bulb hung from the apricot tree, about how, once he was retired and his children had made lives of their own they would have "their own home" and "their own garden," how they would get up after daybreak, read the newspaper in bed, and eat meat and fruit every day, was a lovely fairytale indeed. Mehtap and her brother would get carried away themselves and say how when their father was retired, they would work lots and earn money, they would save a whole lot of money, and with the whole lot of money they saved they would buy themselves a one-story home with a yard, and then their father would never wake up early—never had he slept through sunrise, and when the kids got up, not once did they ever find their father at home, having tea and reading the newspaper. "I'll bring the newspaper to you in bed," Mehtap would say. "You can keep your pajamas on all day if you like." Her father would talk about the dahlias he would plant in the front yard of "their own house" and her mother would demand without question that roses be planted in the front yard too. She loved roses. Roses articulated a woman's unordinary desires. And then, she wanted pine trees in the front yard; pine trees were the trees of dreams, the trees of rich, distant countries. In a page that had fallen out of a foreign magazine, they had seen a Christmas tree: A glowing, colorful pine tree covered in decorations, with a happy family sitting next to it, surrounded by gifts. Ever since that day, for Mehtap's mother, the pine tree had become the symbol of a warm, carefree family life.

Yes, but now, well, her father was retired, and Mehtap was working. Despite the fact that she gave almost all of her money to her family, setting aside for herself only money for transportation and what she needed for clothing, they still were far from comfortable. Even though her father was in no position to be drinking Yeni Rakı any more often than usual, he had started drinking it every night. Only now, when he drank it wasn't pleasant; he didn't even tell that old "a home of our own" fairytale anymore. Mehtap, in seeking the reason for their plight, thought she had discovered it in her brother's marriage. Just when the prince was about to unite with his lover, a witch emerged, playing the part of the giant who broke the spell. Maybe if her brother's income were added to theirs . . . But her mother defended her brother, saying that of course he was going to marry, he had long ago reached the age at which that was the thing to do. "You'll get married too one day," her mother said. "You'll get married too and leave us," her father said, "and then, either you won't work because you'll have children, or you'll have to help your husband. Why should some man, some stranger, look after your mother and father? It's best I go ahead and find myself a job now." Mehtap didn't want to hear a word of this betrayal, which was portrayed as likely, inevitable even. But somewhere deep in her heart, she felt that there was truth to these words, and she resented the unknown enemy who was forcing her to turn her back on her most beautiful beliefs. She grew heavy-hearted because she was unable to change anything, even though she worked all day and took evening classes at the academy in the hopes of eventually earning a better wage, even though she squandered no money, and even though she pushed herself—hard, as if trying to squeeze glasses full of lemonade out of a shriveled summer lemon. Her father became set on the fact that he absolutely positively had to find a private sector job, repeating over and over, "What are we going to do when you leave? The older I get, the harder it'll be for me to find work. It's best I find a job now." Was it all in vain? Had they spent their nights painting those portraits of Mevlana in vain? Had she and her brother sworn to each other and made a pact in vain? Would the fairytale told so many times under the light of that bulb in the backyard of their rundown house in Konya never come true? Were all of those dreams, which seemed so reachable, real and so very humane, in truth only supernatural, like the fairytales with the giants and the fairies, with Mount Qaf and flying carpets, and the wood-chopping girl who marries the sultan's youngest son? Mehtap felt distraught. She felt very distraught. That morning, her father had started working again for a private sector company. He made less than he had working on the railway, and in exchange for even more hours of toil. Someone, perhaps her older brother, perhaps someone else, but certainly *someone* had betrayed them. There was someone out there who had stomped all over Mehtap's childhood, all over her beliefs and efforts, and unleashed that old wolf of her nightmares upon her father, without even batting an eye.

She raised her head and looked at Necip Bey. She had noticed when Necip Bey walked into the bank that the button had come off his golf pants, and she had barely been able to contain the laughter ignited by the few sparks of childhood still left inside her. Wearing a serious expression she had unknowingly acquired at a very young age, she looked into Necip Bey's eyes questioningly.

"How much, Sir?"

She was certain that Necip Bey would be withdrawing money.

"All of it!"

Mehtap was both surprised and saddened by his response. She herself, despite her hardship, deposited a few liras into her account each month, skimping sometimes on socks, sometimes on money for the cinema, in order to do so. She had saved up little money thus far. But even though that money was multiplying very slowly, at an unbearably slow pace, she was determined never to withdraw even a single kurush, unless, God forbid, she should be forced to do so due to death or illness. Sometimes, in an impressive display of fortitude, she suppressed those whims that beset all of her peers; she hoped that once she had finished school and her wages had increased, she would make her bank account grow and get a mortgage for a home (she didn't let her folks know that she was saving up), and surprise them with the apartment she bought; she would cry out, "Look, see, I didn't betray you, all of my efforts were not in vain, look, the fairytale told in the light of that bulb was not a fairytale, it was possible, anything is possible if you just put enough effort into it." But as her money accumulated ever so slowly, the amount necessary for the down payment on a mortgage increased in even greater increments, and what was worse, the prices of apartments skyrocketed. Yes, some things were changing, but whatever did change was always in the favor of that big-headed wolf.

Mehtap looked at Necip Bey once again. This time, the hem dangling over his sock did not appear ridiculous to her; she found it pathetic. It was as if something else had been lost along with that button. The fact that Necip Bey was withdrawing the last of his money put an end to the fairytale that played out over and over again in her mind. The idea that saving money at the bank wouldn't change anything began to take root inside her. If that weren't the case, would Necip Bey, that worldly-wise, perfect gentleman, withdraw all of his money? She began to wonder whether money in the bank, whether there to be constantly withdrawn or constantly saved, was actually a powerless thing, something that could be given up with such indifference.

"At least leave some of the money in the bank, so that you don't have to open up a new account when you want to make a deposit."

Necip Bey looked at Mehtap with an expression of shock on his face. It was always this girl who attended to him at the bank. She was a very quiet, very serious girl. He had never before seen her speak without being spoken to. He studied her face carefully. He couldn't attribute any meaning to the imploring look in her weary eyes, the blues of which had grown watery from staring at so many numbers. How could he possibly know that Mehtap was defending her own fairytale? Feeling that for the first time he was encountering someone who actually took an interest in the dwindling of his funds and who pitied him because of it, Necip Bey refrained from reprimanding her for her display of over-familiarity. Though he considered speaking with shop workers, clerks, petty civil servants and ticket sellers an unforgivable act of frivolity, he answered the girl sincerely:

"I will not be opening another account."

"But why? Perhaps you will."

"No, not anymore. I have no more debts to collect. From now on, I only have debts to pay."

"But just a year ago you had a considerable amount of money in the bank—if only you'd taken out a mortgage rather than emptying your account?"

"I own an apartment building already. But at this rate, I'm going to have to sell it too."

Mehtap's eyes opened wide. Someone who owned an entire apartment building was speaking to her—she, who thought that owning a single apartment would change everything, who had gone to such great efforts, endured such great hardship to that very end—of hopelessness, did not see himself as having been rescued by virtue of the fact that he owned an apartment building, was nevertheless withdrawing his funds, and was saying that he was going to have to sell the apartment building. She was utterly baffled.

"Okay, but, isn't the income from the apartment building enough?"

"Young lady, you mustn't have the slightest clue as to how expensive things are these days. Besides, I've got two kids to put through school. My wife's divorcing me and she wants alimony. This money is hardly enough for the promissory notes I have to pay. And if I can't pay the promissory notes, I'll have to sell the apartment building. Otherwise I'll go bankrupt. What's more, the apartment building is mortgaged. I can't possibly meet the mortgage and tax payments with the rent and the income from the store." And with that, he went silent. He realized that he had spoken much too much, that, like a common, petty man, he had shared his woes with just any random person. His face resentful and angry, thinking that this bank clerk must be among those responsible for the increasingly negative changes that kept occurring, enraged by this girl, just one of the countless examples of the sleep-walking hoard that did not mourn for the good old disappearing days of yore, he stormed out of the bank.

Mehtap watched Necip Bey as he left. *It's a good thing he's not coming back to the bank*, she thought. He was someone who constantly withdrew his money from the bank, who constantly whittled away at a hope, who made cracks in the hope that one day everything would suddenly change thanks to the money in the bank, who rendered the fairytale unbelievable, who sided with betrayal. She didn't like this man who tried to prove that the days when her father toiled endlessly at the riverside only to return home with arms burnt by the welding machine, the days when her father never wandered around the house in his pajamas and always woke up before sunrise, the days when Mehtap and her brother spent all night painting portraits of Mevlana, were better, lovelier days that would never return. She hated him. After Necip Bey left, she ordered herself a tea. The office boy, completely taken aback, looked at Mehtap with an expression of disbelief. Mehtap had never ever drunk tea at the bank.

Once Necip Bey had left the bank, deeming hunger to be at least partly to blame for the increasing unbearableness of the thoughts that plagued him, he decided to get something to eat. He had an ulcer. When people with ulcers get hungry, they see the world as a darker place. For Necip Bey, the world was already a dark place. Still, he was hungry. He decided to get something to eat at Piknik. He always had something light for lunch. For him, maintaining a stylish appearance in this dark world was of utmost importance. How many people still championed beauty?

Grilled meat with grapefruit juice, followed by a bitter coffee. It angered him the way Turkish women grew fat. They did so because they did not know how to eat properly, and they were primitive. He entered Piknik. *Now, I'll stop by the store after lunch, drop off the money, then go back home and take my midday nap. In the early evening I'll go to the club and play a round of tennis. And then I'll have a shower. And then some whiskey on ice.* The darkness within him was allayed, just a little bit. Ultimately, he wasn't responsible for what was happening. He was not responsible for how expensive things were, how merchants were a bunch of cheats, how rare honorable behavior had become in dealings of commerce, how his wife and kids splurged, how his big brother had spent all the gold in the basement of their house in Salonica, how people became more and more rude, more and more inconsiderate, more and more impolite with each passing day, or how the world got progressively worse, becoming an ever more regressive, uninhabitable place. Nor was he responsible for the fact that this country could never catch up with Europe, or for the way it teemed with beggars. He had never taken an interest in politics. He had never borne any responsibility for the governing of this land. Besides, he hated politics. Politics was a lowly job. It was a job for greedy middle class people. He looked around for an empty seat. There was a seat next to a young man and woman. Before ever so slowly and politely pulling out the chair, he asked permission from his neighbors at the table. The male of the neighbors, surprised by this unnecessary gesture, motioned nonchalantly with his head. *How rude!* Necip Bey nearly stomped off to find another place to sit, so offended was he. But upon seeing that all of the other tables were full, he decided against it. He hung his umbrella on the back of the chair. Curling one of his long fingers, he summoned a waiter. The waiter came running. Necip Bey grew very angry at people who ran on the job. For a waiter to run was a sign of carelessness, rudeness and ineptitude. The waiter was standing next to Necip Bey, pen and paper in hand, waiting impatiently for the words to come out of Necip Bey's mouth, when he said something to the other waiters: "Memet, the French fries go over there!" Necip Bey was enraged that the waiter was not paying attention to him. "Son, shouldn't you be serving *me*?" The waiter, having understood that this man was going to be a handful, was about to go take care of things that needed his more urgent attention when . . . Necip Bey grabbed the waiter by the arm, stopping him. The waiter, dumbfounded, stopped. *Another crackpot*, he thought. Necip was determined to educate the waiter, slowly but surely. Although he himself was responsible for none of them, he always tried to correct faults whenever he encountered them, wanted for others to benefit from his knowledge and ideas, and gave all and sundry a lesson whenever he deemed it necessary; he was a citizen cognizant of his responsibilities, just like Europeans, like the Swiss. In Switzerland, a child never sat down on the tram, even if it was completely empty; if a child did attempt to sit on a tram with empty seats, an elderly passenger would be sure to reprimand him before the ticket-seller did. But then if only everybody did their duty as citizens, if only everyone learned not to shake the dust out of their rugs from the windows, if only everyone paid their taxes . . . He turned towards the waiter. And he did not let go of the waiter's arm until the waiter turned to look at him. The waiter, forced to direct his bewildered, distressed gaze at Necip Bey, waited.

"Look son, listen to me carefully, because if you bring me anything I did not order, I will send it back," Necip Bey said, before releasing the waiter's arm so that the latter could take down his order. "Now, I want a completely fat-free sirloin steak. But don't let them leave it on the grill too long and dry it out. It should be medium rare. And with it, boiled potatoes . . ."

Look at this idiot, does he think he's at Washington Restaurant or something? the waiter, by now incensed, thought to himself,

"Sir, we don't have boiled potatoes. We have French fries, or mashed potatoes . . ."

"Son, do you not boil the potatoes before you mash them?"

"Yes."

"Weeelll then, why are you making this so difficult? Your job is to satisfy the customer!"

And just who is going to satisfy us? thought the waiter. *Guys like this aren't only demanding, they're stingy too; they don't even leave a tip.*

"Now go to the kitchen . . . Ask for two boiled potatoes . . . Have them peeled real good . . . Then top them with a handful of parsley mixed with olive oil and lemon . . . Then put some boiled peas and carrots next to it . . . Rub a little butter into the carrots . . . Wait, hold on! Don't get upset, son! Look, I want the order exactly as I have described it. And I want grapefruit juice too. Grapefruit juice, freshly squeezed . . ."

Necip Bey did not even see the fire trucks that had entered the street across from him or the people rushing in that direction just then. The waiter did not even listen to Necip Bey's last words. Instead, he ran over to the window to see what was going on.

Güngör gets ahead by dyeing Easter eggs

Güngör eavesdropped on Necip Bey's conversation with the waiter. *The jackass! He comes in for lunch but ends up ruining the meal, for him and for us, with all of his whining. I know his type. I get my fair share of them at my own store.* Güngör recently opened a furniture store in Çankaya. In this store, he sells items for the home, which he brings over from Europe using "trousseau permits" that he buys from certain merchants. He is planning to open a branch of the store in Nişantaşı soon. That's right, his store is doing so well that he is going to have to expand the business, which goes something like this: Certain merchants and members of parliament would get trousseau permits from the Department of Finance, claiming that they needed them because they were about to give their daughters' hands away in marriage. And then Güngör would relieve them of the permits.

Despite the middlemen, Güngör made a hefty profit because he got the merchandise on the cheap thanks to the permits and then sold it at greatly inflated prices. Not to guys like Necip Bey though, of course. Guys like him would come to the store and prattle on for hours about items they had seen in Europe. They would immediately convert prices to foreign currencies and give you a speech about what all one could buy for the same amount of money in this or that city; they would frown upon the quality of the wood, and find the polish tacky. Most importantly, however: they never ever bought anything. Never. Men of his sort never buy anything new. They never get rid of their old stuff, they're simply too devoted to things of the past. No one has ever witnessed them getting new things, or refurnishing their apartments. These guys needed to be brought down a peg or two, so that they would sell the antiques they possessed yet did not deserve. In his home decoration displays, Güngör combined antiques with modern decor. And the result was very stylish indeed. He had seen examples of it often in foreign magazines. But no, guys of Necip Bey's ilk simply did not cough up their antiques. Oh, but eventually they will, they'll have to. *What in the world is this man good for, other than having to sell his stuff? Sooner or later all of these guys, all the men of their ilk, will run out of the money left to them by their pasha grandpas because they aren't creative. They don't know how to make use of what they've got, or how to create anything new.* Güngör, to the contrary, was a creative person. Thinking about himself, he swelled with pride. *Did I not create everything while possessing nothing? Did I not get my start in business dyeing Easter eggs?*

"Haven't I ever shown you the Easter eggs I used to dye?"

Güngör's fiancee gave him a puzzled look. She had dyed her hair bombshell blonde. And she had had it flattened to fall straight down to her shoulders. She wore sunglasses that covered half of her nose and nearly all of her narrow forehead. She had just had her nails done; she was inspecting her nails, or rather, the ring that Güngör had given her the day before. A new ring. For her, it was a source of one week's worth of happiness. During this time (that is, until she saw something new in the shop windows to become infatuated with), rarely did she allow for anything to come between her and her latest prized possession. She looked at Güngör with astonishment. They would be married soon. Or rather, they were going to get married once Güngör got a divorce. Güngör was a perfectly likeable man. First of all, he was not stingy, and second of all, he took an interest in women's clothing. That is to say, it was particularly important to him how the woman he was with dressed. He always said: "For the woman at my side to dress badly would be akin to my store doing poor business. Just as it is important to me what I put in my shop window, just as I place expensive antiques acquired from the covered bazaar in the shop window without batting an eye, if I am to link my arm in that of a woman without batting an eye, then I must take care to make sure that she too is decorated so as to attract interest and customers."

Güngör wanted to look into his fiancee's eyes. But he couldn't see them. Those glasses didn't suit Melahat at all. Her forehead was too narrow, her nose too flat. They made her look like a dimwit, and rendered her already unimpressive profile flat as a board. They made her look like a Volkswagen or something. *She hasn't answered my question. But then I'm not asking her so that she will answer. I am warning her that she should listen.*

"Have I shown you my Easter eggs, Melahat?"

"No."

Good. Yes, or no. The best answers a woman can possibly give. In either case, the other person can guide the conversation in the direction he desires.

"My first job was painting Easter eggs. Back then, we lived in a basement apartment on Meşrutiyet Avenue."

"In the basement of Gülsen's family's apartment building?"

Gülsen was the wife Güngör was in the process of divorcing.

"Did you marry her because she was the daughter of the owner of the apartment building?"

There she went, talking too much again. Güngör was perturbed. He was about to rebuff her, but then he changed his mind. He had an important appointment at noon—best not to let himself get unnerved.

"Maybe! Why not? How about the fact that you chose this ring out of all the rings at the store? Though you most certainly had cheaper options."

"Well, um . . ."

"Anyway . . . At the time, my father was still in prison for embezzlement . . ."

"Sweetheart, don't say that . . . He was the victim of slander, that's what your mother says. I don't understand why you choose to disparage yourself like that."

"What are you talking about, disparaging myself? Embezzlement is the most righteous action a civil servant can take. Doesn't the state constantly embezzle the money of the citizens? Someone who sensed and saw this took back from the state a very small portion of the money that the state had usurped from a whole slew of people, money to which he was actually entitled, and even if he himself wasn't entitled to it, well, he had essentially taken back the money that was actually the entitlement of a bunch of other people. What's wrong with that? If I were stupid enough to become a civil servant, I would do the same thing. Only, I'd be smarter about it. If you want to embezzle the state's money, you don't necessarily have to be an accountant and get caught and spend time in prison. Look, instead you become a building contractor. You take part in a tender bid, and then you overcharge the state for services rendered. You do everything by the rulebook. All your documents bear the signatures of high-ranking civil servants. Those

same high-ranking civil servants who discovered the poor accountant's embezzlement and turned him over to the merciless hands of the
courts. What's more, you would gain the respect of everyone around
you for being a highly intelligent, competent man. Your wife wouldn't
be ashamed of her husband then, like my idiot mother is of hers."

When he looked up, he found his fiancé inspecting the clothes of
some woman sitting at the next table. Again, she's not listening, he
thought.

"Why are you even looking at her? Her clothing is utterly tasteless. A
person should always dress well. If you've got some free time, study my
magazine collection. That way, you'll learn how to dress more stylishly.
That color doesn't go well with your hair. When a blonde woman wears
pink, it makes her look like a plastic baby doll. A baby doll suits the
basest of tastes, even that of little girls in the slums, because baby dolls
are designed according to primitive tastes. Don't wear pink again."

Melahat was taken aback. Güngör's words upset her. She looked
into her fiancée's eyes with a hurt expression in her own. She gave
him a long, lingering look in an effort to curry favor. She squeezed
her fiancée's hand. She trusted her hands. She believed that when she
held a man's hand, it excited him.

Seeing that he had put Melahat sufficiently on edge, Güngör continued talking:

"I lived in that basement with four siblings, plus my mother. We
didn't have any money. But all of us were impeccable when it came
to how we dressed. We were a beautiful family. Despite everything,
we turned the heads of everyone on that street. My sisters were the
most beautiful girls on it. And neither of them was stupid enough
to go wasting time with the neighborhood lads. And you see how it
paid off, who they're married to now. What's more, their husbands
are much better off now than when my sisters first married them.

Everyone in our family is determined to better their station, no matter how good it may be, and we're quite successful at it too. For those who have a good eye and the ability to make the right decisions, it's really not that difficult. If you know how to aim, hitting the bull's eye is easy. That's always been the case, ever since the first humans began to roam this earth. Back then, people were hunters. Whoever was best at spotting the game and taking aim, and who was capable of flawlessly delivering the fatal blow to his victim, was the one who always had the fullest stomach."

Though bored with Güngör's talking, Melahat was reluctant to withdraw her hand from his, to tear her eyes from his and look in another direction. Güngör was quite temperamental. How easily he had dropped his wife of so many years. What's more, he was always going on about the virtues of changing things. Any item in the store that didn't attract attention, that didn't sell, was never kept around for long. Güngör never hesitated to get rid of such items immediately, selling them for next to nothing, even if it meant losing money. Melahat simply had to be someone who was always capable of attracting the attention of Güngör and others, and who others, men other than Güngör, that is, were prepared to sweep off her feet at any moment. She must respond to Güngör's ambition to own, to possess, to compete at all times. Meanwhile, Güngör would want to consume whatever it was he had acquired. Why would he acquire anything that he wasn't going to consume? Güngör would absolutely positively want to consume her, and he would do everything he could to that end. She would have to resist. She wasn't going to let Güngör consume her the way he had consumed his first wife. The woman had turned over her share in the apartment building so that Güngör could open his first store. And her father had always supported Güngör on his road to success. But at first, he was frequently unsuccessful.

Now, Güngör would be paying her a nice alimony in exchange for the divorce. True, but still she had borne three children, had fifteen abortions, and been worn out, depleted from trying to make Güngör's fickle wishes come true and seeking to keep up with his nightlife. It wouldn't be easy at all for her to find another husband, not after this. Yet she was what many would still deem quite young. Worn out and depleted as she was now though, she meant nothing to Güngör. On this topic Güngör would say, "Look, she and I are almost the exact same age, the two of us shared the same life, but look at her, and look at me. I'm tough as iron. I'm in much better shape now than I was in my youth. In many ways I'm far ahead of where I used to be, and much more attractive. I'm much better than I used to be at speaking, thinking, dressing, doing business, earning money and living well."

As for his wife, when the topic of separation came up, he had explained it to her as follows:

"Don't go on whining about 'Oh, what am I going to do now?'! It's not my fault if you don't know what you're going to do. I'm going to pay you an alimony far greater than the amount your father gave me once upon a time. What else can I do? What if I went and whined and cried to you about how worn out I am? You know what anyone in their right mind would say to that? 'Well too bad, then you shouldn't have gone and worn yourself out!' As you can see, I'm not worn out. To the contrary, I am more attractive now than ever before. After a certain age, everyone is responsible for his or her own looks."

Güngör's wife was unable to stomach her husband's mind-boggling hard-heartedness.

Güngör meanwhile spoke of his wife to his fiancé as follows:

"A bumbling idiot of a woman. So it turns out she's just not as talented as I am. Otherwise, she would be just like me. I mean, look at me, I'm capable of attracting women who are much younger than me. All of them are dying to marry me. But her, she'd have a hard time finding anyone, even an old fogy. Which means I'm out of her league. So why would I stay with her? We're just not a good match, we're not equals . . ."

Captured by a sudden feeling of fear, his fiancee responded:

"But you weren't equals when you got married either. She was the educated daughter of a well-to-do family. You had neither money nor an education. Moreover, seeing as your father was in prison, yours could hardly have been considered a respectable family . . ."

Güngör replied:

"Well, that was for her to think about. And it only goes to further prove my own value. Even though I started out much less fortunate than she did, I always made progress, always moved forward and bettered my station in life. She on the other hand was unable to make proper use of her good fortune, and ended up worse off than she was in the beginning. And that only serves to underscore the massive difference between us."

At that point, Melahat kept quiet. It was no use arguing with Güngör. She would appear to take it lying down, for now at least. But just wait until they got married, then she'd show him what a tough cookie she was; like a fine antique, she'd make sure her value went up and up and up. She'd have him sweating buckets trying to keep hold of her . . .

The waiter brought their food. *Later, I won't let him bring me to Piknik, even if we are in a rush like today; it just won't do,* she thought. It was unfathomable that Güngör should eat at this place, even if it was seldom that he did so. Always the same old standard fare. Always the same, identical taste-alike kabobs, Russian potato salad . . . Yet didn't he always say that everything should progress towards something better, something more unique, something incomparable?

"It's odd that you eat here . . ." she said to Güngör. "There's nothing special at all about the place. The same old stuff all the time. The only thing it has going for it are its location and its service. All the times I've come here over the years and it's always the same old stuff . . ."

Güngör gave his fiance a stern look . . .

"Don't be ridiculous. Right now, the important thing is that we get through lunch quickly. You know I have an appointment with the divorce lawyer. But I can just *not* get divorced, if that's what you prefer, huh?"

"Oh, it's impossible to talk with you. You're always pointing out the faults of others. Don't you have any faults of your own?"

Güngör narrowed his gray eyes, which were now cold as ice.

"No, I do not. Get that into your head—I am perfect!"

Yes, he was perfect. There was no way he could tell this playboy bunny how he had turned what started out as a job dyeing Easter eggs into the business it was today. She wouldn't be able to wrap her head around it. *I'm wasting my breath, losing time. I need to finish eating and get to work on this divorce suit a.s.a.p.. Putting this beautiful dunce on the straight and narrow is a task for later.* Of course he was perfect. Back then, before the neighborhood of Kavaklıdere had become the developed place it was now, when the first Americans had only just descended upon Ankara, before anyone knew how long they would stay, just what they were or what they would bring, he was wise enough to know how to take advantage of this new development and, you see, it was then that he thought of dyeing and selling Easter eggs to the Americans living in Kocatepe.

Back then, he didn't know any English, other than the words "why" and "very good." One day, the local girls—he doesn't recall if Gülsen was amongst them—were sitting on the garden wall, giggling nonstop. Güngör looked in the direction they were facing and saw that the American bachelors who lived of the first floor were making all kinds of gestures at them and blowing kisses. The other neighborhood boys witnessing the same scene were also upset by it. They would have to beat those guys up, just like they'd beat up that boy from Gazi High School who had followed Güneş and dared to set foot on their street. But in this case, the guys had uniforms, and then there was the fact that they were foreigners, and it would be rude to do that to foreigners. Güngör, believing it nevertheless necessary to take action for the sake of the honor of the neighborhood, hiked up his shoulders a bit, held his arms out slightly from his body, and walked straight to the Americans' window. The American sergeants were having a blast as they watched the young man walk up to their window. Güngör reached the window. To the Americans, who were watching him with curiosity, he asked, "Why?" Because he didn't know enough English to respond to the answers the Americans gave him, he sufficed with shaking his head and smiling. And in doing so, he took the first steps towards a peace pact. The Americans invited him into the apartment and offered him a beer. It was a different kind of beer. Güngör really liked this beer, which was ice cold and drunk from aluminum cans. Without responding to the men's talk—but then how could he—he piped in occasionally, doing the best pronunciation he could, with a "Very good," as he drank his beer. Later Güngör began spending almost more time with the neighboring American bachelors than he spent with his friends from the neighborhood. He helped the Americans decorate their Christmas tree. He was invited to their Christmas celebrations. All of this rendered him special. The American gum he carried in the breast pocket of his shirt he gave to those who got on well with him. In a short time, his appearance changed. The Americans had given him a pair of the "blue jeans" they got on the cheap at Piyeks as a present. And he had a colorful, patterned dress shirt and every time he wore it, his mother would tell him, "Son, that's a women's shirt."

In the spring he saw dyed eggs in the Americans' apartment and learned that it was a great hassle for them to dye those eggs. After finishing middle school, he was enrolled in a school for master builders. The truth was, he had a real knack for drawing and all kinds of handiwork. He immediately went and got ten eggs from the corner market and then locked himself up at home. He worked on those eggs for a whole three days. Then he took the painted eggs and showed them to the Americans. He had in the meantime improved his English a bit. He explained to them that if they liked, he could paint a large number of eggs for them. When they asked how much he would charge, he replied, "You are my friend!" The Americans were very pleased and touched that someone from a different religion would show such an affinity for their religious traditions and extend a helping hand, and what's more, that he wasn't charging them for it. They took the eggs from Güngör, but they didn't send him home empty-handed. It wasn't long before Güngör started painting eggs nonstop. He had in the meantime amassed a slew of American goods. Easter went by fast. Güngör, however, remained in possession of goods that were far more valuable than the eggs. Cartons of cigarettes, "blue jeans," gum, shirts. All of which he was able to sell at extravagant prices in a very short time. Wasn't that a phenomenal discovery? Güngör had had the smarts enough to take advantage of the silly coquetry of two stupid neighborhood girls and thereby gotten his start in the world of commerce. A short while later he opened one of the first shops selling American goods on the corner of Meşrutiyet. He didn't carry all kinds of knickknacks like the other shops of that sort did. From his American pals he only bought whatever he deemed purchasable, usable, sellable. The most discriminating customers began to patronize his store. What's more, the financial exchange that he engaged in with his American friends was not only to his but to their benefit too. They were able to earn their spending money for Turkey by selling Güngör goods they bought on the cheap at Piyeks, and in turn, this allowed them to save up a large portion of their wages to be put to use once they'd returned to their homeland.

Always keeping the cogs of his mind oiled and running, Güngör proceeded to open a place named "Gift Shop" next to his store, thinking that when his buddies returned to their country, they would want to display some souvenirs from the distant country in which they had spent several years, much like hunters who hang the stuffed heads of wild animals they have hunted in the desert on the walls of their living rooms for all and sundry to see. Because he had a wide circle of acquaintances amongst them, most of the Americans did their shopping at his store. Sometimes, when they didn't have Turkish money on them, because they knew that he sold American goods, they gave him things in trade. And in such cases, Güngör undoubtedly came out on top of course. Meanwhile, he had married Gülsen. Gülsen's father had helped him open the store, and whenever funds were tight, he gave him money for the business. Then, when her father died, Gülsen sold her share in the apartment building to her siblings. Güngör used the money to open a bigger, fancier store. He spent the years constantly growing his business, constantly making it fancier. Finally, he opened the store on Çankaya hill, where he sold only European goods. American goods were actually pretty tasteless, if you asked Güngör. He didn't need to sell them anymore. Now there were more customers for the Italian, Swedish, and German goods he sold. The customers who bought stuff from the stores that sold American goods were usually middle class people buying odds and ends. It was boring and exhausting bargaining with them over underwear, bras, cigarettes, irons and glasses. Now, those luxury-loving, new generation snobs, those nouveau rich who equated the quality of an item with its price and who were infatuated with European goods, were virtually scrambling to snap up the items he brought in using the trousseau permits. Those whose income was below a certain level could only tour the store, as if touring a museum. Meanwhile, he'd had an apartment building constructed on Vali Dr. Reşit Avenue and bought himself a Mercedes. Güngör considered the Mercedes to be superior to all other automobiles. A good businessman, just like the businessmen in British magazines, should use "conservative," expensive, fashionable goods. Güngör's attire was like that too. He wouldn't be caught dead wearing the Italian fashions that the youth of the petite bourgeois were so keen on, he didn't give the time of day to such exaggerated sensibility—with the exception of Italian shoes. He wore English cloth, and made certain that his clothing was tailored to be nothing less than classic. He wanted to dress like a diplomat and give the impression that the impossible was possible by achieving an appearance that was serious and inspired confidence. In short, the objective of his behavior and his attire was to sell.

That's right, I'm perfect, he thought once again. Squinting his eyes, he looked at the pretty little bird sitting across from him, someone incapable of assessing his success for what it was worth yet prepared to perch upon the blessings of that success. They were done eating. He had to be quick. He called the waiter over. This whole ordeal with his wife, he had to get it over with for once and all. He heard the fire engine siren. The waiters ran over to the window. *There you have it, the typical behavior of useless people. Whenever an ambulance or a fire truck happens to drive by, there they are, gawking. The city starts digging a sewage canal, and they're there in a snap, ready spectators. What's that, a road digger machine at work? They'll spend hours gathered round a-watching—because they don't have anything important to do, they don't have any goals. Everything, all that happens, is beyond them. They're spectators of everything, of the roads that are built, of the homes that burn down, of people who make money. These are common people, I don't have time to be watching people or running over to some stranger's burning building—as long as it's not my store that's on fire. And if it were, I wouldn't be a spectator, not only would I be the hero but I'd come out ahead, because I insured the store for a whole lot of money.*

Güngör paid the bill. He and his fiance got up. As he got up, he knocked Necip Bey's umbrella off his chair. Pretending not to notice, he didn't deign to pick it up. They left Piknik. Güngör walked over to the opposite street where he had parked his car. Melahat trailed behind. She was annoyed at how Güngör marched ahead. Güngör thought he was always ahead of everything, and he liked it that way. The first to get the profit, the first to calculate the exchange rates, always the first, always ahead of the game; and so why shouldn't he be ahead of a woman? *If she's got any sense, she'll come after me.* He noticed that the street was crowded. There were fire trucks. It annoyed him. Now it would be difficult to get his car out of its parking place. Güngör had one goal at that point, and it was to reach his car. He was going to get into his car and go to Ulus to meet with the lawyer. The crowd and the fire trucks that were blocking his way to this goal only angered him. No matter what it was that had caused all of these people to gather here and these fire trucks to clog up the street, it only angered him. His sole goal, at this moment, was to rip through the circle of fire trucks and crowds created by this event and reach his car. No matter what had happened, whether it be a war or an insurrection, for Güngör it was just something that was blocking the path to his car with its crowd of people and its fire trucks, something that was making him late for his appointment with the lawyer. Güngör's strength should eradicate the extensions of this event which were obstructing him from reaching his goal, his strength should bore a path right through them. He walked towards his parked car with determined steps. He parted the crowd. A whistle blew. A traffic cop pushed Güngör back roughly. Blood rushed to Güngör's head. A traffic cop, equating him with the crowd that had nothing to do with him, a crowd that had gathered here for who knows what stupid reason, had pushed him back, coming between him and his goal—the son of a bitch!

Melahat was pleased that the traffic cop had stopped Güngör, who had marched ahead without waiting for her. The existence of things like this, which could stop him, make him wait, made Melahat happy, they comforted her. But in the wake of this brief moment of bliss, it occurred to her that, as a result of missing his appointment with his lawyer, Güngör may not be able to get a divorce, and perhaps he then wouldn't be able to marry her either, and her face fell.

Paying no heed to the crowd or the fire trucks, Güngör fixed his gaze upon his car. Stubbornly he looked at his car, and only at his car. A hand touched him on the shoulder. He turned around, still pissed off by the traffic cop's touch of a few moments earlier, prepared to give hell to another impediment who was just as arrogant and presumptuous as the traffic police.

Recognizing the slightly balding head, sweaty hand and tiny, shifty eyes of Prof. Salih Bey, he quickly pulled himself together.

"You trying to get your car out of here too, Güngör Bey?"

"Yes, of course. Why else would I be waiting here?"

"It's awful, and I think we're going to be waiting here for a while yet."

Güngör was angry at the way Prof. Salih Bey just accepted this whole waiting business. When he first saw this familiar face, he had had hoped they'd be able to join forces against the traffic police and march right over to their cars. He knew Prof. Salih Bey from his store.

Güngör had acquired the purchasing permit that the professor had received after staying in America for two years. According to Güngör, Salih Bey's home was the epitome of tasteless decoration. Still, he couldn't really fathom why Salih Bey would sell his purchasing permit rather than use it himself, but then that was Salih Bey's business, a man was only worthy of what he aspired to desire. When Güngör went to Salih Bey's house to talk about the purchasing permit, Salih Bey explained that the furnishings in the house were from Mevhibe Hanım's father and therefore held sentimental value and so on and so forth, thus probably trying to explain why he wasn't using the permit to purchase things himself. Well, anyway, Güngör Bey knew that Salih Bey used the money he got for the permit to buy a new car.

"Are you going to Ulus as well?"

"Yes, the bathroom in our apartment . . . You know how those old buildings are . . . They fall apart just like that. The bathroom is a disaster. The ceramic tiles are broken. And no matter how much you have the sinks scrubbed, they still resemble anything but a sink. My wife's on a rampage. We spend a fortune on cleaning women. When we were in America, we weren't able to hire a cleaning woman, but still, my wife kept saying how easy it was to keep the bathroom clean. The other day, we had a Belgian professor over for dinner, and when the man asked to use the toilet, my wife became extremely anxious. And rightly so. When you go to the bathroom in Europe, it gives you this feeling of relief. It's almost fancier than the living room or the guest room. When we went there for the most recent European Council, well, believe you me, the bathrooms were so nice, you could just stay inside them forever . . . You think, at the end of the day heck it's just a bathroom, but the truth is, it's not, it really has a huge impact on the health and digestion system. So, I'm going to look at bathrooms, sinks and ceramic tiles and stuff. We're going to completely redo our bathroom. They made the bathrooms so small in these old apartments though, when you renovate, the stuff hardly fits. And so we're going to knock out a wall and expand it towards the hallway. My wife wants ceramic tiles with flower patterns. You had them in your apartment. Did you get them here in Ankara? "

"No, mine came from Italy. They're all European. But now they make imitations in Istanbul. I don't know whether they have them in Ankara though."

"I guess it's best we have a look in Ulus, and then, if necessary, we can order some from Istanbul."

Prof. Salih Bey obeys the rules

Prof. Salih Bey was distressed. If only he'd been able to take care of this before lunch. They were eating late these days because his son and daughter came home late. And when he got back from the university and saw that they hadn't yet arrived, he'd decided to go to Ulus and have a look around. But now he couldn't get to his car. They lived in an apartment building that looked out onto this street. Or rather, the building belonged to them. He wouldn't be able to take care of the ceramic tile business that afternoon, but at least he could get some ideas. This year he'd taken on as few lessons as possible so as not to neglect the office. He would need money this year. Salih Bey was a penologist. His office was in Ulus. He also made money as an expert witness. These little jobs didn't bring him a lot of money individually, but they added up. He thought he might collect debts due to him in Ulus while he was at it. Whenever he found himself having to lay out a pretty penny, reaping the money he had earned gave him that little bit of extra confidence. Though he was better off now than he had been in the past, and though he owned an apartment building, a car and land, and though his office did good business, Prof. Salih Bey still wasn't able to look at the future with full and complete confidence. This lack of security was something that had been with him since childhood.

He had grown up in one of the narrow streets of Samanpazarı. His father had a tiny, fly-ridden shop where he sold a bunch of odds and ends, from sticky apricot roll-ups to shop ledgers. A tiny shop on a street corner. Still, it did decent business because it was the only shop in the neighborhood. The shop's most frequent customers were neighborhood kids who walked in and bought themselves gum and colorful roasted chickpeas. Neighborhood residents considered buying actual food from the corner shop to be nothing less than imbecility and profligacy. They got their seasonal food supplied in bulk, wholesale, from the fruit and vegetable market. And many of them got their foodstuff from relatives back in the villages. The people who lived on this narrow street of Samanpazarı had the practice of getting everything as cheap as possible down to a science. Housewives competed with each other in this field. On summer days they'd gather in one another's houses, make noodles and the ingredients for *tarhana* soup, and dry out fruit rolls. They'd string up eggplant, peppers and okra and hang them on the walls, they'd buy tomatoes by the oke when they were at their cheapest and make tomato paste under the sun. The baskets of plums and cherries that came from their relatives back in the villages would be turned into jam. There was very little they had to buy from the corner store. Rice, flour and soap arrived at their homes in huge sacks, not in the paper bags of the corner store. From the corner store they would buy, when in dire need, a little sugar, cigarettes, cheese, and *sucuk*. And once in a blue moon, a bottle of *rakı*. Most of the men who lived on this street were coppersmiths, welders or small-time merchants. When those men wanted to toss back a few after a hard day's work, they didn't drink at home, they drank cheap wine at the Armenian winemakers' places over at Hergele Square.

Sometimes, when a respectable guest showed up—and unexpected guests were rare in these homes—the man of the house would send one of the kids to the corner store for a bottle of rakı.

If the owner of a corner store in a neighborhood who was so prudent, who had to be so prudent, drew his profit from the neighborhood's rare imprudence, then his profit would of course reflect that. And so Salih Bey's father barely squeezed a living out of his store. Salih Bey was his father's oldest son. That's why his father so desperately wanted for him to get an education. He knew that this fly-ridden, sticky store wouldn't be enough to put food on the table for the family that Salih would eventually have, or the siblings whom he might have to shoulder responsibility for as the big brother. Salih went to elementary school at a small school in Ulus. All of the other school children were like Salih, they were all pretty poor. But even back then, Salih held himself apart from the others, he wanted to be apart from them. He had gotten it in his head to be different from them. Salih was privileged in comparison to the other children in that he had more pistachios, roasted chickpeas and gum in his pockets than they did. But for him, even at that age, even this miniscule privilege was something to be developed and fostered. Based on his evaluation of what he heard and what he was told back then, he thought that he could achieve that development through hard work. To work, to increase the amount of gum, roasted chickpeas and marbles in his pockets so that he had much more than the other children, and then to fill the pockets of his school smock with money, and then to have better shoes than the others so that he could walker faster than them and without tripping in the mud in the winter. Maybe later, after working a whole lot, he'd be able to get on a bicycle and get away, get far, far away from this crowd of shorn-headed children with their black socks held up with white rubber bands.

He was very hard working. He always ranked at the top of his class. He'd bury his head in his schoolbooks at night until the wee hours. Besides, he didn't feel confident unless he'd read over and recited his lessons at least five times, until he was absolutely certain he'd memorized them. True, he had very little confidence in himself, or in anything else for that matter. This was a trait he'd picked up from his father. If you asked his father, everyone was a thief. Everyone in the neighborhood pulled all kinds of numbers to get out of paying for the goods they'd purchased on credit. And so his father found myriad ways to secure from the neighborhood residents—who never volunteered to pay their debts themselves and who considered *not* shopping at the corner store a downright profitable endeavor—the payments that were his rightful due. He'd use thick paper when weighing items, water down the lamp oil, fix the scales. From his father Salih learned to survive by not trusting others.

He memorized his lessons well. Finally, in order to understand whether or not he had memorized them well enough, he'd hand his schoolbook to one of his siblings and ask them to read a random word from the middle of a page. If he failed to recite verbatim whatever came after that word, he'd go over the lesson another five times. He didn't consider himself prepared for the lesson until he was one hundred percent confident that he had memorized it. If he were called to the board or had to take a test when he did not feel prepared, he'd tell his friends that he didn't know the lesson and put a concerned expression on his face. Then, when he got a really good grade, his friends would be angry at him for his lack of honesty. Yet, from his own perspective, he was being honest because his goal was not just to pass, not simply to know the lesson well enough to get a good grade. Rather, he was striving to increase the mite of privilege that he possessed over his classmates. And since the only way to do that was to work, the only thing he had confidence in was work. Working was his everything, his passion, the air that he breathed. If he didn't work hard enough, well, how hard was enough in order for him to achieve the daunting goal of separating himself from the rest? In order to know, he had to reap results, results which proved that the vague difference between him and the rest was growing. Yet so far, the only result he had achieved was to be first in his class. He still lived on a street that was just like the ones his friends lived on, he lived a similar domestic life, ate similar foods and wore similar black socks held up by similar white rubber bands.

One day, while looking at the shop window of a newly opened haberdashery, he saw a child. The child, who held his father's hand, had white socks. White socks were important; Salih had never worn white socks before in his life. Salih's friends never wore white socks either. And the boy was holding a red ball; a squeaky clean, shiny red ball with a velvety surface. Salih on the other hand was holding two live chickens. The heads of the chickens hung down, and because of their screeching, everyone who passed by turned to look. His father had sent Salih over to his friend's, who had a largish chicken coop behind his house on Çırıkçılar Slope, to fetch those chickens. And so Salih had picked up the chickens and was heading home, taking his time along the scenic route. It was obvious that there was a difference between the live chickens that he held and the red ball; this boy in white socks would never ever carry a live chicken. Salih moved closer to the boy in order to get a better view of his ball. The boy, frightened by the chickens, leapt aside. Clearly, he wasn't used to being in close proximity to live chickens. Neither Salih nor his friends, however,

were afraid of live chickens; in fact, when necessary, they even slaughtered them themselves. Salih, even if he was at the top of his class,
was not afraid of these live chickens, and he also wore black socks.
He didn't know whether this kid was hardworking, but so long as
Salih himself did not have white socks and a red velvet ball instead
of black socks and live chickens, his own industriousness would be
insufficient. Because his classmates didn't know this, and because they
never would know this, they thought he was dishonest and so they
didn't like him.

But he didn't like them either. He didn't like any of his classmates.
He didn't have time to like them, for one. To like them would mean
to fall prey to their traps, in other words, to be like them, to continue
to be like them. He never played games in the street. He didn't have
time for that either. He had to continue his work, which had not yet
rendered sufficient results. The only thing he trusted was work, it was
his only friend. Sometimes, he'd fall into step with his friends and
take part in their games, but it wouldn't be long before he'd come to
his senses. He'd abandon his circle of friends and leave the game with
a somber expression on his face, just like that. He would understand
that his friends had set up a trap. They wanted to trap him there,
hand in hand, inside their circles; they wanted to eliminate the faint
difference between him and them by keeping him from working.
They wanted him to remain spinning inside that static, impoverished
circle with the black socks and the white rubber bands and the ball
made of paper. These shorn-headed friends who pushed him into this
trap with their very own filthy hands, he didn't like any one of them.
Actually, he didn't like his mother, father or siblings either. To him,
they too were people who obstructed his development, made it so
hard for him to achieve his transformation. He showed the utmost
respect to his parents; he was scared to death that they might keep

him from studying, and since they made such tremendous sacrifices for someone who was ultimately going to abandon them for entirely different circles, they must be very good people, he thought. At night, in the fantasies he plotted in his cold bed, there was room neither for his mother, with her hands that reeked of onions and had grown raw and red from washing the laundry, nor for his father, who always wore his *takke*, counted the beads on his *tespih*, picked up olives with his bare hands, always burped after meals and then never neglected to express his gratitude to God with a "*Yarabbi şükür!*" Or his siblings who played outside the house naked, not even deigning to wear underwear. In his fantasies he imagined the kid with the red velvet ball and the kid's father. Salih went with them to the park. For Salih, going to the park was a daily habit of other people. He didn't like his mother and father. But he treated them with respect. He deemed it necessary to treat the other elders around him with respect too, so that none of them would stand in his way. Quarreling or arguing with them was only something that would stop his progress and make his life harder. Salih didn't need any obstructions, any difficulties. The only difficulty that he recognized and made room for in his life was work. He put all of his effort into overcoming this difficulty, a difficulty which had to be defeated. Affection was a harmful thing that kept you from working, that got you off track, or at the very least distracted you. If he liked his mother too much, when she ran out of water in the middle of doing laundry, he would have to interrupt his studying to go to the well and fetch more water. If he liked his father too much, he would have to help him at the store, instead of studying. If he liked his sibling, he would have to get up from his schoolbooks and take him to pee. And a thousand and one other obstructions that would stand in his way. Affection would only bring with it new difficulties, it would increase the difference between him and the white-socked boy, it would arrest him in the circle of black-socked, lazy children. And so that's why he didn't like anybody. Later, when he worked and worked and became a completely different person, once he had moved up to a completely different street and a completely different house, his only friend, work, would pay him for his friendship, and then of course he could make other goals for himself and take a liking to this or that . . .

Lots had happened between then and now. His chest swollen with pride, he passed the exams which earned him a scholarship to boarding school and finished high school and then law school, again on a scholarship; he got in his professor's good graces during university by taking on the bulk of the professor's workload and research, and became an assistant to him; and thanks to his industriousness and his respectfulness, he quickly climbed through the ranks to become a professor at a very young age. Because for him the world was a one-dimensional goal, he never learned to think in a multidimensional way, conceiving of interconnections and contradictions, or to think holistically, and so he wasn't in the habit of reading or going to the theater either. Now, that change he had always waited for had happened, and his industriousness had born fruit. He owned an apartment building and a car. He had a good salary. He was part of a co-op for a summer home. Still, he worked nonstop, he earned more and more money nonstop. He never turned down a job that would bring him good money. As he rose through the ranks, because he was forced to form friendships with people around him, he felt the need to take an interest in new subjects. At times one had to speak of philosophy or mythology. As a decorative topic for himself, he chose Ottoman history, the reason being that, during the meetings he took part in abroad, he came to realize that historical subjects piqued the most interest. Amongst foreigners, his knowledge of history was perfectly valid. And so he dove headlong into Ottoman history, and his efforts soon bore results. It wasn't long before the foreign officials that he met both in Turkey and abroad were in awe of this Turkish professor's knowledge of history. Of course, the historical conditions that led to the historical events were of no interest to him. Historical knowledge was, for him, tightwad that he was, freshly minted gold in his pocket. Drawing upon his old industriousness, he memorized details by the dozens. Like what that Ottoman Padishah so-and-so said to his Sultan mother after such-and-such war . . .

As a child, he hadn't liked black-socked children because he didn't want for them to stand in his way. Now he frequently found himself employing terms like "humanity" and "humanism." These were words he had to use. And he had learned what he needed to know about these words. But as for affection, he had forgotten how to show it, how to feel it, at a very young age. He had never exhibited any industriousness when it came to liking people. And so he had zero experience at it. That facet of himself, the one that loved, remained so stunted, had calcified to such a degree that for him to start loving now would be like being someone who had never done gymnastics ever in his life trying doing a somersault. It could break his backbone. Because he was not used to making humanly connections with people, out of concern that they might keep him from working, now, whenever he was forced to express his opinions about the future of humanity, he would recite words he had read in such-and-such book or quote such-and-such thinker. Then he'd slither his way out of it by putting a definitive end to his statement with the pronouncement of generic, unalterable, invariable verdicts which he had documented using all the necessary ibid.'s and c.f.'s.

Salih Bey considered himself someone who had achieved the goal he set for himself in this life, in one way or another, and in this respect, he was, to a degree, right. The shorn-headed little kid who used to go to Samanpazarı Elementary School was now a notable professor occupying an important place in society; he'd married the daughter of a member of parliament; and he had improved his financial situation with the help of the inheritance his wife had gotten from her father, so that it was at least as solid as his social status. He no longer needed any changes in his life; to the contrary, what he needed to do now was maintain what he had, keep everything just as it was, right now. In this respect, he and his wife Mevhibe were in agreement and so they had no intention of getting rid of the furniture left to them by Mevhibe's father, "Big Daddy Mister MP" as a symbol, in a way, of the station of theirs which they sought to perpetuate. When Salih Bey saw Güngör Bey, he recalled the pressure the latter had put on them to sell the furniture and other antiques in their house. But no, they were not going to refurbish. They were only renovating the bathroom, and that because of the foreign guests who had begun to come by frequently on ambassadorial visits or during trips abroad. That is, as required by the situation that they wished to maintain.

If Güngör Bey brings up the topic of selling the antiques again, I should turn down the offer definitively, he thought. Güngör, however, did not exhibit the least bit of interest in Salih Bey; he was thinking about crossing the street. When Salih Bey saw him taking a step forward, he interrupted to ask:

"What are you thinking of doing?"

"Getting in my car and going to Ulus."

"But the traffic cop won't let you cross with those fire trucks there."

"So, I'll do it anyway."

Güngör stomped his way over to the traffic cop.

"Son, look here!"

"Yes, what is it, sir?"

"How much longer are you going to keep us here? I need to get to Parliament. At least let those of us who need to be somewhere get in their cars and go!"

"But what about the poplar!" The words were barely out of the traffic cop's mouth when Güngör exclaimed:

"What poplar, son? You're going to be up a tree soon yourself, I tell you . . ."

And with that, he marched towards his car. The traffic cop was about to blow the whistle and rush after him when chaos broke out over by the poplar. Güngör hopped into his car and put a lead foot on the gas pedal. He was an excellent driver. He masterfully maneuvered his way out, weaving through the fire trucks and then parting the crowd as he virtually flew out and onto the avenue. Salih Bey was still standing right where Güngör had left him. He was not the kind of man who, in order to reach his goal, was prepared to tear down things or make his own rules. To the contrary, the fact that he had obeyed without exception and without fail the rules and those who made them undoubtedly played a role in his patient, calculating, industrious progress.

Mevhibe Hanım stands guard at the walls

From behind the tulle curtains of the window Mevhibe Hanım saw her husband speaking with Güngör Bey and how Güngör Bey, after talking with the traffic cop, crossed the street and then proceeded to part the crowd as he took off in his car. Her husband was just standing there, waiting with the rest of the crowd. Though she thought to herself, *Oh, Salih, what a wuss you are, if only you'd just left with Güngör Bey*, a familiar voice inside her head reminded her of the advantages of setting one's foot upon firm ground. If you asked Mevhibe, though he was rich Güngör Bey couldn't always be relied upon to walk on firm ground; as for Salih, on the other hand, she was certain that he always walked on firm ground, and one of the primary principles of doing so was showing respect to the police. Yet she was angry at her husband for shopping for the new bathroom sets at such an inappropriate hour. *And now he's going to be late for dinner!* The kids would be home in half an hour. Today she was having Nurten Hanım prepare home-made pastries, *puf böreği*, because she knew it would make her son happy. And those pastries turn out awful if you don't fry them right away. She was already in a surly mood when she entered the kitchen. Nurten Hanım, who was cutting dough using a saucepan lid, was immediately vexed by Mevhibe Hanım's presence. Mevhibe Hanım was very demanding. She found fault in everything, no matter what. It made no difference the pains that Nurten Hanım went to since she'd begun working at Mevhibe Hanım's house. For example, she no longer put dirty dishes straight into hot water with detergent. First she would wipe the plates off using paper that hung from the wall expressly for that purpose. Then, she'd take the dish brush and, after dipping it in sudsy water that wasn't too hot (according to Mevhibe Hanım, really hot water scalded the dirt), she'd then use it to clean the plate, and then she'd dip it in the sink full of hot water next to the sudsy water and rinse it. Glasses were to be dried using a clean towel after having been left wet for a period of time, but not quite long enough to dry completely. The towel used to dry the glasses was never to be used for drying plates. Forks and knives were cleaned in separately boiling water. The kitchen towels she washed with boiling water every day before going home, ironing them first thing the next morning when she arrived back at work. She was also not allowed to string vegetables which were to be hung out to dry without first covering the table with paper. Most of Nurten Hanım's time was spent covering things in paper and then throwing that paper away. When Mevhibe Hanım was around, Nurten Hanım was extra careful not to touch the cupboards, or anything for that matter, with wet hands. The refrigerator was cleaned out and wiped down every single day. Food that was to be put in the refrigerator would first be placed in special containers and then put into the refrigerator according to a strict regimen. "The kitchen should be just like a pharmacy," Mevhibe Hanım always said.

Perhaps it was because of this frequent comparison to a pharmacy that Nurten could not bring herself to like the food cooked in this house. It was like medicine; she simply couldn't eat it. All flat, bland meals, all cooked the same way, despite the meticulous care taken in the kitchen.

"How many eggs did you put in the dough?"

"Two."

"One would have been enough, Nurten Hanım."

"With one egg, the cheese ends up too dry."

"Of course it does, if you just go and drop the egg in there like that. You have to beat the egg real good first, so that it thickens. Stop rushing! The patient dervish gets what he wishes, you know . . ."

Nurten Hanım said a silent prayer, asking God to grant her patience. *The patient dervish shits in his britches!* That, by God, was the correct version. That's the version her husband said when he came home drunk in the evenings. "Nurten, girl, c'mere and let me smack you up a little! Nurten, girl, why don't you cry for God's sake . . . C'mon, yell girl! Girl, you're gonna kill me with that patience of yours . . . Look here, now you get this into that puddin' head of yours: the patient dervish shits in his britches . . ."

You can beat a single egg as much as you want, sure, it might thicken, but it still tastes the same. When she prepared this pastry at her own home, she did so with peace of mind, and she didn't skimp on the ingredients. And her kids would gobble it down by the plateful. It was only once in a blue moon that she made pastry at home, but still, when she did, the oil would drip from her little boy's fingers, and his eyes would shine with delight. She couldn't imagine any meal ever being devoured with such enthusiasm in this home. For one, any dish you made was bound to be tasteless if you skimped on the ingredients and stuck to myriad dietary rules. And every meal had to be cooked according to some strict rule. Not once was rice with tomatoes ever cooked in this house. Rice was always cooked like this: First the rice would be boiled in salty hot water, then drained, then a wee bit of butter would be added and it would be left to steep. Olive oil dishes would be put on the stove without any oil, and then, as soon as they were taken off the stove, Mevhibe Hanım herself would attend to the oil. She never let Nurten Hanım pour the oil on anything. In fact, she kept the oil locked up. Nurten Hanım wondered, *Why did Mevhibe Hanım go to so much trouble? Why would someone hire a maid if they were going to stick their nose into everything anyway? If only she'd just do everything herself.* Salih Bey had a delicate stomach, or so she said. The truth of the matter was, there wasn't a thing wrong with his stomach. The whole family was healthy as could be. They had high cholesterol, supposedly. That's why they were on a special diet. She didn't believe a word of it. If you asked Nurten Hanım, there was only one reason for all of this nonsense: stinginess.

Mevhibe Hanım put half of the meatballs that had been prepared for the grill in plastic containers and placed them in the refrigerator. She always made Nurten Hanım wear plastic gloves when she kneaded the ground meat. Then she'd wash the gloves, using measures of cold and boiling water, and hang them out on the balcony so that they wouldn't stink up the place. There were only two meatballs per person left for lunch that day. If the son of the house was particularly voracious and failed to get his fill from the portion allotted to him, then Nurten Hanım would end up with one meatball, or none. "Sorry, Nurten Hanım," Mevhibe Hanım would say, "you'll have to find yourself some other nibbles." But Nurten Hanım could never pluck up the courage to eat something of her own accord in this house. *Actually, no person in their right mind would get upset at having missed out on those meatballs anyway,* she thought. They were nothing but dry, fatless veal, containing neither onions nor pepper. When you grilled them, they turned out like rubber. And they barely had any bread or egg in them either. And the salads, well they were virtually inedible. Mevhibe Hanım would have her slice up the lettuce real fine, then pour on some lemon with a little bit of sugar. She had come back from her last trip to Europe convinced that this type of salad was the healthiest of all.

"Now would you look at that, you've gone and washed the greens too early again. When you do that, you kill them. The greens have to be washed exactly fifteen minutes before we sit down to eat. And I told you not to squeeze the lemon like that. It loses all its vitamins that way. If you don't put the juice on the salad as soon as it's squeezed, it's worthless . . ."

Saying this, she would then point to the clock which hung in a highly visible spot in the kitchen, thus reminding Nurten Hanım that she wanted everything to be done according to the clock.

Indeed, every day she wrote on a piece of paper exactly which chores were to be done when and in what manner, and then hung it up on the side of the refrigerator. *I wonder what would happen if I were illiterate?* Nurten would think each time.

Mevhibe Hanım wandered around the kitchen with a long face. She hardly ever smiled as it were. As she monitored the household chores, she always wore the grave expression of one engaged in a momentous task. It reminded Nurten of the municipal workers who occasionally came to inspect the grocer's stand in their neighborhood. With the graveness of an inspector Mevhibe Hanım reviewed every minute detail in the kitchen. Everything was in its place. It had to be. Mevhibe Hanım wouldn't allow for it to be otherwise. "In my house, everything is always in its proper order," was her constant refrain. *How about you live in a cramped gecekondu with six little bastards, lock them up at home and leave for work, that'll teach you how the order of a house is disrupted*, Nurten thought bitterly to herself now and again. *And then, you can watch your husband arrive in the evening and make a mess of the house you worked so hard to pick up after you got home exhausted from work.*

"Nurten Hanım, did you do the laundry and ironing like I told you?"

"Yes, only the pants aren't dry yet."

"Please, iron those pants right after lunch. I'm going to go to the hospital this afternoon and give them to the kids there."

Nurten Hanım was enraged; the pants that Mevhibe Hanım's son had outgrown were just the right size for her own son. She very well could have given the pants to her. But she had never given Nurten Hanım any hand-me-downs. Mevhibe Hanım kept everything. She kept everything, clean and ironed, in chests. She made use of everything. She kept everything for the inevitable day when it could be used. *If a person can't lend a helping hand to the help in her own home, what good can she possibly be to some stranger's family?* Nurten Hanım thought. She bent over, directing her reddened face towards the pastry.

Mevhibe Hanım was a long-standing member of the Republican People's Party. She had been working for the party's women's branch for years, and she was the head of one of its philanthropic associations. Every Thursday the association directors would go to the hospital, or to an orphanage, or to a circumcision celebration they had organized. On Wednesday afternoons, they played bridge. And they had get-togethers at one of the women's homes once a month. The get-togethers were always amply attended. Ladies from all of the prominent old families of Ankara would be in attendance. Mevhibe Hanım's father had been a member of parliament in Atatürk's day. He knew all of the elite families of Ankara.

She left the kitchen and went to the living room. She glanced at the dining table, thinking, *That Nurten will never learn how to set a table properly. But then if you don't have it in you, if it isn't in your genes, well* . . . Mevhibe Hanım's father was a very strict man. Her heart would beat fast with fear whenever she took him coffee. He was unforgiving, her father. He never forgave a fault, never. And it was thanks to that scrutinizing eye of his that he had won the favor of the famous pasha, Atatürk. According to her mother, Atatürk too was very prudent with his money. He once bestowed upon Mevhibe Hanım's father a few of Ankara's old vineyards as a gift. In his lifetime, Mevhibe Hanım's father had never shown his children a good time. Mevhibe Hanım was never allowed a luxury as a child. And she didn't care for luxury now either. She only cared that her home was always clean, orderly and decorated in a way that befit an honest family of good standing. Her clothes were made by excellent tailors. She didn't even throw out old newspapers. She saved every empty jar. Even though the house was large, all of the numerous built-in cupboards were packed full. Underneath the beds, on top of the wardrobes, everywhere was full of carefully placed stuff. "This place isn't a home, it's a cellar," her daughter would complain. Her daughter was a horrible spendthrift. "Whenever I set foot in this place, I feel like a jar of pickles stashed away in the cellar, only to be used when the time comes. This place suffocates me . . ." she'd once yelled at her mother, who thought: *So she's suffocating. Well, she can just suffocate then, the ingrate. She forgot to pay the installment for her school tuition. And I already gave her the money myself.* Mevhibe Hanım had kept the endowment she had inherited from her father, and which would not run out easily it seemed, all to herself. She never gave her husband a cent of the money she got from it. It was her job to look after the house. Mevhibe Hanım spent her own money—and of course she never misspent it—on expenses that she deemed necessary. And it was she who had given her daughter the money to pay for the installment of her high school tuition. Olcay had graduated from high school the previous year, and now she'd started university. When Mevhibe Hanım's son was in Europe and his scholarship was suspended, she'd sent him money too so he could pay off his debts. *I wish I'd been willing to pay for his university over there too,* she thought. Now it was much worse since he'd started university here. Those kids with their unfathomable ways, of which she did not, could not, approve. She herself was a consummate child of Atatürk. She took pride in her Turkishness, in her father, and she knew her responsibilities, the tasks that were her righteous burden . . . She was hardworking . . . She stood by her word. *My father raised me well.*

Nurten had placed the forks upside down on the table again. Mevhibe Hanım was rearranging them one by one with a grave expression on her face. Olcay entered the room. She breezed by her mother like the wind. Her mother understood that she was heading for the door.

"Just where do you think you're going? I didn't even know you were here."

"It's so hot out, I came back to put on something lighter . . ."

"How did your exam go?"

"See you later."

"I asked you a question . . ."

"Sheesh, how should I know? They haven't posted the grades yet . . ."

"But certainly you have an idea?"

"So-so."

"What do you mean 'so-so'?"

"You're at it again, asking questions that have no answers."

"Where do you think you're going? Your father and brother are on their way, we're going to have lunch . . ."

"Well, I'm not."

"No way, I won't have it."

"How so? It's my mouth, isn't it?"

"Now look here, little lady. Then why am I spending a fortune on the help and all this money on food?"

"So, you can have four meatballs each today. Nothing wrong with that, is there? There's usually never enough for Doğan anyway. And that way, Nurten Hanım will get to eat her own meatballs too."

"You saucy thing you! Nurten is perfectly comfortable here."

"C'mon, Mom. You're not going to try and tell me being a maid is a comfortable job now, are you?"

"Why shouldn't I? Do you know what her house is like? It's got leaks all over the place. The woman's got sciatica, she'd die if she stayed there all day. At least here she can keep warm."

Olcay wants to go to the other side of Mount Qaf

Annoyed, Olcay grew quiet. She had long ago decided that her mother, like most people around her, was one of those people who would never change and were impossible to talk to. And so Olcay would head straight to her room as soon as she got home, and only leave it to enter their midst at dinnertime. She thought, *If only they wouldn't barge into my room and disturb me like they do* . . . Her mother never tired of opening the door to her room every night, every God given night, and telling her that she'd ruin her eyes from reading so much. Olcay was positively certain that her mother did this for the sole purpose of agitating her. Her mother had always come between her and the things she liked and enjoyed. Between her and love. If it was a book she loved, then between her and the book. Between her and colorful balloons . . .

She adored colorful balloons when she was little. Back then, her father had just bought a new car. On Sundays they'd go out to the Atatürk's Farm, to the Dam, as if it were some mandatory weekly assignment they were obliged to complete. Excruciating, loveless excursions they were. Her mother and father's relationship made Olcay feel ice cold inside. Not once had she ever witnessed them saying a warm, reckless word to one another, not once had she ever seen her mother kiss her father on the cheek, not once had she ever observed her father giving her mother a slap on the buttocks, not once had she ever seen them engage in a fight that began with rage and culminated in tears, not once had she ever witnessed behavior that might indicate they had sexual relations. Whenever it occurred to her that they must have slept together at some point, as evidenced by the very existence of herself and her brother, she'd feel ice cold inside. She couldn't imagine those two people being that close, engaged in such a human exchange, and whenever she did try to envision it, she'd stiffen with horror. The thought was akin to the portrait of her long dead grandfather which hung on the wall coming to life, taking Olcay onto his lap and bouncing her on his knee. She'd think of ice-cold hands, dead hands embracing her, and the damp, skeletal legs of a corpse touching her body. Cold and loveless question-and-answer sessions. Conversations and pauses intended only to remind the other of duties and responsibilities. Her parents remained quiet through-out those Sunday excursions. They stood on either side of a silent, loveless wall, exchanging with one another only the most essential information about the side of the wall facing them.

"Did you get the house keys?"

"Did you turn off the gas?"

"Good Lord, close that window, the kid's all sweaty, she'll get sick!"

"Didn't you bring the kid's sweater?"

"This car shakes an awful lot. Olcay never throws up in İsmet Ağabey's car."

"And was it İsmet's wife who bought him his car, hm?"

"How many times have I told you not to slam the car door like that!"

"Look to your right, your *right* I said. There's a truck coming!"

"How many times have I told you not to put those sweaters in the back window!"

"How long will we be staying? I need to know whether I should bring the sweaters or not."

"We'll be back in fifteen minutes."

"Kids, you can't have soda. It'll make you sick to your stomach."

"If you go on whining about wanting a balloon again, I'll whip the living daylights out of you."

Olcay loved balloons. Big, colorful balloons. Whenever she saw a balloon seller holding a bunch of colorful balloons, she felt weightless inside and imagined herself soaring into the sky together with them, up and over that depressing wall of lovelessness. For hours she would beg her mother for a single balloon. "Please, Mommy, buy me a balloon, please, please pretty please, Mommy, buy me a balloon!"

Most of the time her mother would turn a deaf ear to her pleas. But sometimes, especially when she was too tired and stressed to put up a fight, she would buy Olcay a balloon, just to shut her up. And it was at such moments that Olcay would commit one of her greatest crimes. She would go out into the street holding the balloon, and quickly hand it over to the first poor child she encountered. This habit of hers drove her mother crazy.

"Why did you give him your balloon?"

"So he could fly?"

"Who?"

"Him . . . That kid . . ."

"To where, you dimwit?"

" . . . "

Olcay never answered the question. Because the truth was, she wanted to send those poor kids flying with her balloon, like on the flying carpets in the fairytales her grandmother told her, to the other side of Mount Qaf. The reason why she wanted to send those kids flying over Mount Qaf was simple. When she asked why those kids were poor, she was told that that was just the way the world was. "When I grow up, I'm going to be super rich, and I'm going to put all of those kids in a giant house. That way, they won't have to curl up and sleep on the sidewalk . . ." Her mother would respond with something along the likes of, "So it's up to you now to change the world, is that so, you dimwit?" Olcay would grow furious at these responses, which she could only attribute to her mother's stinginess. What child could possibly tolerate her mother yanking her away from toy stores, *simit*-sellers, and ice cream vendors? But whenever she spoke to her mother of the huge, giant house, big enough to take in all the Gypsy kids and the beggars, with a kitchen full of food, the only response she ever got was, "So *you're* going to change the world now, are you, you dimwit?" Even in her responses, her mother was stingy.

Well, if the world really was unchangeable, and if those children really were doomed to a life of begging on rainy sidewalks in this world, then Olcay would tie them to colorful balloons and fly them over Mount Qaf. In the fairytales that her grandmother never wearied of telling her and that Olcay never wearied of listening to, on the other side of Mount Qaf there were princes, and they married poor girls whose hearts' desires they fulfilled, and everyone lived happily ever after. There, when the poor shepherd answered the king's three questions correctly, he married the princess. There, when an orphan plopped down on a rock with a weary sigh, crying, a giant with a maw as big as the sky would appear and bestow palaces upon the child.

From the stomach of a fish caught by a poor fisherman in the lake would emerge a wishing ring, and the fairies that came out of the wishing ring would turn the fisherman's cabin into a chateau. Olcay loved her grandmother, most of all because she told her fairytales about Mount Qaf, where the wall of lovelessness had collapsed. She didn't condemn all poor children to a life of poverty like her mother did; she turned them into princesses, princes and kings.

And she loved colorful balloons too. Colorful balloons, which exploded in wondrous beauty, were like the fairytales her grandmother told. Still, perhaps they could carry the children to the other side of Mount Qaf.

She didn't tell her mother all this of course. She knew that her mother would say that all of those fairytales were nothing but nonsense and that she would accuse her grandmother of messing with the mind of her daughter, who was already a handful to begin with. She would burst the balloon, just like that. "What a dimwitted, hotheaded kid!" "A kid who's always looking for something to cry about!" Such certain, unwavering judgments were always being passed about her. Her mother said that she would never get her a balloon again, because she insisted on giving them to others. And so seeing again and again how nearly everything she said only led to critical commentary and unwavering judgments passed against her, Olcay became a silent child. She began spending more time with her grandmother. She had her tell her the same fairytales over and over again, and frequently sobbed in silence. One day, Olcay's mother saw her struggling to do the *namaz* prayer on her own. She was furious. Olcay's mother came from a staunchly secular family that boasted a Republican People's Party MP. She had been raised to know what was what. But when it came to her daughter, well, she was a different story, and it was all because of that ignorant mother-in-law of hers, messing with the child's mind. At home this problem was addressed with the utmost sobriety and the grandmother was sent off to live with her daughter. Endowed with a monthly stipend of course. Thus did the kind-hearted princes and the princesses who did not hesitate to marry shepherds disappear from her life. The wall of lovelessness was growing higher. For a while Olcay made do with the prayers she'd learned from her grandmother; but the prayers were in Arabic and so Olcay garbled the sounds, not understanding their meaning. Every night, before she went to sleep, she prayed that her loved ones wouldn't die, wouldn't grow ill and wouldn't become poor. Even for her mother, who refused to buy her a balloon.

Those Sunday outings continued, with never a balloon, not one soda, not a single ice cream. Whenever Olcay went out into the yard, she always dreamed of making it over the wall of lovelessness. In her relationships with other children she was the compromiser. She did her best to be loved. And she was always the one to grin and bear it, so that they would let her play. The children caught on immediately. They taunted her, their natural reaction against the weak. They took her ball away from her, and then wouldn't let her play. She wasn't good at any games because she'd been raised in an overly protective environment in which the thought of her perspiring, and thus triggering a series of illnesses, caused enormous concern. She was weak and constantly ill. She grew tired quickly. It was impossible for her to keep up with the other children who, for their part, had no scruples about taking her ball and did not like her. Sometimes, when the injustice of it all became too unbearable, she complained to her mother and got her ball back. And then the children got their revenge by not speaking to her. When that happened, she would beg them to make up with her. But they wouldn't. Once they were finally convinced that they'd made her beg enough, they'd tell her, "Go get us some gum, and then we can make up." And so, unbeknownst to her mother, she bought them gum. She wasn't rich like they thought. Her mother gave her very little spending money. A few times, in order to buy the affection of the other children, she stole money from her mother's purse. Once her mother caught her. The woman was utterly shocked, completely horrified. The idea that someone who belonged to a family such as hers, that the grandchild of Doğan Bey . . . could commit robbery! Olcay was a disgrace to the entire family. It was for this reason that Olcay's mother got her father to hit her for the very first time. It was a cold, traitorous punishment, like an execution deemed imperative. Olcay was locked up in a dark room where she was made to wait until she got her punishment. No one asked her why she had attempted to steal the money. And if they had, she wouldn't have been able to answer. After that incident, it became more difficult for her to buy gum and for her to buy the other children's affection. It cost her, a lot. And the children meted out their own punishment. They frightened her when she went out into the yard. They threw clawing cats at her. And Olcay would scream and scream at the top of her lungs. She was a timid child. She had terrifying nightmares. Again and again djinns, hellhounds, giants and demons would emerge from the shapes of the curtains and attack her. She also grew frightened of going out into the yard. Beneath her bed hid a coven of evil spirits. When it was time to go to sleep, instead of walking to her bed she leapt into it from as far away as possible.

Fear wound around her like a coil. And that coil of fear became her sole refuge inside the darkness of the wall of lovelessness. She locked herself up in her room and surrendered herself to painful, terrifying thoughts for hours on end. Inside that coil of fear, she sought something to hold onto. That's how she started reading. She read anything and everything she could get her hands on. Reading released her, if only temporarily, from the suffocating nightmares. The world she read about in the books and magazines was so much merrier than the terrifying dreams in which she lived. At first, no one paid any attention to her reading. But then when her eyesight began to deteriorate while she was still just in middle school, her mother decided to put her foot down and take control of the situation. Her mother's attempted obstructions, however, only served to fuel Olcay's curiosity. One time, her mother sold all of her books to a junk dealer. For a week Olcay hardly ate a bite and she spoke to no one. Then she started locking herself up in the bathroom in order to read books she'd gotten from her friends. Her mother grew concerned. Her father on the other hand couldn't have cared less. He had work to do, papers and expert witness reports to write. He had no time to deal with an unsound daughter. Finally, Olcay was taken to a psychiatrist. The doctor took Olcay's mother aside and told her that her daughter's mental health was in shambles, that it was imperative she start developing healthy relationships with her peers. Mevhibe Hanım grew frightened. She recalled her brother Mahmut. Her father had loved Mahmut more than any of his other children. Mahmut was always at the top of his class. Their father used to say, "I'm going to send the boy to Switzerland to study." Like his father, Mahmut too would become a member of parliament or, even better, prime minister. And so her father, that incredibly stingy man, went so far as to hire a private language tutor for the boy. Then, upon hitting puberty, Mahmut suddenly grew strange. He stopped speaking to anyone. One day, the *evlatlık* of the house let out a piercing scream, sending the family scrambling. (This story was actually a family secret kept from Mevhibe even. Mevhibe heard about the incident much later on from her aunt.) Mahmut had first raped the girl, and then attempted to choke her to death. A robust girl with arms grown strong from beating so many rugs and washing so much laundry, she managed to grab the boy's leg and pull him to the ground. Having lost his grip, Mahmut proceeded to chase after the girl in a state of frenzy, half-naked, his hair and face a mess, emitting horrific screams. The boy's father and the two guests who happened to be over that night were barely able to restrain him. Later, the boy was taken to somewhere in Europe, and finally, having exhausted all other solutions, he was locked up in an insane asylum. The diagnosis: early dementia. And the girl? How was Mevhibe Hanım supposed to know what happened to the girl? This story had been kept secret, insofar as possible, not only from Mevhibe Hanım, but from all other family members and friends as well. All good, upstanding families have their secrets. Mevhibe Hanım, upon learning about this incident long after the fact, was unable to overcome her horror. And so, her fear that her own daughter might someday suffer a similar illness trumped her stinginess, and she enrolled her daughter in the prestigious Istanbul American School for Girls.

In high school Olcay continued to feed her passion for reading, this time without obstruction. She was liked because of her silent, agreeable demeanor. She neither stood out nor angered anyone. She spent most of her time either reading or studying for class. She was a good student. Sitting at her desk, she declared a gradually escalating war against the whole of her unsound childhood. Wielding her will power, she battled first her cowardliness and then her sluggishness. By her senior year, she was no longer the same insular girl she had once been. She played sports. When she became ill, she didn't go to the doctor, she didn't take medicine. She gradually became sounder, and more at ease in her body. And she began taking part in social activities too. She spread herself unnecessarily thin. She was involved in everything, from theater to the school magazine. Meanwhile, her interest in books had waned a bit. At the time, Camus became her favorite author. Love of humanity and inevitable failure . . . She felt an affinity with this point of view. She read *The Stranger* with unabated passion. For her, the negative fate of unchosen relationships conjured up memories of her childhood and its unhealthiness. She read Sartre's *The Wall*. The wall of lovelessness from her childhood loomed once again in her mind. The book spoke of completely different things, of course, but still it released a kind of pessimism within her, reawakening the fiends, demons and giants of her childhood. The shapes on the curtain came to life once again. Evil, invincible tendrils grew out of the curtains, reaching towards her. At that point, in order not to suffer defeat in the battle she had declared against unhealthiness, Olcay stopped reading.

One day during her senior year, her brother, who had just returned from a trip to Paris, came to see her. It wasn't his first visit. Since he'd gotten back from Paris, he sometimes came out to see her on Wednesdays, when he took trips to Istanbul with his friends. They'd go to the cinema, or sometimes to the theater. The two siblings hadn't spoken much as children. They'd never opened up to one another. Growing up they were detached, separated by the wall of lovelessness. They'd watched the wall with sunken hearts. But their mutual participation in the same process had given birth to an affinity between them. Olcay knew that the kids in the neighborhood had made fun of Doğan too, that they called him a "sissy," and that, despite all their efforts to spoil him, his parents had actually made life a virtual prison for him. His mother never allocated more than two meatballs per person. But she always gave the maid's share to her son, so that he'd have enough. This aggravated Olcay to no end. When her brother got home from school, their mother would take from the refrigerator the dessert or fruit that she had saved for him—and which would have been usurped from the others' share—and place it before him. Because her love for her son was incapable of conquering her stinginess, she made others pay for that love. One winter, she didn't have a new coat sewn for her daughter, even though the latter's coat was nearly in tatters; instead, she had her own old coat altered for Olcay. And then she went and coughed up the money for a bicycle for her son in the spring. It was tiny details like these which had created a rift between Olcay and her brother. Even if they did suffer the same pain, she did not feel as if she were on equal terms with him. That's why when she lay in bed at night, heavy with the weight of her nightmares, crying and pulling her blanket over her head out of fear, not once did she ever go to his room, not once did she ever consider seeking refuge at his side. Still, seeing their mother's pettiness and hearing their father's dry, static, narrow-minded words was something they had in common, and it made them kin.

When her brother showed up one Wednesday, he told her that they wouldn't be able to go to the movies because he was meeting a friend. Did she need anything?

"No," Olcay had said, but then added, "Can't you take me to meet your friend?" She was just as shocked by her own question as her brother was. It was the first time she'd reached out, trying to extend herself into Doğan's circle. For a while Doğan didn't respond, his silence accompanied by a serious expression on his face.

"You still reading?"

"Not for a while now."

"Why not?"

"I read *The Wall*, and it really got me down and so, I don't know, it just seemed like reading was bad for me."

"Read other books. One nail drives out another."

Olcay was stunned by Doğan's response. The Doğan she knew didn't express his thoughts directly; instead, he tried to explain them using long, complicated sentences. She generally listened to her brother with a mixed feeling of alienation and respect. Could it be that the change she sensed in Doğan but could not quite grasp might diffuse the alienation separating them?

"What do you mean?"

"It's easy. If *The Wall* scared you, or rather, confused you, it's silly to give up reading because of it. Running away from the wall isn't the only solution. A wall is something that can be scaled, overcome."

Olcay looked askance at Doğan. He had a thin face and closely set eyes. He was no longer the chubby, chunky boy he'd been as a child. *If only I had a boyfriend like him*, she thought. An old, familiar sense of melancholy fell over her.

"Still, some don't have the legs to scale the wall . . ." She liked this different sort of interest that Doğan was taking in her, and she wanted to make it continue.

"Have you tried your legs out enough?"

Doğan paused. Looking at his sister, he struggled to recognize her.

"Wait, I don't think I did a very good job explaining. I mean, Olcay, sweetheart, what I mean to say is . . ."

Using his hand he drew a circle in the air.

"The world isn't all that complicated. And so, maybe the chaos that you refer to as 'a wall' isn't really anything to be afraid of after all. It's simple, completely understandable. And there are books that can help you to understand. You can read them. And then once you understand, you won't be scared of some old wall anymore. Okay?"

Olcay didn't respond. The two of them remained quiet. They were walking along the Bosphorus. It was spring. Olcay was suddenly overcome by an urge to hop into one of the many caicques along the shore and paddle her way up the strait. Even the Bosphorus opened onto the sea, so why shouldn't the wall be surmountable? Doğan was right. For a while she gazed upon the beauty of the opposite shore, which appeared to draw closer.

"Look, I can't tell you right now why, but your words, they seem right to me Doğan. I can feel it, here."

She pointed at her heart.

"I mean, how can I put it, it's just that, since just now, I love you even more."

Doğan lowered his head. He seemed embarrassed by his sister's words.

"I'll introduce you to Ali, if you want."

Olcay nodded. Together they walked. In her mind she was paddling, using her arms, which she had always thought so weak, those arms which had always avoided struggle. The sun warmed her on the inside and illuminated the darkness that was pregnant with demons and nightmares. The sea was near.

Olcay tries out her legs

Mevhibe Hanım removed the glasses that Nurten Hanım had put in the wrong place and put them where they belonged. Once she had understood that her daughter was about to leave without a proper explanation, she asked, in the shrill voice she assumed in such situations:

"Where are you going?"

"To the party headquarters . . ."

"What party? This is the first time I'm hearing anything about a party?"

"Don't worry, it's not called The People's Party, though it has a lot more to do with the people than that party does . . ."

"What's wrong with the People's Party? It's your grandfather's party."

"Riiight . . . Well, that only reinforces my views."

"As if you could have any views! You're a knee-high little girl. And my father was a brilliant man."

"True, it's obvious from all the land he acquired."

"You think he didn't deserve it? Those men saved this country. A person who doesn't care about their family can't be expected to care about their homeland. You think people like you who haven't a shred of respect for their parents are going to save this nation, do you?"

"I have no such lofty notions. But I can see with my own eyes. And I don't like to ignore what I see."

"Well, I hope with those eyes you can also see how messy your room is. You don't even know how to run a household yet. I'll be disgraced if you get married."

"Disgraced before whom?"

"Who do you think, the mother of the dimwit silly enough to marry you."

"Oh, now that just brings tears to my eyes! But I'd rather not be a disgrace to myself . . . Why are you looking at me like that? Of course, it's all my fault. I should have known better than to think you would ever understand me . . ."

Mevhibe Hanım looked at her fingernails. They were dirty. She couldn't possibly get her nails done before the hospital visit. They took care of all kinds of things there, including diapers. They didn't wash the diapers themselves of course. They accompanied and assisted the personnel and nurses. She could have her nails done tomorrow. *Oh, the stress of it all.* She was sick and tired of having to deal with everything about this house. Wound taut with frustration, she turned to her daughter:

"And just why wouldn't I understand? My father always said I was smart. In fact, he regretted not sending me to university . . ."

"'Regret' you say? If that man ever regretted anything it was that he got the deed for the vineyards of Küçükesat when he could have had the vineyards of Kavaklıdere."

"Of course he did. But to whose foresight do you owe your prestigious high school degree, little lady? My father's . . .."

"*I* never asked to be sent to that private high school though, did I?"

Now red in the face, Olcay looked at her mother's misgendered body, the top half so thin, the bottom half so thick. *Why do I get so angry at her? After all, she's just another person. Besides that, she's my mother. Perhaps, by being so contrary, she's actually helps me to see the truth. If she treated me with the warmth and understanding I wished for, perhaps I'd go soft. I wouldn't be on a quest for love. I wouldn't be on a quest at all.*

She recalled the building attendant Rüstem Effendi, who often carried Olcay in his arms and took her for walks in the garden, and bought her things like candy and gum when she was little.

One day when Rüstem showed up at the door, in a burst of excitement she ran to him, wrapped her arms around his legs, and kissed the knees of his pants. Why would she do such a thing? Her mother had been furious with her. "Aren't you ashamed to kiss those filthy pants?" Later, she locked Olcay up in the storage room for half a day as punishment.

She looked at her mother again. She recalled her mother's directives, given after she'd completed her punishment in the storage room, on how to behave in front of attendants and other such people, sentences like: "You can't understand them, they belong to a whole different world, and if you don't behave accordingly, they'll never respect you, they'll ridicule you . . ." Spoken like she's speaking now, with tautly drawn lips. After that, Olcay never sat on Rüstem's lap again, and she quit accepting the gum. Later, a very short while later, her father fired Rüstem, claiming that he'd cheated them on the money for coal. Olcay considered whether or not her mother was right. Did she really not know these people? She thought of what Ali had said: "People of your class possess a kind of raw naivete. You view issues not from the perspective of class, but with a teary-eyed tenderheartedness. You don't know the people, and you don't try to. And in turn, they don't trust you. Tears and feelings of guilt aren't very important or, more precisely, useful for them. Neither do they feel guilty, nor are they tenderhearted. They're suspicious and, when necessary, traitorous. For them, this has nothing to do with being kind- or evil-hearted; it has everything to do with survival. And that requires heft. They don't care much for the weak. Neither good intentions nor a love of mankind are enough to secure their belief in you. Just the opposite. They'll want proof that you've joined them. They'll want you to break the bonds that divide you from them. That is, your bonds with the system. Because the object known as the heart can suddenly grow hard, and when it does, you can easily slip back into your old ways. And that's precisely why they don't trust you. The whole 'sitting pretty' spiel. And they'll continue to be suspicious of you so long as they believe you could turn around and go back . . ." As he spoke these words, Ali had looked Olcay over from head to toe, eyeing the bag her father had brought her from Italy, her plain but stylish clothing.

In a way, Ali had spoken like Olcay's mother:

"You'll never understand them!"

Olcay was overcome by a new feeling of loneliness. For a moment, she felt like not going to the party headquarters, like shutting herself up in her room and thinking. Would the shapes in the curtain turn into frightening demons again? Would nightmares besiege her once more?

Olcay approached her mother. She understood that upsetting her did neither of them any good. What would it change? She kissed her mother on the cheek.

"Alright, Mom, have a good day. See you this evening . . ."

Mevhibe's long face did not brighten up, not in the least. Whenever her children fell out of step, she would inevitably remain sour at them for some time.

"If you like helping so much, why don't you come to the hospital with me? Look, it's not just talk, it's real work. As my father would say, 'Fine words butter no parsnips.' There are so many children there in need of help. There aren't enough nurses, and the ones they do have are ignorant. There are some who don't even know how to feed a child. So, what do you say? Don't just stand there, answer me. But of course, you look down on such work. You only listen if the words sound like they're straight out of a book. My father was a man of the people. He understood the people. When he was an MP, all the attendants used to come and kiss his hand on holidays. He never begrudged them a helping hand and made sure he had their respect. 'The people, as you call them, are like children,' he used to say. They have to trust you, and know that you're looking out for them. But if you don't discipline them, if you let your iron fist go slack, they don't know what to do. They become disconcerted, aggressive and useless."

"C'mon, Mother, you sound as if you're talking about training a dog!"

"Oh, you young folk, you haven't an ounce of respect for your elders, do you? Call me ignorant if you like, but look, I don't neglect my family, nor do I upset my friends or care only about myself and having a good time. I take part in the party's philanthropic activities too. And that is part and parcel of being a true citizen. Look, I'm opposed to snobby high society types like your aunt too. She's never once come to the hospital, no matter how many times I invited her."

"What difference does it make?" said Olcay.

"Of course it makes a difference."

"I mean, there's not much difference between her behavior and yours. One of you goes blowing your money on seamstresses and gambling, while the other kills time swaddling babies. But that doesn't change anything."

"How does it not change anything?"

"It doesn't, because there are still children who aren't taken care of in hospitals, or rather, who die without even making it to a hospital."

"And? What am I supposed to do about it? Is it up to me to change the world, huh?"

Olcay remained silent. Her mother was right, it wasn't up to her. Olcay was dragging this out. She was getting caught up in a useless debate with her mother. She'd do well to go back to her old ways of childhood and adolescence, when she preferred to keep her mouth shut. *The more Ali criticizes me, the more aggressive I become as I try to prove myself,* she thought. *But acting this way with my mother is a huge mistake. If Ali could see me now, he'd just make fun of me.*

"What's for dinner?"

"Puff pastries. It's what Doğan wanted."

"It's what Doğan wanted." She felt that old jealousy from childhood rise up within her. But then, understanding the futility of the emotion, she shrugged it off.

"I have to go, I promised I'd be there."

Mevhibe Hanım was flustered by the discussion with her daughter, and it had exhausted her. She walked to the bedroom without even looking at Olcay. She locked the door behind her. It was her habit to lock herself up in the bedroom whenever she became upset. And when she did so, it meant that there would be a chilly wind blowing through the house for a week.

Olcay gently pulled the door shut on her way out. But she hadn't forgotten to take a look in the full-length mirror before she did so.

Mevhibe Hanım is enraged

Once in the bedroom, Mevhibe Hanım took off her robe. She was seething with anger. She grabbed a bottle from the dressing table and sprinkled some *kolonya* onto her hand, which she then dabbed on her arms and neck. She lay down on the bed. Her legs were killing her. *Of course they are, I spend all day running myself ragged for those ungrateful* . . . She felt used, misunderstood and underappreciated. She considered calling Nurten Hanım in to give her a leg massage. But then it wouldn't be right for her to abandon the pastry dough just then. Any moment now that all too familiar pain would slice through her skull, piercing her brain. And it would remain with her for hours. But she absolutely had to go to the hospital today. Especially because, just the week before, she'd grumbled about Sevim Hanım as the latter left, "Half the time she never shows up." She opened the bedside cabinet and took out a piece of muslin, then she took two pills from the drawer and swallowed them dry. She folded the muslin into a long strip, wound it around her head over her eyes and then tied it.

She tried to dispel the drove of thoughts that descended upon her mind. Hopefully Salih wouldn't go off and try to buy the first thing he laid his eyes upon. *He doesn't bother himself about such matters; his work, that's all he cares about. I wish I'd gone with him.* Like her father, Mevhibe Hanım didn't trust anyone. She always sought, and found, mistakes in everything anyone else did. Mevhibe Hanım resembled her father in many ways. For example, she was authoritarian, just like him . . . She remembered how her daughter had talked back to her a short while earlier. The throbbing in her head increased. *We never used to talk back to our father. We never even dreamed of talking back. To the contrary, our insides quaked with respect before him.* Yet anyone who knew about Mevhibe Hanım's childhood couldn't possibly fathom why she held her father in such high esteem. Mevhibe Hanım had had an awful childhood. When her father left Trabzon for Ankara as a member of parliament, not once did he bring Mevhibe Hanım's mother over to be with him. He only had his children sent over so he could enroll them in school. Her mother was a farmer's daughter. She was ignorant. She doted neither on her children, nor on her husband, who appeared to have forgotten all about her once he was in Ankara. She lived her life as if it were some kind of fate to be endured. As soon as school started, the children would go to the city to be with their father. There they would move through the house like ghosts, scared shitless of their father's constantly roaring voice. Their father had gotten remarried but, despite the Civil Code, he'd seen no need to divorce his old wife before doing so. Their new mother wasn't a peasant like their old mother, who wore a headscarf. Their new mother strutted about with her head uncovered and attended Republican Balls with her husband. But that was pretty much the extent of her relevance. She, like her predecessor, had no say at home, and their father didn't really give a damn about her either. Most nights he could be found hanging out with his buddies at Karpiç, or having a good time with a fresh-faced *consommatrice*. In turn, the stepmother took her rage out, insofar as possible, on the children, especially on Mevhibe. When she was little, Mevhibe often had the runs. Even back then her stepmother would torture her with unfathomably strict diets. One time, she wouldn't let her eat anything but plain boiled rice until Mevhibe grew so hungry that she stole dry bread from the kitchen. Ever since, she's never liked rice. Mevhibe's skin was always yellow. A greenish yellow. And she had pimples. Her stepmother even objected to her wiping her face with kolonya as a cure for the acne, complaining of the cost of the kolonya and cotton. She objected to how Mevhibe dressed and how she wore her hair. She made her wear her hair neither long nor short, but rather at some abhorrent length, and then comb it backwards. Mevhibe did not stand up to this impeccably administered torture. It never even occurred to her to do so. Because, to Mevhibe, her stepmother wasn't a separate person but rather the extension of their *beybaba*, now also an MP, in the home. For her, the act of standing up to "MP beybaba" would have been akin to treason, something completely irrational. Her father, a man from Trabzon whose word carried weight in the Black Sea region, was doing important things now, big things, they all agreed on that; his relatives and friends in Trabzon, all of them knew what an important man Doğan Bey was. Having forgotten that Doğan Bey used to be just like them, they started worshiping their fellow Trabzonite who had made it into parliament. What did it mean to get into parliament? For donkey's years the mere mention of the word "government" had conjured up in their minds images of people at unreachable heights, like sultans, ministers and pashas, and so in their minds they similarly glorified Doğan Bey. That is to say, Doğan Bey had become a real big-timer, a genuine heavyweight. And for them, an important guy like that was, in brief, someone in whose presence you rose to your feet, whose hand you kissed, whose every word was a command to be followed. Both the wrath and the benevolence of great men was to be met with the same acquiescence as any act of God. His wrath should be considered no different from a natural disaster, a flood or a storm, while his benevolence counted as nothing less than an undeserved blessing. That's what Doğan Bey's relatives and fellow countrymen thought. And so Mevhibe, who spent her summers with those same relatives and countrymen, was naturally of the same mind. This being the case, how could one possibly oppose him? They were mere mortals. And in Mevhibe Hanım's eyes, her stepmother too was just someone else responsible for carrying out orders. Didn't she ever wonder why her father, being the great, important man that he was, didn't give her a better life? No, she did not. For her, simply being the daughter of such a great, important man was enough.

And so Mevhibe, for this reason, spent her adolescence as an unappealing shadow, sickly and sallow, wandering about in ill-fitting clothes. No one thought she'd ever find a husband. But if a young woman has a father like Doğan Bey and is therefore surrounded by an influential circle and bound to inherit a considerable fortune upon her father's death, then an ambitious, sober, prescient young man, someone of the likes of Salih Bey, will always be willing to ask for her hand; and just such a young woman was Mevhibe.

Mevhibe really could not have cared less whether she got married or not. If she hadn't, she simply would have lived out her days as a respected lady, dusting off the silver-framed photo of her "MP beybaba" and going to get-togethers at the homes of her father's old buddies' wives and daughters. Indeed, Mevhibe's father's legacy would be tremendous—and not only in terms of worldly possessions, mind you!

If it just so happened that Mevhibe Hanım spent her adolescence as a pale, pimply faced, shabbily dressed young woman, then, according to Mevhibe Hanım, it was because her father wanted it that way, and that was just fine. It was perfectly acceptable, for it was just as her father saw fit.

"If beybaba sees fit!"

It was a sentence spoken to Mevhibe every day and the truth of which she accepted without question. "MP beybaba" knew what was and was not fit to do. "MP beybaba" always deemed appropriate that which was fit to do, because "MP beybaba" was the government, the state. And Mevhibe was the daughter of the government, the state. So of course she was going to respect the government, the state. If she didn't, who would? Standing up to "MP beybaba" was, in a way, the same as standing up to the government, the state. Mevhibe Hanım had understood, had gotten into her head at a very young age the exalted nature, the immunity, of the government, the state. And with time, her incessant vocalization of the importance of respect for the government, elders and the law became a core characteristic defining her personality. And everyone, both in her home and outside of it, was obliged to silently perform his or her duty in the same manner that she dutifully dusted the silver-framed portrait of her beybaba.

Mevhibe never ever moved the silver-framed portrait of her beybaba from its spot. From behind his glasses her father peered down upon one and all there in the guest room, always from the exact same height, always from the exact same spot.

For Mevhibe Hanım, moving that portrait would have been akin to rocking the foundations of the state. According to her, the government was exactly like that portrait: something that had to remain always in the same place at the same height, always just as it was. It did not change, it was the unwavering representative of immutability. Mevhibe Hanım didn't care for the word "change." She never had, ever since her "MP beybaba" had been left out of the cabinet due to a change in government. It had come as a huge blow to "MP beybaba" and those close to him. They just could not fathom how such a change was possible. Would "MP beybaba" now become just another person, just like anyone else? How could the government change? How was it possible that "MP beybaba" would no longer be an MP? The official car would no longer arrive at their door, the ministry janitors and civil servants would no longer line up to kiss his hand. It was difficult to conceive of this change. Ever since then, Mevhibe Hanım disdained the concept of change; she was fully aware of the ill fortune that accompanied it. Her father died only a short while after being deposed of his seat in parliament. Perhaps because he couldn't stomach this new state of affairs. It is to that great, great injustice that Mevhibe Hanım attributes his death. And that is why she has felt nothing but anger at each person who assumed her father's ministry post in his wake. She's also upset with the People's Party for the same reason. But her father, when still alive, had registered his daughter with the party, just at the time when the issue of equality between men and women had made its way onto the agenda. It could hardly be said that, in his personal life, Doğan Bey truly and sincerely embraced the issue of women's rights. But by registering his daughter, who had just finished high school, with the party, without seeing any need to consult with her about it, he had set an example regarding the vital importance of women's participation in social life. And thus did he create an immutable situation in Mevhibe Hanım's own life. From then on, for the rest of her mortal days, of course Mevhibe Hanım would be a member of the People's Party. It was a situation as immutable as the silver-framed portrait of her father hanging there on the wall. This situation did not, however, really require Mevhibe Hanım to take an interest in politics. Politics was something else altogether, something dark. Politics was nothing but contradictory newspaper headlines, forever in a state of flux. And politicians who abused her father's legacy, and inspired zero trust. A politician should be like an iron fist, like her father. Actually, a politician should be a servant of a firmly entrenched state, of a government of never-waning power. And the other citizens should not dare to stick their tongues out at these superior beings who have only the best interests of those citizens in mind, and they should not stick their noses into business that they do not understand, business that they did not spend day and night grappling with. And indeed, Mevhibe Hanım was a party member who did not stick her nose into such dirty business. Her father had made a choice for her. And any change in that department was now out of the question. Divorce too was a deplorably immoral act. Whether a person chose his or her own spouse or not, upon becoming married, he or she became entrenched in a situation. Situations should not be radically changed; to the contrary, situations needed to be constantly reinforced. That was her philosophy of life. The photo inside the silver frame on the wall could not be changed. But the silver of the frame should be polished once a week. That was true of marriage too. Over time, the couple should become increasingly bound to one another by bonds more important than marriage, such as an apartment, a few children, acquired possessions. In Mevhibe Hanım's home were possessions left to her by her father. That is, what was left over after everything had been dispersed to everyone else. But because there was such a large amount of possessions in her father's home, which was actually never really lived in, she had still ended up with a lot of possessions. And of course changing those possessions was out of the question. Such stuff could not be given away; giving it away would be tantamount to denying her lineage. And it was the stuff that one possessed which defined one's lineage. For example, Salih had been successful in his lifetime, but there wasn't a single item in the house passed down from his family, and that only went to show that his family wasn't a "good" family. Even a single armchair passed down from one's father was proof that one had a family, that one wasn't a bastard. Mevhibe Hanım had preserved the items in her home for years by changing the upholstery when it got worn out, or polishing it when it lost its shine. Spending money on household items was done for the purpose of reinforcing those items, so as to prevent even graver changes from happening. If you don't get the armchair reupholstered, then you have to buy a new armchair. The cause of such change is neglect. And people pay a high price for neglect. Mevhibe Hanım has no tolerance for neglect that produces such results. And just as important as conserving one's possessions is getting maximum use out of them. If you've got tomatoes at home, you use tomatoes; if you've got cucumbers, you use cucumbers. So long as there were two cherry trees in Mevhibe Hanım's father-in-law's tiny garden, she would never attempt to make strawberry jam. In the end, this philosophy led to a state of monotony in the home of Mevhibe Hanım and her family which drove her children to insurrection. The same jam is made in that home every season. Certain meals are cooked in certain seasons, and the items in the cupboard occupy permanent spots.

Her husband's water for shaving is always heated in the same bowl. Hand and face towels are always hung from the same spot. Hair and nails are always done by the same barber. If you ask Mevhibe Hanım, changing something only results in a longing for what one has given up. Therefore, frequent changes of apartment building attendants or maids are not to her liking. She only makes such changes when deemed absolutely necessary. The right thing to do is to make the attendant and the maid contributors to the reinforcement of the order that reigns over the apartment building. And Mevhibe Hanım is quite successful at doing this. Very few maids who have worked for her have ever dared to cheat or rob her, or ask for a raise. She has little trust in those acquaintances who move often or frequently hire new employees to replace the old. Actually, an honest person should remain exactly as he or she first introduces him- or herself to be, otherwise, it's akin to committing fraud or an act of deception. Whenever Mevhibe Hanım's stringent espousal of her theory of immutability becomes too extreme, Salih Bey starts to get upset. Had he himself not achieved great changes in his life? During a harsh spat between the two about getting new furniture and appliances for the home, Salih Bey had said: "In that case, if it were up to you, I would have spent my entire life in Samanpazarı." Mevhibe Hanım in response had said that she did not think that way when it came to honest, hardworking people, that of course there were exceptions.

Despite this right to change which Mevhibe Hanım recognized under special circumstances, both Salih Bey and the children had clearly understood that it was necessary to move through the house in an unwavering pattern, like the hour and minute hands on a clock. And as bored as they may become of the monotonous progression of domestic time, they never attempt to push either of the hands in the opposite direction. It is only outside the clockwork regimen of home that the children consider abandoning the beaten path. Mevhibe Hanım views her children as pieces of this domestic clock. They were meant to stay put, so that the hour and minute hands might continue to turn in the same direction. Without getting their hands or shoes dirty. For them to do something on their own would only obstruct the routine. Seeing as, so long as they remain inside the machine, the children have no choice but to ensure the smooth running of the machine, they can only escape their roles as instruments ensuring constant rotation in the same direction by severing themselves from the machine as a whole. But Mevhibe Hanım knew that if that were to happen, the machine would no longer function. And she had no intention of turning a blind eye to such a possibility. Meanwhile her children, knowing that they are in fact part of a specific machine, live on the edge of a no-win situation filled with the fear that, even if they do manage to rend themselves from this machine, they might end up meaningless, lonely parts, or that they won't be able to fit into a machine they do like, or that they might not like the machine they do fit into.

Mevhibe Hanım lifted the muslin headscarf from her eyes. She looked at her watch. She must have taken a five-minute nap. Salih still wasn't back yet. Had he made it to Ulus, she wondered. It looked like this bathroom renovation was going to cost a pretty penny. But it would make their home more dignified, more appropriate to their situation, which would in turn be reinforced. *I was mortified when that professor came for dinner the other day. We need to do this for the sake of Salih's career. If we neglect this bathroom business, it would be bad for Salih's situation.* Again she considered going to the kitchen and calling on Nurten Hanım to come massage her legs. She walked over to the window to see if her husband was back yet. She parted the tulle curtains and looked out. What a disgrace! She was furious. Once again the wife of the apartment building attendant Mevlût Efendi had put up a clothesline between two poplars in the garden and hung her clothes on it, on the side of the building facing the street for all and sundry to see. She opened the window to yell at Mevlût, to call him up and rake him over the coals good.

Doğan and Ali

Doğan was standing with Ali in the middle of a crowd. They were on the sidewalk. They were so wrapped up in their heated debate that it occurred to neither of them to investigate the reason why so many people had gathered there on the sidewalk. And there were people blocking their view. They couldn't see a thing.

"Look, it's time you stopped talking like a book," Ali said. He wore a tense expression on his face. Doğan's corduroy pants, beige sweater, the collar of his sport shirt sticking out over his sweater, and his suede boots clearly contrasted with Ali's attire. Ali wore cheap, tacky shoes from Sümerbank on his feet. Ali didn't care much for them himself, to tell the truth, but his mother had bought them and, after all, they were super cheap. He wore a nearly threadbare suit with pants shiny from being ironed a few times too many and a white-striped navy-blue jacket that wasn't at all appropriate for the spring weather. The suit hadn't been tailored for Ali. It hadn't been tailored for anyone. They'd given it to his father once when he landed a government job for a stint. Now they'd had it adjusted to fit Ali. It was one of those suits which, in its attempt to mimic reserve and decorum, only served to emphasize the poverty from which it sprang. Ali had lost weight recently. The double-breasted jacket was too big for him. His shirt had grown yellow. And the tie he wore around his neck was a present from the son of a relative who'd gone to Germany as a guest worker. It was an awful tie made of shiny, fake silk. Ali was tall. Though thin and bony, his was a strong, limber body. The back of his pants hung baggy over his rear. Thick veins were visible on his bony hands and arms. He had a Roman-like nose and hazel eyes that rarely blinked. Those eyes inevitably compelled the person he was addressing to say something, to explain or to defend themselves. His curious, patient gaze, far from being distrustful, was filled with great warmth. Sometimes when he spoke, Ali's eyes would well up with tears. He'd get upset at the tears that streamed down his face, despite all of the gravity and calmness of his words, and after wiping them away with the backs of his hands, he'd continue speaking in calm, measured sentences, as if he hadn't shed a tear. Yet his graciousness, intelligence and attentiveness were not enough to quell his exuberance and sentimentality. Anyone who looked into Ali's eyes immediately understood his power to love and to exude passion, and after listening to him speak, they would be shocked at how someone so emotional could speak so logically. One day, when Doğan asked Ali how he managed to do so, Ali replied, "I'm not one of those people who puts his heart up for sale. I hate the idea of deceiving others with the pain and the passion that it holds. It needs to learn to endure pain because I have to teach it to bear not only its own pain but that of countless others as well." When he spoke, Ali, whose eyes might well up at the slightest thing, never delivered sentimental pleas, he never raised his voice nor gesticulated. He was straightforward and unpretentious.

Sometimes he explained his appearance as such with the following words: "You don't need to make paintings about the power of dynamite in order to make dynamite explode."

In this respect, Ali's composure was even more striking when he was debating with Doğan, who in contrast was in a constant state of gesticulation. They'd been debating there on the sidewalk for half an hour. Standing next to Ali, Doğan kicked and stomped like a racehorse chomping at the bit to kick off the race and desperate to reach the finish line as soon as possible. Ali listened to Doğan with a calm, thoughtful expression, giving ear with affectionate tolerance to his exaggerated sentences and the conclusions he reached thanks to his sharp intellect and vibrant imagination. Ali dug in his heels, defending his doubts about the finish line of the race that Doğan was so eager to commence and in which he strove so mightily to engage Ali as well; Ali drove Doğan crazy with his simple questions, squelching Doğan's enthusiasm for the race. In the face of Ali's obstinate realism, Doğan's exuberance began to subside, and when the constant motion of his hands and arms, something which generally added more punch to his forceful elocution, eventually became devoid of meaning, suddenly no longer knowing what to do with his hands and arms anymore, he just stood there, looking like an adolescent boy who'd been given too much of a hard time.

Ever since he was a kid, Ali had been careful to calculate the firmness of his foothold. He'd take a good look around and, once convinced of the steadfastness of his position, he wasn't easily dissuaded. When he was a kid, his father occasionally took him to the park. His father was unemployed then; whenever he went into the city to look for work, he took his son with him, but sometimes, rather than take him along to this or that office, he left him at a park. Ali would spend a while watching other kids climb up the stairs and glide down the slide, over and over.

They would push and shove each other in a race to get to the top of the stairs first. Before trying to ascend the stairs, Ali considered whether he'd be able to make it up. He'd been taught not to attempt the impossible. He was a proud child, and he didn't like to be rudely reminded when something didn't belong to him—and he had learned at a very young age that many things did not. First Ali thought about whether or not the slide had an owner, as many things did. He'd never encountered a toy that did not have an owner, a toy that everyone could play with. Then, upon observing how all the kids in the park shoved each other around as they attacked the swings and slides, he decided that these particular playthings did not have an owner. First he began making his way up the stairs leading up to the slide, expecting all the while for someone to grab him by the ear, or slap him on the cheek. One day out of curiosity he'd climbed onto the top of one of the taxis that rarely drove through the neighborhood where he lived, and he was quickly met with a slap on the cheek from the taxi driver. His pride was so hurt that for the longest time he'd made a habit of not even turning to look at a taxi.

He ascended the first step. He tried it out, made it his own. Then, with slow determination, he ascended the second and the third steps too. The children behind him didn't push, they didn't dare, seeing the determination in his eyes when he turned to look at anyone trying to pass him, stopping them in their tracks with a mere glance. Finally, he reached the top. Now, knowing what the slide was, he was certain of his next move. Ali was just about to slide down when an impatient, impudent child bolted up the steps, trying to get ahead of him. With a swiftness that contrasted with his previous patient movements, he grabbed the kid by the armpits and pushed him off the steps. The child hit the ground, and blood flowed from a gash above his brow. In tears, he wailed. His mother ran to his side, and the attendant blew the whistle. In no time Ali was surrounded by angry-faced people yelling and screaming at him.

147

The park attendant latched roughly onto Ali's ear. It wasn't difficult for the attendant to discern that Ali didn't have a family that would come running to his defense. He ripped Ali from the slide before Ali had had a chance to go down it. Ali made a beeline straight out of the park. His father returned to find him sitting on the sidewalk. His face was red, his eyes damp. But he wasn't crying. He wasn't in the habit of complaining. And so he didn't tell his father about what had happened. If he wasn't able to deal with something when it happened to him, he would wait until he had the strength to do so. He wanted to rely on his own strength. He never sprinted to the front, unless he was absolutely sure of himself. And when he did take to the front lines and met with defeat, he'd think long and hard and blame himself most of all.

"Why aren't you playing in the park?"

"No reason . . . I don't want to come to this park ever again."

He didn't respond to his father's question as to why. He was thinking of the owners of the park who had emerged at the last minute.

Doğan took offense at Ali's accusation that he "spoke like a book." They had been friends for two years. And both of them were avid readers. Except, because Doğan knew foreign languages, Ali urged him to read books written in them, asking him to then present him with a summary in Turkish. He asked so many questions that Doğan, afraid he wouldn't be able to provide all the answers, labored over the foreign books until he knew he had it all down pat. Even though it was Ali who pressured him into reading the books, Doğan reveled in the pleasure of being able to tell Ali about them, to teach him things thanks to the books he had read, and Ali appeared perfectly content as a humble, patient listener. But now, this unexpected scolding about "talking like a book" had angered him. Yet he didn't want Ali to see that it upset him, and he was more than a little miffed at his inability to suck it up. He blushed.

"What do you mean, 'you talk like a book'?"

"Exactly what I said. You're standing there trying to be a book, you're trying to create a book with your words. Yet the truth is, you can't write a new book by forming sentences about the books you've read."

"Are you denying the existence of general truths? What I've just told you isn't something I just made up, my sentences are based on truths . . ."

"But you're drawing it out. And when you do that, you lose your footing in reality, in real phenomena . . ."

"So you're denying the truth of my starting point?"

"What you call your starting point is not some random point you just pulled out of the air, it's based on certain truths, certain realities. And unless you can prove the truth of the train of thought you produce, you sever yourself from the truth and the believability of that point . . . . You understand what I'm saying?"

"No, you're just trying to make things difficult."

"Expecting you to back up your statements is not 'making things difficult.' And books aren't easy to write either."

"Now what does that have to do with anything?"

"I mean, I'm not objecting to the book, I'm objecting to the 'like'. Book sentences shouldn't be rendered abstract. They haven't been written as the result of abstractions; they're the outcome of real events, situations, realities. You can only develop them based on reality and specific situations. Otherwise you're turning concrete results into abstract starting points."

Ali fell silent. He felt that he'd gotten caught up in sentences. He was always cautious to avoid the wiles of words and the boundless possibilities they offered. He tried to pull his thoughts together:

"Let's say there's a door here. A door that is the only door to a full room. The room is full, and those inside need to get out. First those inside try to push the door open, with all their might. Then they understand that the door's locked. They try to think of other ways to open it. Once they understand that the door can only be opened with a key, they start looking for the key. If they find the key, they open the door. If they can't find the key, then they continue trying to force it open, because the problem is not that they need to find the key, it's that they need to open the door. Now what I'm opposed to is abstracting myself from the room, the door, the people who need to get out, by proclaiming that I have the key. Because the question that needs to be asked in this case is, which key belongs to which door? That question must be answered. In order for the people inside to get out, if you get what I mean, the important thing, what makes the key important, is the fact that they're locked up. You see?"

"So you're belittling the key? But doesn't that mean that you're belittling theory? Without theory—"

"Did I say anything of the sort? What I mean to say is that the key is important for letting the people out. The objective is for them to get out, it's that simple, for them to get the key, so that they can open the door. Otherwise, the fact that the key has the power to open the door is in and of itself useless. So I mean, now look, don't get angry with me, but what you've just been doing is molding key after key and lining them up on a key ring. But where does the key ring hang? From the belts of the stewards whose job it is to keep the food in the cellar locked away from everyone else."

"That's taking things a little far, isn't it? I mean, you can't possibly claim that I had any such objective . . ."

"No, that's not what I'm saying. I know that's not your objective, that's why I'm trying to warn you, to keep you from arriving at unde-sired conclusions."

"Thanks . . ."

They remained silent for a while. The dense crowd on the sidewalk lurched forward, dragging Doğan and Ali along with it. Ali instinctively tried to keep others from bumping into Doğan. Doğan was touched by the effort.

"They've cordoned off the road. There's something going on over there, but who knows what."

"We'll know soon."

"We'll be waiting here for a while though, I guess."

"So it seems. But it's probably nothing important. You know how our people are, always up for a spectacle."

"We could go back to Piknik, if you like."

"No, no. I'm curious now to find out what's happening over there."

"We can ask."

"No need, everyone'll just tell you something different anyway. Let me try to make my way up to the front."

"No, wait, it looks like the crowd's dispersing."

For a while they just stood there, considering what to do next. Ali was clearly lost in thought about something. Then he turned to Doğan:

"Do you believe a person could stab himself in the stomach, just like that?"

"Now where did that come from?"

"There's a guy in our neighborhood. He had an ulcer. He was in horrible pain.

"The ulcer was at an advanced stage, but he didn't have the money for surgery. One day, we heard these piercing screams coming from his house. Later, his wife said that the pain had become so awful, so dreadful that he stood in front of the mirror, looked at himself, and said, 'Lord, if it weren't for this stomach, I wouldn't be in such pain,' and so he grabbed his wife's tailoring scissors from her hand

and drove them into his stomach, to cut his stomach out. And that's exactly what he did . . ."

"And? Did he die?"

"Of course he did. But the important thing is that the man had decided that the pain was definitely coming from his stomach. And that the pain had gotten so bad that he would try to gouge his stomach out. That whatever it was that determined his thoughts, and his pain, had concentrated in his stomach . . ."

Ali stopped speaking. Doğan was looking elsewhere. Such was his habit. He rather preferred speaking himself, in monologues. When he spoke, he did so well, and he sounded knowledgeable, and in fact, he was more animated, effective, and colorful than Ali was when he spoke. Ali liked listening to Doğan. But now, the fact that Doğan wasn't listening to him upset him. The truth was, Ali rarely spoke. And he was used to Doğan's habit of not listening. His eyes would suddenly veer off into a different direction, he would cease listening to whoever was addressing him, and just like that his attention would be rapt with the new thing he was looking at. He was interested in so many things that their very multitude made Ali uneasy, and he would grow saddened by the thought that the topics which were the foundation of his friendships, including this friendship, were only a few of the numerous topics that interested Doğan.

Doğan had a very multifaceted personality. It was as if because he wanted so desperately to extend beyond that clock of his mother's that always rotated in the same direction that he himself extended in every direction in the hopes of escaping that circle via any crevice possible. It was because of his desire to overflow beyond the confines of that tedious, suffocating circle that he burst out in every which direction. He had fostered curiosity in all sorts of things ever since he was a child. When he was around ten years old he took an interest in silkworms and got so caught up in this curiosity that his room became chock full of the cardboard boxes he kept them in. He would watch the larvae for hours on end, and read anything and everything about them that he could get his hands on. One day he considered trying to stop the silkworms from becoming butterflies and leaving their cocoons, and to obtain silk from them instead. He learned how to do it. But then, foreseeing the inevitable consequences of trying to manufacture silk at home, his mother put a stop to things. He wasn't able to obtain any silk, and the foul smell given off by the dead larva in their cocoons permeated the house. And then one day, for some reason or another, the silkworms ceased to be of interest to him. The silkworms' boxes lingered in his room for some time. Later, when his mother disposed of them, Doğan didn't even notice. And ships, he liked ships too; he used to collect pictures of them. But then that curiosity later gave way to a fondness for postage stamps.

In middle school, Doğan expressed interest in helping with the wall newspaper that his officious Turkish teacher had the students produce, largely for the purpose of showing off to the inspectors. He got good grades in Turkish, and at first his teacher pressed him to manage the newspaper. But then later he got so caught up in the whole thing that his curiosity about actual newspapers soon verged on obsession, and the next thing you knew he was wondering about their editorial directors, and seeing himself as one in the future. All those aspects of the regular newspapers that he liked he started copying in the school newspaper. First it was caricatures, and then comics, and then editorials, and then sports pages. The wall newspaper just got bigger and bigger. This state of affairs started to get on the Turkish teacher's nerves. Finally, the teacher put restrictions on the topics that the newspaper could cover and the total number of pages it could contain. These restrictions put a damper on Doğan's enthusiasm, and so he turned the wall newspaper over to someone else. Yet he nevertheless continued to foster his interest in newspapers for some time thereafter. His room was full of newspaper clippings. He cut out the articles he liked and pasted them onto the blank pages of a magazine of his own making, changing and updating the design at his will. This fixation of his began to make a bigger mess of his room than the silkworms had. His room became an utter wreck, with paste, paper and newspaper clippings everywhere. It was around then that he watched a documentary about missiles. He was simply bowled over by those missiles which traveled unfathomable distances at astounding speeds. And so on that day he became interested in physics. He forgot all about the home newspaper. The newspapers that he had collected in his room were abandoned in a stack in some corner. The dusty stack was eventually disposed of by his mother and the servant. Doğan of course hardly took notice. Physics was his new passion. He dreamed of becoming an atomic physicist and continued to feed his interest in missiles. He read all the relevant books and magazines he could get his hands on, never growing the least bit bored. And he got good grades at school too. He was on the honor list every year. Mevhibe Hanım bragged to the neighbor ladies whenever they gathered at her house that her son was going to become an atomic physicist. Doğan finished high school at the top of his class. He won a scholarship and went to Paris. In the two years that he spent in Paris, he grew bored of physics. One of the main reasons for this was that in France he felt that he lagged behind his classmates. He realized that he owed his superiority back home to the fact that no one there took any particular interest in physics. In Paris, however, his knowledge did not render him exceptional in the least, for there was simply nothing extraordinary about harboring an interest in atomic physics in that city. Doğan's friends at university were well ahead of him. In Paris, being a physicist was not something that mothers bragged about when the neighborhood ladies gathered at their homes. It wasn't long before Doğan realized that he would only be successful if he devoted himself exclusively to his faculty lessons. Only if he confined himself to a narrow circle . . . But had he not spent years trying to climb out of a constricting circle? Had he not sought to overcome the tedious monotony that had oppressed and suffocated him for years via interests that he had fostered for this very reason? Finally, he stopped attending the faculty lessons and started spending all his time in the coffeehouses of Paris. There he met a slew of people who had perfected the art of being special. They spoke of poetry, politics, women, problems, of how life was ridiculous and something that shouldn't be taken seriously, they made fun of everything, produced gossip of the highest level, and were depressed beyond repair. That was when he took an increasing interest in art. Actually, everyone at those coffeehouses was interested in art. He took an interest in film. He wrote to his family, telling them that he had given up on atomic physics and had decided to get a degree in cinema instead. Because he stopped attending lessons and taking exams, his scholarship was cut off. He asked his family for money. His father refused, telling him he had no money for such ventures. Mevhibe Hanım had money, but there was no way she would be sending him any of it; as soon as she heard of his exploits, she wrapped a piece of muslin around her head and locked herself up in the bedroom. So that son of hers that she'd been bragging about, the one who was going to become an atomic physicist, had decided to become a filmmaker, just another good-for-nothing bum, huh? If Doğan had asked for money to study atomic physics, Mevhibe Hanım would have coughed it up in a second, but she was a responsible mother, she couldn't possibly promote her son's adventures in bumhood with her own money. The grandson of no one less than the grand "MP beybaba" was to become a filmmaker. No, there was no way she could stomach that. How could a person possibly join the ranks of the riffraff of one's own accord? A filmmaker or an acrobat; six of one, half a dozen of the other. There's this memory from her childhood that Mevhibe frequently recalls. When Ankara was still a thinly populated city and Kavaklıdere and Çankaya were rural garden areas, Mevhibe Hanım's family lived in Kocatepe. The hills behind their house were bare. One day, she heard a pack of children running uphill say that acrobats had erected a tent up there, and so she followed after them. The children sat down around the acrobats' tent, which had been set up on a flat area at the top of the hill. Two acrobats walked back and forth across a rope tied taut between two poles. They did somersaults. A woman in garish makeup and a hideous costume, the lowest of lowlifes, sang a song. Then, after the short-lived performance, the acrobats began walking amongst the spectators, asking for money.

"Ladies and gentlemen, you have watched our show. Although we usually collect our fee in advance, as a courtesy and privilege to you we did not collect money at the entrance this time. Now, please, place in this tray as much as your generosity can afford . . ."

The acrobat gathered the money, alternating between gestures of humility and intimidation. Mevhibe didn't have any money on her. Embarrassed, she ran away. Now, for some reason the thought of her son becoming a filmmaker kept reminding her of those acrobats. Actually, being the sophisticated, cultured lady that she was, having attended the theater, concerts and the ballet with her husband, Mevhibe Hanım knew that art was something else of course. But still, she couldn't help it; for her, the mention of art conjured up a combination of destitution and banality. Ultimately, it was something she equated with that fallen woman and those acrobats who were more like bandits than anything else. Now how could she possibly accept it, Doğan, holding out a collection tray like that? Of course it wasn't exactly the same thing, but still . . .

"Don't be stupid," Olcay had said. These words only riled Mevhibe Hanım up that much more. "I too know good and well what fine art is, of course I do. And nobody loves a good movie more than me. But, come on, let others make them! It's a dirty business, you never know how things are going to turn out in those murky waters. Besides, sweetheart, this is Turkey, nobody gives two figs about film-making here. In Europe, sure, fine. But here, nobody would get it. The whole spiel's run by bandits. And the so-called 'actors' are anything but artists; they're nothing but a bunch of whores. What does Doğan know? He comes from a good family. In the end he'll be impoverished and disgraced."

"So if so-and-so can't do it for this reason, and so-and-so can't do it for that reason, then you tell me, who's supposed to make good movies in this country?" Olcay said. "Why not Doğan?"

Oh, and the thought of her son's former academic success, now that just sent poor Mevhibe Hanım into the very depths of despair.

I mean, if he hadn't been such a good student, then fine. Maybe then she would have thought otherwise: "Well, seeing as he'll never finish school, and he'll never become a proper man anyway." But why would a boy like Doğan, a boy with such a bright future ahead of him, up and decide to become a *filmmaker*? As if he were some unedu-cated kid who hadn't had a proper upbringing! "What's wrong with filmmaking?" Olcay countered. "It's an occupation, and a difficult one at that. Just look at the respect the state theater actors get. Even the president holds dinners in their honor!" "Oh, now I know good and well what I'm talking about," Mevhibe Hanım replied. When beybaba was an MP, he had taken her to a dinner held at the Çankaya Palace in honor of a foreign ballet troupe that had come to Ankara.

He had kissed the hand of the lead ballerina. But Mevhibe Hanım knew that beybaba would never have let his own daughter become a ballerina. Everyone should choose a job that was right for them. The daughter of a beybaba MP could not become a ballerina. "Fine, then who can?" Olcay asked. "Oh, I don't know, the children of other families, families that don't give their children proper educations, or children of the divorced, people who don't give their children a proper upbringing, or talented children of the common folk, I mean, those who have no other opportunities to make their way in life . . . Of course art is a beautiful thing, but like I said, it's no occupation for someone from a decent family."

Even when Doğan failed to change his mind about becoming a filmmaker and it became apparent that this passion of his was not going to fade away anytime soon, Mevhibe Hanım refused to soften up. Although she had upon several occasions sent money to her beloved son so that he could pay off his debts—because she could not stand to have someone of her own blood in debt to everyone and his brother—she adamantly refused to send him money so that he could pursue his passion. Finally, Doğan, after having picked up enough about art and cinema in the cafes of Paris and having seen enough decent films, had no choice but to return to the homeland, bearing a bevy of books about cinema and an amateur camera he had bought using the last bit of money his mother had deigned to send him.

For some time he wandered the shantytowns of Ankara, wielding that camera. He became an active member of Sinematek. He wrote a few articles about cinema for a couple of literary journals. In a short time word that "he knew his stuff" spread among cinema lovers. Together with a few amateurs who shared his mindset, he started a film collective. And then they started publishing a journal in order to disseminate their ideas about cinema in general, and their thoughts about Turkish cinema in particular. A few female university students who, though they shared their passion for cinema, didn't know enough about it to make films themselves, but who nevertheless were enthusiastic participants in the collective, willingly took on the duty of selling the journal. The girls succeeded in doing so with the help of their extensive circle of acquaintances and also the help of those who were too bashful to turn them down. As their first activity, the collective decided to organize a week of screenings during which they would show a few of their amateur documentary films. That way, they would be able to both make a case for their assertions regarding filmmaking and sound out the response to their beliefs in public opinion. To this end, they would have to rent a cinema for a week and find spectators. The money earned from the journal wouldn't be enough for this purpose. Again with the help of the assisting girls, they tried to gather money and sell the tickets for the screenings beforehand. Finally, borrowing money from a variety of sources, they managed to gather enough for the screenings. Doğan had managed to get his mother to cough up a small amount by telling her that it was for something else.

For the opening they had produced a brochure of declarations full of ambitious and assertive statements. The brochure contained a ruthless criticism of Turkish cinema, followed by views regarding the place and duty of cinema within society, as well as information about contemporary cinema, and concluded by calling upon Turkish filmmakers to perform their duty vis-à-vis the Turkish people. The evening of the screening, frequenters of the Sinematek and a few bookstores that had advertised it, in keeping with their habit of making sure they weren't omitted from such events, filled the cinema. Finally, after a forty-five minute delay, the screening began.

Before it began though, Doğan and his friends mingled in the foyer with spectators, most of whom they already knew, and repeated the statements that they had put forth in the brochure in even more fervent sentences. They became so caught up in their own statements that the show was only able to go on after a few impatient spectators whistled.

They had not done a trial run for the showing that night with the projector they had rented from one of the summer cinemas in Küçükesat. Their friends who had agreed to show the film were unable to get the projector to work. The lights went out several times. Each time the lights came back on, Doğan and his friends dashed over to the projector, but they were incapable of doing anything but looking at it, their hands firmly planted in their pockets. Finally, their friends who had assumed the duty of doing so were finally able to get the projector working. The lights went out again, and the film began.

It was a documentary about Altındağ. Doğan had spent six months wandering the neighborhood of Altındağ, camera about his neck, and it was there that he had used up most of the raw film he had brought over from France. In his head he had a scenario that he'd finally crystallized after ample discussion and debate with his pals in the collective. The film was going to depict in detail the people of Altındağ; their butt-naked children playing outside, laborers heading off to work at the crack of dawn, women rushing to feed and clothe their children before dashing off to serve someone else, old people napping at front doors, chicken coops, kelims woven of old scrap cloth, a funeral in the middle of the neighborhood, a circumcision celebration, an imam-blessed marriage, and this and that. Doğan would narrate the film with the voiceover of someone who did not live there but was touched by the sights. There would be a stark, irreconcilable contrast between the narrator, who presented the images in what he himself deemed a beautiful, poetic narrative and the actual images on the screen. The viewer, sensing this irreconcilable contrast, would think of how impossible it is to explain these places, of how they could only be experienced, of how insufficient mere spectatorship was. The documentary would conclude with a quatrain on the guilt of the spectator. Doğan had heard this quatrain from a young poet friend of his in Paris, and liked it a lot. While the quatrain was being read, the camera would draw closer and closer to the face of a mother crying in the wake of a coffin of a child who'd died from deprivation, and as the voice of the person reading the quatrain softened, the sound of the woman's weeping would become louder.

Following hours of discussion with his friends, Doğan had made some modifications to these ideas of his. Consequently, when he put his film in his camera and went to Altındağ to record, he was of the firm belief that he now knew very well what he was going to do. As soon as he arrived in the neighborhood, he found himself surrounded by kids. Before he was able to capture the images that he had already laid out in his mind, he himself was captured by the children, to the point that he could neither take a single step, nor look left or right. He had come here as someone concerned about them, so of course he could not reprimand them. For a while he rushed to answer the series of questions the children threw at him. Once he was convinced that he had done all he could, he tried to leave. But the children, who had ruthlessly besieged him, had no intention of letting him do so:

"Film me, brother . . ."

"No, not him . . . film me brother . . ."

"Film us brother . . .."

All of them were hopeful, as if this was their chance to become movie stars and escape this neighborhood, to become famous like Ayhan Işık and possess enormous homes and fancy cars. This was such a hope, such a rare boon that had fallen at their feet, that they had no intention of being so stupid as to let it escape. The children's begging and pleading soon became contagious, and the bigger kids joined in too. They also drew in closer, to see if the good luck might rub off on them. Doğan began to sense that those surrounding him would not let him do a single thing here until they had wrenched away the rights that they were so determined to obtain. Next came the mothers. They too had spread their wings like falcons over the rights of their children. It was absolutely clear that they would not allow filming of either themselves or their front- or backyards, so long as the hearts of their children remained discontented. Doğan, thinking that he would never be able to film the things he planned to film, like circumcision ceremonies and funerals, unless he made sure he was in the good graces of the neighborhood folk and, arriving at the conclusion that he had no other choice, he succumbed to the will of the children. But in doing so, he made one of the gravest mistakes of his life. The children's requests knew no end. They all wanted him to film more of themselves. Just as he would be getting ready to film one of them, another would pose with his plastic pistol and start tugging at his pant leg, while another would be shoving aside the kid he was filming and thrust himself in front of the camera. One of the kids silently watched Doğan for some time, water pistol in hand, his silence punctuated by occasional outbursts of talk and laughter with his pals, in an attempt to attract attention. The boy's initial silence was really only to size Doğan up. It was a characteristic that most of the children here possessed. When confronted with a stranger, they would first stare him down, and then they would follow him for a while, and once they were convinced that the stranger they were trailing was not a tough guy and would not beat them up, they'd start badgering him, knowing good and well how to get him to do their bidding. And so once he had completed the surveillance phase, the boy with the water pistol latched onto Doğan's jacket:

"Make a movie about me too, brother!"

At that moment, Doğan was preparing to film the boy with the plastic pistol who was wearing a hat made out of newspaper. He had just started filming when the kid who had completed his surveillance routine soaked Doğan good with his water pistol. The lens of his camera also got wet in the process. While Doğan was drying off the lens, this time the kid whose recording had been interrupted came up and started yanking at his jacket. Now certain that it was his turn, the kid with the water pistol soaked the boy with the plastic pistol this time. The boy's paper hat was ruined, which infuriated the hatted boy, so he pounced upon his adversary, snatched the water pistol from his hand and chucked it into a nearby chalk well. The two boys dug into each other full force. Suddenly the fight grew. It spread throughout the mass of the children. They started throwing stones at one another. One of the stones hit Doğan in the head. Doğan, who up until that point had just been standing there dumbfounded, uncertain as to whether to shield himself or his camera, had blood streaming down his head. The children's mothers too had become engaged in the battle. Hurling unspeakable curses at one another, they too began to take part in the competition that was raging between their children; each of them wanted her child to be filmed. They had no intention of seeing the rights of their own children being usurped by some twerp, and in the belief that you can beat the treat out of another's mouth, they cheered their children on, urging them to land their punches first. Meanwhile, they also cautioned Doğan, who was busy wiping away the blood streaming down his forehead, not to deny their own children's right to be filmed. Finally Doğan, now thoroughly fed up, decided to film all of the children together. Everyone marched over to a nearby field, and the children sat on the grass. This time, they wouldn't sit still; they kept trying to get in front of one another, and the ones behind kept giving donkey ears to those in front. It was a daunting task, but Doğan finally managed to film the children. He hadn't the strength to see or film anything else. Meanwhile, the children and their mothers, having joined forces to guarantee the future of their film careers, hurled questions at him right and left:

"When's this movie going to play in the theaters, brother?"

"Brother, did I make into the movie too, huh, brother?"

"What theaters is it going to be shown at, brother?"

"Brother, when are you going to film again?"

"Brother, you'll tell us when it hits the theaters, won't you, huh, brother?"

Meanwhile, the hour was approaching evening. Several men returning from work also took an interest in Doğan. A few of them invited him to their homes for coffee. Doğan, unable to bring himself to refuse their polite invitations, sat and had coffee. He responded to their never-ending litany of questions with a heap of fanciful lies. For he had quickly discerned that honest responses would make no sense to the bearers of the questions. They were expecting a concrete, tangible movie like the ones they watched at the neighborhood theater. One young man asked, "Whose life is the film gonna be about, brother?" Doğan, pleased to have an answer for that question, replied, "This neighborhood." One of the men gave Doğan a suspicious look. "You must take us for a bunch of idiots, brother," he said. "A place doesn't have a life." A frustrated Doğan replied: "I mean, I'm going to film the life that is lived here." This time, another one of the men took offense: "Just what is it about our life then, son; you can't go messing in people's private lives." Doğan, by now worn ragged, let the words slip from his mouth, "I mean, for example, I want to film your funerals and stuff." This response upset the man even more. "Now look here son, you don't want things to get ugly. A funeral's no theater. That's blasphemy!" Doğan fell silent, and so did the other men sitting with him. There was no way he'd get to film the funeral bit now, that much was obvious. Now that the feeling of discord between him and the locals had become quite concrete, he didn't have the courage to ask if there were any circumcision ceremonies on the horizon. He thanked them, took his leave, and headed home. He was tired.

He didn't speak with anyone at dinner that evening. When he returned from Paris, he had taken the university exam. He knew that his mother was dying of curiosity to learn the results. He had learned the previous day that he had gotten into law school. That upset him too. What he really wanted to do was make movies. He found university education pointless. If he wasn't going to get to learn about what he was interested in, then what was the point? And it would be especially meaningless to go study at that school for scriveners, he thought. But if he said this to his mother now, it would only cause more unrest. She didn't want to hear of even the mere possibility of her son not going to university. His father was strict about this point as well. Of course he had to continue his studies, after all, he was the son of a professor! And then, ultimately, his mother and father would get into it. His mother would accuse his father of spending way too much time dealing with other people's children and neglecting his own son. "Why don't you educate your son instead of writing all those papers about education!" she would complain, and then his father would storm off, Mevhibe Hanım would lock herself up in the bedroom, and this discord would continue for days. The only thing that made Doğan think twice was his military service. If he didn't enroll in university, he would have to do his military duty, and then the whole filmmaking business would go up in smoke. The unpleasant feeling of suffocation that marks the onset of defeat wrung his heart. He got up from the table. *I'll probably end up enrolling anyway*, he thought. He shut himself up in his room without telling his mother that he'd gotten into law school. He lay down on his bed. He thought of Giselle, whom he'd had to break up with when he was forced to return to Turkey because he'd run out of money, of her amber skin, her wholesome face, her hazel eyes. At the Paris coffeehouses where they hung out, when asked about their love affair, they had responded with a nonchalance they deemed imperative, "What do you mean love? We're together, that's all." Giselle was better at expressing such thoughts than Doğan was. She would say: "We ran into one another. It was something like a car wreck; if a car runs into you, you can't just continue along your way. Now we have to stay together until we've recovered. And then we'll both move on." That's the kind of word-smithery they did; they said that they were watching one another. "Spectating is important, but it shouldn't be something static. If a car wreck is happening here, then somewhere further away a war is happening, and even further away, a revolution. Spectatorship should transform events and locations . . . In order to do that, you have to reach the speed of sound, in which case, let's look into one another's eyes and leave it to others to foolishly refer to it as love . . ." Doğan spoke in a similar fashion so as to please Giselle; after a certain point, it's so easy to fashion such speech. Like drinking a lovely, bitter, acrid French coffee . . . Relaxing, painless . . . Fun! Yet when he went as a spectator to the slums in Altındağ in order to shoot a film, he hadn't been able to watch anything or make any of the explanations necessary for the film . . . He had only grown weary. That, and he'd been watched. He'd gotten sick of the suspicious gazes shot at him, and the quick-wittedness he'd displayed in the Paris coffeehouses had vanished, leaving him incapable of devising believable, confident responses to the questions directed at him. Suddenly he missed Giselle, missed her very much. For all their big talk, parting had been difficult. He'd struggled to suppress his tears amongst the crowd that had gone to see him off. And now, lying there with his eyes closed, he tried to bring to life the image of Giselle's hazel, speckled eyes and her taut body. But the persistent gazes of the children chasing after him kept cutting in front of Giselle's eyes, suffocating him with their mix of suspicion combined with questioning-pleading-hope. Pressing his face into the pillow, for the first time in a long time, Doğan cried.

So that's basically how he had shot the film he showed that night. He'd gone back to the same places a few more times, cringing, afraid of looking like a thief, and recorded a few random scenes. The section with the children was clearest. Besides, most of the film had melted. Consequently, he edited the film, inserting images of children sticking their tongues out at the camera, giving each other donkey ears, and shooting water pistols, splicing them with the various sequences shot at the hilltops of the shantytown, and named the film *Shantytowns and Children*.

Once the spectator issue had been resolved and the lights went out, Doğan's film began. After pressing the start button on the tape player, and thus launching Haydn's Symphony of Toys, which he had chosen as the film's background music, Doğan realized in horror that the film had melted just after the children's faces appeared. The lights came back on. Doğan stopped the music, in his flustered state pressing down on the button with unnecessary force. It wasn't long before the lights were turned off again. The film began anew from where it had left off. And Doğan started the music again. But this time, the tape was dragging, Haydn's music was too slow. But since the speakers weren't working right, the problem with the sound was barely detectable anyway. Then someone yelled out, "Sound!" Someone must have fidgeted with the speakers in response, for suddenly Haydn's music, now unrecognizable as the sound of it rose and fell, filled the cinema. Just as the child with the water pistol began shooting at the camera, the sound spontaneously ceased. A few people laughed loudly. Doğan, glancing around nervously, noticed that a young man sitting at the end of one of the rows was watching him carefully.

There was something about the young man's gaze that reminded Doğan of the children in his film, and so he became even more nervous; Doğan had noticed the same young man while he was walking around in the foyer before the screening. He was wearing a brown, rather worn out suit. Doğan had noticed, while walking past him, that he wasn't wearing any socks. He also took notice of the young man's bony face and his piercing gaze. Everything about him set him apart from the intellectual mass crammed into the foyer. While everyone else was talking, debating and sniping at each other, he stood silently in a corner, soberly concentrating upon the brochure. Hardly anyone else read the brochure. Doğan was unnerved by this boy in rudimentary attire.

Once the other films, all of which suffered misfortunes similar to that of Doğan's during the screening, had been shown, it was time for the "discussion" session, as announced in the program.

The topic of discussion was how social dynamism could be propelled by means of documentary films. Doğan's film was to be taken up as an example.

Doğan and three of his friends sat in front of the screen, their feet hanging down over the edge of the stage. As usual Doğan was wearing corduroy pants and a turtleneck sweater. In his hand he held a pipe, which he had recently started smoking. He frequently lit the pipe, which frequently went out, and did his best to appear relaxed before the audience, most of whom he knew, to some degree at least. But he wasn't relaxed. The boy in brown was sitting there in the audience, looking at him with a patient, deliberate gaze. His was the most solemn face in the room.

When the discussion began, some of the spectators, who up until then had been chatting and giggling with their friends, suddenly sobered up. First was a discussion of the role of documentary film in Turkish society. Once the issue of how Yeşilçam had corrupted the people's taste in a deliberate attempt to weaken their consciousness had been addressed, they moved on to the next topic: the dialogue between cinema and the masses and the importance of the dynamism that would be fostered via this dialogue. Doğan appeared to have forgotten the fiascos that had occurred during the screening of his film. And also the fact that the film he had made had nothing to with what he had really intended to do. He said that "the children were a reflection of dynamism," and that "in interspersing static images with this dynamism" he intended "to show the potential, future force of these children," and that "children were the force capable of eradicating these images of poverty . . ." The truth is, he was making it all up as he went along. At one point, the discussion seemed to come to an abrupt end. But then, the voice of that solemn-faced, reserved spectator broke the silence. He spoke in a soft, quiet voice, enunciating each individual word. But Doğan seemed to sense the built-up anger that propelled his words:

"Look here!" he said to Doğan.

In a way, it was the command of someone looking to pick a fight, yet the face, the voice said otherwise.

"Who gave you the right to make fun of those children?"

"What do you mean, 'make fun of them'?" Doğan replied, stuttering in shock. "It seems you weren't listening to the discussion we just had."

"I did listen to it, I most certainly did, but first, I watched the film," Ali said.

That was Ali, and that's how Doğan came to know him.

"I can say this much about the thing I just watched. Those brainwashing flicks they show in the open-air theaters of poor neighborhoods of the likes you've just shown us, well, they're a thousand times better than the film you made. As for the damage such films do, well, at least they add some color to the kids' lives. Sure, they don't have much in the way of toys, but at least they can imagine themselves as Malkoçoğlu or some other hero for a few days after watching one of those films. But if they were to watch this film—and they never would, mind you—but if they did, they'd boo it and hurl soda bottle caps at the screen in disgust. And if the kids you filmed were to watch this, they'd stone you for tricking them into thinking you were making a movie. But then it's clear from the way they stick their tongues out at the camera and make donkey ears that they never really fell for your trick in the first place. Now let me tell you what I think about this film. It's pretty much the same result any amateur slinging his camera around there would get. Because those kids would be hard-pressed to let you film anything else before making you film them first. And so you filmed them, and because of all the trouble you endured doing so, you couldn't bring yourself to go back and really dig in, and so you recorded a few shots from a distance. And then you spruced it up a bit, and now here you are talking about dynamism. Even those kids were on to you, they could tell you were nothing but an amateur, and there may be some people here who appear to have fallen for your little trick, or who have no qualms appearing to have done so. But like I was saying, those masses you want to ignite would simply explode into a volley of soda bottle tops if they were here to see it. That thing you call dynamism is important, I know, but in order for the exchange of dynamism to happen, I mean, for it to reach the spectator from the screen, something has to happen on the screen. Now if I stand up here and say, 'This is the best weapon to kill a pig with,' and then I show you that water pistol the kid was using in the film, you'd just laugh at me. I'm really sorry pal, my words might be hurtful. But I watched your film, patiently, and I also read what you wrote in the brochure. And I did my best to find a connection, a consistency, even the most basic, between your words and your work. But in order to assess the degree to which you were able to achieve what you claimed you set out to do, one would have to watch the film properly. That wasn't even possible. You rile on and on about Yeşilçam, which is fine, pal, but, seeing as you've chosen to respond to film with your own films, then in that case you've gotta show something decent up there on the screen. You can't tell an enemy you're gonna kick their ass and then show up with a wooden sword. I expect this film to at least be as clear and understandable and to have the same continuity as the Yeşilçam movies. Plus, you can't go making such grand claims in a frivolous place like Neşe Cinema, switching the lights on and off every few minutes during the show. What really surprises me is that none of the spectators here have had a word to say about any of this. The only conclusion I can draw is that they don't take you seriously. Who amongst the spectators here would be content to find themselves confronted with such a film in any cinema theater if they'd actually paid for their ticket? Those people here who have spoken so seriously without taking tonight's failures seriously are no less guilty than you are. Serious words deserve serious spectators. The nonchalance displayed here is something serious. If you take this film and show it to the people, the masses, you'll find that they're not as nonchalant as you are. If they pay a lira, they expect a lira's worth of film, you know, I mean one with an obvious beginning and an end that you can actually see. It is only after such an exchange that the transfer of dynamism is possible. Am I wrong, pal?"

Ali had been leaning forward as he spoke. He was looking straight at Doğan. He had said some harsh words, but in such a soft, unembellished tone. It was a talk that in no way resembled that of those who had spoken before him making grand assertions about Turkish filmmaking. The audience had shown the same disregard for those who spoke before him as they had for the film itself, but they all listened intently to Ali's words. Ali was one of those people who begged to be heard out, because there was something that he absolutely had to say.

Doğan realized this as Ali spoke. Deep down, Doğan was upset by Ali's words, but at the same time, he couldn't help but agree with him. There were only a handful of people there that night whom Doğan held in high regard. But they had slipped out as soon as the film was over, after saying a few encouraging words to Doğan. None of them had presented an explicit criticism like Ali had. The more he thought about this, the more enraged Doğan became, and the greater the feeling of failure, which he often fell prey to these days, became. He thought that, with his corduroy pants and his pipe, he must look like an inept child. One who, decked out in the pretty clothes his mother had tailored for him, forgot his lines at the school play.

Ali had fallen silent. He was looking at Doğan, patiently waiting for a response. Doğan had no response to give. Actually, he could have said a lot of things, if he had employed his usual quick-witted repartee. He could easily have changed the direction of the conversation. But he felt that if he did so, that cursed feeling of failure would pervade him completely. He no longer wanted to be the unsuccessful actor in a bad movie; he wanted to leave this cinema, to leave it behind.

He jumped off the stage and walked straight towards Ali. He sat down next to him, and said nothing. A few people attempted to carry on the debate. But their words remained up in the air, meaningless. Doğan kept quiet, as if he were not one of the people responsible for organizing the screening. After a short while, the crowd dispersed.

Doğan and Ali left together. As if they were old friends.

"You're not angry with me, are you?"

Doğan looked at Ali's face, trying to discern whether or not he was being mocked. His comrade's long narrow nose, dark shiny eyes, and honest gaze immediately drove the thought from his mind.

"No, actually, I should thank you."

"For what?"

"You gave me the chance to accept something that I was already aware of, the nonsense of it all. The matter of cause and effect."

"If that's what you think, then so be it. But still, you shouldn't be ashamed of the work you've done."

"Even if it's bad?"

"Yes, as long as long as you've understood that it's bad, even if it is bad. My father always says, 'More good comes out of action than of doing nothing at all.'"

"Would you have a drink with me?"

"No."

"Why not?"

"I don't have the money for a drink."

"But I'm inviting you."

"That's all good and well, but it's important that I don't have money."

"You can invite me another time, buddy."

"That's the thing, I won't have any money another time either."

"Then whoever has money will treat. It's nothing to fight about."

"Of course, unless you're the one who doesn't have any money."

Doğan fell silent. He wondered if Ali was offended. He both desired and feared Ali's friendship.

If I were him, I wouldn't be friends with someone of my class. Doğan was fond of rigid thinking. But he could sense that Ali was capable of viewing issues differently depending upon the context, and that this variability in his assessments lent him a kind of flexibility. Later, when Doğan asked Ali, "Shouldn't people of your class be more hard-nosed?" Ali had responded, "Just the opposite. It's people like you who address the issues strictly through reading who are rigid. People like that usually don't possess the necessary power of change and adaptation when it comes to a particular issue. Because in truth, they're guilty and cowardly. Only those with something to hide are so eager to build walls. It's actually because of their feelings of guilt that petite bourgeois intellectuals fail to rein in their thoughts and instead plunge forward full-throttle. Their fear of being unable to change themselves supposedly gives them the audacity to change everything in one stroke. Sometimes they use theory as a wall to conceal their fear and culpability. In situations in which action and flexibility are necessary, they succumb to the power of that strict, stagnant wall and, unable to deal with the pressure of events, their fear and guilt become menacingly apparent." That's the answer he gave. But what had happened between then and now?

"The plane tree is collapsing, I think," Ali said.

Doğan looked at Ali. *Had he changed? Has Ali changed for me since that day?* No, after all, it was he who had informed Doğan that the tree was collapsing. Doğan meanwhile, standing there in the midst of the crowd on the sidewalk, was reconsidering his relationship with Ali and wished to define something at the moment that the plane tree collapsed. But what? Ali? It was clear who Ali was. His relationship with Ali? Or maybe what was to happen after the tree collapsed, after the avenue was cleared of people? But how?

After exiting the cinema, they had walked together in the cool air of the Ankara night. Doğan didn't want to part from Ali. He was afraid he might never see him again. Ever since he'd returned from

Paris, a feeling of distress which had started in Paris but which there amongst coffeehouse humor had day by day gradually been rendered numb and unable to break out of its shell was unfurling within him. And along with it, his failure, his meaninglessness. He'd wanted to study film, but he hadn't been able to. Maybe he hadn't wanted it badly enough. Maybe there wasn't anything that he wanted badly enough. The truth was, the numerous books he'd read had only served to confuse him, or rather, to cause the things which plagued him to multiply. He hadn't been able to become a link in any chain. He was neither a student, nor an artist, nor a real bourgeois. The things he had written for the brochure now seemed ridiculous to him. In the first few months after he'd returned from Paris, he'd gone to Yeşilçam. There he'd met famous directors and producers. He'd tried to impress them by relaying all the things he'd heard in Paris. They'd listened to him a few times, without taking him very seriously, and then they'd started making fun of him. None of them had given Doğan a chance. As if they'd made a secret pact to conspire against him, all of them told him one had to have experience, to rack up hours as an apprentice, and they claimed to have already been privy to approximately the exact same words that Doğan so beautifully expressed, but insisted that the market itself was something different, and that that "something" had to be taken into account. And now, with Ali walking next to him, Doğan thought that those men were right not to give him a chance. What, were they supposed to grant him unlimited freedom, when they themselves were hemmed in by strict laws? He had this indecipherable feeling that Ali was going to open one of the doors he thought closed, and with his everyday simplicity, his lack of pretense, show Doğan how to get out. Because Ali was someone who would definitely do what was possible. He looked at Ali's hands. They were hands which, should the lights go out, would immediately repair the blown fuse; he wouldn't allow the darkness to get to him.

Doğan once again feared that he might never encounter Ali again. Did Ali sense this fear of his?

"We can go to our place if you like, buddy. My ma'll still be up waiting for me. She'll fix us some tea."

This made Doğan happy. He was just as delighted at Ali's invitation as he had been the first time Giselle had invited him to her room.

"Your mom won't mind?"

"Not at all. What mom minds her son coming home?"

Doğan was about to say something, but then changed his mind. His own mother would get very upset whenever he brought guests over out of the blue. "A real man doesn't go to someone else's house without a proper invitation," she'd always say. Because a home might be in any state at any given moment, and it wasn't proper for a stranger to be privy to just any state of the house. She couldn't possibly conceive of the idea that a person might have a friend so close that one could share anything with him. Therefore, she wrote off any of Doğan's friends who happened to come over at an inappropriate time, and once she had done so, that was her final judgment and there was no looking back. Consequently, whenever such a friend would call Doğan, his mother would inevitably be rude to them, and do everything in her power to wreck the relationship. A little while earlier, when Ali turned down his invitation to go out for a drink, he considered taking him home with him, but then, recalling his mother's disposition, had quickly changed his mind.

"Alright then, let's go to your place," he said to Ali.

They walked in silence, first to Ulus, and from there to Dışkapı. Ali turned onto one of the back streets in Dışkapı. It had grown very quiet. They could hear the rustling of the trees on either side of them. "There are lots of gardens around here," Ali said. "They call them the Kazıkiçi Gardens. That's where they grow cantaloupes and melons. Cucumbers, tomatoes . . . Shit Creek runs through it. That's the reason for the smell. We're used to it though. Besides, it's good for the cucumbers and tomatoes." He laughed. It was the first time he'd laughed since they met. It was a warm, natural laugh. They arrived at a one-story home. The stone paving at the entrance was wet. Seeing Doğan look to the skies to discern whether or not it had rained, Ali explained. "It's my ma, she's in the habit of washing the entrance every hour. Until the whole family is in for the night. Whenever I come home and see that it hasn't been washed, I immediately get depressed. I think my mom must've run away, that the house has been abandoned. Like when I was a kid. Anyway, I'll tell you about that later." Ali lifted the doorknocker, sounding their arrival, and the door opened. Ali's mother, who must have been in her forties, had the typical look of an immigrant woman, blond with prominent cheekbones. She wasn't wearing a headscarf. With her round, blue eyes she gave her son a fond but censorious look. She was wearing a loose-fitting *entari*. *This woman must have been a knockout when she was young*, Doğan thought. *A wholesome-looking woman with her feet on the ground*.

"So you finally found your way home I see."

The woman's reproach did not have the same sting of cold needles that his mother's did. This was a game familiar to both mother and son.

"And? Now if you don't go on and make us some tea, and I mean good tea, I'll head right back out. I told this guy we've got tea at home, so don't you dare disgrace us."

"At my age, I'm in no condition to be disgracing anyone, it's up to you now to disgrace this family," she replied, letting out a laugh just as heartfelt as Ali's had been.

"Is Dad asleep?"

"Of course he is, the poor guy. He has to work for a living, early to rise . . ."

"Right, right."

"We'd best not disturb your father." The words were barely out of Doğan's mouth when Ali's mother replied:

"Now what kind of thing is that to say? Who'd be disturbed by decent young men like you? Our home is always open to them, be they one or one thousand. We do get a little worried when this nutcase here is out and about though . . ." Then she began doing those little things a hostess does to make a guest feel at home. She put a pillow behind Doğan's back. She took out a cigarette, and then from a cheap glass cabinet she took out a crystal tray, one of the household's most luxurious possessions, and placed it in front of Doğan before going to make tea. Doğan looked around him. It was an immaculately clean room with whitewashed walls. Handmade white doilies on the divan and pillows edged in lace with violets embroidered on them. Doğan thought that, despite his mother's fastidiousness, their own home did not appear as clean or heartwarming as this one. The floor consisted of wooden boards that were a shiny yellow; it was obvious that they were frequently scrubbed down using soft soap. Cheap, ugly baubles here and there. Three coffee tables. Four yellow chairs lined up against the wall like soldiers. On the walls a clock, a *Saatli Maarif* calendar, and next to it, a catchpenny carpet made of fake silk depicting lions. The most visible spot in the room was occupied by a cheap cupboard with a mirror in the back, clearly purchased from one of the furniture dealers in Samanpazarı. Inside the cupboard a few coffee cups, a wedding candy tin, and a few gilded lemonade glasses. *All of these items, taken individually*, thought Doğan, *are cheap, ugly, common things. Yet there is something about this home as a whole that is heartwarming, comforting.*

His own home, filled as it was with antiques passed down from his grandfather, was like a grim, suffocating museum in comparison. He never had liked his home, even as a child. In elementary school he had drawn a picture of a home that was pitch black and written on it, "Our home, black home."

He settled into the divan. Overcome by a sudden but gradually growing sense of ease, he looked at Ali. It was as if he'd been coming to this house ever since he was a child, as if he'd spent many a night sleeping on the divan he was sitting on now.

Ali walked into one of the side rooms, whistling all the while. He returned wearing pajama bottoms instead of pants, and slippers on his feet. He did as he did every night, as if there weren't a guest in the house. Doğan assumed that when someone of a different class came to their home, people like Ali and his family would grow tense and flustered, unsure of what to do. Like the university janitors or building attendants who came to his family's home. Whenever Doğan went to the building attendant's apartment to let him know that the heating wasn't working properly, the attendant would be baffled as to how to behave and, clearly feeling ill at ease, would make Doğan feel ill at ease too. An unscaleable wall would rise between them. Yet Ali wasn't like that at all. You could tell from his actions that he felt much more at ease than Doğan did. Doğan wondered as to the source of this ease. Ali lit a cigarette and looked at Doğan.

"So, welcome to our villa!" As he said this his eyes wandered over the room, with a gaze that somehow said, "I know how tasteless all this is, but I don't care, in fact, I embrace it."

"It's all according to my ma's taste. All bought by sucking the life-blood out of my dad . . ." he said with a laugh. "And despite how ugly it all is, my dad had a hard time paying it off. He nearly got fired from the atelier he was working at because of that cupboard right there.

Oh, right, I forgot to tell you: My dad works at a turnery. He was always asking for a raise at the most inconvenient times. But he had no other choice. Because of the stones, of course . . ."

Seeing the bewildered expression on Doğan's face, he explained: "I mean the stone pavement in front of the house, buddy. Whenever my mom gets something in her head, like for example she got obsessed with that cupboard there once, she'd go running off to her mother's in Konya. She's a strange woman, my ma. She could go hungry for a week and not whine a bit, she can wash a mountain of laundry without a peep, but for some goddamn cupboard she'll dig her heels in and hold out for as long as it takes. And so when she got upset about not being able to get that there cupboard, she took off. And so of course the stone pavement in front of our house was abandoned to the mud. Anyone who came by could tell from the filthy entrance that my mom wasn't here, you didn't even have to knock. It's horribly dismal that way. Must be why my mom got into the habit of washing the stones all the time."

"So your mom used to run off, huh? Just because of the cupboard, or were there other reasons?"

"No, because we were broke. They'd fight over it. For days. My dad was a hard worker, but he was a bit too generous with his money. I'll never forget this one time they fought over milk. Back then my dad worked at a factory. And so he was entitled to one liter of milk each day. During one holiday one of my dad's friends from work came over to our place. He was a worker with five kids, and all five of them were sick. The man kissed my dad's hand and thanked him for the milk, right there in front of my mom. So it turned out that my dad had given the man his own share of milk, though of course my mom didn't know about it. Once the man had left, all hell broke loose. In those days we spent three days hungry for every day we were full. My mom was crying, 'How can you give away your share of milk when my children are going hungry?' And then their fighting got so intense my mom up and ran off to her mom in Konya."

"Your mom was in the right, if you ask me."

"But my dad was in the right too. He was right not to ignore a man he had to stand next to every day, a man who was constantly moaning about his sick children. So both of them were right. They were both doing the best they could do. My day worked all day and my mom kept us kids and the house clean. Whenever they'd be up all night fighting, I'd cry in bed, afraid that my mom would run off to Konya again. But I couldn't bring myself to be angry with either of them. I'd feel bad for both, and pray that God would give these two good, hardworking people more. As time went by and my prayers weren't answered, it was as if, inside, I grew dark with gloom, full of frustration and desperation. I'd get enraged and just blow up at everybody. And when my mom ran off, my dad and I would sit together and weep. It was so sweet, the way my dad wept. And so then I'd get angry at my mom and start cursing her. But then my dad would get mad at me and tell me to stop it, that my mom had put up with so much, and that it wasn't her fault. And so I'd ask whose fault it was then. My dad would just make a tight fist and remain silent. He didn't have an answer for me."

Ali told all of this in an unembellished manner, as if it were all par for the course. Doğan felt awful. It was as if someone was choking him. Just then Ali's mom entered the room, her blue eyes twinkling. The blue of her eyes reflected off the tray, making it shine all that much more. The copper tray had been scrubbed spotless. She brought the tea in a spotlessly scrubbed teapot. The tea glasses too were clean as could be. There were spoons inside them, and beneath them plastic saucers with a flower pattern. The sugar bowl was made of yellow plastic. The lace doily on the tray, and everything else, conveyed tremendous love and care.

"In the Caucasus we bring the teapot out when we serve tea. That way everyone can have it as strong as they like, and as much of it as they like. And we don't use sugar either. Like they say, if the tea's any good, no need for sugar . . ."

"Oh, come on now, you're just saying that so we'll use less sugar."

"Well, would you listen to that . . . As if you aren't the one who refuses to drink tea with sugar in it!"

"That's another topic . . . But there's nothing you wouldn't do for sugar, now is there!"

Doğan sensed that this was some kind of inside joke between Ali and his mom.

"You see this mom of mine? She was once sold for exactly one kilo of sugar. One kilo of sugar."

"Oh, c'mon now. I took a liking to your father as soon as I set my eyes on him at the Konya bus station, and that was that."

They both laughed. Ali took the tray from his mother and placed it on the coffee table. He poured the tea into the glasses. The blood red, boiling tea warmed Doğan's insides. He breathed in the scent of the steeped tea. He recalled his own mother's watered down, tasteless tea that she forced the family to drink, claiming that anything stronger was "bad for the stomach, and makes one irritable." But this tea filled him with a sense of contentment.

"How were you able to steep the tea so perfectly in such a short amount of time?"

"There's always tea brewing in our house, son. The whole family has a weakness for tea. The truth is, we should all like the best of everything. All of us humans should consider ourselves worthy of the best we can do."

"That's right," Ali said. "Mom thinks us worthy of the cleanest sheets, that's why she does the wash every single day."

Ali's mother gave him a hurt look.

"Poverty doesn't equal filth," she said. "It doesn't cost you to wash the laundry now, does it!"

"Soap isn't free though. And if you get ill from all that work, they don't take care of you for free."

"It's *my* back though now, isn't it? It's my pain to bear, and my wash to do," his mom said, feigning anger. She filled a glass of tea for herself, picked it up, and left the room.

Doğan reveled in every sip of his tea. He hadn't put any sugar in it. For some reason, he hadn't wanted to. Though he assumed it would be bitter, he quickly grew used to it.

"You don't want any sugar?"

"No."

"Because I don't take sugar?"

"No man, I wanted to try it like this."

"Because of the way my mom and I joked just now?"

"Why do you think that?"

"I don't. I'm just asking. Asking questions is a good thing. That way you avoid mistakes. I'll tell you the story that the joke comes from, if you like."

Doğan was downing his tea in big gulps now. He nodded.

"So my dad, he's just a common laborer, right? Actually, no. You see, at some point, somehow, he became the running champion of the Balkans. And when he got back to Konya, the governor and all the big wigs, all the schools, they all welcomed him with flowers. At the time, my mom was a student at the Konya school for teachers."

"Your mother's a teacher?"

"No, she didn't graduate. But that's another story. My mom's family are immigrants from the Caucasus. They lived in Konya's immigrant neighborhood. It's full of immigrants and Gypsies living together. You ever been?"

"No."

"Oh right, of course not. Why would you? Maybe we'll go together one day."

Doğan was pleased by this suggestion. So it seemed Ali wanted to establish a real, constant friendship with him. There was something, some things they would be doing together after this. Doğan felt the feeling of failure inside him ebb.

"So my mom's family was living in the immigrant neighborhood. My mom had gotten into the Konya School for Teachers. It's real cold in Konya in the winter. My grandma knit my mom a pair of mohair socks. Then she boiled them with onion to bleach them. Yet one of the socks ended up a light color and the other dark. They made fun of her at school because of those socks. And so my mom never set foot in that school again."

"Because of a pair of socks?"

"Yes, because of a pair of socks. Sometimes what they call fate all depends on a pair of socks. How much does a pair of socks cost? Not much perhaps. But even that much can be important for a person. Anyway, before my mom dropped out, hers was one of the schools that went to welcome my dad. The Champion of the Balkans! And it was my mom who handed him his flowers. Now, our Balkan champ was a distant relative of the man who was governor at the time. The governor hosted his relative, the champion, in his home. My dad saw my mom at the station and couldn't get her out of his head. He begged and pleaded with the governor, who finally tracked her down for him. At the time, you couldn't get sugar anywhere. And so again making use of the governor's influence, he found a kilo of sugar and took it to my mom's. My mom's family was so impressed by that kilo of sugar that they immediately agreed to give my mom's hand in marriage . . ."

"And then?"

"The expected. No one had asked about my dad's education or employment of course. And so when the governor moved away, my folks were left to fend for themselves."

"In a way, it's kind of like your mom was deceived."

"Maybe. But wasn't my dad deceived too? The way they celebrated his return with all that pomp, welcoming him with a musical band and flowers, hailing him champion of the Balkans. Later whenever they fought, my dad would try to rattle my mom by saying he'd got her in trade for a kilo of sugar. He was exactly twenty years older than her."

"Your mom must have been a real looker back in the day!"

As soon as the words were out of his mouth, Doğan regretted having said them. Ali might not be too happy about such a reference to his mother's beauty . . . But Ali didn't seem offended in the least.

"Yes, she was. I could never get my fill of looking at her. And I was really jealous too. So much so that at one point, I became convinced that my mom was cheating on my dad. My mom used to take me out for a walk every day. We wouldn't go anywhere in particular, just wander around. We'd sit on the bench at the square. There was this young lieutenant, he used to tag along after us whenever we went out. My mom pretended not to notice. But it drove me crazy. I really gave my mom a hard time about that. Yet those walks were my mom's sole source of entertainment. She didn't much care for going to other people's houses, and we rarely had guests over. My mom turned a lot of heads whenever she walked down the street. And so I didn't want to go out into the streets, and once we were out, I'd do everything in my power to resist. I'd kick my mom, she'd buy me a simit and I'd promptly throw it onto the ground. If my dad thought my mom looked pale when he arrived home in the evenings, he'd tell her to take the kid out and get some fresh air. My mom would look at me and laugh. I used to get so angry with my dad because he let my mom go out like that. Because there weren't many rooms in our house, I slept with the two of them, and so I was a lot more aware than I should have been about certain things. You get what I mean?"

"Yeah," answered Doğan. As he did so, he looked at the tea glass he had just refilled, and thought about how he had never considered his mother in conjunction with the word "love," let alone felt any kind of jealousy over her.

"Right, you get it. So, I knew everything, but because I didn't understand it, I would misinterpret it. I'll never forget, it was right around when I started middle school; one afternoon I was sitting next to the window doing my lessons when someone threw a letter in through the window. I thought I would die right then and there. I couldn't bring myself to open it right away. My entire body was shaking all over. Finally I worked up enough courage to open it. It was a love letter written to my mom. The truth is, it was obvious from the letter that the love in question was unrequited, that my mom had absolutely nothing to do with it, but what difference did that make to me? To me, my mom was a whore. I stopped talking with anyone at school; I'd watch the other kids playing, so carefree, all the while I was eating my heart out, thinking, *Of course they're going to play, they've got nothing to worry about, their mothers are honorable women.* I hated my mom. At the time, we were in pretty bad shape financially. My dad kept changing jobs. He just couldn't bring himself to put the whole Balkan championship thing behind him. He wanted to continue being that man greeted at the station by a cheering crowd. He couldn't handle being scolded by his bosses. And so whenever he got ticked off, he'd hand in his resignation, just like that, regardless of the kids and the doctor bills. Then when he'd get home and see my mom, he'd understand that he'd made a mistake, but by then it would be too late . . . One other time, shortly after my mom had given birth, she had a fever and I had the measles, and we had neither medicine nor money for food; since it was the first of the month, my mom told my dad to buy us some fruit when he got paid that day. But my dad came home late. He'd been drinking. As soon as he saw us he started to cry. He'd gotten angry at his boss for something he'd said, and quit. Without taking that month's salary, you see? And then he borrowed some money from a friend and went drinking. My mom couldn't take it, she just kept screaming. My dad kept yelling at her to be quiet. He always knew when he was in the wrong. 'I know, any man worth his salt would take his salary and come home with all the stuff we need. But that guy, he up and called me a jackass, out of nowhere, a jackass, that's what he called me, and just at a moment when I was so burned out—a jackass! The dwarf, one punch and I would've sent him flying across the room, it's because of *him*, Şükriye. I was thinking of you guys and how I'd bring two kilos of oranges home, and so I must have gotten lost in thought, when the bastard comes and plants himself in front of me and says 'Get to work, jackass.' And I just lost it, believe me, Şükriye, if I hadn't quit right then, I would have killed the guy.'

"If only you had, if only you'd gone and killed the guy and ended up in prison. And then I'd be a whore.' I went ballistic. I leapt out of bed and started beating my mom. The poor sick woman, I was beating her like crazy. The word 'whore' echoed in my mind, thousands of mallets pounded at my temples. At first my mom just froze. And my dad was too shocked to react. My mom fixed her blue, bewildered eyes on me. I'll never forget the deep sadness that I saw in those eyes. My dad, drunk as he was, just sat there in a chair. My mom shot straight out of her sickbed, put her coat on over her nightgown, grabbed the newborn, and left. My dad cried all night long. He sat me down in front of him. The first time he went to my mom's house, my mom offered him coffee, which she carried on a tray. She was wearing a hand-knit woolen dress. 'Below where her petticoat ended, her knees shined beneath that knit dress. Your mom's skin, it was so smooth and shiny, your mom's skin, why did you hit your mom, she always took such good care of you, I'm not worthy of Şükriye, I'll never be a real man, oh, if only you'd hit me, knocked some sense into me, son. My dearest comrade, my son, why, why, why?' he moaned, weeping that heartfelt weep all night long.

"'Don't cry,' I said. 'What, are you supposed to let them call you a jackass? What business does she have out on the street anyway? She should stay at home, look after her baby. It's a good thing she's gone, good riddance to her.' But even as I said spoke those words, I was thinking about my blue-eyed mom, outside in the middle of the night, already ill, and I was scared to death something bad would happen to her. My dad doused his head and then fixed himself up. We went out together and started searching for her. Finally, we found her at the station. She didn't have any money. When she saw us she turned her head the other way, facing the wall.

"'I'm going to Konya,' she said.

"'But you don't have any money,' my dad said. 'I promise you, Şükriye, when I find some money tomorrow I'll buy you a ticket and send you myself.' 'How are you going to find the money? You'll have to go and be someone's slave again. And as long as you're willing to do that, then what was the point in spouting off to your boss today?'

"Both my dad and I felt relieved. The fact that my mother was talking, complaining, was a good sign. It was when she was silent that she was at her most dangerous. She possesses the stubbornness typical of blondes, as we say; she had no intention of backing down. 'I'm going to beg till I've gotten enough money for my bus ticket,' she insisted. But in the end, she came along with us, silently. That night my dad made love to my mom. And then my mom cried, almost silent wails, calling my dad 'crazy, you crazy, crazy man.' That night, I understood that my mom loved my dad dearly, and that she hadn't cheated on him. The next morning I told my mom I was going to work really hard and rescue us from our poverty."

"What did your mom say?"

"She looked at me for a long time with those blue eyes of hers. 'You silly fool,' she said. 'If you had any wits about you, you wouldn't go beating up your mom, now would you? Silly fool, you think your dad's lazy, do you?' she asked. 'No,' I replied. 'Well then? What'll change then if *you* work?' she said. Her words really got to me. I mean, it meant there was no hope—no hope that my fear of my parents' separation, which befell me at the end of each month, would ever subside. The fear would already set in at the beginning of the month. That's when the debt collectors came by. My mom would put them off, telling them to come back around the following month. Because if we paid our debts, we'd go hungry. More than half of my childhood was spent trying to find a solution to this problem. There was something that made even people like me, my mom, and my dad, people who loved each other dearly, turn into monsters and lash out at one another, make criminals of out them, a kind of sickness maybe, something I didn't know, that I couldn't understand. I had to find a solution for it. But even with my child's mind, I could sense that I wouldn't be able to find a solution to something whose cause I didn't know."

"And did you eventually find it, the solution?" Doğan asked. He was on his fifth glass of tea. Ali stood up. With bare feet he paced back and forth over the İsparta rug with flower designs. He looked at Doğan with gentle eyes and then, as if simply asking him, "Would you like some more tea?", as if speaking of just any other everyday thing, he said, "Of course I did. Do you believe there's anything for which there isn't a solution?"

Doğan didn't get home until the break of dawn. He and Ali had talked all night long, without drinking alcohol, and without talking nonsense. When Doğan left, Ali's mom was washing the stones at the entrance. He could hear the birds twittering in Bostan. He felt almost weightless. He and Ali had agreed to meet up again the next day. Doğan learned that Ali was studying law, and so he decided to enroll right away himself. He seemed to know now what he was going to do. Or even if he didn't exactly know, he sensed that he would find out very soon, and he could tell at least what he *wasn't* going to do.

"Where have you been?"

"I was at a friend's."

"If you're already staying out all night drinking at your age . . ."

"We drank tea."

Mevhibe Hanım looked at her son with unbelieving eyes. Doğan always came home late like this on nights when he'd been out drinking.

"What, daytime isn't good enough for drinking tea anymore?"

She looked at her son with suspicion. She sensed that he'd changed in some way. If Doğan had been out drinking, she would have complained a bit but then just taken the situation in stride. But here he was, her son, having returned home in the morning completely sober, looking her straight in the eye and saying that he'd only drank tea. As usual, Mevhibe Hanım was not happy with this change. It annoyed her.

Doğan went to his room. The brochures they had printed for the film screening were scattered about here and there. He gathered them up, took them to the kitchen, and threw them away. Upon seeing Doğan himself finally trash all those pieces of paper she had been wanting to get rid of for how many days now, saying that they dirtied the room, Mevhibe Hanım became quite peeved.

"What's wrong with you?"

"I'm fine."

"What do you mean you're fine?"

"Mother, for the first time in my life I'm saying that I'm fine, and you're not even happy about it!"

"No, dear, it's just that till now, whenever I ask if you're okay, you always say, 'What's there to be okay about?'"

"That's because I wasn't okay."

"Why do you insist on confusing and upsetting me like this!"

"Why not? It would do you some good to be a little upset. You know what, Mother, you need to make yourself really, really uncomfortable and forget all about that thing you call peace of mind."

"And just why should I be uncomfortable?"

"You will be, there's no other way. You will be uncomfortable!"

"It's always bothered you, my comfort, my ease."

"Of course it has, because it's annoying. What's more, it's not even real. You're not comfortable, nothing about you is at ease. You don't even know the meaning of these concepts."

"Sending you to Paris was a huge mistake. The only thing you learned there was how to belittle your parents."

"No, I learned other things too. I learned about darkness. About twilight. It may not be complete darkness, but twilight is awful. You bump into all sorts of things. And now I'm learning about darkness, pitch-black darkness . . . Tonight someone told me, 'Those who don't know complete darkness cannot recognize a light that will illuminate the whole world, and they don't search for it.'"

By this point Mevhibe Hanım was thoroughly suspicious.

"Were you with that movie bunch again? Nothing good will come of them."

"No, Mother, I was with someone from the university."

Mevhibe Hanım was completely taken by surprise. Doğan hadn't said much about the university. All he'd said was that he had no intention of studying law.

"I'm enrolling today. The friend I was with last night is studying law there too."

"Thank goodness for that."

Now instilled with the hope that her son was finally getting on the right track, the expression on Mevhibe Hanım's face softened.

"He must come from a good family, seeing as he doesn't drink and he's going to university."

"His parents are working class, they live in the slums."

"Is that so!"

Mevhibe Hanım blurted out those last words. Then, thinking that her son had probably just said that to anger her, she shrugged her shoulders and walked away.

Alone now, Doğan walked over to the window. He looked outside. It was the first day that he had paid any attention to the poplar in the yard. It was a very old poplar. It must have been planted there long before the apartment building had gone up. The front wall of the yard had divided the poplar's thick, dry roots, which could be seen just above the earth. The tree's leaves were dead. Its trunk was cracked here and there. Living sap seeped out of the cracks, and the dry, moldy, dead insides of the trunk were visible. Doğan wondered why they hadn't cut down the poplar when they erected the apartment building. It must have been his mother, she wouldn't have allowed it. "That way, there'll already be a tree there in front of my home." But it couldn't be said that the tree had benefitted from this life that it had been allowed, or which had been bestowed upon it. With its sickly, ugly appearance, it was in perfect harmony with the facade of the apartment building, which was completely tasteless itself. Rather than a beautiful living being, one of the last remains of what had been a steppe, the tree was simply an extension of an ugly building. After gazing upon the poplar for a while, Doğan said to himself, *That tree will dry up soon.*

The crowd rippled, first forwards and then backwards. Ali had his eyes set on the traffic police who were trying to keep the crowd of people away from the areas where the tree might land if it fell. Just then, he saw Güngör Bey get into his car and take off, completely ignoring the police. "Look at that swine," he said. "He knows how to find a solution, but only for himself."

Doğan hadn't seen Güngör.

"The tree that's falling down is the poplar in front of our apartment building."

Ali laughed.

"The tree's falling down, and the man's flying the coop."

"Who, who's flying the coop?"

"Just another somebody, anybody. Like that poplar of yours. It's just any old poplar, for now, any old poplar about to fall down!"

Olcay and Ali

After that day, Ali and Doğan became inseparable. They always went to university together, and whenever there was any political uproar, they would go to Ali's place and drink tea and debate until morning. Ali didn't much care for going to Doğan's house. He thought it better that Doğan come over to his. Olcay too had been over to Ali's a few times. Mevhibe Hanım didn't approve of Doğan's friendship with Ali. She held Ali responsible for the unpalatable changes she saw in Doğan. And so she got really angry when she found out that Olcay had also been over to Ali's. Olcay immediately took a liking to Ali. Doğan had found his sister's fondness for Ali disturbing, but had avoided thinking about the reasons why. Perhaps it was some kind of extension of the jealousy of a child who didn't want to hand his toy over to his sibling. But Ali quickly caught on, had understood that it made Doğan uneasy, and so he stopped telling him to bring the *bacı* along with him. Olcay was upset with both Doğan and Ali for leaving her out of their friendship and discussions, and frequently accused them of having "feudal" mindsets. Whenever Doğan would start to criticize Olcay, the latter would tell her brother that he had no right to do so, because just as he made no effort to further her progress, he completely left her out of everything that was going on.

"You need to find your own way!" Doğan had told her.

"Fine, if everyone's to find their own way, and those who claim to know what's happening and to try to change things bear no responsibility towards those who don't know, then you're right. But anyone who thinks that way hardly has the right to criticize others."

A short while later, Olcay too became part of Doğan and Ali's friendship.

Ali was fond of Olcay's presence, but it also made him nervous. He felt that Olcay was in awe of him, unnecessarily so, and that she would never be able to evaluate him in a completely realistic way. One day, he shared this concern with Olcay: "You're friends with me just so you can oppose the things around you which bother you, and which you oppose anyway, that much more. You think that just by liking people like me, you achieve some sort of change within yourself. All kinds of little behaviors of mine, which couldn't possibly be otherwise anyway, inspire some sort of awe in you. It bothers me to have my natural behavior held in such high esteem, because these aren't skills, they're just the result of the conditions under which I've been raised. And you also make too much of the fact that I come from a working class family, whereas that too is no skill of mine. If we're to have a healthy relationship, you need to stop seeing me in the light of your falsely acquired complexes. You need to judge me outside of that, just me, plain and simple, according to my qualities which I myself am responsible for." Olcay hadn't responded to Ali's words. In a way, Ali was right, because no matter what Ali did or said, he appeared to be right, and because of some feeling of inferiority that she couldn't explain, she decided before Ali even did anything that whatever he did was right. Sensing this, Ali was wary of his friendship with Olcay. He was wary that this friendship was something created by Olcay's own personal issues, and so he was afraid that once Olcay had overcome her personal issues, their friendship would lose its meaning. Olcay meanwhile was of the opinion that Ali belittled her family, the way she had been brought up, her daily habits, the way she dressed and the way she talked. "He sees me as a degenerate extension of a degenerate system, that's why he doesn't trust me," she said. This mutual discomfort cast a shadow on their friendship. Nevertheless, after some time they began meeting up, just the two of them, without Doğan. When they were together, they felt the crushing weight of something outside the two of them, something that bore enmity towards them and their relationship. Ali liked Olcay. He liked her tall healthy body, her dark honest eyes, her slim sentimental hands, and her sentimental words. He was aware of the fact that he was fond of her not only as a friend, but as a woman too. And this fondness bothered him. He thought that no matter what, Olcay would never be able to establish a real intimacy with him, and so he did his best to suppress his feelings for her. Olcay sensed Ali's interest in her, but she couldn't figure out how to overcome the distance that Ali insisted on planting between them. It had soon become clear to her that Ali would not grow close to her of his own accord. Olcay didn't want to remain a bacı forever. She felt intensely close to Ali, and she wasn't fond of any other man, not in that way. She realized that it was up to her to strengthen their relationship. But because she was afraid that Ali would disapprove, she couldn't bring herself to take that step. What if he told her, "I thought you were a bacı, so what's up with these feminine bourgeoisie pretenses?"

Usually whenever they met they would go for walks. Because Ali didn't have any money, he couldn't take Olcay out. And whenever Olcay offered to take him out, he unequivocally rejected the offer, saying "It wouldn't suit an Ottoman like me." Olcay responded by telling him that underlying this behavior of his was an Oriental attitude that viewed women as inferior. And when she did so, Ali would retort, "You may be right, but now's not the time for resolving such issues." One day when they were walking by a construction site, Ali pointed out one of the laborers. "Do you think there's any sense in telling this guy about male-female equality?" he had said. "Or his wife? If a home becomes too small for you, first you knock down the walls. Next you build a new house, and only after that do you think about a chimney." They'd walk for hours debating such topics. They'd usually head out to the Eskişehir Road. They enjoyed the walk back, watching the sun go down. On these return journeys, Ali would treat Olcay to a glass of tea, telling her, "I'm not that hard up just yet!" They'd sit down and have their tea at one of the *kıraathane*s in the slums. The coffeehouse regulars would cease playing backgammon for a moment to give these unusual customers the once over before continuing with their game. "We've given these guys a shock. Actually, we don't have the right to shock them, to wear them out like that for nothing," Ali would say. "But I don't feel comfortable at the patisseries, bacı. I can't stand those snobs who show up there everyday like it's their job to sit around and gab. I can't take pleasure in the tea or the company." Olcay had blushed at the words "take pleasure in." With Ali . . . it was going to be wonderful, of this she was certain. In her high school days, back when she greedily devoured any book she could get her hands on, she had read Freud, and for a while had exaggerated the importance of sex, thinking that freedom in this regard would resolve personal problems. But the narrow-mindedness and hypocrisy she had witnessed surrounding this issue, especially amongst her own family members, made her think that the things that annoyed or depressed her had to do with sex. And that's why her first rebellion against those close to her was to break such taboos. As a result, she had some relationships early on, which she pursued indiscriminately and without much thought. Those relationships did nothing for her, except to increase her frustration and make her feel like a failure. She had put an end to that period of her life, still bearing certain false generalizations regarding love, a pessimistic attitude and a feeling of emptiness.

After getting to know Ali and starting to think again about a slew of topics, this time in a sounder manner, she understood that declaring a one-woman war on sexual taboos was not going to change the underlying unsavoriness of it all. Such behavior would only assist the system in accelerating her own degeneration and consumption. The interest she took in Ali was of a different nature. For the two of them to become physically close would not change the character of their relationship. Olcay believed that such a union would only serve to strengthen their friendship through a new form of sharing, that it would propel them towards a more creative, more complete togetherness. At least, for her it would be that way. Or, in short, she desired Ali, in any way she could have him, no matter the consequences.

It was on the return journey of one such long walk that Olcay suddenly stopped in her tracks.

"What is it, bacı?"

"Why do you insist on using the word 'bacı'? What does it mean?"

"For goodness sake, it means friend, sister, buddy, so, that's what it means, my bacı!"

"Would you call the woman you love 'my bacı'?"

Ali remained silent for a while.

"I never thought about it before. The truth is, I've never loved a woman."

Upon hearing these words, Olcay, under the impression that Ali had tried to cut her down to size, blushed. She was horribly embarrassed.

Upon seeing Olcay blush, Ali understood that he had put his foot in his mouth in a major way. He took Olcay's hand in his own. Both of them acted as if it was something they always did, the most natural thing in the world. The blood coursing through two bodies separately suddenly began coursing simultaneously, making for a bigger, more beautiful, more stimulating journey. They walked, filled with the joy transmitted to each other via the touching of their hands, as if the sap of their very beings flowed into one another.

They didn't speak again until they reached Dışkapı. When they arrived at Ali's house, Ali said to her, "I'm going to make you tea." Olcay knew that Ali's family was away in Konya. Still, Ali felt the need before stepping inside to inform her that his family was away in Konya. In his usual plainspoken, honest, frank manner.

While Ali was in the kitchen preparing tea, Olcay walked over and stood by him. She told him all about her previous relationships, the emptiness she felt inside, and her fears of decay and degeneration. And then she asked: "Will you love me anyway, despite all that?" Ali took Olcay's head in his hands:

"Actually, I feel closer to you now, not just because you don't like this system, neither with your heart nor your mind. You're a victim, just like me, a victim whose salvation depends on change."

Olcay had rolled up the sleeves of her blouse. Her blue veins were visible beneath her dark yet thin skin. Ali slowly, gradually grew to know those veins; for awareness of blood coursing as one is a familiarity that requires patience. Olcay pressed her cheek against Ali's, and slipped into a feeling of rest. She felt not only that she hadn't rested like this in a very long time, but also the creative power of her renewed cells.

They laughed as they filled their second glasses of tea. They were sitting naked on the divan, their backs to one another. Their backs were cool.

"We're like Siamese twins."

"Does it bother you not seeing my face?"

"I can't get enough you. I share the flow of your blood, the beat of your heart. I *live* you, I mean. And so it so it doesn't matter if I see you or not."

"Let me make the tea this time."

"Okay, bacı."

This time, Olcay was delighted by the word "bacı." So it seemed that their relationship hadn't lost its former friendly, sibling quality.

"So nothing's changed?"

"No, of course it's changed. Is it possible for something not to change after such a wonderful experience? Everything's changed, for the better."

"You're right, it was just a silly fear I had for a moment."

"Don't be afraid, fear isn't for those who can see the light, even if just a glimpse of it. Kids in the dark are afraid. We're neither kids, nor is it dark."

"Until recently I used to get scared at night."

"Will you be now?"

"Not while I'm with you."

"No, you have to not be afraid even when I'm not around. Like courageous people, that's how we must hold on to one another's hands. Not to greet one another, or to lean on one another. Look, Olcay, they may take you away from me, but only I can rip you out of me. It's the same with courage, and belief. Now, for example, you've got a slew of habits—can you give them up?"

"Yes." Olcay said the word hesitantly but with a desire to appear determined.

"Right, so, I don't want to be one of those habits. One of your ties to the system. I don't want to be your toothbrush in the morning, or the deodorant you spray under your arms, or your egg shampoo. These may comprise only tiny parts of your daily happiness and comfort. I have no desire to comprise a larger part of that same daily comfort. I mean, I can't give you support in order to make you more comfortable, or to make you unafraid, for example. Once you've severed all of your ties to the system, and that takes courage, once you've shown that courage, you'll no longer be someone who's afraid of the dark. And when that happens, if you still love me, I'll accept that love as genuine. Okay?"

Doğan is of two minds

Olcay was a natural part of Doğan and Ali's friendship by now. When Doğan understood that an affinity between Ali and Olcay, of which he could not be a part, which he could not share, had begun, he was worried at first. He was cold toward Olcay for a while. He behaved like a child seeing others trying to play with his toy. Many times he nearly lashed out at Olcay, "How dare you! I found him first!" Towards Ali he felt a little resentful. But still, the three of them were together, always—with the exception of Ali and Olcay's romantic relationship, which was not something they hid but which remained in Doğan's eyes a clandestine affair. Except for the occasional times when the couple was alone, together the three of them discussed and debated, worked and shared life to the degree to which they were able to understand it. Did he take the relationship between Ali and Olcay to heart so much because he viewed it as something singular, a selfishness that interrupted their union? At first Olcay and Ali didn't sense this change in Doğan. For a while, they didn't notice the change in his behavior. They assumed that this stillness on Doğan's part was just a passing phase of his rollercoaster personality. But soon they began pondering the possible reasons for Doğan's quiet but peevish behavior. It unnerved each of them in different ways.

Olcay found in his behavior something that reminded her of the "big brother rights" that she was frequently reminded of in her childhood. Old sentences came to mind:

"Olcay, don't go into your brother's room!"

"He's a boy, and he's older than you, it's his right!"

"Your big brother is right, the man is always right!"

"He's a man, he needs it, he's a man, he needs a good education, he's a man, he can do it, he's a man, it's his right . . ."

And on and on they went, those sentences belonging to her childhood memories. No matter how much those sentences infuriated her, the truth is, they had conditioned her. And so now, she felt guilty towards Doğan, she couldn't help it, because Doğan was acting as if his rights, which he had rejected in his mind but which had long become a part of his daily habits, had been taken away from him.

Ali, on the other hand, felt a completely uncalled-for sense of despair, something he had no desire to feel. Doğan didn't believe in him like he used to, that he could sense. He acted as if he had detected some great weakness in Ali, as if Ali had disappointed him. It was as if Ali's taking an interest in Doğan's sister had somehow revealed Ali's "desire to jump up a class." As if Ali secretly yearned for those things which only people of Doğan's class possessed, like sports cars, and had revealed this side of himself at the first chance . . . It was as if his sister were one of those possessions, one of the rights that another class would own, and Ali had betrayed his own class by aspiring to them. Meanwhile Ali wanted to take Doğan aside and scream at him, "Is Olcay some *thing* that belongs to you, man, is that it, huh?"

Ali couldn't reconcile this attitude of Doğan's with the mentality that had helped to secure their friendship originally; he found it crude. So it seemed that most of Doğan's thoughts were superficial; Ali had believed that he could change Doğan's class values. But a simple incident had quickly revealed that the foundations of Doğan's beliefs were anything but solid. Ali thought back: *All those discussions we had about the bourgeoisie's perception of women, what was that about? And wasn't it Doğan who frequently brought up such topics? Didn't he take such things much further than I did? Was it not he who insisted that change in this regard was imperative, while I maintained that such topics were a mere luxury for the time being? But now, in refusing to accept my relationship with Olcay, what difference is there between him and Mevhibe Hanım, who views her daughter as if she were some crystal plate?* But Ali was getting a bit carried away with such thoughts, going a little too far, due in part to that uncalled-for sense of despair. Doğan's feelings had nothing to do with him looking down on Ali. It was actually nothing but a simple case of jealousy. Doğan had absolutely no desire to share with anyone else the light, which he falsely assumed he and he alone had seen after years of meaningless struggle inside a labyrinth. Fueled by a desire to possess, a desire he had failed to squelch within himself, he wanted to seize for himself and himself alone a thought, a discovery, a salvation, belief, enlightenment, friendship, love, even these most human of things, the most important things we have to share. He was partially aware of this. But still he was yet unable to deal with these feelings. And his failure to deal with them set him back, making him feel all over again those old feelings of failure and hopelessness. It was as if he was losing the self-confidence he had only so recently gained, and at the conclusion of hours and hours of pointless and exhausting thought, he would reach a point of ridiculousness to the degree that he thought it possible Ali never thought anything of him from the get-go, that perhaps the only reason he took an interest in Doğan at all was because he was actually interested in Olcay. He recalled the snobs of former days who, back when Olcay was in high school, having taken a liking to her used to invite him here or there but who then only showed an interest in Olcay, and by dwelling on such thoughts, Doğan was in a way equating his friendship with Ali with the relationship he had with those kids. Deep down he knew that they weren't at all one and the same. And he didn't even get angry with those snobs. He thought it quite natural that they would use him to get to Olcay. Just as he had thought it quite natural for other kids to snuggle up to him just so they could get their hands on his football. For Ali, Olcay was not some football, and Doğan sensed that the relationship between them was not your run-of-the-mill bond. Still, he couldn't help but be of two minds.

Unable to decide upon a course of action, Doğan kept his distance from Olcay and Ali for a while. But what started out as keeping his distance from two individuals started to turn into something else. He started keeping his distance from university, demonstrations, debates and discussions. When Ali admonished him for this one day on the telephone, he knew Ali was right, though he didn't say so. The day Ali called, Doğan was pacing around his room in frustration, trying to concentrate on the cinema magazine he was holding. It was one of the most recent to come out in Paris and Giselle had sent it to him. When his mother reluctantly told him that Ali was on the phone for him, Doğan couldn't help but feel a sense of joy, but then suppressing the feeling, he took the phone and said in the coolest voice he could muster:

"This is Doğan."

"Where have you been, buddy?"

"Where do you think?"

"I don't know. The only thing for certain is that you haven't been at the places you should be; I wouldn't know about the rest."

Doğan was overtaken by a sudden rage. *Who did Ali think he was anyway? An inspector? Who was he to tell me where I should and shouldn't be?*

"At least I'm not out skirtchasing!" he said, and as soon as he did so, he regretted it. Ali remained quiet for a while. Then, in a gruff voice, he said:

"I hope by skirtchasing you're not referring to Olcay."

"Why should I be?"

"You know where you picked up that word, and you know the kind of mentality it stands for. But know this too: Olcay and I share a bond, at least as close as the two of you do. I mean, I'll defend her against you if necessary."

There was an uneasy silence. Once again Olcay had come between them. Did Ali even have anything more to say anymore, other than making speeches about Olcay? Had he picked up the phone to call Doğan, or to defend Olcay? It was Doğan, barely able to contain the irrational burst of rage inside him, who broke the silence.

"Is there something that needs defending?"

"Yes, there are things we need to defend, to stand up for. Or there were, I guess. Isn't that so, Doğan?"

Ali felt his heart sink as he spoke those words. Why was he saying these things to Doğan on the phone? *Why haven't I taken Doğan aside already and spoken with him frankly, face-to-face? Instead, here I am, attempting to solve some silly, emotional problems, which we could easily overcome in a single sleepover at my place, via a telephone call that is bound to be cold and inadequate. Am I genuine enough when accusing Doğan? If I really wanted to rescue Doğan from going "going astray," shouldn't I already be aware that the matter at hand is too serious to be addressed on the phone, and shouldn't I behave accordingly? And if that's the case, then what to do? Could it be that the distance Doğan has put between us actually means for me, in a way, the shedding of a ball and chain in my relationship with Olcay?* As if intuiting Ali's thoughts, Doğan exploded:

"Nobody's forcing you to put up with me!"

Ali was shaken, like a child caught in a guilty act. He immediately pulled himself together.

"What do you mean 'put up with,' buddy? There's no such thing as 'putting up with' for us. With us, it's about pitching in. Striving towards what's right, for more . . . Why are you making me repeat things you already know?"

It was a great misfortune, his use of the term "pitching in," Ali thought. *Calling up like this was a mistake, definitely. I need to have a proper talk with Doğan as soon as possible. I am the last person who should doubt my own sincerity. "Things you already know," what a tactlessly tacked-on phrase.* "Don't make me repeat things we already know," he mumbled into the phone this time.

"Go ahead, repeat it. You'll derive great satisfaction from it."

"Now look here Doğan, all of this reeks of evasion."

"And just what is it I'm supposedly trying to evade?"

"I don't know, but surely the reasons for you deserting us are as concrete as the reasons you had for joining."

"Who said I'd deserted you?"

"Then how do you explain the fact that you never join us anymore?"

"Maybe I'm busy doing more useful activities."

Doğan felt distressed by the lie he had just told. Moreover, his words were far from convincing. He'd forgotten how to lie, how to subtly and sweetly deceive like he used to. In the past, despite the throngs of idiots and bores around him, he'd believed that living was only possible by lying, that one couldn't possibility feel ethical responsibility towards those who were stupid and ugly. Yet for some time now, ever since he'd come to believe that stupidity and ugliness were variable, he no longer felt the superiority he once felt when faced with either. The concepts of beauty and intellect didn't mesh with such feelings of superiority. Still, he felt guilty towards Ali, a feeling that would perhaps stay with him for some time, and so spurred on by his guilt, he defended himself, going on the offensive as he did so.

"You still owe us an explanation."

"Why?"

"Because . . . Wait, no, there is no 'because,' now is there, buddy? At the end of the day, aren't we on the path we believe to be right?"

"So?"

"So, in that case, I mean, if we're sincere in our intentions, then anyone who finds something better, something more right, has to tell the others about it. That is, if that person isn't trying to make 'what's right' his own personal property."

Ali's use of the word "property" angered Doğan. Why was he always harping on about property? Why was he always on Doğan's case about his family, even at the most inappropriate times?

Yet that wasn't the case. Doğan knew it too. How many times had Ali told Doğan that such issues could be overcome? The important thing was one's ties to class. Anyone opposed to a class would eventually sever its ties with that class. It was he himself who felt an unnecessary feeling of inferiority because of the family and circles he came from. And it was Ali who had tried to get rid of this unnecessary feeling of guilt that he constantly harbored. The whole issue revolved around his love for Ali. He had loved Ali so much that he couldn't bear for someone else to be at least as close to Ali as he had been, and so in avoiding the situation he sought refuge in various pretexts. He had gone back to being the same old suspicious Doğan. And it distressed him.

"I have no explanation to make. I've come up with a program for myself. I'm reading."

"That's great. So let us benefit from what you read too. We've really gotten behind on reading recently."

Doğan, having the feeling that Ali was making fun of him, became enraged.

"But of course, we're the petite bourgeois intellectuals, aren't we?"

"Now where did that come from? Why shouldn't we benefit from one another? Doğan, look, I've got things to tell you too. Wouldn't you like to learn some things from me as well?"

By this point, Doğan had softened up. The fact that Ali had persevered, hadn't stopped talking despite Doğan's rebuffs, had alleviated his suspicions. Still, though he agreed to meet up with Ali, he said he could only do so two weeks later, because he was studying for exams. It wasn't a convincing excuse. And Ali wasn't convinced. As if talking with Ali would somehow keep him from studying. How had their getting together in the past, or rather not in the past, but up until recently ever kept him from studying, or doing anything? In short, what had it ever obstructed? Nothing. To the contrary, spending time with Ali had always invigorated Doğan. But these days, Doğan was confused. And he wanted to resolve this confusion on his own, before confronting Ali. Meanwhile Ali blamed himself for Doğan's postponing their meeting for two weeks. Doğan was of two minds. *But what about me?* Ali wondered. *I thought that by talking big like this on the phone I was giving my friend support.* But no, he wasn't. As soon as he was able to get away from all the work he was doing for the labor union strike, he intended to go straight to Doğan and pull the latter out of his shell. That was his final decision. And so he didn't make a big deal out of Doğan's avoidance.

A couple of days after their telephone conversation, Doğan found out that Ali had been taken into custody along with some of the workers who were on strike. He was suddenly overcome by a feeling of loneliness. Ali, who had spent night after night patiently listing to him talk about all the things that had happened to him, all the mistakes he made ever since childhood; Ali, who had helped him to recognize all of the dangerous twists and turns in his mind; Ali, who, by explaining that complicated labyrinths only existed in nightmares and that there was always a way out, had rendered Doğan's boredom meaningless, had fallen prey to the police, or rather, he was doing things which had landed him in police detention while Doğan remained outside of it all. He didn't even find out about it until long after the fact. It was at that moment that Doğan felt the great distance between himself and Ali, their alienation from one another. And next to this feeling, the situation with Olcay seemed so very insignificant. Doğan felt ashamed for having gotten so caught up on the issue. *At the moment when friendship, when faith, is most important, we always get caught up on some insignificant detail and quibble, throwing the important stuff to the dogs in the process,* he thought. In those days, Doğan did a lot of thinking, but that's all he did was think.

Olcay enters the labyrinth too

The following week Doğan wanted to approach Olcay and ask for news about Ali. But he just couldn't bring himself to do it. It was he who had introduced Olcay to Ali and he didn't like the idea of having to ask Olcay for news about his best friend. The day before he and Ali were to meet, Olcay walked into his room and quenched his curiosity.

They had just finished dinner. Doğan was in his room struggling to write a letter to Giselle, but try as he might, he wasn't able to write anything sincere. Suddenly he was struck by the realization that he had forgotten Giselle's face. Just as he was pondering whether he should be shocked or pleased by this, Olcay walked into his room, carrying a tray of tea.

As always, she took measured, calm steps and placed the tray on Doğan's desk. And then she sat down on Doğan's bed. With her head she motioned for Doğan to take his tea. Doğan noticed on his sister's face, which was usually pale, a slight blush. She had pulled her hair back tightly into a ponytail. It made her slanted, dark eyes, and her Romanesque nose even more pronounced. Olcay was a pretty girl. *Ali's got good taste, I'll give him that*, Doğan thought. But Giselle was pretty too, and now he didn't even remember what she looked like. There was something unusual about Olcay's behavior. For some time now there was something unusual about everything. Doğan realized that Olcay wanted to talk. He decided not to push her with any questions.

"That's my girl. And just when I've got a craving for tea. But it doesn't look like you have any intention of pouring it."

Olcay gave him a plaintive smile, and then rose, walked over to the tray, and filled the tea glasses.

"You don't want any sugar, do you?"

Doğan looked at Olcay. Ever since they had met Ali, both of them had stopped taking sugar with their tea. Olcay knew good and well that Doğan had stopped taking sugar. By asking him if he wanted any now, was she trying to understand if he had reverted to his old habits since he'd stopped seeing Ali? He used to put no less than four lumps of sugar in his tea.

"What kind of question is that, you know I don't."

"I was just asking. It's been a while since we drank tea together."

There was no mockery, no reprimand, or any such thing in her voice. It was more as if she wanted to have a heart-to-heart, or a confession. Finally, she spit it out.

"Ali gets out tomorrow. They're going to release him in the morning. His mother said so today."

"Is that so!"

So that meant Ali would be able to make their appointment for the following day.

"How did you find out? Did you go their place?"

"No, I ran into his mother yesterday," Olcay said, wearing a guilty expression. "I really should have gone over to see her while Ali was in prison, but, well, I just didn't have the courage."

"Why not? I thought you and Ali's mother got on well."

"We do, but I thought she might be angry with me, since Ali and I are on the outs."

Doğan just sat there, giving Olcay a stunned look. He was in shock. Ali had been taken into police custody. He was on the outs with Olcay. And Doğan had been unaware of any of it.

"When did it happen?"

For a moment it occurred to Doğan that Ali may have called him in order to smooth things over with Olcay.

"It was wretched timing. The day before Ali was taken into custody."

Doğan was relieved. Olcay burst into tears. Doğan silently watched his sister, and he realized that the more she cried, the more relieved he felt. And this bothered him. He picked up Olcay's tea and handed it to her.

"C'mon, drink your tea now. You can tell me about it later. You want a cigarette?"

Olcay wiped away her tears with the back of her hand. She began to sip her tea. But it was useless trying to rein in her emotions. Her sobs grew increasingly louder. This annoyed Doğan to no end. He felt a kind of alienation between himself and his sister, and he found the way she was crying repulsive, vulgar even. *Another idiotic bourgeois girl!* he thought for a moment. *Why put on the 'deserted woman' act? If you left him, then you left him. It's not like anybody forced you, right?* He grew more and more enraged. At that moment he likened Olcay to one of those temperamental children of the guests who used to come to their home when he was a child, the ones who weren't content with wrenching his favorite toy from his hands but had to break it too. *She'll shut up once she's found a new toy.* He started drinking his tea, paying her no mind. He relit his cigarette. He thought that from now on, his sister would always feel like a stranger to him. Something had changed. *Olcay, me, Ali, we've all changed. From now on, we won't be able to be close, to know exactly what the others did and why, like we used to. We'll reproach one another, wrongfully accuse one another, slip into side streets and lose each other in the labyrinth. Even if we grow close again, there will always remain these untold, misunderstood things between us. Doubt and mistrust will remain, because we failed to experience an important change, an important event together. Who knows which whim of hers led Olcay to leave Ali and withdraw back into her beloved shell. I took refuge in books. What about Ali? I don't know. He ended up arrested though. He must have done something wrong.* This thought scared him. He sensed that he was trying to erase the feelings of guilt he harbored with regard to Ali by claiming that Ali must have done something wrong. *Why might Ali have done something wrong? What exactly was the wrong that he did?* He forced his mind to come up with something. *Well, first of all, it was a mistake to fall for this girl. Who knows what kind of silly, unnecessary lengths he'd gone to in order to make a good impression? His thoughts revealed a constant tendency to blame Ali and Olcay. He couldn't help himself.* He refilled his tea glass. Rediscovering the disinterested look he thought he had abandoned back in the Paris coffeehouses, he turned a half-mocking gaze to his sister.

"So what's the big deal? It's not like you're the first girl who's ever broken up with her boyfriend."

Olcay grew quiet. She had sensed the change in Doğan's voice and attitude. Why had she come into Doğan's room anyway? As if it was Doğan she'd ever turned to for support whenever she was unable to bear the exhaustion, dejection and sadness that lingered in the wake of relationships that had made her feel as if she'd dived into a swamp and sunk headfirst, all in the name of standing up against this or that! From now on, she would be able to discuss only superficial problems with Doğan, like back in the day when they used to stand outside the *kolej* and talk about books. About books and music and the things they wanted to do. Would those days when they'd sit in Ali's low-ceilinged, stuffy room and drink tea till dawn, picking at their own wounds till they bled, offering their very souls up to one another, as if offering up a bowl of dried fruits and nuts, getting right to the heart of things without digression or embellishment, putting every aspect they possibly could into words—would those days never come back? Olcay felt an indescribable sense of melancholy. So much so that she found herself incapable of tears. She couldn't stand that old familiar look in Doğan's eyes, a look of disinterest, of indifference. Now if she told him that she broke up with Ali because she was afraid, he might make fun of her. At that moment, she was afraid of Doğan. Her former fears were raising their ugly heads once again. Who was this disparaging person sitting across from her? This person who, no matter what she said, twisted everything around until it sounded ridiculous. *Am I like that too? Is this what Ali thought when he listened to me talk?*

With Doğan sitting across from her now, the things that she wanted to tell him started to seem ridiculous, meaningless. How could she possibly tell Doğan right now that she was afraid of inviting Ali over for dinner, that she was loath to force her mother into it? How could she tell him something so meaningless, without embellishment, without evasion, but rather simply like it was? If only everything were so simple, so cut-and-dry. She'd been afraid to invite Ali over to their house. It suited her much better to go over to Ali's instead. She didn't have the strength to tell her mother about Ali, to try and convince her to accept him. Now Doğan would question her about the "getting their mother to accept Ali" bit—was it really necessary? *As long as I continue to be a*

*part of them, a compatible part of a harmonious whole, then getting my
mother to accept Ali is pretty much equivalent to getting her to accept me. Or
is it that I'm growing weary of leading a double life? Afraid of splitting into
two increasingly divided, alienated parts, striving hopelessly and in vain to
patch up the pieces.* Perhaps it was because of this deception that she had
felt it necessary to have her mother accept Ali. Because she was unable
to propel her fractured self forward by disposing of unnecessary sand-
bags and then to piece it all back together again. To experience Ali's
system together with Ali. For a few hours. And then later, after parting
ways, to go back home, to take a hot, bubbly bath, to go to the opera
with her parents, to wear pants now and then. And then to have her
hair done on her way to the opera. To go to the tailor's together with
her mother. A little bit of this, a little bit of that, to take a spontaneous
trip to the salon for a pedicure just because she felt like it, because it
already existed as a possibility in her mind; and then, to toss all of that
to the wayside and pull her hair back in a ponytail. To be one instant
here, the next instant there, behind the door, living the life of a broom.
She wasn't bored when she was with Ali, no, not all, she liked the daily
habits she acquired as a result of the worldview and the thoughts she
increasingly shared with Ali, as a result of Ali's friendship, as a result
of being with Ali; those habits became hers and she was happy to claim
them. In fact, she took refuge in the simplicity, straightforwardness
and warmth of his system. But then later, she would close the door with
a thanks and a goodbye. She would return to the fakeness of the home
that she grew up in, to the forced comforts created inside those walls
of lovelessness, walls to whose existence she had long become accustomed. She went back to other clothes, other conversations, other
relationships. When she was at Ali's place, Ali's mother would listen
to their conversations, neither expressing surprise nor interrupting. Yet
the very idea of Mevhibe Hanım ever listening to a conversation

between herself and Ali was simply inconceivable. Mevhibe Hanım would instantly try to take things into her own hands, and no one would be able to convince her to do otherwise. And that wouldn't be all she'd do. She would do everything in her power to obstruct a relationship containing such conversations. Still, Olcay wanted to invite Ali over. She wanted to be able to say to her mother, "Look, this is Ali, the person I'm closer to than anyone else. And this is what he and I think . . ." But she didn't believe she possessed the strength to make that happen. The mere thought of the volley of questions she would be subjected to should she dare to say to her mother even, "I want to invite Ali over for dinner" was enough to overwhelm her. The responses to those questions would lead to a fight and, worst of all, that fight would not cause even the smallest change in her mother's thoughts. She could invite Ali over in spite of her mother. But in that case, both she and Ali would feel ill at ease. Because everything, everything in this home, was a part of Mevhibe Hanım's system. Mevhibe Hanım's laws were in effect for everything, from water glasses to forks. In this home, it was considered improper to slurp one's coffee, like Ali did. And as for belching after a particularly filling meal and then breaking out into joyful laugher, as Ali's father often did, that too was unheard of. As was putting on your pyjamas and then curling one leg under you at the dinner table, for example. How many times had Ali, in Olcay's presence, put on his pyjama bottoms and sat on his right foot, holding onto the foot with his left hand, while he ate? Olcay too had grown used to eating like this. But in this house, it was most definitely the left hand that held the fork. And meat was always cut immediately before being placed in the mouth. Yet Ali cut all of his meat up beforehand into tiny little pieces, and then taking the fork into his right hand he'd proceed to gobble away. So many details that seemed so unimportant! But Olcay knew that if Ali were to eat like that in their home, just what kinds of looks her mother would give him, and the kind of biting remarks she would make. Should she tell Ali, "At our house, do this, don't do that," to avoid any awkward situations? What a ridiculous thought. She couldn't force Ali to become a compatible part of a system he despised just for the sake of having a meal in peace. And if she couldn't force him, then it would be nothing short of ridiculous to even try; the dining room, with its forks and knives and its everything, would resist any and every attempt to destroy Mevhibe Hanım's system of culinary consumption. Ali would sense this resistance and ask Olcay why she had brought him here into the enemy's midst, why she had thought an attempt at compromise necessary. It would cause unnecessary exhaustion for the both of them. And so, it was best if Ali didn't come over. It wasn't necessary that he did. But what about the hours that Olcay spent apart from Ali inside a circle that was antagonistic to him? There was a part of Olcay that lived within that circle, that is, a part of her that was Ali's enemy, that was alien to Ali. Whenever she parted company with Ali and went back home, she soon found herself brazenly perpetuating her old habits, her old behavior. She perpetuated her antagonism, her alienism. Olcay was gradually coming to understand that so long as she failed to rip this antagonistic alien piece out of herself and get rid of it, so long as she failed to rip out that piece of her that breathed inside that circle, that could not live without being in that circle, or dispose of the circle altogether, her love for Ali would be lacking in some way. Believing that such a relationship would inevitably be deficient somehow, irreconcilable in fact, she became afraid that this irreconcilability would gradually intensify. Her fear, her uneasiness, had increased over time. Especially since that day, or rather night, when Ali had shown up at their house unexpectedly, just like that. Ali's sudden appearance had frightened Olcay. He never made sudden appearances like that, perhaps because he didn't want to upset Olcay by prompting any unpleasant behavior on her family's part. Ali hadn't stayed over that night, he'd told her to stop by the party offices the next day and then left right away. Olcay sensed a feeling of relief at Ali's rapid departure. The next morning, at the party offices, they didn't talk about what had happened. They spent all day writing down the addresses for the magazines that were to be sent to Anatolia. That evening, Olcay was to go to the opera with her parents. Recently she and her mother were on the outs because of the work Olcay had been doing for the party. And so she had felt obliged to join them when they went to the opera. Her mother had also made an early evening appointment at the hairdresser's. Olcay would have to abandon her work in the late afternoon in order to make it to the appointment on time. But did she really have to? Exhaustion! She and Ali had fixed stamps to the envelopes all day long, drinking tea after tea, and it was now nearly evening, but they still hadn't finished. At one point Ali said to her, "If you want we can go have dinner at our place, and continue afterwards."

"I, um, I have to leave in a little bit."

"Where to?"

Olcay remained silent. She couldn't tell him, "To the hairdresser." If she had, Ali would have thought nothing of it. Whereas he should have something to say about it. He should tell Olcay that she was being inconsistent in her life. Anyone who can't change herself . . . He should have screamed, right in her face, that by going from the hairdresser to the opera and perpetuating habits that she didn't believe in, habits of a circle that she didn't believe in, the curtain would be pulled back, revealing her insincerity for all to see. But Ali was incapable of such a thing. He simply would have replied, "Is that so? Well, in that case, I'll have to work on my own tonight. Come by again tomorrow if you have time though." The more Olcay thought about how the scenario would play out, the more frustrated she became. By acting this way, wasn't Ali actually showing that he didn't take Olcay seriously? Perhaps he considered Olcay nothing but some pretty ornament serving merely to embellish this exhausting battle. It was with great tolerance that he put up with the way Olcay threw herself into his beliefs, into his struggle. "For now we're going to have some stunning, hedonistic spectators," he'd said one day. Perhaps he was convinced that Olcay would never, *could* never leave behind her own community, her own system. And so in constant deliberation with herself, and with not a little bit of fear that her thoughts might come true, she had not told Ali that she had to go to the hairdresser because she was going to the opera. In a way she'd kind of expected Ali to stop working and object to her leaving, to ask a litany of questions and be insistent. But he hadn't asked a single question. Upon seeing that Olcay had left his question "Where to?" unanswered, he had quietly resumed working. After a brief silence when Olcay prepared to leave, she looked into Ali's eyes, searching for a glint of accusation, of doubt, of mistrust.

Yet Ali had simply looked at Olcay with his usual gentle, affectionate gaze, and said "Goodbye." To Olcay it had seemed as if this "goodbye" contained a hint of "do whatever you like" disregard. Why had he said "Goodbye"? *In his eyes, I'm not all that important anyway, and so he simply doesn't expect much of me. In fact, he probably thinks he gives me more attention than I deserve as it is. "What's that, m'lady, you want to come? Well of course, come! What's that m'lady, you want to go? Well of course, go!" That's what he thinks of me.* Otherwise, if he really trusted her, really took her seriously, then on that day, when there was so much work to be done and they were so close, such good friends, he should have asked her why she was calling it quits and leaving, should have contested her, criticized her harshly, pushed her to choose between one or the other. But what was it that Ali always used to say? "We should expend our energy not to satisfy our whims or for the purposes of what we imagine might possibly be possible, but for what truly *is* possible. For what could happen, for what is within the realm of possibility. It's our job to make what's possible, possible." That's what Ali would say in debates with Doğan. And did he think Olcay "possible"? Olcay's head throbbed, pounded by these thoughts. Ali hadn't pushed her at all, really. Never. He had with great generosity opened up his own world to her. He had let her share everything, her thoughts, her beliefs, her life, all of it, with him. He had wanted this, it's true. He had invited her into his own system. And Olcay had accepted the invitation and refused none of the abundance of offerings presented to her. Seeing as he was opposed to Olcay's system and her habits, he didn't expect her to reciprocate in this regard of course. That is, he didn't expect Olcay to invite him in the same manner. But what he might have expected in return was for Olcay to also dedicate herself to this animosity, this state of opposition, this existence outside the inner circle. By not wanting to do so, Olcay had effectively decided to perpetuate the appendages of a system, the enemy as it were, that Ali opposed, or at least to have reconciled herself to it. This, in turn, showed that there was a significant part of Olcay that he held in disregard, that he completely ignored. He knew and loved only the Olcay who was close to him, who was together with him; he thought it perfectly natural that there should be an Olcay he didn't know, one who was the daughter of Mevhibe Hanım, whom the women who came to Mevhibe Hanım's home get-togethers called "cutie pie," who attended opera galas, who had her own room and a maid to make her bed, whom the apartment building attendant called "little miss," who took her father's car to go on vacation and stay at various touristic hotels during the summers, who played bridge in the evenings, who when speaking with her parent's circle of friends used very different sentences from the ones she did when speaking with

Ali; with the love he felt for Olcay, he saw her as someone to whom one could say "goodbye" with a hint of melancholy, and that was all. For now, she was a stranger whose presence was appreciated. Olcay thought of all of these things. All night at the opera she followed neither the music nor what was happening on the stage. Butterfly, who died by committing hara-kiri, really got on her nerves. *That's how he sees me, as someone like her, a butterfly that has alighted at his side for the time being. And he's not waiting for me to commit hara-kiri. Could I even commit hara-kiri? Could I disgorge myself of all the habits that have seeped deep down into my being? Could I take my life in a single stroke? I thought I could. Ali gave me the confidence to do so. But by not pushing me to, he showed that he doesn't trust me in this regard, that it isn't even worth asking for.* Olcay didn't sleep a wink all night long. And when they met at the party headquarters the next day, she suddenly blurted out at Ali, "It would be better if we didn't meet from now on, it's the only honorable thing to do." Ali looked into her eyes, smiling, with an expression of disbelief that said, "What's up with the dark humor?"

"Is that so? And which paper did you read that in?" he teased.

"Don't make fun. You know that I spend at least ten hours of each day in a system that is completely different from yours, that is the enemy of yours, and which you patiently oppose. You can try to ignore it all you want, but I can no longer be a part of this travesty. So long as I fail to sever my ties with these things, in my eyes my relationship with you will be lacking, it will be missing something. And I don't want to be a hypocrite. I don't want any lies anymore." Unable to hold them back, she burst out in tears.

Ali gently stroked her hair. In a calm, still voice, he said, "You people, always in such a rush. Just because you conceive of something, want something, doesn't mean that it's going to happen right away, okay? Bonds as strong as those don't just break on any old

Wednesday afternoon, bacı; now if you want for it to happen, but you haven't been able to make it happen, then that means the time hasn't come yet. You think I don't care? That we don't care? The day will come, Olcay, I'm telling you—you just have to want it, you just have to know how to want it. The real lie is to think you have severed those ties before you actually have, before the time has come . . ."

Then, upon seeing that Olcay derived no comfort from his words (to the contrary, she was only crying more loudly now), he remained silent for a while, before speaking again in the most compassionate of tones.

"Or . . . or are you scared, sweetheart?"

Again he hadn't gotten angry with Olcay. Again he hadn't scolded her. And in the end he had sought out the traces of fear underlying Olcay's distress. The fear of letting go of the system. The fear of falling outside the system. Could that be it?

Perhaps it was. Otherwise why all these statements, all this touchiness? Or she was simply incapable—incapable of letting go, of breaking free. Because she slept in the bed of that house, because she had the servant of that house wash her clothes, and because she ate the meatballs of that house. And so long as that was the case, she would continue to be incapable. It was her mother and father who supplied for the system that was their household. So long as that was the case, would she be able to present herself to them as she was and be accepted? It was these thoughts that ran through her mind.

"It would be best if we stopped seeing each other."

This time Ali looked at her with a hurt expression.

"Now look here, this isn't a game."

"You bet it's not, that's precisely why we have to stop."

"Please cut it out with the pretentious talk and just say what you mean."

"I can't go into details right now, not when you've got so much work to do."

"Anything can be explained at any time, so long as it is the product of a clear mind."

Meanwhile Ali continued to affix stamps to the envelopes. It was as if he hadn't taken Olcay's words seriously. *As if we're just joking around here, after all, you know, you're sitting pretty, no worries at all, you don't have to engage in all these internal battles with yourself like I do.* She'd gone on and on like that to herself, and eventually whipped herself up into a rage. Perhaps the fears that she'd been repressing had taken on the form of anger. And then she stormed off, without bidding Ali farewell. She would call Ali in a few days, for sure. But would anything have changed by then?

As she had pulled the door shut behind her and walked out into the street, she was crying. Ali meanwhile was most certainly continuing to affix those stamps with the patience of a saint. For a long time Olcay was unable to forget the sadness she felt that day.

That was why Olcay had gone to Doğan's room, to tell him about all of this. Doğan would be able to understand many things that Ali could not. Doğan shared with her this house, these habits, and every now and then, sometimes more than others, he too tripped up on some part of this system. It was possible for him to help Olcay. But Doğan's attitude had caused her to revert to a previous state, one that was introverted, one that lacked self-confidence. For a while they sipped their teas in silence.

"So they're releasing Ali tomorrow."

"Yep."

"Will you see him again?"

"I'll stop by party headquarters tomorrow, I'm sure to run into him there."

"I'm meeting up with Ali tomorrow."

Olcay wanted for Doğan to ask her to come along, and when Doğan failed to do so, she resented it. *They view me as some kind of decoration, an accessory that can be picked up and put back down just like that, some insignificant piece of the game.* Olcay glared at Doğan for some time. The wall of lovelessness belonging to that fortress in which they had grown up rose between them once again.

Ali and Doğan meet over by the collapsing poplar

Ali and Doğan met up at Piknik, as they had agreed to do on the phone.

"Looks like you've bounced back alright!"

"What do you mean? Have I been ill or something?"

"Oh, c'mon now, buddy, I mean, you know, from what happened to you . . ."

"Oh, that . . . Well, if anyone needs to be on the mend, it's those who aren't on our side. They're the ones who need to get better."

"I feel like you're blaming me."

"No, no, not at all. My health is perfectly fine, that's all I meant to say."

"And so you mean to say that I'm ill?"

"C'mon, man, what's going on here? This isn't about you and me, you know."

They each ordered a beer. Ali had lost weight.

"You look tired."

"Well, they did wear me down a bit, of course. And there were so many people to talk to."

"Where?"

"At the police station. And then in jail."

"How long did they keep you for?"

"First they took us to the police station, where we spent the night. Then we were taken to court and arrested. We spent fifteen days in jail. Then the order came for my release. We still have to go to trial though."

"How did they treat you at the police station?"

"What does it matter? This country's working class has been taking beatings at police stations for years. Not because the police are bad guys, just because it's the status quo, it's what everyone's used to. The only thing that's changed is that it's happening to different people now. That's all."

"Don't say that. How can you say it doesn't matter?"

"Look, when I was at the station, in the room next to me there was this little Gypsy boy. Exactly nine years old. You heard me: nine years old. He'd been caught, red-handed, pickpocketing. They put that boy on the falaka and beat his feet, again and again, but it was no use, they couldn't get him to confess. Later, while he was resting, his feet swollen up like balloons, I asked him, 'Son, you were caught red-handed, why didn't you just tell the truth and avoid the beating?'

"For a moment he glared at me suspiciously, the same way he had at his interrogators when they were beating him. He didn't say a word. I gave him money so he could order himself a kebab. Only then did he talk to me.

"'Don't be such a greenhorn, brother, nobody tells the police the truth.'

"'Why not?'

"'Wouldn't do us any good. Look brother, there are three places where you should never tell the truth, not even your real name: one, the police station, two, the holding cell, three, in court.'

"'C'mon, why's that son?'

"He shook his head as if angered by my stupidity.

"'It's the only way to survive, brother, the only way to get by. If I tell them the truth, I'll be up shit creek, nod my head and there goes the paddle. And who's gonna feed me when that happens, huh? Better to just take my beating here so I can get out and find me my daily bread, okay?'

"Would something like that ever occur to you? Or to me for that matter? He keeps his mouth shut just so he can get out of there and get his next meal. He's willing to put up with the beatings. He doesn't succumb, doesn't turn himself in, he knows that doing so would keep him from getting by, from scaring up his daily bread. He knows perfectly well the bounds outside which he stands. He makes his living by virtue of his very marginality, so why should he play by mainstream rules? Just look at what this nine-year-old boy is willing to put up with, if it means he'll go hungry otherwise. Because hunger is more unbearable than any kind of physical pain."

"The lumpenproletariat are the mud of the system; we can't arrive at political conclusions based upon their behavior."

Ali was galled by this response. They finished their beers. Doğan, sensing that Ali was displeased, said that he had to go home. He paid. They got up to leave. They had no choice but to wait on the sidewalk together with the rest of the crowd. As they did so, Doğan provided a whole litany of the characteristics of the lumpenproletariat. Finally, Ali burst out at Doğan: "Stop talking like a book already, would you!"

"I'm right though, aren't I?"

"You know how just a few minutes ago, you said that they were the mud of the system? Well, if you ask me, they best represent just how depraved and misguided the system is. Their behavior is a kind of defense against that very depraved, misguided system. Nobody has severed their ties with the system in the same way or to the degree that they have. They have no hopes of becoming a spoke in the wheel of the system or anything else of the sort."

Ali paused and took a deep breath.

"You know what I think, Doğan? Someone like you, for example, no matter how much you read, no matter how much you think, in fact, no matter how involved you become, it's still damn near impossible for you to sever your ties with the system. Let's say you were tried and found guilty for a political crime. In the end, you'd be a 'political prisoner' from a good family, and then become a good lawyer or something. Your family would visit you, take care of you. But if you, I don't know, were to commit some petty crime, like the lumpenproletariat do, pickpocketing, or shoplifting, drug dealing, scalping tickets or something like small petty crimes, not like murder, because murder's still considered an honorable crime amongst the people, well, there was this driver who was in prison for murder, everyone respected him, the prison guard who beat up the pickpocketers every day couldn't lay a hand on him, but then one day, the guard was about to mess with him, and the driver said, 'Look here, you're dealing with someone who's killed a man, I will kill to protect my honor, that's how valuable it is, and I've proven it, so there's no way I'm going to put up with a tongue-lashing from some namby-pamby guard like you.' He's got that sense of honor that murderers possess; I heard a lot about him when I was in prison, but anyway, I'm getting off track. What I mean to say is that those pickpockets, the so-called lumpenproletariat, even there they're outside the system, they're the mud, the dredges of the prison system; they aren't considered worthy of such adjectives as moral or honorable, and in response, they easily claim honorlessness for themselves, because that's all that's left over for them, and so that's what they console themselves with. They don't possess any of those values that even the guy who's committed murder still possesses, despite the fact that he's committed murder, and they can't; if they do, they won't survive. It's as simple as that. Take yourself for example, only if you commit a crime like theirs, only then perhaps would you be able to break out of that castle of yours."

With his hand he motioned towards the apartment building where Doğan lived. That's when he noticed Olcay, who was standing amongst the crowd gathered on the opposite sidewalk. She was standing near the fire truck. The avenue had been evacuated. The firefighters had tied a thick rope around the poplar that was about to fall, and they were pulling it in the direction they saw fit for it to fall. They had completely evacuated the spot where they had decided it should collapse, and marked it off with a police cordon. Olcay wouldn't be able to make it over to the other side until the poplar collapsed.

Doğan was looking at Ali, his expression one of shock. It was the first time he had witnessed such aggression in Ali. Noticing that Ali had diverted his attention to the other side of the street, he too shifted his gaze to the same direction. He saw Olcay. *Is Olcay the real reason he's acting this way towards me? Because they broke up?* He felt a growing sense of exasperation. Being stuck in the midst of the crowd was suffocating him. It began to drizzle.

"Seems it's going to rain, that's probably why I've been feeling so out of sorts."

"Well, now that the rain is falling, you must feel some relief, right?"

"No, not at all! Is it that simple?"

"No, it's not."

"Oh, right, simplicity suits me, doesn't it?"

"Why are you being so touchy, Doğan?"

"I don't know. It's just so frustrating. If that poplar's going to collapse, I just wish it would get on with it so that we could cross the street."

"We don't have to wait, if you don't want to."

"No, I definitely have to stop by the house."

"You do realize that the poplar is right in front of your apartment building, don't you?"

"Yes, and it's rather surprising that it's remained standing as long as it has. When the apartment building was being built, my mom said, 'a poplar is a poplar,' and wouldn't let it be cut down, so it is to her that it owes its present existence. But of course, since there wasn't enough room for its roots, it's since dried out."

"So you didn't plant it."

"No, perhaps it dates back to when Kızılay was still a swamp."

"So you mean it's an old, meaningless poplar which has nothing to do with you?"

"Exactly. Why are you smiling?"

"No reason . . . For a moment . . . It's a ridiculous thought . . . It's just that, you know, I made this connection between your house, all of those things, and the poplar. But it's just an old poplar it seems, and so its collapse doesn't change anything."

"What could it possibly change?"

"I don't know. That's all . . . A ridiculous analogy. Something I picked up from you guys, just so you know!"

"We're going to end up soaking get if we keep standing here like this. Maybe we should go inside somewhere and have another beer?"

"No, I like the rain. Olcay's going to get soaked though!"

It's Olcay, that's what on his mind. That must be why he was so cross with me just now, because he's angry at Olcay for breaking up with him. Ali is also letting himself get carried away by his emotions. And he's capable of being ridiculous too. Like he was with the whole poplar analogy.

"When you went on about the pickpocket just now, were you trying to tell me that you don't trust me?"

"No, not at all. Why shouldn't I trust you? And besides, what difference does it make if I do?"

"It makes a big difference."

"Look, this isn't about you and me, Doğan. How many times do I have to tell you that?"

"But why shouldn't it be? I mean, on one level, it is about you and me. If we're to act together . . ."

"To trust you or not to trust you . . . Now, how should I put this? I don't know exactly what you're capable of. How far can you go? These are abstract matters, actually. We've done so little together. We haven't had the chance to test one another."

"So test me!"

"How can I? And who am I to do so anyway? You have to test yourself in certain situations. I can't create those situations. I can observe you, make judgements about you, or perhaps influence you in any given situation. But my trust in you is something subjective, you're going to do whatever you're capable of in any given situation in the end anyway. Regardless of my trust in you, or lack thereof . . ."

Ali suddenly grew quiet. He didn't care for his situation.

"We're being ridiculous, standing out here on the sidewalk talking about things like this. Are you going to come with me after you've stopped by your place?"

"I don't know. I'm confused."

"If you're confused, don't come."

Doğan swung his arm through the air in a sweeping arc, indicating the apartment buildings across the street. In doing so he had disturbed a few members of the crowd, who grumbled in response.

"You think everything ties back to my roots. I know the way people like you think. I know it by heart. Because you harp on about so-called petite bourgeoisie roots. And I'm sick of it, you understand? Of the way you misunderstand everything and your narrow-mindedness. But you will never get it. Now, you're going to think I'm trying to wile my way out of this because I haven't been able to break free of all those things you go on and on about, my bourgeois habits . . . But you know what, I'm sick and tired of these stereotypical accusations."

"I didn't accuse you of anything though. Those are your words, it's you who's getting angry."

"Even if you don't say it, you think it. It's obvious from your every action. And you can't deny how easy it is to make such accusations. Even you yourself have complained about it!"

"That may be so. But you shouldn't get angry about it, just as you shouldn't get angry at anything that's a fact, anything that we need to face up to. You live in that apartment building over there, you grew up amongst a bunch of habits. Are these facts, or not? You, and all of us, have to face up to these things. Just like we have to face up to other situations as well."

Doğan wasn't listening to Ali.

"You expect me to do a bunch of silly things in order to sever my ties. Even, in fact, to sever them in some crude way by committing petty crimes like theft. You think I won't be able to break free of the environment I come from without first doing something improper like that. You don't trust my mind, or my heart. Say it, you don't, do you?"

"I do."

"Well, in that case, why the example of the pickpocket?"

233

"No reason in particular . . . .. It was just a thought . . . Like I said, you guys got me into the habit of playing with thoughts. But enough of this right now, Doğan. Are you coming with me or not?"

Doğan continued speaking, almost yelling really, in the midst of the crowd that pressed more and more tightly against them.

"Well now. I'd say it's the perfect time to test me. Shall I nick somebody's wallet to please you, to prove myself to you? And you can yell, 'Thief!' Let's play the 'outcast' game together. Or rather, you help me get caught red-handed while pickpocketing someone. So that Mevhibe Hanım's son, the beybaba MP's grandson, is caught pickpocketing in broad daylight!"

He burst into laughter.

"Hey, you know what, that's not such a bad idea after all. You've got a damn good head on your shoulders, you. Now look, I'm going to nick that guy's wallet. And you're going to scream . . . But how can we make sure I get beat up at the police station? Truth is, I really don't think they'd beat me for a crime like that. That only comes later, after I've got a record . . . What would you call me then? Right, 'seasoned criminal Doğan . . .' Will I be considered a real, red-blooded man then? Well, will I?"

The more Doğan spoke, the louder his voice got. Rain ran down his face like tears. Ali wasn't looking at Doğan, he couldn't. He didn't want to. He was sad. He should say something to him, help him. Doğan really needed that right now. Otherwise . . . He was losing it, he was slipping away, right there before Ali's very eyes. Ali should say something that would enlighten Doğan's confused mind, something straightforward and obvious, to calm him down. And he blamed himself a bit for this state of affairs. *I really touched a sore spot with him a while ago with those stories I told; truth was, it wasn't the right time, not at all. I didn't intend for this to happen, not at all. I wanted to probe him, myself, us, in a friendly, proper way, that was my intent. No, I didn't mean to get on his case, go after him and him alone. That's the last thing I wanted to do.* He had wanted to share with Doğan the things he had reconsidered during his short time in jail, to talk not about "you and me" but about situations. *But what have I done? I wanted to push the envelope. But was that the right thing to do?* He had pondered the question throughout his time in jail. Yes, it was necessary to push the envelope, that was for certain, but rushing things? That's what he had done, he had rushed it. *I got on the boy's case via the shortest route possible. Without having a proper discussion.* The firemen's concentration was trained entirely upon the poplar. Ali, now vexed, watched the firemen for a while. *Here, where I stand right now, I've mistaken rushing for pushing the envelope. And in the end, something happens, an unimportant poplar collapses, outside of us. While we watch, the firemen will succeed at toppling the poplar in the manner they see fit. The poplar will have collapsed before we're even able to cross the street, before Doğan and I are able to have a proper conversation. What comes to pass will be exactly what the firemen, those tackling the issue, want. Who will benefit? Not us. Or rather, who will suffer? If we could know what has gone to waste, or rather, if we were the ones who suffered, really suffered, if we understood our inability to have any impact on that simple collapse of the tree, we would be ashamed of our current spectator status.* He was ashamed, he needed to start all over. He needed to talk with Doğan again, this time, without rushing things. But for now, perhaps the best thing to do would be to slip his arm through Doğan's, silently, and have a couple of beers with him. To not foolishly attempt to capture lost time, but to wait for a while.

Doğan wrested his arm from Ali's.

"Look at that sucker over there, it's his wallet I'm going to nick. Take a good look!"

Doğan spoke loudly, attracting the attention of those standing nearby. But still, everyone was more interested in the poplar. A tall, pepper-haired gentleman standing a short distance from them in golf slacks wore a solemn expression as he watched the firemen attempt to topple the poplar in the direction they saw fit, so that he could explain later exactly what it was they did wrong. "How about that 'gentleman' over there? Exactly the type of guy I'm looking for . . ." He began to walk towards Necip Bey. He stepped on the foot of Hatice Hanım, who was standing next to him and observing him with an expression of awe, shock and loathing. Hatice Hanım was just about to unleash the rage she had built up in her mind since leaving The Big Store when she heard Doğan speak, in exactly the manner that Hatice Hanım would have approved of, that she would praise, saying of him, "Now there's someone who's had a proper upbringing, who comes from a good family." She saw him, watched him as he strung together just the right sentences: "I'm very sorry ma'am, please accept my apologies, it was entirely unintentional. How can I make it up to you?"

Shoeshiner Necmi hopes to score some money from the spectators

The Gypsy Necmi had set up shop at his usual spot, right next to the entrance of Piknik, which directly faced the front yard of the apartment building where the poplar was about to collapse. A crowd is a good thing for shoeshiners; sure, it's a good thing, but not at times when such an important event or spectacle is underway. At times like that, everyone suddenly forgets all about their stinking shoes, they forget all about their clothes, their jobs, their families, for a moment and completely lose themselves in the sight before them. And such was the case at this moment. Right there, during all that time, not a single soul amongst that packed crowd thought for even a moment of going ahead and getting their shoes shined, which would have been a perfectly logical thing to do, seeing as they were just standing there waiting. Necmi looked at the crowd in disgust. But then a crowd is nothing to be fond of. *Those people don't have the slightest idea what they're doing*, Necmi thought. Necmi had considerable experience watching crowds, and he had long ago arrived at the verdict that crowds were horribly unstable, unreliable, unpredictable, silly things. They'd get their shoes shined at the most inappropriate times, but never when the timing was right. Whenever an unimportant event, like this one, the mere collapse of a poplar, happened they'd simply lose their wits and forget all about the money in their pockets. Yet they knew good and well exactly how much money was in those pockets. And so now, seeing as they had to stand there anyway, why not go ahead and have their shoes shined, rather than just watch that meaningless poplar collapse. But no, if that crowd weren't standing right there, if the firemen weren't dashing right and left in an effort to ensure that the poplar collapsed at a fitting angle, it would never occur to them to watch the poplar collapse. They wouldn't even notice it, they'd just march right by without a second glance. They had nothing to do with the poplar; if you asked them what good a poplar was for, they wouldn't have the first clue. Gypsy Necmi, however, knows what a poplar is good for. There were plenty of poplars back in his hometown, Konya. Necmi knows that you can make a pretty penny just growing poplars. There were men who owned fields full of them. Just owning a single poplar meant something, actually. It's a good tree, the poplar. It's cheap. It's easy to take care of. It's not picky about the earth it grows in. And it has plenty of customers. Get on a bus and head towards Konya, and see for yourself, all those telegraph and electric poles. Weren't they all made of poplars? So, one day, a poplar was cut down to make a pole. Did a single person in that crowd ever take an interest when that poplar was cut down, made into a pole and erected on the roadside? They couldn't care less about how a million poplars were grown, pruned, skinned, made into poles and erected and they had been perfectly happy getting their shoes shined while that happened, but let them actually witness some stupid poplar collapse and they forget all about having their shoes shined. Why? Out of curiosity? Not at all. If you asked Necmi, a crowd has no curiosity of its own. It was a scramble for curiosity, they scrambled after curiosity about this and that. Just like now, some officious soul had informed the fire station that a poplar was about to collapse on people. And off the news went, spreading from this person to that. Telephones rang, normally idle civil servants dashed about. And then, finally, they commanded those poor firefighters, "Get moving, a poplar's collapsing!" What choice did the poor guys have, they're just servants at the beck and call of their masters—what was the poplar to them. Let it collapse. How much do those guys make anyway? They exist to obey commands, and so they put their helmets on, whip seven neighborhoods into a fury as they speed to the site in their firetrucks and get to work. Necmi looked at the sweat-drenched firefighters yanking on the rope tied to the trunk of the poplar with all their might in order to make sure it toppled in the desired direction and at the police running around trying to keep the crowd under control. *That's the way these people are,* he thought. *Press their buttons and they go ballistic. As if the poplar were their own rightful inheritance. Neither the poplar, nor the yard where it stands, nor that apartment building belong to you, so why the hell are you sweating over it, you idiots?* But God hadn't put any sense into those guys' heads. If they had, they wouldn't be firefighters or police. They'd be landlords. And then, when the annoying forty-year-old poplar in their yard started to collapse, they'd pick up the phone and start ranting and raving to the officials, all of whom would be their relatives or at least acquaintances. Telling them to hurry up, their poplar was collapsing. Who were the officials anyway, but a bunch of guys who'd become officials thanks to the business cards of this or that landlord. And so then they'd start yelling left and right, putting these guys to work. C'mon men, there's a poplar collapsing on such-and-such street, in whatever yard, God forbid it fall onto so-and-so's car! Lest so-and-so's garden gate suffer a dent! And these guys, for goodness sake, they wouldn't think to ask whose car, whose cutesy daughter the tree was about to fall on. Did they have the right to ask? They'd already sold all their questions, their minds, their ideas, for just enough money to scrape by from month to month. They put on their helmets and dash about, sweat dripping from their ass cracks. If you ask them how much they make, they stare at you like an idiot. They don't understand the question. These petty servants are such dunces, judging by the fervor with which they rush to the rescue, you'd think their mothers were being slaughtered. And then they infect the crowd with their panic. The crowd senses from the way these servants are dashing about that something's happening, something's going on. Because, as a rule, this entourage of servants only dashes about like this when something major happens to major men. And the crowd, well, heck, they sure take an interest in major things that happen to major men, thinking that maybe, just maybe, they themselves will suffer a dent in all this damage. And so they pile themselves into curious masses. That is, until they're finally convinced that no part of the incident at hand is going to touch them, not even a wee little bit. It's because of that very fear that that they become meek lambs in the face of that crew of servants, stopping and starting just as they are told. Otherwise, none of the police currently containing this massive crowd could barely stop any one of these people, on any given day, to so much as inquire after an address. That would be unthinkable. But now, they're aware that behind the servants' tither lies esteemed commands. Whoever gave the order could not have done so out of the blue, of course. It's only because they see some reflection of the commanders in the persons of those firefighters that they show them any respect at all, and even then, only in situations like this. That's why they're showing this entourage of servants some respect right now, when the truth is that in any other situation, they would look down their noses at them.

He took a bottle of vinegar, its mouth stopped with a piece of rolled up newspaper, from the side of his shoeshine box, wet one of his rags with it, and began polishing the mirrors on the side of the box. Gypsy Necmi's shoeshine box was extra fancy. It was decorated with carvings and mirrors. The carvings were painted in myriad colors and polished. The box Necmi had made himself, with his own hands; it had taken him a full three months. But there wasn't another box like it in all of Kızılay. He took out a Harman cigarette and lit it. No matter what, Necmi liked fancy things. Like Harman cigarettes, for example. *I'll smoke whatever the hell I want, goddamn it. Even if it is expensive. What is life, after all? It's just one day at a time. Any Gypsy worth his salt knows the worth, and the worthlessness, of money, whether he likes it or not. Money is the meat in the mouth of the lion. And it is a tough piece to seize. You have to be vicious like a lion, but once you've seized that meat, you gotta swallow it straight down, without even chewing, otherwise another lion will come and snatch it from you.* Using his lighter, he lit his cigarette. He gazed at the lighter for a while. He'd bought the lighter six months ago from the smugglers in Diyarbakır's Enayi market. He'd bought his wife silk in Diyarbakır too, before their wedding. They'd told him that in Diyarbakır they had shiny silk that was cheaper than water. He'd earned the money to buy the silk from gambling. Necmi could play cards with the best of them. That was another art of his. He was one hell of a cheater. Everyone pretty much knew more or less that he cheated. Because he always won. But he did such a masterful job of it that his opponent could never be quite sure, and so the latter would drag the game out, thinking he'd be able to catch on to Necmi's tricks, and as a result lose over and over again. But even simply watching Necmi play cards was a pleasure.

Some people went so far as to seek out opponents for him just so they could watch him play. He almost got into serious trouble a few times because of this card-playing business. In fact, once one of the taxi drivers on the corner of Sakarya became so enraged by his antics he nearly sent Necmi to kingdom come.

After eleven at night, taxi driver Hasan would open his trunk and lay out dinner. During the summer, it was rakı, ice, melon and feta cheese. He'd cook some *menemen* on his little spirit burner. An evening of slow eating, drinking and card-playing would ensue. The games would be played tag-team. Whenever one of the driver's shifts started, he'd turn his hand over to his partner. Hasan had heard of Necmi's fame and invited him to play. That evening, hash was on the menu. Using a pocketknife, Hasan cut the brown hash, which resembled an apricot fruit roll, into small pieces, mixed it with tobacco and rolled it into joints. The drivers then took turns taking hits inside their taxicabs. In an effort to disguise the scent, Necmi mixed vanilla into his own. A sweet, pleasant smell filled the cab he happened to be in. Necmi took hit after hit as he played. And Hasan got more and more upset as Necmi won round after round, but then he didn't want to ruin his reputation as a gracious host. Necmi was relaxed as could be. He was thinking about the silk he was going to buy from Enayi market. He imagined, in a state of ecstasy, the playing cards and lighter he'd buy there as well. Every now and then he'd take a hit inside one of the taxis, but he never went overboard. Whenever Hasan came over to rouse him, "C'mon, it's time to play," he'd feign resistance and pretend to be much higher than he actually was. Hasan meanwhile thought he'd surely be able to catch on to Necmi's tricks, with the latter being as high as he was. At first Necmi would lose a couple of rounds on purpose, then he'd take Hasan for all he was worth. In the end, he ended up with every cent of Hasan's thousand liras. Hasan hadn't taken a single hit of dope that night. The sun was rising; the birds atop the trees on Sakarya Avenue had begun singing. When fishmonger Rıza, who'd come in early to open his shop, saw Necmi playing cards, he spouted off a few teasing words. He was a good friend of Necmi. Necmi sometimes stopped by his shop and bought a bonito, which he'd then garnish with some red onion, and tomatoes if they were in season, and then send it over to the baker in a nearby alley. And then he'd chat with the fishmonger until the fish was ready. Rıza got a kick out of chatting with Necmi. But then again, everyone did. Necmi ate his fish with his hands, the nails of which were stained black from shoe polish but never gave the impression of being dirty. For one, the black on his hands was not from dirt, and besides, he was very particular about his appearance. His mother tailored his dress shirts. Necmi would go to all sorts of lengths to find some colorful silk, and then he'd stand watching over his mother's shoulder till the shirt was sewn. He always combed his dark, curly hair at least a dozen times, and in addition to his bottle of vinegar, he never failed to carry a bottle of lavender too. The latter he would occasionally sprinkle over his hair. He always wore pants the color of which contrasted with his shirt, and whenever he didn't have any customers he would take the opportunity to shine his own shoes till they sparkled like mirrors. He was always shocked at how so many well-dressed men with so much money walked by wearing shoes that clearly needed a shine. And Necmi had a fine voice. Not a Gypsy wedding passed in the immigrant neighborhood in Konya at which Necmi didn't sing and dance. Necmi would tell fishmonger Rıza about those weddings and about dalliances from his youth. "We, well, we learn everything, every little thing, when we're still just kids," Necmi would say. "For us Gypsies, there's no such thing as keeping the sexes apart," and then he'd tell about how he'd made love to his present wife when they were still kids, and how he tricked her, telling her, "Girl, I'm gonna teach you how to make a bear dance!" Necmi has a ton of bear stories. He'd tell about how his father, a true blue Gypsy, would wrestle bears, and then how he'd take his wife, who'd looked on with such admiration as he did so, right there on the floor mattress, in front of the kids. Rıza reveled in these stories that Necmi told, reenacting each scene. Necmi's father was illiterate. But when he died, they found a notebook inside his mattress. Necmi told the story like this: "My father's coffin was barely out of the house when she stopped her wailing and went and cut open the mattress and took out the notebook. My father had forbid her to touch it during his lifetime. It was a yellow shopkeeper's notebook and on its pages were pasted our neighbors' family photos. Our home in Konya looked out over a courtyard. And the photos, they were of the other Gypsy families whose one-room apartments looked onto the same courtyard. My mom recalled that my dad's brother had been a street photographer who hung around the municipality gardens, and so my father had had him take the neighbors' family photos on the cheap. At the time, my mom wondered why my father had been so insistent that the neighbors have their family photos taken, and when she finally saw the photos, she understood. My father had used an ink pen to draw horns on the heads of all the men." Necmi would laugh when he said this, revealing his gold teeth. Rıza would ask, "Did your dad really cuckold all those guys?" "Of course he did, and those horns in the notebook document it! Stamps aren't the only thing a man can collect, you know." Necmi would also impersonate his father doing a bear dance. There would be a bear, and a bear-handler:

"How does a woman faint in a Turkish bath?"

"How does a Gypsy bride dance?"

"How does Mehmet the Kurd wrestle?"

That morning, fishmonger Rıza was simply looking to tease Necmi as he passed by:

"You gettin' a bear to dance again, are ya, Necmi?"

Necmi looked at the money in front of him and then gave Rıza a wink: "Oh, and what a bear it is, a real, true bear!" But the words were barely out of his mouth before Hasan pulled a screwdriver on him. "What fucking bear, you're the fucking bear, you Gypsy pimp you!" The other drivers, having leapt out their taxis, were barely able to rescue Necmi from Hasan's wrath.

It wasn't hard for Necmi to forget all about this incident, because he was all about results. If a man didn't risk something, then he was bound to lose. You only live once. But if you risk your life, then you're bound to reap a reward. You could only die once, but whoever risked his life always came out ahead. Either you possess wealth, or you put your life on the line without blinking an eye. The only other option was a life of servitude. Life, Necmi would proclaim, is just like gambling. You gotta lay your life out just like that too, and most of the time, life fell for the bluff. Because rarely does anyone put their life out there like that. And besides, if the bluff doesn't work, well, dying is better than living the life of a dog. Rather than dying a slow death, you die the death of a pasha, with fame to boot. Like in the story of the bird of prey and the vulture. The bird of prey asked the vulture, "How many years will you live?" And the vulture replied: "I'll live a long time." Then the bird of prey asked, "So what do you eat?" The vulture responded: "I a eat shit, and I a eat carcasses, and I a eat rotten meat." To this the bird of prey said: "'At's great, just great, you go righta on and live a long life then, 'kay? I live a short life but I a eat quail, and I a eat partridge, and I a eat rabbit." *So you see, in this life, you have to be a bird of prey. You gotta aim for the heart every time. If you've got money, then put your money out there, but if you don't have money, then you put your life out there. But you gotta keep your eye on the heart of your enemy. He'll be so worried about his own life, he won't even realize you've put your life on the line. Just when he believes he's made his escape, he'll fall into your trap. I'm a philosophizer, that's what I am. Philosophizer Necmi.* Once Necmi had rescued himself from Hasan's screwdriver, he came out with a pretty profit and so he headed to Diyarbakır to put together a trousseau for his fiance, and bought exactly three kinds of silk: one, pomegranate flower; two, blood red orange, and three, rose pink. And he picked up a lighter and a set of cards for himself too.

Necmi began making some noise, banging his brush against his dye box in the hopes that, perhaps, someone in the crowd, hearing him, would have his shoes shined. *I'm not going to be able to scare up enough for rakı this evening.* He found himself gazing at Olcay, who was standing on the sidewalk opposite. A pretty girl, pretty but cheerless. Those "refined" types, for whatever reason, always wearing the expression of an undertaker. The Gypsy girls that he grew up with and flirted with as a youngster, they were all cheerful. There wasn't a one of them who didn't laugh, who didn't swear, who didn't sing and dance at weddings and circumcisions. *These Turkish girls though, that's just the way, so somber you'd think they were carrying the weight of the world on their shoulders. That's what they consider desirable. Just tie one of those around your neck and jump into the sea. It's the best way to get to the other side with a frown on your face. You're a pretty girl, for goodness sake, would it really kill you to smile? I tell you what, if I were to find my woman wearing a face like that when I got home in the evening, I'd send her packing, put her right in the donkey's saddle and say "Off ya go! You just take that face of yours and put it on when those women you wash for hand you a pile of menstrual cloths!"* But that's the kind of girl those folks *like.* Having spent so much time on the street corner watching the passersby, Necmi had come to ascertain certain things about human faces. He understood in a snap, just from the expression on a man's face, whether or not he would have his shoes polished, and if he were the miserly type. *For one, a man who smiled was guaranteed to be generous. The frowners, they were actually the stingy sort. And they made up the majority. I mean, any man who would begrudge you a simple smile was certain to begrudge you money. Most of these city types who pass down this street would never do anything for free. Not even smile. If they smile at all, it's at their beau to get a snuggle, at the butcher to get a good slice of meat, at their boss to get a raise, or at the people to get a vote. They're incapable of smiling for free, like this. And they get suspicious of anyone who does smile for no apparent reason. When they see that, they put on a frown, thinking, "Now that guy's definitely going to want something from me."* Necmi loves a good laugh. Whenever Hüseyin, a taxi driver who works at the same corner as Necmi, is at the taxi stand, the two of them listen to the police radio on Hüseyin's car radio. They sing songs together and laugh and laugh. If he laughs too much, potential customers are scared away. Necmi sees them scurrying and hurls a series of curses at them. *You prick you, think I was taking the piss out of your ten cents, did you! Any rakı bought using your shitty money wouldn't be worth swallowing anyway.*

The crowd was staring at the poplar. Necmi knew that poplar well. After all, it stood right across from him every God given day. *These dumbasses on the other hand, they hadn't once taken the time to look at that tree before now. They didn't even know it existed. Now that it's about to collapse, they all stand there staring straight at it. What the hell is there to look at? It's a tree, collapsing is in its nature, so is drying out. It's not like it's going to ask you first, now is it? Is it not alive? Aren't your foul-smelling bodies going to make their way to the boneyard, letting off a stench as they go? The tither these folks are in, it's all about themselves. Now, that poplar is collapsing, right? Even if it's just a poplar, they can't bear to see something collapse, they can't bring themselves to accept mortality. It wouldn't suit them at all, because they're going to die too. Every one of them would be more than willing to take the place of that poplar, become a prison bar staked onto this earth for eternity. But every single one of you is going to die, so take that, ha!* he thought. *These guys aren't just depressing as hell, they're enough to send the devil running. Man, the whole lot of us joyful Gypsies are going to have to lift these guys' spirits in hell too. There's no way this bunch of scarecrows is making it to heaven of course. Damn it brother, they'll be dragging us down all the time on the other side too.* Necmi laughed. He wasn't one to let such thoughts get him down. He imagined the feet of the crowd surrounded by flames, how they'd hop, skip and jump trying not to get burnt. *Now let's see you not get those shoes shined.*

He looked at Olcay again. She was a pretty girl, no doubt about that, a little flat-chested, but there was no hurt in that, after all, it wasn't like he was going to be getting it on with her. But the eyes, the brows, they were alright. He let his gaze linger on Olcay's sad expression and smirked, thinking, *Seems the girl's got no one putting a smile on her face.*

Necmi's wife would spend half an hour giggling when they went to bed at night. If she didn't, Necmi would get upset, thinking, *You mean to say I don't even have what it takes to make a woman laugh?* He imagined what would happen that evening. Their one-room apartment next to Recep Usta's gecekondu. His wife would fry a slew of long green peppers. Necmi wouldn't sit down at a dinner table that didn't have peppers on it. Add some rakı, and some watermelon, and he'd be in a fine mood in no time. You gotta look at this world through a cloud of smoke if you want it to have any flavor, otherwise it is unbearable; you gotta have smoke, you gotta know how to get to the right altitude. And then he'd strike his hand on the table and start playing the *darbuka*. Once he was really into it, he'd slap his wife on the butt. "Dance, girl." At first his wife would play coy, until Necmi let out a whoop. Once Necmi let out that whoop, his wife would start dancing. He looked at Olcay once more. *That one wouldn't dance if her life depended on it. She'd sit straight across from you, looking you square in the eye, drudging up memories of every goddamn bad thing that's ever happened to you.* He looked in the direction Olcay was looking, and saw Ali.

"Well, if it isn't our Ali! What business has he got in this part of town?"

He whistled to get Ali's attention. But Ali was engaged in an animated conversation with one of the little patisserie bastards. Necmi called all of the well-dressed young men who were always busy "hanging out" patisserie bastards and believed that all of those boys idled the days away spending their daddies' money taking girls to patisseries. He couldn't wrap his head around this patisserie business though. If you've found a broad loose enough to go to a patisserie with you, what the hell business did you have going to a patisserie? There had to be four walls somewhere in this great big city where you could have some time to yourselves!

Necmi knew Ali well. *Our boy Ali, he's a swell kid. What business has he got with those sissies?* He recalled his wedding. He'd invited Ali. He knew Ali from Konya. Ali's grandmother lived in the same immigrants' neighborhood as him, and Ali frequently stayed with her. On Necmi's street. He and Ali would play pickpocket. Necmi could have been a first class pickpocket if he'd wanted. He'd learned all the tricks. From the trash pickers. Cart drivers were second class Gypsies. And that's where most of the pickpockets came from. Necmi in turn had taught Ali all that he'd learned from the trash pickers. Their pickpocketing was all a game though. They'd bump into Ali's grandmother and make her mad, just for fun, until the woman would finally drive them off wielding a pair of tongs. The grandmother, who was Circassian and had one heck of a temper, would say she was going to turn them both into the police and see to it that they rotted on the roof of the prison. The truth was, Ali and Necmi actually kind of sort of wanted to land in prison. For them prison was something very exciting. Especially the prison stories that Necmi heard from those around him . . . So many of Necmi's fellow Gypsies had landed in prison, and the children who ended up behind bars with their mothers would go on and on bragging about it once they got out. Their "when I was in prison" stories were pretty much the equivalent of the "when I was in Europe" stories told in other neighborhoods. And so Necmi and Ali would imagine what they'd do when they landed in prison:

"We'll pickpocket," Necmi would say.

"They'd throw us in prison, man."

"Can you get arrested in prison?"

"Ah, right, anything goes there."

"There, anything goes."

The stories they heard made them think that prison was the freest place on earth. And so they'd have a jolly time imagining themselves emerging from prison rich from pickpocketing. But there was no way they were going to land in prison, Grandma wasn't turning them in and their pickpocketing schemes never went beyond teasing grandma. After all, Ali was a good kid. He knew the meaning of a bad deed.

When he was getting married the previous year, Necmi heard that Ali had gone to Konya to visit his grandmother, and so he'd invited him to the wedding. Ali showed up bearing a pressure cooker. They held the wedding in the courtyard of the building where the bride's family lived. All their relatives and Gypsy pals had shown up for the wedding, Gypsy women decked out in colorful dresses sat in the chairs lined in rows in the courtyard, clapping their hands and singing. Everyone danced, the bride included. And then they brought out the henna. That's when everyone really started to whoop it up. A five-year-old boy played the tambourine, while some of the men showed off their skills, some playing the lute, others the *kanun*. Most of the relatives played at weddings, and whenever Necmi was hard up he too would go to a wedding to play music or sing and dance for money. Any Gypsy worth his salt played music and danced; if nothing else, those Gypsy folk could get by with a shimmy and a shake. Necmi had unloaded a few bullets into the sky and then danced with gusto. He'd tried to get Ali to dance too but Ali, being shy, refused. That's the way these guys are, they haven't a clue how to have fun at their weddings when it's time for the henna; instead, everybody stands around crying, it's like they're made of mourning from head to toe. Especially their womenfolk, they dance stealthily like they're trying not to get caught in the act, as if they're stealing bread from the cellar or something. Eating, loving, they do it all in secret. Even when they drink water they crouch down with their backs to you. They live their blessed lives that the sweet Lord bestowed upon us as if it were a crime. *But as for us, we know the value of the only thing ever given to us for free, and that's why with us, two things are a free-for-all: joy and commotion. We Gypsies abide by what we call the law of commotion. Anyone can yell and scream as they damn well please. Women belt out songs while they're washing laundry in the courtyard. Our fights, everything we do is completely out in the open; we've got no possessions to hide, nor any savings. Gypsy girls don't have trousseau chests. We sling our sacks of possessions over our shoulders and take off as we please. For us, there's no such thing as pining after the homeland. A home, a table, a chair, we get attached to none of it. What's a chest to us? Who wants to sling a chest over their shoulders, it'd be like hauling your own coffin around with you. We don't like having too many possessions, but we do like donkeys. Because donkeys carry us, and our load, wherever we want, just like that. Is there something that's made us upset, something that's got us feeling strangled? Well, then we just hop on our donkey and off we go, brother. Our weddings are of the clean-slate sort too. Any man who takes off for some other part of the world ain't coming back. And Gypsy womenfolk don't sit around fretting after them, no siree. She gets herself knocked up, doesn't want that womb to go to waste. A Gypsy woman is the mother of the child she gives birth to, the child she nurses. Once she's unleashed the child onto the world, she forgets all about it. The only person you gotta carry in this life is your own good self. Your belly full, your head held high. But take your talent and your joy with you. Your talent keeps your tummy filled, and your joy keeps you heart happy. Talent's important to us. We don't have anything to do with that studying business. You can graduate from thirty schools if you like, what difference does it make if you don't have talent? We don't belong to those types that lug around a bag full of books yet fail to put food on the table. A Gypsy is someone who knows how to use his hands. He has the hands of an artist, he's skillful, and handsome too. A Gypsy is good-looking because he has learned to use his hands, every part of his body; we own our bodies, not a bunch of stuff.* He recalled his wife's narrow waist, the way she danced in that orange silk blouse at their wedding, and he laughed heartily. Even if he's going hungry, a Gypsy will find a way to get his hands on some olive oil to put the shine in his hair. That's just how it is. This mass of misers who can't be bothered to shine their shoes doesn't have the first clue about how to live. He looked at Ali again. *He doesn't see me.* He was very fond of Ali. Ali wasn't like those other haughty bastards from their neighborhood, the ones who looked down on Gypsy kids. Actually, even as a child Ali was serious, and smart. The boy had tact—that's the word, tact.

Ali saw Necmi. He waved, smiling. Then he made his way through the crowd and over to him. With Doğan at his side.

"What're you up to, you good-for-nothing Gypsy, you?"

"Nothin', just directing traffic."

Ali laughed. "How's business?"

"Good, real good. You just keep right on studying. You better become a statesman though and make it the law that you have to get your shoes shined. That way the government'll do us some good for once."

Ali laughed again.

"So you're still studying, huh?"

"That's right."

"Ali, man, what a shame! What you're doin', it's a real pity. How long does this thing called life last anyway? You gonna spend half of it studying? Just so you can make a few bucks in the end. If it's all about making money in the end, why don't you start from the end? Earning money is a different skill altogether, the earlier you get started, the better you get at it. You're gonna step into the market with half your life already behind you and find that all the tykes out there are fiercer than you, all of them like vicious birds of prey. Ready to rip you to pieces."

"C'mon Necmi, the world isn't just full of people all looking to rip each other apart. The world can't go on like this, it's going to get better."

Necmi looked Ali over from head to toe, displaying obvious displeasure with what he saw.

"Brother, you gotta get yourself into shape first. The world'll get its turn later. What good can come of any person who denies himself everything?"

"Necmi, you big poser you, all you think about is appearances. But what we're saying is: how about we pretty up the inside first."

"Ali man, you're talking like a greeting card. The plainer the clothes, the darker the heart. He who doesn't see beauty can't understand it. He who doesn't understand beauty can't make another soul happy, because he doesn't know how a soul is made happy."

"*Maşallah*, I see you still know how to run that mouth of yours."

"Everything we got, we keep in tip-top shape, brother. We Gypsy folk don't wear out, we die."

"How's your wife?"

"She'll be glad you asked, brother. Come over some evening so she can fry you some vegetables. Not in that pressure cooker of yours though. I'm sorry but, man, we hawked that thing off straightaway. We're not the sort that has delicate stomachs that can only handle boiled whatever. Real food's got a sizzle to it. The whole room's gotta smell like fried veggies. We'll fry you a bunch of peppers. Some melon, some rakı, whaddya say?"

"I'd say that sounds just fine. But I don't know where you live."

"Ah, what kind of an excuse is that? You just stop by here again near evening. I'll take you there. We'll pick up some fish on our way."

Doğan looked on, baffled by the conversation happening before him. Ali had so many different friends who were so different from one another. How was it that he got along with each of these different people who were so unalike? To Doğan it seemed symptomatic of a lack of character. You know, like when you have a certain character, you can only be friends with those who have kindred characters. Otherwise, you have to make concessions when it comes to your own character. If he were to explain this to Ali just now, Ali would respond with something like, "And just what is character, something superhuman, separate from humans? If it's first and foremost something that makes humanity what it is, then it should be understandable to everyone," he'd say. *That's how he is, his always holistic, embracing, open character has me standing next someone like Necmi, whom I would never take an interest in if it were purely up to me, whom, in fact, I would never even see. He changes me, makes me do things I wouldn't otherwise do, opens me up to things I wouldn't see, wouldn't hear otherwise. Perhaps that's why I need him. Like a blind person needs a dog.* Doğan knew that he was mistaken in comparing Ali to the dog of a blind beggar. He knew it was unjust, both to himself and to Ali. But now, just a few moments ago, he felt the power to open doors that he himself would never be able to open on his own. This power wasn't the power of guidance, it wasn't his, and it wasn't Ali's either, it was another separate, immense power, something that came from a much larger circle, from people in situations similar to his own; Ali knew how to take from this power, and how to give it too.

But it completely rattled Doğan whenever Ali gave to others, like he was doing now. Doğan realized that he felt uncomfortable with how chummy Ali was behaving towards Necmi. He hated that feeling. *Why am I so stingy, I can't even share a friendship. No, Ali can't change me; in fact, perhaps, in a way, he reinforces who I am.* Ali and Necmi were still joking around.

"You watching that poplar collapse too?"

"Aren't you?"

"So what if we do watch it, Ali? I've been shining shoes on this here corner for an eternity, and that there tree's been standing right across from me the whole time. It's not like its standing there has made any difference in my life, so why should its collapse mean any-thing to me?"

"Oh, c'mon, you some kind of fortuneteller now? Just look at all the people gathered around because something's happening. This isn't some chalkboard, it's life—and it's changing."

"Don't you pay any attention to those folks, Ali. The only thing they're curious about is whose roots will go to pot when that poplar collapses. I've got a box, and it travels, and when I can no longer make a living on this street, I'll go to another, doesn't matter whether there's a poplar tree or a fig tree or none at all."

"That poplar's in our yard . . ." Doğan said.

He had no idea why he had spoken these meaningless words. But he was ticked off by the fact that Necmi paid him no attention, that he behaved toward him with the same indifference he behaved towards the poplar. That's right, perhaps he'd interjected in order to draw some of Necmi's jubilant anger onto himself. With his dark eyes Necmi gave Doğan the once over.

"Well, in that case why are you just standing here? Why don't you do something for the poplar yourself rather than making those poor workers run themselves ragged trying to prop the thing up?"

"I don't care. Its roots are dried out anyway."

"Then you should've cut the thing down. Then we wouldn't have had to put up with this godforsaken crowd in the middle of the day."

"I told you, I don't care."

"Then why do you say it's yours? It's either yours or it isn't, the end. Are those shoes yours?"

"Yes, they are," Doğan said, taken aback.

"Great, then take an interest in them. Just look at them, who knows when they last got shined."

"True, so you think I should have them shined?"

"I do the shining, you pay the fee."

Like a child Doğan immediately put his foot on the box to have his shoe shined. Ali looked on, smiling. He found it both entertaining and saddening the way Necmi took Doğan into his clutches and instantly had him doing his bidding. *He sniffed out Doğan's lack of self-confidence*, he thought. *The gambling Gypsy. He observes people with the shrewdness of a gambler. He can tell who's going to lay it all on the table, who's going to make a run for it. And he plays accordingly. You'd be hard pressed to explain to Necmi anything beyond gambling, anything beyond cutthroat existence or that the world is not static. Even if he were to lead Doğan away from this poplar, which in its present state caused so much doubt and unrest, it would be nearly impossible to keep new, similar plane trees from sprouting up. So why bother?*

Necmi sang as he shined Doğan's shoes:

"Your lovely face heaven-sent, did you I love to my heart's content . . ."

Oh yes, love, true love, only possible to the heart's content, Ali thought. In a mood of delight, infected by the joy that Necmi radiated, he continued to watch the poplar.

Aysel shows off for Ali

Aysel grumbled as she waded her way through the crowd blocking her path to the Ulus dolmuş stop. She'd had her hair cut short. Her large mouth, her far too darkly lined eyes, her bra which lent to her bosom the ridiculous appearance of sharply pointed projectiles, everything about her gave her away at first glance. She chomped much too loudly on her chewing gum while utilizing her handbag in an effort to part the sea of people before her. She bumped into men with her shoulder and then screeched at them, as if she herself had not incited their reaction to begin with:

"Watch yourself, asshole!"

There was something about her every movement that provoked, in one way or another, everyone she encountered. She owed her liveli-hood to her provocativeness. She had to provoke. If she were to get anything out of anyone, she had no choice but to prod and poke a bit. The truth was, if you didn't press down hard enough on their bruises, most people couldn't be bothered to react. If you wanna empty some pockets, you gotta shake the pants they belong to. Ever since she was a little girl, Aysel had either had to yank at her elders' skirts or throw a temper tantrum in order to get anything. Sometimes for something as simple as a slice of bread, or a glass of water. Even as a young child she had come to grasp the fact that adults had no intention of taking an interest in anything, or giving anyone anything, unless you somehow managed to push their buttons.

Just behind Yıldırım Beyazıt, in the neighborhood of Hacı Doğan, she had seen how Huriyegil and Nazangil had pulled no punches in attempting to protect their baby dolls made of old socks from the envious evil eyes of the other children. Yet hardly a day would pass before the babydolls had been deprived of limbs, having been subjected to vicious tug-o-wars: "At is mah babydoll!" The rule for any child that grows up in Hacı Doğan is this: Once you get your hands on something, you snap it up and run as fast and as far as you can. Just like a street dog that's found a bone and wants to gnaw on it in peace, far from the other canines. For one, in such a neighborhood, it was impossible for a child to own anything that was unusual for the neighborhood; and second of all, if such a thing were to come to pass, it wouldn't spell out good news for the kid. It would end in them falling prey to attacks upon property—"Give 'at here!"—and being pummeled by other children and, finally, being deprived of her possession, such that the child wouldn't know whether to cry at the loss of an irrecoverable windfall or at her physical pain. One day Aysel's family's neighbor, a porter named Rüstem, had given his son a real ball, though how he got his hands on it no one knows (the neighbors claimed he stole it). Imagine it, in a neighborhood where even paper to make balls (the kids there played with paper balls) was hard to come by (after all, newspaper was something valuable and adults wouldn't let kids anywhere near paper), a real, genuine ball! When he got home the following evening, he found his son with a busted brow and a gash in his head, and then proceeded to beat the crap out of him because he'd surrendered his ball.

Aysel had learned as a young child the tremendous difficulties that came with possessing something. Anyone incapable of getting the best of at least a dozen people like herself had no right to possess anything. Getting a beating was a law enforced daily, and just as was the case with any daily matter, a beating too would come to a resolution depending upon the attending results. And then there was the police station, a place that did not alter the results of the beating, but certainly had everything in the world to do with beating. For some reason, though the beater and the beaten never switched places, there were those who had taken it upon themselves as a duty to intervene in this whole beating business by adding a helping hand into the mix. She was afraid of the police—because the police could rescue neither the rag doll nor the ball from being shred to pieces, but they would beat up whoever was beating and being beaten. She could not fathom why her elders, who harbored no qualms when it came to breaking each other's teeth and chins and smashing each other's faces in, simply could not deal with the police. As soon as the police showed up, they'd abandon their fights and turn into meek little lambs, and then tagging along after the police officer who was usually much punier than them, their eyes red and their noses runny, they'd go to that place called the station, and there they would silently take their beating. Numerous local punks known for pulling knives in response to so much as a dirty look would not make even the slightest attempt at self-defense at the police station. As soon as they set foot in the station, they instantly became putty, automatically opening up their palms so that the police might smack them. From this state of affairs Aysel had arrived at the conclusion that the police hailed from a neighborhood full of punks much more powerful, more remorseless and burlier than the rough-necks in her neighborhood. The roughnecks in her own neighborhood were afraid of the roughnecks from that other neighborhood. Not the police themselves, but the other neighborhood's roughnecks. In Aysel's neighborhood, everything had to pass through the police, the station; it was the sole path to officialdom. Births, marriages, mis-tresses and their "sponsors," mother-in-law-daughter-in-law quibbles, debts and dues. Every night one of her neighbors would beat his wife. And the wife would step out the front door and yell "Police!" And then the husband would creep up behind her and shove a trash can over her head to keep her from being heard. The police would come and take them both to the station. After a while, having given their depositions, they'd return. The same incident would then be repeated a few days later. Aysel could not figure out why on earth the woman continued to yell, "Police!" when every single time she suffered the same beating and had the same trash can shoved over her head. As but a young child Aysel had come to realize that the police did not exist in order to change situations. Especially not troublesome situations! The police station was somewhere within the orbit of trouble and those who got caught up in trouble inevitably found themselves caught up in the same orbit. Trouble was everywhere. Trouble existed all the time and at every moment. You had to be on alert at all moments in order to keep both trouble and the police at a distance, and you had to put trouble on someone else before it had a chance to get its claws into you. A listless person could never shake off trouble because the bird of trouble always alighted on the heads of the stagnant. Aysel saw as a child that trouble existed in human form. As your mother, your father, your sibling, your friend. You had to fend off each and every one of them, giving as good as you got, and the police were just one of the indispensable spectators of this clash.

Aysel didn't have many relatives who weren't trouble. Her father had violated her older sister, and from that union Aysel was born. That is to say, first her father was trouble for her sister, and then he got Aysel in trouble by being the cause of her birth. The mother of her mother then kicked her pregnant daughter out of the house. Aysel's mother/sister began working at a fifth rate *pavyon*. This allowed her to take care of her daughter, upon whom, by means of her pinching and cursing and pushing and shoving, she released all of the hatred she harbored for this world. Aysel would have to spend hours begging, crying and pulling at her mother/sister's skirts for a mere morsel of bread. Aysel would cry until her mother/sister first smacked her for crying, before finally handing over a few cents so she could go buy bread. Her mother/sister was rarely to be found at home. Meals were never cooked there, and even salt was nonexistent. Aysel envied the salt the neighbor kids would put on their bread. Her stomach, it could be said, had never experienced the pleasure of a hot meal in all her life. On the extremely rare occasions when her mother/sister was at home, she would sometimes send Aysel out to get watermelon, cheese, cucumbers, tomatoes or halva. Other than these occasional delicacies, bread served as her sole source of sustenance. And on the rare occasions when her mother/sister did buy such foodstuffs, she wouldn't give any to Aysel straight away; only after Aysel had yanked on her skirts sufficiently, crying, "Sissy, gimme!" would she bestow upon Aysel some of the foodstuffs she had sent Aysel out to buy.

She had just turned eleven years old. Her sister came home with two men. Aysel hadn't yet gotten her period. One of the men gave Aysel a piece of chocolate. It was the first time in her life that she'd ever had chocolate. She gobbled it up so quickly that she was only able to taste the chocolate after she had finished it. It wasn't until after there was no chocolate left to eat that she understood chocolate was a wonderful thing, and so she desired more chocolate. The man did not give her any more chocolate, but he did hurt her, a lot. Aysel toughed it out, in the hopes of getting more chocolate. She knew good and well that nothing could be had in this world without toughing it out, and that everything came with a price. And so then she asked the man for another piece of chocolate, thinking that she had earned it. And the man said to her, "Come with me tomorrow, and I'll buy you all kinds of chocolate." Heaven only knew just how much more he would hurt Aysel, but then her sister hurt her too, beating her all the time like she did. Plus she starved her, and she never ever bought her chocolate. The next day she went off with the man. The man sold her to some people. And without buying her even the smallest piece of chocolate. This time, he let the men he sold her to hurt her. Aysel was not in the least surprised at this. But still she whined and begged for several days, thinking that maybe, just maybe the man would get her some chocolate. Finally the man lost his patience and slapped her smack in the middle of her face. This too came as no surprise to Aysel. This was the system as she knew it from her mother/sister, the only system Aysel knew, and so of course it would continue. Finally, the man sold her off once and for all. Then some other men took her to Antakya. They locked her up in a hotel room. They never opened the door to her room, they slipped her some food now and then, and occasionally sent a man inside to be with her. Aysel asked each and every one of the men for chocolate. Most of them never came back. After some time, Aysel got the sense to ask for chocolate to begin with. If the men who entered her room failed to deliver chocolate, she'd resist. She was agile and able to handle the men, who were usually drunk. But then one of the men who had locked her up in the hotel came and beat Aysel until her face was a bloody mess. Aysel sat in her room crying for three full days. She thought of her absolutely positively miserable childhood in Hacı Doğan. How she wandered the streets on an empty stomach, the neighborhood brawls . . . But she hadn't been out of that room for months. Her stomach was full now. At first, she found this state of incarcerated satiation preferable to her days of wandering the streets hungry. But then when the men who beat her up because she had demanded chocolate left Aysel hungry for three days in an attempt to starve some sense into her, she began to feel her lack of freedom the same way she had felt the lack of chocolate. And so she wised up, and became determined not to give up something she had tasted, but rather to resist until she got it. On the fourth day, a taxi driver who had visited her before came bearing chocolate this time, because Aysel had insisted upon it the last time he was there. Aysel was reaping the rewards of her resistance. She thought that perhaps there were things she could do to obtain freedom as well. She begged the man to get her out of there. Begging was one of the things she knew best, for she had honed this particular skill in the course of groveling before her sister for a morsel of bread.

The man promised to get Aysel out of there. Of course that would cost her too, but she had to get out of that room. She would die, simply die, if she didn't get out. One evening the driver came to her window and told Aysel to grab onto a sheet and let herself down. Aysel fearlessly performed exactly as told—death was everywhere, so why should she fear it? She had already seen countless dead bodies as a child. Once a man had been stabbed to death right before her very eyes. The man had been spying on the lavatories, and word had spread through the neighborhood that there was a peeping tom in their midst. And so one day a laborer decided to stay home from work and catch the guy in the act. When the laborer's wife entered the lavatory, he cornered the approaching peeping tom and stabbed him then and there. The police came and arrested the attacker. Meanwhile everyone in the neighborhood had walked up and spit in the face of the peeping tom. Aysel could not fathom why the police had taken away a laborer for killing a man into whose face everyone spit. Moreover, the laborer's son suffered from tuberculosis, and died a short time after his father was arrested. And so all of this had awoken within Aysel the idea that it was best to stay away from the police. While in Antakya, not once did the idea of going to the police even cross her mind. If the police had shown up in her room, she would have resisted, without even asking for chocolate, let alone complaining about the conditions she was being held in.

They got in the driver's taxi around midnight and took off. Towards Ankara. On their way there the men who had locked Aysel up began trailing them. They even fired some shots at them from behind. The driver put the pedal to the metal. Meanwhile, Aysel belted out tune after tune at the top of her lungs. She had memorized the songs she could hear rising from the *gazino* during her stay at the hotel. Once the taxi driver had managed to lose the guys who were pursuing them—he knew the streets like the back of his hand, that's why he had dared to run off with Aysel like this in the first place—he pulled over and stopped the car. He mixed some marijuana with a little tobacco and rolled a joint. And then he turned to Aysel and asked, "So do you sing?"

"Of course I do, why shouldn't I?"

"You got your docs?"

"What docs, hm?"

The driver wrinkled his forehead and thought for a few moments.

"Do you have your papers, from the census bureau?"

"What kinda papers you mean, hm?"

"Every person's gotta have papers. Otherwise, they're not considered a real person."

"In that case, what are they considered, hm?"

"Would you quit saying 'hm' all the time? They're not considered nothing, you see. The police'll take you in if you don't have papers."

"Well, ya don't say! So you mean those papers are 'lose the police papers.'"

"Well, whatever you wanna call them, if you don't have them, then you can't sing, and you can't get a job. You'll go hungry."

"And so I can't get me chockylit either, hm?"

"What are you talking about, chockylit! I just told you, you'll go hungry!"

Aysel began to weep. Everywhere she went she encountered this specter of hunger. And now she was going to go hungry because she didn't have her papers. How was she supposed to find these so-called papers? She thought of her older sister.

"Why don't you ask my sister if I've got papers?"

"You got a sister?" the man asked suspiciously. Aysel had understood, in her infinite astuteness, that the driver didn't much care for the idea of her having relatives.

"Who else you got?"

"Like I said, my sister, and my mom, they're one and the same."

"What the hell is that supposed to mean, you little tramp?"

"It means my mom and my sister are the same, oki?"

"Girl, don't go pushing my buttons. Now what the hell is that supposed to mean!"

"Nothing, it don't mean nothing . . . My dad attacked my sister, and I was born a bastard . . ." She told her story the same way the kids in the neighborhood told it. The taxi driver listened, shaking his head, and then told her, "I'll talk with your sister once we get to Ankara."

Once they got to Ankara, the taxi driver locked her up at his place, telling her, "I'm going to your sister's." When he got back, he was wearing a long face.

"You don't have no papers or nothing."

"So whadda we do now?"

"Everything'll be fine, as long as the police don't find out."

Thanks to her keenly developed intuition, Aysel immediately understood that the driver feared the police just as much as she did. Whoever best conceals their fear and transforms it into the appearance of toughness, wins. And so that's exactly what Aysel did.

"Brother, if you lock me up again, I'll run straight to the police."

"And I'll rip you a new one," the driver said. But he didn't lock Aysel up again.

She began singing at the gazino at Gölbaşı, drinking with the patrons there, and occasionally going off with the ones her bosses approved of. She was thirteen years old. She had learned every trick you could turn in bed, every cuss word imaginable, how to smoke dope and how to drink. She had no ID. One night, the police raided the gazino. They took Aysel in. She was sent for an examination. Then upstairs to detention. They didn't know what to do with her because she didn't have her papers. She spent some time in prison. She wasn't sentenced. They had x-rays of her taken, in order to determine her age—according to the x-ray, she was fifteen years old—then they released her, and again, she didn't have any papers.

Aysel had been heading to Kızılay that day to get papers from the barber Hüsnü. From one of her regular johns, a person of high standing, she had learned that Hüsnü, one of the best barbers in Kızılay—and who also happened to be the neighborhood *muhtar* at the time—sold identity papers. She had siphoned off a bit of the money she was supposed to hand over to Hüseyin so that she could afford the identity papers. She was still living with Hüseyin. But he didn't wear the britches like he used to. She didn't let him get away with so much as a pinch on the ass anymore. He occasionally got angry, sometimes drank too much, but he was no longer able to beat Aysel like he once did. When they threw Aysel in the slammer, they'd roughed him up good at the police station too for pimping her out. But they hadn't been able to prove anything. Yet after that beating, Hüseyin was a wreck because Aysel was in prison. It seems he'd developed a fondness for the money Aysel brought in. And so he had no intention of letting her go.

Aysel had looked scornfully at the face of the man who was sad because his revenue had been cut off. Hüseyin was no longer the man who ran off with her in a grand escape, raining gunfire upon his pursuers as they sped out of Antakya. Yet this incident had for a long time continued to have a certain hold on Aysel. And Hüseyin himself told the story frequently, always with a proudly puffed up chest. But now, Aysel had learned the ins and outs of the male species, that they too could get their feelings hurt and that they too had a price. Aysel supplied Hüseyin with plenty of money for his marijuana-lined cigarettes. And in that respect, she was his master. It was thanks to Aysel that he'd been able to soup up his lemon of a car. He was completely smitten. He was a completely different person with Aysel. And Aysel was no longer the child he drove to tears as she begged for a piece of chocolate. She was a person who knew how to play with men's nerve endings. That was her job. The male body was to her what a car engine was to Hüseyin. She knew good and well exactly when and how it worked. "No man can so much as lay a finger on me if I don't want him to," she would say. "A single word from my lips is all it takes." Men had bought her, and they continued to buy her, but now she sold herself knowingly, and named her own price.

At the police station, on the night that they made Aysel stay because she didn't have any papers, one of the policemen started to put the moves on her. He pressed himself up against her while taking her fingerprints.

"Hey, back off!" Aysel had said.

The other policemen laughed.

The humiliated one responded:

"What's that, pretending you've still got a shred of honor are you now, you whore!"

"Honor, now that's something I can live without! It's a luxury I've got no use for. Even so, I can always do better than some lowlife like you. Hell, I could buy the honor of a lowlife like you with just a single night's wages."

When the enraged policeman lunged forward in retaliation, Aysel grabbed the bottle of ink used for fingerprints and doused him with it. And that's when all hell broke loose. The chief, who turned out to be an acquaintance of Aysel's from the gazino, intervened and calmed the officers down. He also invited Aysel into his office for some tea in a bid to calm her down as well. While drinking her tea, Aysel insisted that she was going to sue the police. The chief knew just how particular women like Aysel were about their flesh; after all, it was the one piece of property they owned, and therefore they depended upon it for everything. Their bodies were their only capital, and they'd gouge the eyes out of anyone who impinged upon it. There in the chief's office, Aysel sat nonchalantly sipping at her tea, as if she were anything but a criminal in custody. And it was indeed true that she had nothing to do with the concept of crime. *If it's a crime to make a living, then you can just fuck off, brother. What am I supposed to do? Ain't like I'm going to just give up and die. Better you die than me, brother, then they can say, "Oh, he died so innocent."* She had one leg crossed over the other, and she swung the leg on top, occasionally popping her chewing gum and thus interrupting the routine chatter in the chief's office. Aysel watched the police coming in and out of the chief's room with the same scornful look in her eyes that she'd acquired as a child. *So you brought me in here—now what? Won't I be right back at work, at the exact same place tomorrow? Won't your chief being paying me a visit like always?* They make their living from playing with other people's livings. When they were bringing her in, she had said to the policeman who handcuffed her, "Catching prostitutes—you call that a job!" and then she learned that the policeman had been doing this same job for the past ten years. "For God's sake, and have you been able to wipe out prostitution in those ten years, huh?" "Nope." "Weeelll, in that case, your job isn't combatting prostitution; this isn't a solo job, takes two to tango, you know. Who do you think we're plying our trade with? With your superiors, that's who. So why don't you go combat them, if you've got the balls!"

Stunned, the policeman fell silent.

"Now look here, get this into your head, would ya? If they'd pay me without me having to sell my body, then I wouldn't sell my body. But as long as there are buyers out there, what do you expect me to do? Should I go hungry, when I got paying customers out there, huh?"

Since she lacked an ID, this wasn't the first time she'd been taken into headquarters. *That's just how men are, they'll pay you to do something and ban it at the same time. They're a bunch of idiots who constantly contradict themselves. Some men probably get paid because they're idiots. So they can be ordered not only to catch a thief, but to let him go too.*

After explaining to Aysel that it would be useless for her to file harassment charges against the police, the chief did her a favor by revealing to her the name of a barber who sold fake IDs in Kızılay.

Once again, Aysel was baffled by the course of developments. "Now just look at that! They bring me in her for not having an ID, and then they show me how to get a fake one. Unbelievable!" And so it was that the contradictions she encountered on a daily basis erased any semblance of the concept of crime that she might once have possessed, for she had seen how the same concept always assumed different characteristics in different situations. And now this chief, by referring her to someone who was committing a crime, was in effect showing her how to commit a crime in a more seemly manner. But he himself, the policeman, wasn't a criminal. Yet if it weren't for criminals, he wouldn't have a job. *In other words, both he and I, we make our living off crime.*

Aysel saw Ali as she waded through the crowd opposite Piknik, making her way towards the *dolmuş* stops. He was someone she couldn't possibly ever forget. While she was waiting to be taken in for a physical examination at the station, they'd deposited Ali right next to her. The boy's eyes and face were swollen from the beating he'd just received. Aysel had taken a liking to him at first glance. There was something different about that boy. Something about him that was different from the male species she was used to interacting with. *He's not just a regular guy, he's a decent man*, she thought to herself. She poured some of the pine-scented *kolonya* with thyme that she always carried in her handbag onto a handkerchief and used it to dress his wounds.

"Thank you, sister," Ali had said. Without looking at her, at any part of her, but with genuine sincerity.

Aysel was used to men looking at her, at every bit of her. She couldn't bring herself to ignore this gesture, a gesture which was warm, but in a very different way. She usually addressed men with a scowl and a "hey man" or a "hey buster." But in this case, she said to Ali: "They beat you up pretty bad, huh, brother? I hope those bastards' sperm shrivel up and die, I hope they drown in their own blood, I hope they choke on the bread they buy with the money they make from beating up others, I hope their children suffer by Go—"

"Don't go cursing them like that, sister, it's not their fault."

"Whose fault is it then?"

"It's the fault of those who give them no choice but to do these things."

"And just who are they?"

"Look, do you like doing what you do for a living?"

"Why shouldn't I like it? It's better than going hungry, isn't it?"

"Of course, as things stand right now, you have no choice but to do what you do, and so it's the system that forces you to do it that's guilty. Those responsible for this sys—"

"You mean the guys who abducted me and took me to Antakya?"

Ali laughed.

"Yes, and no. In a way, they didn't have a choice either. You see, you being taken to Antakya is also a consequence of the system doing its thing."

"No, I ran off with those guys because of my mom/sister. It's all that woman's fault. The things she put me through . . ."

"Now look, sister . . ."

"Call me Aysel."

"Now look here Aysel, you do the work you do in order to stay alive, right?"

"No, I do it for the fun of it. You think anyone would put up with all those assholes for the fun of it?"

"Right, that's exactly what I'm saying. So wouldn't you prefer to do a different job, and still make a living?"

"But I can't, I don't have my ID papers."

"Why not?"

"Cause I'm a bastard. The bastard child of my father and sister."

Ali fell silent.

"That's no fault of yours. No matter who you are, you too have to the right to go to school, to work at a decent job, to live a decent life, and so, you see, it's those who don't give you those rights, who refuse to give you those rights, that are guilty."

"Tell me, just who are those sons of—" She was going to curse, but seeing the look on Ali's face, she changed her mind.

"It doesn't really matter who they are, I mean, their names and whatnot. It's not difficult to figure out who benefits from these injustices. But it wouldn't do us much good to tackle each of them one by one."

"Nah, brother, that doesn't fly with me. If someone punches you in the eye, you gotta punch him right back in the face. You gotta put a fear of death in 'em, otherwise, it's no use. You gotta find those guys who punched you in the eye and you gotta beat them so bad that—"

"It's no use getting angry at the guys who gave me a black eye. They're just doing their job . . . Same as you, just trying to get by . . . The important thing is knowing why they gave me a black eye."

"So why'd they give you a black eye?"

"Where'd you grow up?"

"Hacı Doğan."

"Were there blue collar workers over there?"

"Course there were."

"And how did they live?"

"Are you kidding me, brother? They lived the way everyone lived in our neighborhood."

"Okay, and so did they work a lot?"

"Course they did. In our neighborhood, if your back wasn't sore from working, your belly didn't get full."

"You see, that's 'cause they didn't get their rightful due. What I'm saying is, they have rights, and they have to get their due and enjoy those rights."

"What's it to you? In our neighborhood, nobody looks out for anybody else. Just the opposite, everyone's always looking to get a piece of someone else's pie."

"That's because they get so little already. And because of hopelessness and desperation. If they knew how to go about getting what's rightfully theirs, then they wouldn't go wasting their energy fighting one another."

"Oh, sweetheart, you got it all wrong, it's just the way those bastards are. A leopard can't change his spots, after all. It's written in their stars. What a pity if that's the reason you got yourself all beat up like that. Those guys only know how to beat the shit out of each other, and now you've gone and let them beat the shit of you, but they ain't lifting a finger to defend you."

"They're bitter because they're oppressed, but then they take it out on each other because they don't know why they're oppressed. If they knew, well . . . Well then they'd go out and fight for their rights."

"Oh yeah, well, in our neighborhood, everyone protects what's theirs, by God. You must've thought they was idiots or something. But oh no, ain't nobody where I come from would let their neighbor nick even a dime off of them"

"But you see, that's the point: it's not their neighbors who are cheating them out of their rights. It's the ones who have them at each other's throats that's cheating them, and so you see, because I try to explain how this all works . . ."

"Oh, I get it! You hate rich people. Well, ain't you clever! So, now you've done all your explaining, does that mean Hacı Doğan's full of rich people now, huh?"

"Look, sister, it's not that simple. And it's not just a matter of rich versus poor. For anyone who's looking to get what is rightfully his, first he has to figure who's depriving him of it, right?"

"I get it. So you mean those guys who are depriving others of their rights had you beat up so you wouldn't go ruining their plans. Well, those pussies!"

Ali laughed.

"Can't you speak without cursing?"

Aysel took offense.

"What's that, you don't like the way I talk? After all that talk of yours about standing up for one's rights. Where I come from, if you don't know how to curse, there's no way you're getting your bucket filled at the fountain, let me tell you."

"Don't be offended, I didn't say it to offend you. But if you're unhappy with your life, you're not going to gain anything by cursing . . . If you're happy though, well, that's another story."

"And why the hell should I be happy? Hold on, let me dampen that eye of yours again. So you think a street dog can be happy, is that even possible? I mean, like the song says, 'C'mon world, is this your idea of justice . . .'"

"But the world doesn't have to be this way. I mean, it shouldn't, and we should do something to change it."

"If you're saying we should all go and get the crap beat out of us like you did, well then you can count me out! There's plenty of that happening in Hacı Doğan as it is. Thank you very much. At least I'm surviving without having the brains beat of me."

Ali laughed again. His head hurt. He closed his eyes.

Aysel wet the handkerchief with kolonya once more and used it to massage his forehead. She felt immense compassion for Ali. This emotion, so unfamiliar and new to her, rattled her self-confidence.

"Close your eyes, get some rest," she said. "Otherwise you'll be bitin' the dust before you've had your fill of this crappy world."

Ali drifted off to sleep, rousing every now and then, to find Aysel by his side each time. Every time he woke up, he tried to pull his feverish and exhausted mind together and explain to Aysel just who and what was responsible for all of this mess. Finally, Aysel quieted him: "Forget about it, brother! It's no use getting yourself all worked up over those sons of bitches. One day you'll get the chance and you'll give it to 'em real good. Better than letting them beat you to a pulp like they done did." Ali struggled to right his throbbing head before asking in a saddened voice:

"Don't you believe me, Aysel?"

"And what if I don't? We gettin' hitched are we? Am I handing over some deed to you or something? Cause if not, what difference does it make whether I believe you or not? It doesn't matter either way."

"Alright, so let's say I got in trouble. Would you hide me?"

"From who?"

"I mean, would you turn me in?"

"To who? To the government?"

"Sure, the government, let's say. Would you?"

"No. Why should I?"

"Why not?"

"Oh, sweetheart, what's the government to me? I don't recognize it, so fine if it don't recognize me neither. What good have we ever done one another anyway? But I know you. You're a good kid. And you haven't done me any harm."

"Okay, now let's say they give you something in return for turning me in?"

"What?"

"Let's say . . . an ID!"

Aysel pondered this idea for a moment.

"Now don't get upset with me brother, but, I don't know. An ID's pretty much my ticket to making a living at this point. And so maybe, in that case . . . But no, I still wouldn't turn you in."

"Why not?"

"I don't trust them. I mean, I don't trust them to give me an ID."

Again Ali laughed.

"You're an honest gal. I'm going to come visit you one of these days. You work at Gölbaşı, don't you?"

"You betcha. So, seems I got me a new john! But then everyone I meet becomes my john."

"No, I don't mean like that, I mean as a guest."

Aysel took offense at his words.

"So I'm not good enough for you, is that it, brother?"

"No, that's not it at all. It's not you, it's your line of work I'm opposed to. People being sold—I mean, I can't, you know . . . Not when I'm angry at the fact that you're forced to make a living off of this . . . You get it . . . I mean, I can't take advantage of your situation."

"Well it's not like I do it for free, sweetheart."

"Still."

"Ali, brother, it's a good thing the rest of the male species ain't like you. Otherwise, I'd be in the poorhouse."

"Don't worry, if it was up to me, you'd have another job."

"In that case, why don't you find me one now?"

"It's not that simple. You have to have patience, Aysel, patience."

"Oh boy. And just what am I supposed to do while I'm patiently waiting till I find another job? Is God going to take care of me, huh?"

"That's not what I meant by patience. I meant to say that we need to have patience if we're ever going to make things right in the world."

"You know what they say: Curiosity may have killed the cat but patience killed the saint."

"We'll talk more later," Ali said, before drifting off again, a stream of semiconscious thoughts running through his mind: *I talked with that girl like those fanatics who went to the Industrial Market crying,*

"We're here to enlighten the workers!" only to get the crap beat out of them by the small business owners there. But she's a good person, after all, she looked after me instead of just cursing at me and minding her own business. But he was tired, too tired to think any more. Unconsciousness descended upon him like the heaviest of slumbers.

They took Ali away early the next morning.

"Thanks for your help, sister. See you later."

"See ya!"

Aysel wondered if Ali would really stop by and see her at Gölbaşı. The idea of being alone with him excited her. So he was going to stop by, be her guest, or so he said. *You young buck, you think you're pulling my leg, but I know better. Get a couple glasses of rakı in ya, and next thing you know* . . . But that business about being her guest, that had really rubbed her the wrong way. Why? Because . . . because she wanted for Ali to be into her. It was the only way in which she could imagine a man liking a woman, the only way she knew of. Her thoughts swung like a pendulum between excitement and rage. He won't show up; guys like him are too stuck up. *What a fool, champagne taste on a beer budget . . . They were right to beat him up, he had it coming, sticking his nose into other people's business like that! Let him come to our gazino singing that song. Çarliston Nuri would plunge a knife in him for sure, by God! He'd be done for!* Aysel daydreamed:

Ali comes to the gazino. Not like he'd shown up at the station, in those shabby, tattered clothes. No, this time he's wearing a white linen suit. For Aysel, stylish attire for men means only one thing, and that is a white linen suit. So Ali shows up in a white linen suit. Aysel ignores him. She's laughing boisterously, having the time of her life. Ali sits down at the table next to Aysel and says something to the waiter. Aysel doesn't give him the time of day. Ali orders a bottle of champagne, ice bucket and all, and has it delivered it to Aysel's table.

Aysel empties the bottle of champagne onto the floor. Ali stands up, walks over to Aysel and grabs her by the elbow. "Come with me, I'm here to rescue you," he says.

And then, Çarliston Nuri, Tiki-Tiki Niyazi and Koço all descend upon Ali, pouncing him, clobbering him until he's a thousand times worse off than he was at the station. Just as Çarliston takes out his straight razor and makes to slice into Ali's face, Aysel screams: "Stop it, you fucking oaf!" As soon as Aysel intervenes, Çarliston Nuri and Koço release Ali, before bowing down in a reverent salute to her.

After kicking them all out, Aysel instructs the waiters to prepare a fancy table. The waiters dash back and forth, decking the table with a slew of mezzes. And then Aysel orders a big ice bucket of kolonya to be brought to the table, together with a bunch of towels. Aysel places Ali's head on her lap and tends to all his wounds. And then, sitting across from one another, they drink, Ali pausing to kiss Aysel's hand again and again.

Buoyed by self-confidence thanks to her newly issued ID, Aysel made her way through the crowd on the sidewalk that day with her head held high. She didn't give the poplar even the merest glance. Today she had gone from being an undocumented, unregistered someone to a documented, registered someone, a right proper citizen! As if, for Aysel, any other change could possibly match this, let alone surpass it. No, the collapse of the poplar meant nothing to her. She had to reach some certain someones as soon as possible and shove her new papers under their noses. She was going to show them! And she'd raise her prices now too. It was with these thoughts running through her head as she waded through the crowd that she saw Ali. Ali, who was speaking with Necmi at the time, hadn't even noticed her. Aysel paused for a moment. She considered speaking up, saying something to Ali. *But what if he snubs me? What would I do? Nothing.* This place wasn't hers, it wasn't her country, here she had no powers that she could use against him. Better to wait until he made it over to Gölbaşı. She walked to the dolmuş stop.

She sat down on the front seat of the dolmuş, placing her bag next to her to indicate that she didn't want anyone sitting beside her. Nobody gets to touch this for free! An older man, probably a retired public servant, who was sitting in the back asked the driver the reason for the crowd. Just at that moment Aysel, who'd been watching Ali, saw him make his way to the other side of the street, where he grabbed a sharply dressed, clearly well-heeled girl by the arm, and pulled her into Piknik and out of the rain. Suddenly, without even realizing it, Aysel began to curse.

"So what if that poplar collapses . . . So be it . . . I hope it falls smack on the heads of all those sons of bitches . . . And they all go to hell . . . And their dicks fall off, inshallah!"

There was a moment of silence in the dolmuş. The driver, sensing the passengers' disapproving shakes of the head and their rising anger, opened the door and ordered Aysel to get out.

"Go take that filthy mouth of yours somewhere else!"

Aysel got out of the dolmuş and strutted off, popping her bubble gum along the way. She stopped at a spot where she thought Ali could see her. With a showy swoop of her hand, she stopped a taxicab and got in.

The madman of Sakarya Avenue hears the marching band

He walked down the avenue in his old coat, which reached all the way down to his ankles. His beard and hair, which looked like it had never seen a comb, were a tangled mess. The end of his long scarf dragged along the ground. No one took the least bit of interest in the fact that he was wearing a long coat despite the hot weather, or in his scarf, or in his jumbled hair and beard. He walked down Sakarya Avenue towards Kızılay, stopping every three steps to yell out something or other. They had accepted him like this, as he was. There wasn't a person around here who didn't know him. They didn't think about it, didn't even go to the trouble to turn around and look at him. He walked down Sakarya Avenue at the same time every day. Sometimes he asked drivers for a cigarette or some other item. And sometimes, though rarely, someone from one of the stores would give him something to eat. The truth was, no one knew what he ate or drank. No one had ever seen him eating anything. Once in a blue moon he would put something that someone had given him to eat in one of the torn pockets of his coat—he wore the same coat all year round—but whether or not he ever ate it, no one knew. He was an otherworldly creature never expected to change, and he was accepted as such. Indeed, this street only accepted otherness on the condition that it continue as-is, that it never change. Perhaps if he too ate like the other people on this street, if he behaved like them, his otherness wouldn't be accepted. That's why no one ever found it strange that he didn't eat; just the opposite, that's how it was supposed to be. For the people of Sakarya Avenue, that is.

He stopped over by the taxi stand. The drivers were standing by the door of the taxi at the front of the line, gathered around the radio, listening to a football game. Five drivers, their faces red, their eyes fixed on the radio. As if their entire lives depended on the words that would come out of that radio. The expressions on their faces so taut with tension. He walked up to them. He stopped. The drivers, who always teased him, who had made it a habit to yell out a taunting word or two every time he passed by, didn't even see him. Because he was a daily event. The sound of "goal" that they would hear from the radio, on the other hand, would bring change to their lives. After standing silently behind them for a while, he suddenly started yelling out in that shrill voice of his:

"I am neither a martyr, nor a veteran! Planes! The planes of Mevlana. Go back martyrs. Go back veterans!"

One of the taxi drivers jumped at the sound of this scream emitted at the back of his neck. It had frightened him. The change had not come from the expected place. Suddenly he swung around with a swiftness born of both anger and fear. Upon finding before him the street's familiar madman, he felt relief, but also rage. They were used to him, he did them no harm, but just now he had crossed the usual boundaries and surprised them. He had never taken a beating but he might very well take one now. The taxi driver took a few deliberate steps towards him, grabbed him by the scarf and shook him.

"Get the fuck out of here! We don't have time for your bullshit!"

The man broke out in uproarious laughter, as if having this taxi driver shake him up like this was something he had been expecting, as if he walked down this street every day just so that someone would grow angry and try to strangle him, as if that's what he'd been waiting for all this time. While he was being pushed around, one of his pockets ripped open, and a wrinkled, faded, bitten apple fell onto the ground. The driver, unable to contain his rage, kicked the apple. The apple rolled off into the distance, over to the fishmonger's display trays. Upon seeing that his apple had been kicked, the madman ceased laughing and ran, and began searching for the apple. The driver turned his attention back to the radio.

"Basri's got the ball. There he goes . . . There he goes . . . Well, I never . . . Well, I never . . . Listeners, I'm telling you . . . Right . . ."

Each time the announcer said "Well, I never," the drivers slapped their knees. Their faces grew even redder. They stuck their sweaty necks out.

Upon seeing the madman wandering about the trays, the fishmonger's apprentice tried to drive him off. But the madman resisted. The apprentice, not understanding what the madman was after because he hadn't witnessed the previous incident, thought he wanted fish and was surprised by this. In all this time, never once had the guy been so impudent as to ask for anything. What was up with him? He shoved the madman in the chest a couple of times. But the madman was resisting forcefully, looking at the apprentice with fierce determination, motioning with his hands and making strange sounds. The way he did when he was upset. The apprentice, frightened, yelled out to his master.

"Ağbi, he's not going away. What should I do?"

As he asked this question, the last thing he wanted was to get the police involved. No matter what, you never want to get the police involved. Without waiting for his boss's response, he sought a solution himself:

"Ağbi, he wants fish. Should I wrap him up a few mackerel? They've been here a while as it is."

Absorbed in calculating the figures on the ledger before him, the boss only half heard his words. He brushed him off with a brief motion of his hand to indicate that he wasn't to be bothered before proceeding to bury his head back in the ledger.

The apprentice meanwhile touched the madman, who was still crouched in his search for something on the ground, on the shoulder. The madman stood up. He looked at the apprentice. After motioning for him to wait, the apprentice wrapped up two mackerel and held them out to the madman. The madman took the package, opened it excitedly, and upon seeing the mackerel, dashed it to the ground. The fish rolled over a few times before landing next to the street gutter. Two of the cats that hung out around the fishmonger's place darted over to the fish fast as lightning and gobbled them up in no time. At this point the madman started grumbling in an even louder voice as he made his way back towards the trays. The unnerved apprentice was at a loss for what to do next. He grabbed the madman, who was once again crouched down, by the collar and lifted him up:

"C'mon! I've had about of you already. You madman!"

As soon as the word "madman" came out of his mouth he took a fright. He wasn't used to speaking the truth. Speaking the truth got you in trouble. He couldn't tell how the madman would react to being called a madman. His bewilderment only served to intensify his rage. The punch that he threw fueled by that rage landed right on the madman's chin. The madman's toothless mouth caved in. A streak of blood streamed out of the side of his mouth. The sight of it drove the apprentice absolutely crazy. Having lost all control, he pummeled the madman with unabated fervor.

"You son of a bitch . . . Get the hell out of here. Fuck off!"

While raising his right hand in an attempt to fend off the apprentice's punches, the madman crouched down again, and that's when he saw, next to the feet of the raging apprentice, his apple. He snatched it up, put it in the giant pocket of his coat, and stood up. Slowly he exited the apprentice's battle ring. The apprentice, believing he had succeeded in driving the madman to away, rubbed his hands together. He began righting the fish trays that lie scattered on the ground. As the madman walked away, a smile beaming on his face, he was struck by a brief moment of lucidity that flickered in his eyes, and he stopped and yelled:

"Red Lake!"

The apprentice, paying no attention to what was clearly one of the madman's usual outbreaks, continued to arrange the fish displays.

The madman had returned to memories of his childhood. His parents were always angry with him and kicking him out of the house. And he was running through the fields. Then he was standing breathless beneath an oleaster tree. The oleaster tree was on the slope next to "Red Lake." It was into this "Red Lake" that the lords of yore once dispensed with the heads they had cut off beneath the same oleaster tree, or so it was said. And so all the children of the village were afraid of the oleaster tree and always made a point to keep their distance from it. The sun was descending in the far distance beyond the fields. The executioners he had waited for all day did not come. He had waited all day for the executioners to come and cut off his head and toss it into Red Lake. His bloody head would swim all the way across Red Lake and land on the fields. A child, seeing his head there, would snatch it up and run straight to his parents . . .

He was napping in the growing shade of the oleaster tree. A long slumber during which the executor, for some reason or another, never made it over to cut off his head.

His eyes closed. The end of his scarf got tangled in his legs. He nearly tripped and fell. There under the midday sun his consciousness, which he had left back under the oleaster tree, splintered into countless pieces once again. He stuck his hand in his pocket, took his apple into the palm of his hand, and walked over to the taxi drivers. He stood behind the driver who had kicked his apple. Again red faces leaned in towards the radio. The driver took out his handkerchief and wiped his neck. The madman leaned forward.

"Boo!" he yelled in an attempt to scare the taxi driver, who immediately leapt into the air in response. For a brief second the latter had mistaken the sound for that of "goal!" He was on the verge of elation. But before the feeling of elation came to fruition, he suddenly understood where the sound had come from and what it actually was. His eyes nearly popped out of his face. With fury in his eyes he looked around, searching. He picked up the first stone he found and threw it at the madman. At that point the madman had turned around and was walking toward Kızılay. It seemed he felt no pain when the stone hit him in the small of his back. He passed the greengrocers' displays. Once he had neared the boulevard, he began yelling once again:

"Executors! The blood of martyrs! We've set sail! I'm neither a martyr nor a veteran! I'm the captain, the captain! The Muslims have drowned. The ships are approaching. The caskets are marching forth. Long live the executioners! Goddamn! Goddamn doomsday. Doomsday is marching forth. Be quiet . . . Listen . . . Be quiet . . . Listen!"

He finally reached the boulevard. He stood next to the lottery ticket seller who was set up at the corner where the drugstore was. The ticket seller was yelling:

"Just one day left . . . One day left until the numbers are drawn . . . Just one day left until half a million liras could be yours!"

The madman fixed an attentive gaze on the avenue. He smiled at the sound of an approaching band. The marching band was drawing closer. The trumpet section all decked out in red was already visible. The band drew closer, drowning out the sound of the ticket seller's voice. The madman stood smiling on the sidewalk.

The band had already passed Kızılay. The conductor was throwing his wand up into the air, whirling it about, putting on a masterful performance. Feet marched in time with the sound of the trumpets and drums, and then, after briefly marching in place, they opened up like a fan, boots pounding the pavement, keeping tempo with the sound of the trumpets. The madman began walking down the sidewalk alongside the band. He was having trouble wading through the crowds that had gathered on either side of the avenue. Sometimes he bumped into someone who was applauding the marching band's colorful, rousing performance and was shoved this way and that. Nevertheless he managed to make it all the way to Piknik together with the band. The rain had let up. Meanwhile the crowd gathered around the fire trucks and the police cordon too had heard the sound of the band. Some children let go of their mothers' hands and ran over to the boulevard sidewalk to watch the parade. Some simit sellers had even found their way into this newly forming crowd and started yelling "Simit!" The crowd watching the poplar was divided now. Those who had grown bored of watching the poplar, whose collapse was certain anyway, and the direction of its fall now obvious, gathered on both sidewalks, from whence they lost themselves in this new spectacle. The time lost was not of much importance. Just another day gone by.

The madman, unable to walk as he pleased there in the midst of the dense crowd, had already forgotten all about the band. He turned onto Sakarya Avenue, where he walked freely, occasionally taking his wrinkled apple out of his pocket and looking at it. Each time he saw that the apple was still there, he flashed an empty smile.

The poplar collapses

When Mevlût, the apartment building attendant, arrived back at the building, weighed down by his shopping basket, the firefighters had not yet arrived in order to render the poplar innocuous. That the poplar was about to collapse had only been conveyed to the necessary authorities a short while earlier. And the wobbling poplar had only yet attracted the attention of but a few spectators. In order to give his weary arms a rest, Mevlût set the basket on the garden wall for a while. It contained only ten loaves of bread. Though it wasn't hot out, Mevlût was drenched in sweat. But he was used to it; in fact, he rather liked his daily shopping task, during which, as he bought the items requested by the building residents, he squabbled a bit here and chatted a bit there with the storekeeper, the grocer, the butcher and so on. He pushed the iron gate open with his foot. Picking the basket back up, he began walking towards the apartment building. He was lost in thought. *I'm not going to shop from that İhsan anymore, he's gotten too big for his britches, just watch me stop buying from him and I bet he comes down a peg or two.* He beamed at the thought of how İhsan's face would fall upon seeing Mevlût walk into the store next door. At just that moment he shivered; something cold and wet touched his face. He nearly dropped the basket. Angrily he raised his head; it was the washed diapers of his fourteen-month-old son which were touching his face. Blood rushed to his head. His wife had hung the laundry in the front yard again. She had hung up a clothesline, extending from the trunk of the poplar to the annex where they lived, and hung from it rows of diapers, towels and bed sheets. Even though Mevhibe Hanım had warned Mevlût time and again, "Tell that wife of yours not to go hanging her laundry in the front yard!" He dropped the basket and marched into the annex. His wife was crouched down in the middle of the room washing laundry in a tub. She had bound up Ömer to a small reed chair. Upon seeing his father, Ömer began to cry. And then he threw the crust of bread, which was wet with his snot and tears, onto the floor. Hatice glanced briefly at her husband. Because she knew what he was going to say, she pretended not to see him, not to notice his anger. It was this behavior of his wife that upset Mevlût most of all. Hatice never got into a fight so long as she could avoid it, but found instead a way to silently say her piece, insofar as possible. Mevlût looked around for something to do in order to shake his wife out of her silent obstinacy, to keep her from taking refuge in the laundry. Hatice had given Ömer anything she happened to lay her hands on so that he would sit still while she did the laundry, and he in turn had thrown everything given to him left and right. There wasn't space to budge in this room, which served as their living room, dining room and bedroom. To the right on the floor lay the bedspread belonging to the large brass bed situated next to the wall. Ömer had yanked the bedspread off before his mother bound him to the chair. On the table was a bowl of yoghurt, half of which Hatice had managed to feed to Ömer, and next to it a half-drunk glass of tea. Flies were landing on the yogurt that had spilled onto the table. One of the chairs was toppled over. This particular chair, which had one broken leg and which Mevhibe Hanım had given to Mevlût thinking he might use it, had been repaired the previous night by Mevlût. The collapsed chair was now broken in the same place it had been broken before. Hatice had curled up one end of their İsparta rug with the flower design so that it wouldn't get wet, but because there wasn't enough space in the room, she had placed the water pail on the curled up rug. Mevlût had only recently bought the rug from one of the stores in 19 Mayıs, on an installment payment plan. Mevhibe Hanım was paying the installments, the amount of which she then deducted from Mevlût's wages. Mevlût would be hard pressed to forget this good deed on the part of Mevhibe Hanım. The rage he felt towards Hatice, who had placed the water pail on top of the new rug, boiled inside of him until he completely lost his wits. He kicked the pail and yelled, "What business does this goddamn pail have doing here, goddamnit!" Because he kicked a little harder than he had intended, the pail fell over, spilling boiling water onto both the rug and Hatice's clog-clad feet. Hatice leapt up in pain. War had been declared:

"Goddamn you! I wish you'd choke on your own blood!" she yelled. "What harm is that pail to you, you hard-hearted infidel! How else am I supposed to wash laundry in this rat's hole?"

She knelt down and began rubbing her scorched feet, moaning and crying. Ömer, seeing his mother in tears, began screaming his heart out. Mevlût, bewildered by the staggering amount of noise, took his rage out on Ömer this time. In two swift steps he planted himself in front of his son and slapped him in the face:

"Shut the hell up, you son of a whore!"

"You're the whore, you pimp!"

"Now look here, Hatice, don't get me riled up or I'll burn this whole damn place to the ground."

"If you're gonna burn it down, then burn it the fuck down! Drunken bastard! It's not like it's my daddy's property, now is it?"

"Too bad you didn't think of that earlier. You cow-brained idiot. Why the hell do you go hanging laundry outside, leave it waving out their like flags, as if this is your daddy's house, huh?"

"Where else am I supposed to hang the laundry? From my head?"

"Hang it inside!"

"Just show me where in this godforsaken hellhole I'm supposed to hang the goddamn laundry! I went through hell all winter trying to dry the goddamn laundry. You see, I don't spend all day running around town the way you do. Washing your little bastard's shitty diapers is so much easier."

"Well, you shouldn't have had him then, now should you?"

"*Inshallah* God'll take your son's life, that'll teach you!"

Hatice's words sent a wave of shock through Mevlût. The truth was, he was very fond of his son. He'd said that bit about wishing she hadn't had him to piss his wife off. He'd wanted a son. Hatice had hit him in his weak spot.

"Shut the fuck up. Just shut your mouth! Why would God want to take that innocent boy? Inshallah he'll take your life!"

"I wish he would. What good is this life to me anyway?.." And thus did Hatice embark on one of her tirades. The more she complained, the more her wounds festered, and the more her wounds festered, the louder did she cry. Meanwhile, Mevlût had come to his senses. Mevhibe Hanım tended to get quite upset when he got embroiled in a yelling match with his wife because the yells and screams generally made their way past the thin walls of the annex and out into the street. Mevhibe Hanım would say, "Look, Mevlût, you're the keeper of this apartment building. You're responsible for the safety and comfort of all these people. You should treat this entire apartment building as if it's your own home. Now if someone walking into this apartment building thinks someone's being strangled over there in your place, how is he supposed to feel safe? How is he supposed to trust you to keep watch over this place? How is someone who can't maintain peace in his own home supposed to look after someone else's?" And the woman was right. Tilting his head to the side, Mevlût would try to calm her down: "I'm not strangling anyone . . . It's Hatice, she's still the same boor she was when she first got here, a peasant, I tell you. She hasn't got a mite of manners, doesn't know how to sit properly, doesn't know how to speak properly. You need to talk to *her*, ma'am, not me. But does she listen? Is she any help to me in my tasks as this building's keeper? She spends all day crouched in front of the door, suckling her baby. I don't know how many times I've told her, 'Don't go crouching in front of the door like some peasant woman.' She's perfectly happy to spend all day gawking at the street. I warn her once, I warn her twice, and then I beat her. But just one slap and off she goes, screaming to the high heavens; one curse from me gets ten from her. I swear to God, I regret ever taking her for a wife. But she's a distant relative of the family, you see. And so, well, I put up with her, 'cause I have to."

"You just hang in there. Look, you've got a healthy, hardy son," Mevhibe Hanım would say.

And then, as soon as the words were out of her mouth, she'd proceed to tattle on Mevlût's wife; either she'd been hanging laundry in the front yard, or she'd let their son wander in the front yard in his underwear, or she'd emptied the dishwater into the front yard. She was sure to throw in a few words like, "Look, I like you, I really do, you count as one of the owners of this apartment building, but if you don't knock some sense into that wife of yours, you'll have to fend for yourself somewhere else." Whenever he got the feeling that his job was in danger, Mevlût would completely lose it and come down hard on his wife yet again. It was the same dead-end path over and over. A no-win situation, whether he yelled at his wife or not. His job was always in danger. Whenever her husband started ranting and raving, so long as he didn't hurt her physically, Hatice responded with the silent treatment, an ability she had acquired as a child, to disregard what was happening around her; she gave no indication that she even understood what Mevlût was saying, let alone respond. And it was this behavior of hers that transformed Mevlût's desperation into boundless rage, and so after going out and tying one on, he'd come home to beat Hatice until she screamed her lungs out—not without saying her own piece in the meantime though. From this both of them would derive some relief, growing too exhausted to even think about their hopelessness.

The pain in Hatice's scorched feet had subsided a bit. And so she grew quiet. She went to the bathroom and fetched a bucket and a rag. She silently began wiping the floor. It was clear to Mevlût that his wife wouldn't be making any more noise. But he still hadn't gotten the rage out of his system, nor had he resolved the laundry issue.

"You donkey's ass, you. Listen to me, or else I'll do you up real good. I am the attendant of this apartment building, you hear me? I count as one of the owners of this building, you hear me? Say something. Even a cow has more conscience than you do. Look here, you best prick those ears of yours up and listen to what I've got to say. If I see that laundry hanging out there in the yard one more time, I'll put the both of you out on the street, just like that. Who the hell tries to keep a man from putting food on his own table? But with that thick head of yours, you don't understand the first thing about what it means to put food on the table, do you? The bread we eat, it doesn't come from that shitty ass of yours, you know, it comes from the lion's mouth. Just let me get fired and you'll see. You think it's easy being a building attendant in Kızılay? You don't know the first thing about being an attendant. They pulled all kinds of fast ones in that furnace course I took, everyone trying to get their grubby hands on the next guy's meal ticket. You know how much money people *pay* just to get a job like this? I'm telling you, any man would sell his own mother for a job like this one, to be an apartment attendant, *in Kızılay* no less! God only knows how many jealous souls have set their evil eyes on this here place of ours. You can't imagine how many infidels are out there praying I'll get the boot because of some lowlife like you. This is Kızılay, *Kızılay* I tell you! But what difference does that make to a peasant cow like you? How would you know the difference between Kızılay or Cebeci or Yenimahalle? You just keep crouching down out there in front of the door, watching the passersby with your mouth hanging open like some idiot. I'm telling you, if they give me the boot, I swear on my honor I'll cut you up into a thousand little pieces!"

But Hatice meanwhile was completely absorbed in the task at hand. She picked up the bucket and walked to the bathroom. She emptied the water into the toilet. She shoved a sugar cube into the mouth of her son, who was now crying just for the hell of it. Then she crouched back down and continued washing the laundry. Hopelessness trampled Mevlût's heart once again. He straightened himself up tall, as if trying to shake off the pressure on his heart. In a single step he arrived at Hatice's side.

"Girl, I told you to go out there and gather up that laundry!"

Hatice didn't make a peep. She began wringing the sheets, which she had decided were finally clean. When Mevlût grabbed her by the arm, the sheet she was wringing fell back into the washtub. Water splashed out.

"Go gather up that laundry or else!"

Hatice stood up. She wrung the sheet out standing up this time. Mevlût grabbed the sheet from Hatice's hands and flung it against the wall. Hatice bristled.

"What the hell, have you completely lost your mind?"

Mevlût had just decided that it was about time he deliver a good hard slap when he heard Mevhibe Hanım's voice: "Mevlût! Mevlût Efendi!"

Suddenly Mevlût recalled the shopping basket he had left out in the yard. Mevhibe Hanım had told him not to be late. He postponed Hatice's beating until later that night. His despair, or more specifically, his irrepressible anger towards Hatice, whom he saw as a primary cause of his despair, was transformed into fear, and then into timidity. He picked up the basket and entered the apartment building. Meanwhile, the fire trucks had gathered in front of the building, and a crowd had formed. But Mevlût saw none of it; he proceeded towards the sound of Mevhibe Hanım's summoning voice.

He made his way up the stairs as fast as he could and was breathless by the time he got to the top. His basket seemed to have gotten lighter. When he arrived at Mevhibe Hanım's door, out of habit he wiped his feet on the doormat before ringing the bell. He had made it his custom to wipe his feet on the doormat before ringing the doorbell, even if he wasn't going to be entering Mevhibe Hanım's home.

Mevhibe Hanım opened the door. She wasn't in a good mood. Her face twisted into a grimace.

"Where on earth have you been, Mevlût!" she squawked. "Did you get the rye bread I asked for?"

"They were out at the bakery in Sakarya. I bought French bread instead."

"Oh no, but I don't eat French bread, son. How many times I have told you. Why didn't you try the delicatessens?"

"They didn't have any at Köroğlu either."

"You mean to tell me Köroğlu is the only delicatessen in all of Kızılay?"

Mevlût tilted his head guiltily to one side. He remained silent.

"Answer me, son. Did you look anywhere else or not?"

It was as if Mevlût had swallowed his tongue.

"So buying a loaf of rye bread is too much of a challenge for you, is that it, Mevlût Efendi? You can't be bothered to walk even two extra steps, now can you! You know how to whine about not having enough money, but when it comes to doing the work, you give up just like that. Who gets a free meal ticket these days, huh? So why should you expect to? I tell you, Salih Bey is a very important professor and I swear he works more than you do. The poor guy's laboring over his books while you're down there snoring in your sleep. Look, I'm telling you one last time Mevlût Efendi, either you put your heart into this job, or . . ."

The lower Mevlût hung his head, the more unbearable did the weight of despair become, until it weighed so heavily upon his heart that it seemed his heart would never beat again. His heart felt to him as if it were a piece of road kill, run over by countless cars. In a weak voice he sought to resurrect the dead animal inside.

"I'll go get your rye bread for you now, I'll be back before you know it!"

"It's already afternoon. Thankfully we're eating late today. Oh! I almost forgot to tell you. Your wife hung laundry in the front yard again."

Mevlût had found something he could place between himself and despair, between his heart and the force that was squashing it. He gathered some strength.

"Well I tell you, missus, that's exactly why I'm running late. That peasant, God only knows how many times I told her. I was just about to smack some smarts into her if you hadn't called for me!"

"God forbid, Mevlût. How many times have I told you I don't want any fighting or uproar of any kind in my house. Look, if I hear that you've beaten your wife again . . ."

No, he was mistaken; again he found himself facing despair head-on, all on his own.

"Oh no, ma'am, please, I beg you, don't put us out on the street with our little son. God will reward you for your good deeds. Now I'm going to run and get that rye bread and be back before you know it. And I'll take down that laundry straightaway too."

"Hold on, not so fast. First deliver the renters their orders. And let me tell you, just so you know, everyone's complaining. They say you don't buy the stuff that they ask for!"

"I swear to God ma'am . . ."

"Look, you don't even know how to write properly. If you learned how to write, you could make a list, and then you wouldn't get the orders mixed up. How long have you been in Ankara? You have to know how to read and write if you want to be a building attendant these days. But your kind's too lazy to go to the trouble. And then you go tossing around God's name trying to make up for it. You think God doesn't see how lazy you are?"

Mevlût was hanging his head again. There was no beating this despair, the bastard.

"You go on now and deliver the orders. And then you can bring me my rye bread. And don't forget about the laundry."

Mevlût heaved the basket up, using all the strength that could possibly remain in a body with such a deflated heart. Dragging his feet, he descended the stairs. He wiped his feet on the doormat before ringing each bell. Finally, the basket was empty. He left the empty basket at the building entrance. *I should go get that rye bread now*, he thought. Apartment number four had asked for parsley, and gave Mevlût a good tongue-lashing because he'd forgotten it. Actually, truth be told, they hadn't really asked for parsley, but still. He walked out into the yard. The firemen were in the avenue, yanking with all their might on the rope they'd tied to the trunk of the poplar. Mevlût looked at the firemen, at the crowd, at the rope, with a blank expression in his eyes. The only thing on his mind was that rye bread. The laundry had been gathered. But the line that his wife had hung between the annex and the tree was still there. He walked into his home screaming, "Hatice! Go take down that laundry line, woman!" His wife wasn't in the room. She yelled out from the bathroom.

"I'm busy with the boy, he's got to pee!"

Mevlût cussed. He didn't have the luxury of carrying out Mevhibe Hanım's wishes only halfway; he was in no condition to do so. The woman had just said to him . . . He recalled her implied threats of just a few moments earlier and was overcome by a crushing feeling of despair. He dashed out into the street in a bid to stand up to the despair that squashed his heart into a piece of paper thin as a membrane. He wanted to take out his anger on that laundry line his wife had tied onto the poplar, he would rip it down, just like that. He didn't have the patience to untie the knot—no he did not.

Shoeshiner Necmi was watching the crowd scurry over to the boulevard to catch sight of the marching band. They'd forgotten all about the poplar now. *There's no way these people are going to have their shoes shined*, he thought. *Whenever there was a parade or a car wreck or something of the like, they lost themselves completely, and forgot all about their shoes in the process. But in a little bit, once the poplar has collapsed and the marching band has passed, they'll realize that they're late for work, and that they've forgotten to have their shoes shined. Serves them right!*

He'd had enough. Ali and that naive boy he had with him had taken off together with the girl he'd seen across the street, telling him, "We've gotta run." His anger at the crowd, dashing from this spot to that, continued to swell up inside of him. *If I had the power, I'd create a disaster every single moment and rout those suckers like a caged bird landed in a forest.* He began watching the firemen, who meanwhile had lost a good a portion of their audience to the band. They were yanking at the rope they'd tied to the poplar, pulling it towards a previously decided direction; the poplar was just about to collapse.

At precisely that moment Necmi saw Mevlût, the attendant of the apartment building across the street, dash out of the annex. Necmi knew Mevlût, and couldn't stand him one bit. Every now and then Mevlût would bring over the shoes of the building residents for Necmi to polish. He'd spend hours haggling over the price. Annoyed, Necmi would come down hard on Mevlût, "What the hell is to you, man? Since when did they put you in charge of the treasury! Not like it's *your* money, now is it?" But then finally he'd give in and take whatever Mevlût offered because Mevlût was as stubborn as a mule. Even when Necmi tried a little sweet-talking, Mevlût wouldn't budge, wouldn't come down a cent from the price Mevhibe Hanım had frozen the service at. For Mevlût, Mevhibe Hanım was something akin to the municipality in its role as price-fixer. He thought that everyone, not just he, had to abide.

Mevlût grabbed onto the laundry line and began pulling on it furiously. The poplar began to shake, not slowly like before, but quickly now. Upon seeing Mevlût, the firefighters yelled for him to get away. But it was too late. Mevlût was in no state to hear anything, to see anything, or to give up on ripping down that laundry line. It was as if that laundry line were the despair that kept him bound so tightly he couldn't move, and if only he could break free of it, he himself would be free like a slave that has shed his shackles, and his heart, now smashed flat like a piece of paper, would assume the dimensions of a human heart. He simply did not want to lose this position of his as an attendant, right here in the heart of Kızılay, no matter what.

The firemen blew on their whistles. One brave firefighter ran towards Mevlût, waving his hands and arms in the air. But time was so short. The poplar's day had come. The warning came too late. The poplar, unable to stand on its rotten roots any longer, swayed once to the right, and once to the left, made a loud cracking sound, and then, with the swiftness of the final, decisive moment, when it is too late for anyone to change anything, fell on Mevlût.